C000164011

Praise for Patrick
RAIN MU

"A musical, mystical tale spun in the sh... ...
Rainforest. This book is perfect for readers who love ghost stories,
myths, and mysteries."
— Louisa Morgan, author of *The Secret History of Witches*

"Patrick Swenson directs it all in *Rain Music*: a sense of place (you
won't have to go to the Quinault Rain Forest after reading this, but
you'll want to), the joy of creating music, and compelling love magic.
At the same time, he blends in edge-of-your-seat tension like discordant
harmony. You'll both love where you are and be afraid to look around
the corner. From its opening notes to its crashing finale, *Rain Music* will
sweep you in."
— James Van Pelt, author of *Summer of the Apocalypse*

"Swenson artfully blends music and mystery into a haunting tale set in
the rainforests of Washington State. I loved this book."
— Brenda Cooper, award-winning author of *Edge of Dark*

"Swenson unites the magic of music and the power of emotion in this
unique, slow-building fantasy thriller. Composer Truman Starkey is
starting over after a messy divorce by visiting his friend's resort in a
beautiful Washington State rain forest to focus solely on writing the
new symphony that has been eluding him. Within minutes of his arrival,
he hears a voice in the rain that becomes his muse—and calls him to a
magical destiny . . . the many tangled threads of the plot come together
in a satisfying conclusion. It's a rewarding tale."
— *Publishers Weekly*

"I loved the story, the characters, and the overall structure. Swenson
gives a good sense of setting and great details. The musical pieces are
the strongest parts, weaving the whole thing together. Strong, emotional
content."
— J.A. Pitts, author of *Black Blade Blues* Praise for Patrick

Also by Patrick Swenson

The Ultra Thin Man
The Ultra Big Sleep
Slightly Ruby

RAIN
MUSIC

RAIN
MUSIC

Patrick Swenson

FAIRWOOD PRESS
Bonney Lake, WA

RAIN MUSIC

A Fairwood Press Book
November 2021
Copyright © 2021 Patrick Swenson

All Rights Reserved

First Edition

Fairwood Press
21528 104th Street Court East
Bonney Lake, WA 98391
www.fairwoodpress.com

Dust jacket and interior case artwork © 2021 Nikki Rossignol
Cover and book design by Patrick Swenson

Hard Cover Edition ISBN: 978-1-933846-14-9
Trade Edition ISBN: 978-1-933846-13-2
First Fairwood Press Edition: November 2021
Printed in the United States of America

In memory of John Pitts & Jay Lake

To the Morrisons & the staff at the
Rain Forest Resort Village
& to the writers of the
Rainforest Writers Retreat

A NOTE ON THE COVER ART

Every spring I run a writing retreat at Lake Quinault on the Olympic Peninsula. It's held at the Rain Forest Resort Village where this novel is set. My good friend Nikki Rossignol, a wonderful artist, signed on to do the cover art for this novel. As it so happened, she decided to come to the retreat in 2020 (just weeks before lockdown due to Covid-19).

Nikki works primarily with watercolors. While at Quinault, she gathered rainwater and sent several bottles of it back home to Montana. She completed a black and white drawing to start, which graces the hardcover boards underneath the dust jacket.

The cover art for this novel was painted using actual rainwater from Quinault. That means every copy of this novel is infused with the magic of the rainforest!

We both hope you enjoy the experience.

PRELUDE

Into each life some rain must fall,
Some days must be dark and dreary.

—Henry Wadsworth Longfellow
The Rainy Day

MUD AND RAIN

WHEN JOEL HINES FINALLY RAN OUT OF PATIENCE, HE dropped the woman from the end of the pier, feet first, straight into the mud flats exposed by the low tide. She sank into the mud up to her waist.

The second woman who remained on the pier let out a muffled scream. The duct tape had something to do with that. He smiled appreciatively. He had bound her hands and feet tight enough to keep her from doing much more than curling into a fetal position.

Her long dark hair obscured one side of her face, and her ankle-length, sheer white cotton dress was scrunched up around her knees. He'd thought he might duct tape her to the old rusting folding chair on the pier, but decided she didn't need to be comfortable in any way.

Witch, he thought. *Goddamn witch.*

His truck and fifth wheel sat at the top of a bluff overlooking the ocean. He liked that he could come and go with it whenever he wanted—squat for a while without anyone giving him a hard time. It was quiet out here. Sometimes, tourists drove by and checked the view. The pier at the bottom of the bluff had been there for years on a foundation of rocks and gravel in the middle of the mudflats. The pier extended past it, so when the tide was out, as it was this morning, nothing but mud lay beyond. He wondered who had taken the time to build the pier, and why.

The woman stuck in the mud tried to scream, but Hines had duct taped her mouth as well, and her whining protests sounded like a wounded animal.

He yelled down at her, brandishing the knife he'd used to carve some symbols into her flesh. Blood ran down her face from several of the cuts. "No one's going to hear you, Serena darling." He crouched low and smiled. It was getting dark, and he had a little trouble seeing her down there. "Now don't you wish your friend had reconsidered? Don't you wish you'd at least told her what I wanted? Helped out a little bit? I can be a nice guy. You could have handed over the box of Moss, given me a little *respect*, and I would have killed you quickly."

He grew more desperate for the Moss—the magicked drugs he'd been given at his weakest—as his power waned.

If he didn't have his power, the darkness would completely overtake him. The witch understood; she was *like* him, even if she wouldn't take Moss unless absolutely necessary. You didn't just run out and buy Moss from a dealer.

"The tide's coming in," Hines said to the woman on the pier, but loud enough so that the other woman in the mud could hear him. "The water's rising. Serena will have water to her shoulders, neck, chin. Soon she'll go under. Way under." He cocked his head to one side, then adjusted his Olympic Rainforest baseball cap, turning it just slightly askew. "What do you think? Do you think you might tell me where the Moss is? What do you say? Do you want to live?"

Hines raised an eyebrow when she mumbled something through the duct tape.

"What?" he asked, putting a hand to an ear. "What?"

The woman nodded at him.

Yes, she knew. She'd tell him where, the witch. She'd tell him, then he'd chain her to one of the pilings. Probably have to chance leaving the fifth wheel on the bluff and take the truck and search. Make sure the Moss was where she said it was. Then, during the next low tide, he'd come back to the pier, unchain her, and toss her into the mud, too, next to the other, who'd already be dead. Neither of the women had given him any respect. None whatsoever. Without Moss, he had no way to gain his own respect, or light the way to redemption and healing. *Mother, I'm coming for you.*

He bent, pulled her to her knees. She moaned a little, then looked at him with dark brown eyes. A deep bruise had formed on her cheek where he'd hit her earlier to shut her up. Muffled screams continued in the mud below. He wished she'd die already.

He straightened and put his hands on his hips. He looked out over the ocean bay and took a deep breath. The sun, on a collision course with the edge of the world, had turned the sky orange and red. The smell of saltwater invigorated him. He exhaled and smiled. The coming darkness would give him a distinct advantage over her if things got out of hand.

"My God, it's a beautiful world we live in, Kachina. Too beautiful even for the likes of you." He looked back at her. "If you lie to me, I will whittle you away with a knife and drop pieces of you into the ocean." He ripped off the duct tape, and there was a slight redness around her mouth. "Tell me. *Now.*"

The young woman didn't answer him. Instead, she sang. It started in the back of her throat, like her earlier moaning, but grew louder, as if someone were turning up the volume on a radio. She was singing something he didn't recognize. No words. Her voice was dark and rich, the sound seemingly all around him. He didn't like it. The music made him nervous; the witch's voice was too damned melodic, too chant-like, a handful of notes rising higher and higher. He'd heard her sing in town. Watched her dance and sway.

"Shut up," he said, his words growling at the back of his throat. "Goddamn witch, shut *up.*"

She didn't.

And the rain began.

"No, no, no," he said, looking up at the sky. "Stop!"

The rain poured from the sky, battered the wooden slats of the pier, and drenched Hines. He searched the pier for the piece of duct tape he tore off the witch, but couldn't find it. It must have gone over the edge into the mud. The music hurt his ears. If he'd been at his greatest power, he'd have thrown some wind at her and blown her off the pier. Weak as he was, he should just kill her the old-fashioned way, right now. He could keep looking for the Moss on his own. The box was close by, away from the ocean, but she couldn't have had time to hide it well. He'd find it. Better to chance it than listen to the witch sing.

He shook his knife at her and walked closer, but she only intensified her singing, scrambling backwards on her knees, away from him. The rain had made the pier slick. He kicked her side, hoping that would shut her up. He couldn't kill her yet; he needed her. He flicked his knife across her forehead and barely caught the flesh, making a thin red line that curved downward.

She didn't miss a beat and kept backing up.

"There's nowhere to go," he said. "Just forget it."

Her feet reached the end of the pier and dangled over the edge. She stopped moving but sang loud and confidently as he dropped down on his knees in front of her.

"Last chance," he said, wincing from the rain slashing across his face, the shrill singing pounding at his ears. He pushed the tip of the knife against her throat. "Stop it. Stop it now."

She sang louder, the notes rising, rising, rising. The thin cut on her forehead stood out like a frown.

He spat the words at her. "Stop. Now."

And miraculously, the singing stopped.

The rain stopped too.

Joel Hines sighed. Closed his eyes a moment. When he opened them, the woman stared at him, her wide, dark brown eyes so much like a deer's, studying him as if he held the key to something enormously important. But he knew better. He knew the rest of the world meant absolutely nothing to her.

Rainwater trickled down her face. An instant later, in front of his eyes, the young woman vanished.

FIRST MOVEMENT

And all my days are trances,
And all my nightly dreams
Are where thy gray eye glances,
And where thy footstep gleams—
In what ethereal dances,
By what eternal streams.
   —Edgar Allan Poe
    To One in Paradise

1

THE QUINAULT RAIN FESTIVAL

The Previous Year

O N THE LAST DAY OF MAY, TRUMAN "TIP" STARKEY LEFT his Seattle studio apartment with a single suitcase, a guitar, and enough money for bus fare. Unbelievably, it had been two years ago to the day that his old high school buddy Jacob Platt had retired from Microsoft, sold his stock options, bought a small resort on the Olympic Peninsula, and asked Truman to join him. Now, he was finally taking Jacob's offer.

Truman had split with his ex-wife Melissa, a fellow musician and composer, a year before the decision to join Jacob in Quinault. He called her Hurricane Melissa because whenever they were together, he got caught up in her whirlwind lifestyle; inevitably, he came out on the losing end, his things scattered in the wreckage.

Stolen: one symphony, after years of working on it together. Culprit: Hurricane Melissa.

Now here he was again, alone, coming out to see Jacob's resort. It was better than sinking in despair, nothing to show for his thirty years of life, and fighting the feeling of failure at having lost both Melissa *and* his symphony.

"Tip," Jacob said on the phone, "you've *got* to come out here.

Quinault's beautiful, it's quiet, and you've wallowed in your poor-musician routine long enough. You're thirty years old. You're over Melissa, right?"

He was over her, he said. But not her betrayal.

But Jacob was right. He could quit playing open mike gigs and dig in on writing some serious music. A symphony. Make up for what Melissa took from him.

"So you coming? My busy season's coming up and I could use your help. And God, it would be great to see you again, my friend."

Truman paused, thinking about the phone messages his land-lord had left him during the past week—he was two months behind on rent. He glanced wearily at his studio apartment and figured he could cram most of his important stuff in a suitcase. The rest he could sell or leave behind, and Jacob had offered to deal with the back rent.

"Yeah, I'm coming," Truman said.

"How soon can you get here?"

"Give me a few days."

"Awesome. You know where we are, right?"

"Mostly. I'll figure out the fine details."

After two long hours on the bus out of Seattle, he arrived in Aberdeen, a sad, quiet town forty miles south of Quinault. He transferred to a city bus. Four other people boarded the bus between one side of town and the other, but no one got off on the way to the Quinault River valley. Forty minutes later, the bus topped a rise on U.S. Highway 101, and Lake Quinault lay in the valley before him. This was the heart of the Olympic Peninsula, and that meant rain. Lots of rain. But as he descended into the valley during the last breath of May, the sun shone like a sign from God, nearly washing out the green of the tall cedar trees lining the road.

The bus rambled past a sign announcing entry into the National Forest, then coasted into the small town of Amanda Park nestled at the foot of the lake. A river outlet cut past several houses before crossing the highway. Pulling out the map he'd picked up in Aberdeen, Truman traced the river's course with his finger through tribal reservation lands until it merged with the dark line of the Washington coast and the blue ink of the Pacific. The bus slowed down, and when he looked up from the phone, the bus had crossed the river and was pulling over at its stop on the highway, a hundred feet from a rustic general store. Besides the store, there was a cafe, a pizza joint, liquor store, and a bar. On the other side of the highway was a gas station.

Truman stood up. He hefted his guitar, grabbed his suitcase from the overhead rack, and moved to the front of the bus. He asked the driver how to get to the Cedars Resort.

"Go back to the highway, head back the way we came, across the bridge, then take the first left past Amanda Park. That's the South Shore Road, and it'll take you to The Cedars. It's a good three miles or so. You don't have a ride?"

"It's okay."

He thanked the driver, picked up his guitar, and stepped outside. He was grateful for the directions, but, looking up at the sky, he wished the bus's route wound down around the lake instead of further north up the highway. The earlier sunshine had lost its brilliance. An odd sense of foreboding came to him then, like something had reached from behind and grabbed him by the collar. Gray clouds stretched across the valley like a wool blanket, and rain dripped onto the pavement. He walked quickly, but by the time he'd traveled a mile down the South Shore Road, the shower became a downpour, soaking Truman to the skin.

Rain. More than he'd ever experienced. If he hadn't had to walk miles in it, he might have found it soothing, like the first snow of winter. He opened his suitcase and fumbled for a hat. Luckily, his guitar case was waterproof. He discovered he hadn't packed a hat and stopped searching. He didn't want to drown his modest collection of clothes, books, and music staff paper. He closed the suitcase, swearing at the rain.

Then he heard someone say something.

He jumped, his heart pounding. Was someone following him? He glanced at the dark line of trees on either side of the road. He wished he were inside, banging out power chords on his guitar, or at the piano, filling up the entire rain forest with his music, drowning out all the uncertainty in his life. Had he imagined the voice? That would figure. Come out here to find himself, write his music, and start freaking out.

But no, there it was again. Quite loud, nondescript, but definitely a voice. Raindrops trickled down the back of his neck, but the sudden voice caused the tingling sensation running up his spine. Male, female? No, wait—*two* voices. One male, one female. But where the hell were they? He was in the middle of a rainstorm, for Christ's sake, so they had to be within yards of him. They had to be *right there*. He spun in a circle, squinting into the rain, and his heart pounded a little faster.

No one out there. He tried to filter out the sounds of the rain, listening for the voices, and he managed a nervous laugh, ready to dismiss the voices as some stupid trick Jacob had played on him.

It was not a trick. Voices were speaking, even though no one lurked nearby. The rain hit his bare face, and he ran headlong down the South Shore Road. He needed to find shelter. Get out of the rain, away from the voices, wherever they were.

He ran until his legs refused to carry him any farther, his lungs aching and his breath wheezing out in ragged gasps. He came upon a small garage and gas station, and it was closed. He leaned against the wall under the eaves of the building, his back against hard cedar shakes, but the voices didn't go away. His skin crawled with the cold, and shivers wracked his body.

Had to be crazy. Hearing voices out here in the middle of nowhere? He slid down and sat on the pavement, his knees tight against his chest. Maybe it was to stop the shaking he felt inside. The rain didn't let up—in fact it came down harder, and was it his imagination, or had the voices become louder? Yes, but still undecipherable. He listened so intently, his head hurt. When he was about to give up making sense of it, he made out a single word:

Dancer.

No mistaking the word. It had come through loud and clear, maybe because both voices had said it together. The female's voice was soft and melodic, and now that he paid closer attention, he could tell she was actually *singing*, and he thought it just might be the most beautiful thing he'd ever heard. In contract, the male's voice was harsh and ragged and angry.

Truman held his head in his hands and sighed, suddenly weary. He didn't know if the voices were really intended for him—it certainly didn't seem possible, considering he had just arrived. He had come here to work for Jacob, rent-free. He could finally write his music. Okay, so hearing voices was really fucked up, and it scared him. Especially after feeling the call to Quinault a few days before *getting* the call from Jacob. The voices seemed to echo some mystical, almost magical current that thrummed inside him, but he was wasn't sure it was a good thing. He was afraid, but he had to know what hearing these voices meant.

The garage's parking lot had transformed into a system of tiny ponds and running streams. Reaching out with one foot, he tapped his tennis shoe in a nearby puddle. He gazed back up at the sky, blinking water out of his eyes, and waited.

About thirty minutes after taking refuge next to the garage, the voices stopped. The woman's unintelligible song and the man's harsh, guttural voice weakened little by little, then died completely. The next half hour the rain went on without its musical accompaniment, and an unexplainable sadness came to Truman. During the entire hour, no cars drove by the garage. It was as if everyone knew to avoid the rain. That it wasn't safe to be out in it. *The voices will get you.*

When the rain dwindled enough, he looked down the road, and

there, maybe 500 feet away, was the sign for the Forest Lodge, a resort owned by some big corporation. A half-circle driveway arced around a large cedar, and in the middle of the circle, just off the road, was the Lodge itself.

He cursed himself, upset he hadn't struck out a little farther during the rainstorm. Inside the Lodge he would've been completely out of the rain and, he assumed, cut off from the voices. He could have used their phone, called Jacob, and told him to get the hell down there and pick him up. He considered going in there now to look around, but the rain had stopped. No excuse not to be on his way. Looking down the road, he also spotted the Quinault Ranger Station. That could have been another possible sanctuary to wait out the storm.

He had another mile to go before he reached the Cedars Resort. If he waited any longer, he might get rained on again, so he picked up his suitcase and guitar and continued down the road.

The Cedars Resort was its own community on the east end of Lake Quinault. Truman came upon the resort after rounding a long bend in the road. On one side he spotted a two-story motel, painted a brick red, then three cabins painted the same color, and a store and gift shop. Just past that was a post office and a laundromat. A restaurant and lounge hugged the lake road on his left, and an expansive lawn sloped gently down to the beach. The sun managed to peek through the ominous clouds, and the lake sparkled. Two Hobie Cat sailboats sat on the beach, sails gone. Jacob had told him they had an RV Park and campground, so he figured that was down near the beach somewhere. Jacob had also told him that, somewhat famously, the resort was home to the world's largest spruce tree.

If he'd kept walking, he'd find himself in Olympic National Park. The park bordered the lake on the north and east, with Forest Service land on the south, and the Quinault Indian reservation on the west. The Cedars Resort was one of the few independently owned properties on the lake. The previous owners of the Cedars had lived there for twenty years before Jacob Platt bought it, ready to retire from Microsoft and get out of Seattle.

Truman climbed the steps to the store and walked in. Grocery store on his right, gift shop on his left, registration desk in front of him. Doors behind the desk on either side led to the back, probably to the resort offices.

A thin woman who looked to be in her fifties hurried through the left door, closed it behind her, and found her way to the counter. She smiled broadly. The lines around her mouth were laid out like tiny frontage roads. "Sorry to keep you waiting. Can I help you?"

Truman stepped up to the front desk, put down his stuff and said, "Yes. I need to see Jacob Platt?"

The woman stared at him for a moment before saying, "You're Truman, aren't you?"

"Yes. Guilty."

She put her hands on her hips and shook her head. "The guitar gave it away." She smiled again. "It's great you're here. I'm Andrea Cook, Jacob's mother-in-law. Jacob has told me all about you."

It was Truman's turn to smile. "Probably guilty there, too, whatever he told you. Is he here?"

"He's down in the RV park working on the sewer hookups."

"Can I just walk down there?"

She came around from behind the desk, nodding. "Sure. You can leave your stuff here." She led him back outside, and on the front steps she pointed across the street, to the right of the lounge. "Follow the road down between the cabins until it loops around to the right. You'll see the RV park there."

"Thanks," Truman said.

He found Jacob hunched over a white plastic sewer pipe next to the restrooms. He had rubber gloves on and wore a blue wind-breaker with the resort logo printed on the back in white. The logo, a circle containing the outline of the shoreline and Olympic mountains as seen from the motel, was printed in white, the words Cedars Resort in flowing script beneath it.

"I wouldn't have expected the owner to have to deal with this shit," Truman said. "So to speak."

Jacob Platt turned, saw Truman, and broke into a grin. "Tip!" He stood and extended his gloved hand. "How goes it?"

Truman pursed his lips and scrunched up his nose as he considered Jacob's offered hand. "It's going," he said, waiting for Jacob to take off his gloves. "Don't you have help for this kind of thing?"

Jacob laughed, removed the gloves, and they shook hands. He was thin and gangly, and his dark brown hair hung straight past his shoulders. He had a young face and a soft voice. He didn't quite fit the image of a resort-owner, but more of the young kid he'd hung out with in high school.

"Sure, I have employees who help out. And a few in-laws." He stared out at the lake and was silent a moment; he seemed to breathe in the sudden appearance of the afternoon sun. "But there's nothing like getting in there and doing it yourself. I get a little shit on my hands, fix leaky roofs, wash bedsheets, run the cash register in the store, work in the kitchen, and pour drinks in the lounge. Tip, this is *my* place. *My* dream." Jacob spread his arms suddenly. "Is this beautiful, or what?"

"It's beautiful. And peaceful. Thanks for having me out here."

"Peaceful? Oh yeah. Just the calm before the storm."

Truman thought back to the wild rainstorm he'd already endured, and the other storms he'd endured with Melissa and his family. He *wanted* calm. "It's going to rain again?"

"Sure it will," Jacob said. "This *is* the rain forest." He started back up the hill and Truman followed. "No, what I mean is, *tourists*. Be here in a few weeks for the summer season. We're booked solid every night in July and August. You're going to be working with Andrea at the front desk. Did you meet her?"

"She sent me down."

"Lisa, when she's not working the books, will also put in shifts."

Truman had met Jacob's wife only a few times in Seattle.

"You'll be swamped when you're on shift," Jacob continued. "But afterwards? The place is yours. You'll bunk in the living quarters above the store. Room and board and fifteen bucks an hour, like we agreed. You've got anything you want from the restaurant or store for meals and, most importantly, you'll have time to write your tunes."

They walked past the fireplace cabins, all with cedar siding, painted a dark red. There were several large ones, some smaller ones, and they all sported covered porches with cedar railings. Many were occupied. They crossed the lake road back to the store. Jacob stopped on the front porch.

"We brought Lisa's piano out here," he said.

"Yeah?"

He pointed in the general direction of the store. "I had it moved upstairs where you'll be staying. We close up at 8:00 right now, 9:00 starting next week. There's a buzzer by the door for late check-ins. You'll hear it upstairs and down. You'll have to deal with that. Lisa and I live in the house behind the store."

Truman nodded, getting a little misty-eyed now, taking in this outpouring of generosity from his old friend. "It's perfect," he said. "I can't believe you're doing this for me."

Jacob grinned. "It was your choice. But someone had to save your ass."

The rain started again, but so lightly that it was little more than a mist. Truman heard no voices.

"You don't mind the rain?" he asked Jacob.

"Gets a bit much during the Quinault Rain Festival."

"When's that?"

"September 1st through August 31st." His grin spread across his face like a crack in the clouds. "Actually, the summer's not too wet. You know how much rain Seattle gets in a year?"

Truman shrugged. "Forty inches?"

"We average a *hundred* and forty inches. Twelve feet a year."

"Jesus," Truman said.

"In contrast, just a stone's throw from here beyond the Olympic Mountains is a small town called Sequim. Their yearly rainfall is only twelve inches because it lies in the middle of the rain shadow."

Maybe he should've found a job in Sequim instead. At least he would have stayed dry.

"It can be depressing," Jacob said, "no question. The locals—well, I'm a local now—but the old guard, those whose families homesteaded here, they'll tell you the rain's like an old friend. A comforting presence, like a faithful dog that'll fetch your newspaper and slippers, curl up next to your chair, and chase away the bad mailman when asked."

Sure, Truman thought, thinking of the man's voice in the rain, but what bad mailman attacked him this afternoon? "Do you ever hear voices in the rain?" he asked.

"Voices like what? Kids outside during the rain?"

But he'd made up his mind to drop it. He shrugged it off and asked if he could settle in upstairs. Jacob said sure and led him back up the hill and inside the store.

He couldn't talk to Jacob about it. Voices. The rain people out to get him. It struck Truman as the dumbest thing he'd ever let himself believe over the course of his life. So determined was he to leave his past behind him in Seattle, he decided to keep this new madness secret from one of his oldest friends. He wished he hadn't heard the voices. That he hadn't heard *her* voice.

The woman's song in the rain had been too brief, like an unfulfilled promise, even in the long, interminable agony that had been that rainstorm. It threatened to drown him.

After getting squared away in his room above the store, he ate in the restaurant, nursed a beer in the lounge, and walked around the resort. He climbed back upstairs later. His bedroom faced the lake road. The piano was here, pushed up against one wall near the door. Another room in the back had a large TV, couch, a Soloflex weight machine, and an exercise bike. He plunked out a few notes on the piano, an upright Yamaha that had excellent sound. Jacob came up a little later and found him improvising some jazz tunes.

"I had a piano tuner come up from Aberdeen and work on it."

"I can tell," Truman said. "Thanks. It'll make a difference."

"If you get hungry," he said, "grab something from the store. You saw the kitchen downstairs. Bathroom and shower are down there too. I gotta get back up to the house. We'll break you in downstairs tomorrow."

Truman thought about doing some actual composing, but his heart wasn't in it. He stripped his still-damp clothes, crawled into bed with a paperback borrowed from the gift shop, and read until he nodded off.

Truman says goodbye to his parents at the front door, anxious for them to be on their way for the New Year's party. Their decision to let him stay on his own, trusting him to watch over his sister Tina, came only after he spent the last several days convincing them it would be okay. I'm fifteen. Go, already, I'll be fine!

He closes the door, then gazes out the living room window, watching until they've pulled out of the driveway and disappeared down the street. Rain is falling and it seems the weather might worsen before the night is through.

Truman turns to his six-year-old sister. She's sitting on the living room couch, all smiles. The woodstove is burning the logs his dad stuffed in there before leaving. It would be fine just left alone. The room is warm and cozy.

"Do you want to play a game?" he asks.

Tina nods vigorously. "Clue?"

"Well, it's a pastime for kids and grownups, played on a board,

or with cards, or online, a competition to while away the hours—"

"No, the game *Clue."*

Truman smiles. "I know. Just kidding."

A gust of wind rattles the house. Tina looks out the window, eyes widening.

"It's okay," Truman assures her. "So let's play. Clue it is. But," *he says, pointing a warning finger at her, "I get to be Colonel Mustard."*

He woke in the night, and the rain came down hard enough to rattle the windows. He frowned. That was weird: almost exactly like the dream, which had already faded from memory, as most of his dreams did. He remembered enough to know it was about a fateful night that fractured his family. A loved one gone. Perhaps the dream faded so quickly because Truman had never wanted to remember the truth of that night. Had never mourned the loss—

Truman shook his head and refused to think about it. He pulled himself up on one elbow and squinted at the clock on the side table next to the bed. Three in the morning. On the wall next to the door, he spotted himself, vague and insubstantial in the full length mirror. He groaned and lay back down, staring at the knotholes in the ceiling.

The rain pounded against the house, and it wasn't letting up. It insisted he pay attention to it, and he did, crawling out of bed and stumbling to the double-hung window. He unlatched it and pushed up the bottom pane.

The rain fell straight down, so he stayed dry, but there it was: her song washed over him. He'd really expected to hear it—*hoped* to hear it—and she hadn't disappointed him. Her voice slashed through the window and it had more power this time, more clarity. Low, dark, with a hint of vibrato. The man's voice wasn't there, he realized, and her voice came through clear.

Dancer.

The word breezed in through the window with such force that he backed up a few steps. New words came through now.

Moon.

Key.

Truman closed his eyes and concentrated on the song, trying desperately to understand more.

Circle.

Lake.

She continued singing, but no more words came through. It wasn't until he gave up trying to make out her words that the realization hit him. He'd been so intent on her words that he'd completely ignored the one thing he should have naturally paid attention to.

The song itself.

Now that he listened closely, the melody carrying the words through the rain had such a beauty to it that he felt sadness and joy all at once. Few melodies had ever moved him. Samuel Barber's *Adagio.* The intermezzo from Mascagni's *Cavelleria Rusticana.* Like that, but without the strings or the underlying harmonies. Seven simple notes, all different, ascending in various intervals.

"My God," he whispered, leaning out the window. The rain had let up a little, and the drops hitting his face kept a soothing rhythm in time to the song. "You are *beautiful*," he said.

He left the window open, ran to the back room, opened the two windows there, then rummaged through his pack for music staff paper. Quickly, before he forgot it, he plinked the piano keys until he found the exact notes.

He had it. He wrote it down.

His symphony had begun.

2

≫⟫

UNDERCOVER

KAT GREGORY STARED AT THE ENTRANCE TO THE QUINAULT Ranger Station, not wanting to go in. Something had stopped her. The rain had tapered off, so she wasn't getting soaked.

She hadn't been north to see her dad at the station for a few weeks now, and that was fine with her. She wished she got along better with him. Her mom had left him unexpectedly last month, sending divorce papers in the mail from God knew where, and he'd become moody and standoffish, burying himself into his work for the Forest Service. He'd practically disowned her, but at the same time, he didn't begrudge her a place to stay when needed.

Kat had moved out years earlier, but recently the starving artist shtick had forced her to give up her apartment and divide her time between her best friend Serena Ralston's couch in Aberdeen and her dad's place—not his house on the North Shore, but on a cot in the ranger station when he worked long shifts.

To help Serena out with costs, Kat sang at Duffy's Tavern on Main Street, a dive bar that boasted music by local bands. She wasn't in a band herself, but she'd sing some evenings. She gave a split of her earnings to Rand Mills, who played electric guitar with Deluge, one of Aberdeen's most popular bands. He played acoustic guitar for her, though, while she sang solo at the mike. Rand didn't mind the extra work, and he said he loved her voice.

People always said that. She didn't expect any big breaks though, not any time soon. Deluge had their own vocalist and they'd never asked her to join them.

"Come *on*," Serena said earlier that evening as they sat in the bar. "You're a natural talent. Your sound is so—"

"Don't say it."

"—*magical*. You'll be hitting the big time before you know it."

Kat sighed, suddenly very tired. She always felt that way when anyone complimented her. What use was a *magical* voice in a sleepy place like this? "No one will hear me out here. In Aberdeen? Nothing good's come out of Aberdeen music-wise since Kurt Cobain."

"Harsh."

Kat had just come off stage, her last set completed at 7:00 p.m. on a slow weekday evening at Duffy's. She sat at one of the rickety tables, her backpack on the chair across from her, Serena on her left. Serena had ordered her a coffee, and it steamed on the table next to her. In ten minutes, Kat would grab the bus to Quinault and try and nap during the hour-long ride.

Rand swung by the table and stopped to give her a quick hug. "Lovely as ever," he said.

She wondered if he meant her or the music, but she didn't ask.

Then he waved and was gone. Rand moved quickly. He didn't stay in one place long. Sounded familiar. Her mother had travelled all over the country before settling down with her dad. That didn't last, and now she was gone. Kat bussed between the remaining landmarks in her life, an hour at a time. At least her dad mostly stayed put.

"Rand likes you," Serena said.

"He likes the way I sing."

"Sure. But he also loves the way you *dance*. You know. On nights when Deluge plays, and you've had a few drinks, and you've got your skinny self out on the dance floor, all that black hair whirling around you." Serena fanned herself, as if aroused. "Even I get pulled into what you're doing. You really lose yourself."

Kat *did* lose herself when dancing. The singing, too. Maybe that's why she hadn't had much luck in the business outside this solo gig at Duffy's. Too centered on her own problems. Too much time trying to escape them in the best way she knew.

"Oh shit," Serena said, her voice barely above a whisper.

Kat looked back at her. "What?"

"That guy—that mossy guy—is here again." She flicked her eyes left.

Kat squinted that way, past the chair with her backpack. There he was, at another table, looking in her direction, almost shyly, his face nearly obscured in the semi-dark room because the brim of his green Olympic Rainforest baseball cap was tugged down low over his eyes. She'd seen him in Duffy's before. More than once.

He offered a faint smile.

Kat glanced away, then frowned at Serena. "Um. Mossy?" she asked.

Serena shrugged. "Looks soft. Seems strange. Hangs around in dark places. Not sure whether you should touch or not."

"Please."

"He might be on drugs."

Kat laughed. "You say that about every stranger."

"Every stranger who looks *mossy*." She leaned closer to Kat. "Maybe Allie knows him. A client maybe."

"Allie doesn't peddle drugs."

"That you *know* about. When has Allie told you anything remotely plausible about her weird shit? I love her, but she puts out some strange vibes."

"Because she's a psychic."

"Well, that's what she advertises anyway. It might be a *front*."

Kat rolled her eyes for Serena's benefit, but Kat knew Allie *did* have something else going on besides the psychic gig. Allie had told her of an untapped power several weeks back.

"Something is holding you back," Allie had told her months

ago. Allie was relatively young for having so much knowledge about the world—early forties, maybe—and psychic power, whether just advertised or real, still gave her a perceived wisdom Kat felt she could never achieve on her own.

"I don't know what it is." Kat told Allie that but thought of her broken family.

"You must practice what I've shown you. Find your song. Where is it, Kat? Why is it so mute?" She tapped Kat's chest. "It's in here and you won't let it out."

"I sing every few nights," Kat said.

"Not your *song*. You're covering it up with all this other noise."

"Noise—?"

Allie taught Kat ways to find it. She'd hated Serena using the word *magical*, but that was exactly what it was. A song was akin to passion. If you manipulated the song? If you found the correct intervals and the proper order? All Kat needed was the way to express it.

Allie had some options.

She offered some magicked drugs, but she warned of severe side effects and possible consequences if she abused them. Kat said no way. She'd seen her own mother fight with addiction. Plus, she had a hard time believing in magically synthesized drugs.

The other option didn't seem likely either, which, according to Allie, meant using her body as a focus to find her song, joining with a willing participant.

"You mean, *sex*?" she asked Allie.

"Yes. As a *focus*." Allie smiled. "It has been done. You can create wonderful things—*change* things—with the power of a telos."

"Telos?"

"I will teach you."

And so, without telling Serena, Kat had visited Allie many times to learn this option. She felt the need to do so. She was Allie's student, and there was more to learn. She needed to find her song.

Here at Duffy's, letting her coffee grow cold, the bus soon to arrive, Kat didn't think she'd ever hear it. Not as long as she slid back and forth from Aberdeen to Quinault. She was like a pendulum, wound up, but unable to find the center.

She chanced another look across the room. Moss Man was still at his table, but he stared at Duffy's menu in front of him. She could only see the top of his cap.

"Listen," Serena said, "he's here two or three times a week. I've only seen him in here when *you're* performing."

"Oh, come on."

"He's checking you out, that's what he's doing."

"Not necessarily a bad thing." She harkened back to Allie's option. No. Not this guy. Not as her willing participant, even if she ever found herself ready.

"Maybe not." Serena grabbed Kat's forearm. "Oh! Maybe he's undercover."

"A cop?"

"A scout. A *music* scout."

Kat scoffed. "Please."

He was looking at her again. Smiling. Serena was right about something being off with him. She glared until he shrugged and studied the menu some more.

"Maybe he's just hungry," Serena said.

Kat waved it off. "Hey, c'mon. Walk me to the bus stop."

They left Duffy's, and luckily the Moss Man didn't follow. At the bus stop, a block away, the rain came down hard, and neither of them had an umbrella. Serena pulled them under cover, huddling against the plexiglass of a transit kiosk, and there they waited until the bus arrived. Kat gave Serena a hug, promised she'd text her later, and clambered on.

Now, in front of the ranger station, the rain had lessened, just a light drizzle that misted in the lights of the parking lot. Something seemed wrong. Something seemed off. It had nothing to do with the dread of seeing her dad, or wishing her mom was around. It wasn't even about the creepy guy at Duffy's. *Something was—*

She looked up.

Up into the drizzle.

—*calling her*.

That couldn't be right. As soon as she thought it, she was suddenly certain that, as strange as the feeling was, it was in fact *not* a calling. It was—

An echo.

Her body tingled, and goosebumps ran up and down her body. Not from the chill of the rain, but from the almost palpable sense she had of being somewhere else. Out there, outside herself. As if she'd heard an echo of her own voice.

The rain picked up.

The echo was no longer an echo, but a strong voice.

"Kat!"

Kat blinked and saw her dad at the door of the ranger station. She did a weak wave and shuffled over to him. He gave her a hug, but she kept space between them. She turned her head to the side and saw his nametag—*Andy Gregory, Olympic National Forest*—and the US Forest Service patch on his sleeve.

"Come on, for heaven's sake," he said. "You're cold. You'll catch your death out here."

Kat always thought that a strange saying. Maybe she was a bit chilly, but she wouldn't catch death. It was spring, after all. The rains would slow down, and those who worked around the lake would prepare for the upcoming tourist season.

Her dad turned to the door, and they went in. Her cot awaited.

3

A BEAUTIFUL WORLD

DURING THE FIRST FEW WEEKS, TRUMAN LEARNED THE ROPES at the Cedars Resort. Business picked up gradually, not slamming them all at once, and he learned the fine nuances of customer service, not once losing his cool and taking it out on the guests. Jacob called it impressive.

He found he liked the work. He was even good at it. They'd get a little rush, sometimes when Andrea had taken a break, and he'd make do.

"Truman!"

He had zoned out. Andrea's cash register was going a mile a minute on the grocery store side.

"Take over here," she said. "I've got to check in a guest." She rushed over to the front desk side of things, and he rang up a new customer's stack of junk food, chips, and beer.

Both registers worked nonstop for half an hour.

After the rush, Andrea laughed and said, "You wait. That's nothing. Once July rolls round, and it gets warm, you'll be *begging* me to let you stock the beer cooler."

Later that evening, he ate a store burrito and chips for dinner, then locked up and headed upstairs. He was physically tired, but he needed to pop into writing mode and lock himself in the piano room. Face the music.

Write a symphony. Not an easy thing for even the most seasoned composer, but he relished the inevitability of it, the pre-printed empty staves and clefs daring him to continue. Like a novel writer who wrote everything longhand, he liked composing music on paper, not on the fancy computer composition programs. He didn't have a computer, and he preferred the visceral connection from head to heart to hand to paper. It took more effort and forced him to concentrate more closely on the music. He found he could keep the sometimes debilitating loneliness at bay.

The previous week, during a heavy rainstorm, he'd heard his muse yet again. She called for his music in the darkness. That's what it seemed like to Truman. She sang words Truman could wrap his mind around. *Moon* and *key*. *Circle* and *lake*. He searched his phone for a Circle Lake on the Olympic Peninsula, but found nothing. He kept reminding himself to ask Jacob about it.

This time, a few other words seeped through the rain. *Magic, spirit* and *love*.

He liked the almost palpable sexual tension of *spirit* and *love*.

The beautiful melody belonged to his muse, but he called it his own as he wrote it down on staff paper. After that, the symphony's first movement took shape in a whirlwind of activity as he found a perfect counter melody to accompany it (a blend of muted trumpet and oboe), then discovered he could play it backwards, transposed, and make another melody. He was using the classical sonata form, and he already had his exposition: the seven notes of the melody, which he'd base his whole symphony on, had the tonal key of B minor. He'd milk the main melody throughout the first part of the movement, modulate to the dominant key before heading to the development and any number of variations. Reach a pivotal chordal moment with the entire orchestra kicking ass on it, then suddenly cut them out, leave the oboe playing alone on the exact note that started the backwards melody. Work that over, then get both melodies in together somehow, relegate the counter melody to the cellar, a half time bass line.

Potential. Lots of potential. He'd wished, not for the first time, he'd brought a metronome, so that he could click out some tempos to work with. He could parse it all in his head, but he liked the rhythmic tick of a metronome. He thought about running into Aberdeen to look for one.

June ended. The resort was busy, and the weather drier now. Almost no rain had fallen the last week, and it was hot—temperatures into the 90s—and dry. Park rangers had already upgraded the fire danger status from moderate to high. It was way too early to have that happen, late June.

No rain.

No muse.

No music.

During his short time in Quinault, he'd begun to rely on the rain as a crutch. He couldn't compose without it. How had that happened so fast? He'd lacked commitment to Melissa in all aspects of their relationship, but now, less than a month in his new surroundings, he had lost his will to compose.

That had to be some kind of record.

He shouldn't have assigned so much importance to the rain. Hadn't it scared him to death that first day? Yes, but hadn't the rain, in the voice of his muse, given him the melody of his life?

Shit. It was *summer*. It didn't rain every day.

Maybe he should try sitting at the piano bench and force himself to compose. He had the melody. He had the counter melody. But coming up with something meaningful to weave the threads together eluded him. He could not cut through the tension he had built with his initial variations.

On a cooler evening on the first day of July, a light rain fell, barely more than a mist. Truman rushed up to his second story room after his shift and opened the window, hoping to catch a hint of her song in the rain. Funny how he now thought of the music and the rain as inseparable. The presence of ghostly music emanating from the rain seemed a reality, not a figment of his imagination, even though he still kept this from Jacob.

Maybe he was crazy, but it was *his* crazy, and it had helped him so far.

Then: Something made him jump.

He had no idea what. Right afterward, it felt like he was being watched, but no one could possibly be there. Not up in his room. Not down below on the street. Not anywhere but in the rain.

The hairs raised on the back of Truman's neck. He turned away from the window just as a gust of wind blew through, ruffling the curtains.

He faced the full-length mirror. For an instant. For a breath. He thought . . . No. The mirror was a mirror. Still, he had a strong urge to come up close to it and look within the reflection, or maybe look behind it. His breathing quickened, and his pulse raced.

Truman closed his eyes, waited a couple heartbeats, and looked again. Nothing. Only Truman's reflection. But in his head, he had a thought. It came to him in a whisper, and he wasn't certain if it was his own or not.

It's a beautiful world we live in, Kachina.

What the hell? Kachina?

Just then, the lights winked and dimmed, and an instant later they went out, leaving Truman in a darkness as impenetrable as a cloudy, starless night.

He called Jacob. He couldn't find a flashlight, so he had to feel his way downstairs to the registration area.

Truman waited in the chair downstairs behind the front desk, silent and unmoving, trying to calm his breathing. After ten minutes, the lights on the pop and beer coolers came on, and the motors started humming in their own voices, harsh and out of tune.

"Tripped the main breaker," Jacob said when he entered the store through the front door a few minutes later, flashlight glowing.

"Tripped how?" Truman asked.

Jacob shrugged. "No idea. Just some kind of surge, I suppose."

"That happen a lot?"

"Not a lot." Jacob headed for the front door. "Night's cleared up. Drizzle's stopped."

Great, Truman thought.

"Get some sleep," Jacob said. "Resort's full tomorrow."

"Like every night this summer."

Jacob waved and closed the door behind him, disappearing into the night. Truman saw Jacob's flashlight on the counter. He snatched it and made his way to the door, but when he stood outside, he couldn't see his friend at all, and no reply came back when Truman called for him.

He looked above, blinking at the stars that shone through the gaps in the dusty clouds, and with the memory of that phrase—*it's a beautiful world we live in, Kachina*—burning in his head, he pleaded with whatever force was out there to make it rain soon. If it didn't, he believed he might take it upon himself to force the issue: run out into the street one night and dance his heart out.

4

~~~

THE HAND THAT FEEDS YOU

J OEL HINES THOUGHT BACK TO THE MOMENT IN HIS LIFE WHEN
he emerged from obscurity.

The obscurity had started at birth. He came into the world without much trouble, but his mother died a few days later due to complications of the birth, and he never forgave her.

His father was a logger who drank himself into a stupor every
evening. Hines remembered the long nights curled up on one end
of an old, ratty, puke-green couch—the only furniture in the living
room—watching his father drink on the other end. His father would
drink and demand Hines give him his undivided attention. He'd
quote lumber mill statistics one moment, spout gibberish the next.

You know how many lumber mills there are in this country?
He'd point the bottle at Joel. *Maybe five hundred. Six. Fuck if I
remember for sure. Guess what state produces the most lumber?*

He didn't know.

Guess.

He guessed Washington.

Shit no. Alaska.

He wasn't surprised.

Oregon and California are next.

His dad quizzed him whenever he could, never expecting a
correct answer.

You know Russia has the largest forest area of any country?

But the U.S. of A. knows what to do with it, by god. Hell, we've got thirty percent of the world's forest.

So, he'd almost make sense like that, and then before Hines knew it, he was on to something else. Something he didn't understand a word of.

His father never said a word about Hines' mother. Never. And, for all his drunken nights, he never touched Hines, and rarely yelled at him. He rose every morning to work in the woods, where a single stupid move could kill or seriously maim him. Hines decided early on that nothing in that house—not even his father—belonged to him, and he left it all behind when he turned sixteen. He kept his legal name for when he needed it, but a few years after leaving, he changed his last name from Walters to Hines.

He survived for years on the streets, pulling odd jobs in the woods, sometimes retail jobs in town, and peddling anything he thought he could sell to make a buck. When he was twenty-four, he bought a trailer—a fifth wheel—and moved around Gray's Harbor, never settling down anywhere for long.

Fucking ten years of that life. He figured his dad was dead by now. Drank himself to death, or maybe a tree had fallen on him. Hines never heard anything, never saw an obituary. He was still angry about his mother leaving him, and he had a strong desire to wish her back among the living and reunite with her. Ask her why. Why the hell?

Hines started dealing on the streets. Made himself known. Didn't get on the manufacturing side of things, like cooking Crystal or that sort of thing. He sold it though. Not right away. First just weed, then Molly, then Oxy. Later he hit on the idea of moving cocaine, and that got him into a couple of rings that kept Aberdeen and the rest of Gray's Harbor feeling good.

He was comfortable, but also footloose and fancy free. He had clients, he had his fifth wheel, and enough money so that he didn't live like a bum.

He was thirty years old now, and he'd been hanging out at the local taverns, gawking at women, certain one of them would re-mind him of his mother, but he didn't have anything to go on, so it was mostly an exercise in futility. He especially liked Duffy's, and just tonight he'd seen the dark-haired girl sing again. Kat. In-troduced as Kat Gregory. When he saw her dance on nights she came to listen to the bands, he stared at her longingly, her move-ments like self-contained miracles, but when she was up on stage and *sang* . . . Now *that* was something. Her voice moved him and frightened him at the same time.

Didn't remind him of his mother in the slightest, but he could mess with her head.

She left with her friend—he knew her name, too—and that was that. Bye-bye for now, Kat and Serena. He decided to take the long way around to his truck so he could walk in the rain. He'd un-hitched the truck from his fifth wheel, as he usually did, the fifth wheel parked out of town.

He was getting drenched, but he didn't mind. His ballcap helped some. Trusty old cap. Cutting through the alley behind Duffy's, he walked north to take a circuit around the block. Before he was half-way around, however, he decided to head east and cut through an apartment complex, weaving his way around side streets and alleys until he came out on another street that had old houses, some trail-ers, and very few working streetlights.

The night was welcome. The rain, too. The unfamiliar sur-roundings. Kat, he thought. What am I going to do with *you*? Are you a dark angel barring my mother's way back?

He heard something faint. Far away, like an echo. That was weird. There was a voice. It was—*singing*. How strange. What a soothing sound. It came and went, though. There. Not there. There. But always as if from somewhere else. He had a shitty singing voice, and couldn't hold a tune, but he tried to hum a couple of the tones he could center on.

Then the music stopped.

"Huh," he said.

He tried a few times to replicate the song. Most of it. Didn't think it was so bad.

Before he realized it, he'd left the street and stood in a small clearing amid some evergreen trees. A little park he'd never come across before. No one else came here either, he suspected. There was a rusted grill top over a fire pit, and that was about it. The park was eerily silent.

He took off his cap.

He looked up and the rain wet his face.

A wind blew suddenly. He liked the sensation of it against his skin. Wind. *Wind.* There was power there.

It whispered to him, said, "Hey, look out," and with the warning came fast-approaching footsteps on the slick grass. The next whisper was a jacket rustling behind him and at once he felt a pinch in his side, but a pinch with a metal claw.

He fell, turned onto his back, and the attacker was on him, knee on his chest. A big man, bald head gleaming in the rain. Long overcoat—what Hines could see of it. He held a knife, and its serrated edge already had blood on it.

Hines recognized him but couldn't remember his name.

"What—?" Hines managed to say. He raised his head to glance around, see if anyone might help him. He put a hand to his side and grimaced when he found the wound.

"A message and a farewell," the man said. His voice was deep, like an organ's pedal notes. "From Bill Hand."

Oh shit.

Oh shit oh shit oh *shit.*

Bill Hand was a career criminal who'd left Chicago to build a drug ring in the Pacific Northwest. A ring Hines had joined, doing sales on the streets. Hand was frustrated with rings moving in on his territory, so he took on new sellers to escalate business.

There was one thing Bill Hand hated more than anything.

"Unless you have that five thousand on you," the bald man said, "the message starts now."

"I was going to get it back to Bill," Hines said. He remembered the man's name now. Jake. Jake someone. "Honestly, Jake, I was. Look, take what I have. It's not much but—"

"Skim and you pay the price," the man said.

Hines thought that the funniest thing he'd heard all week. He lay his head back in the grass and laughed.

"Fucker, what's so funny?"

"Is that the message? Skim and you pay the price? *Really*?"

Jake frowned. "It's not the message. It's an—admonition."

"My. Fancy word, Jake, but I don't think it's an admonition."

"Then what is it?"

"Maybe an aphorism."

"Aphorism? What's that?"

"A saying? Moral? An adage?"

"I don't care what the fuck it's called. The *message* is, you don't ever skim from the Hand that feeds you." Jake brandished the blood-covered knife. "Farewell, Joel."

It happened so fast that Hines didn't have a chance to fight it. There was all that joking around about vocabulary, and then *violence*. Jake brought the knife down into his gut, stabbing him deep. Before Hines could shout out in surprise, the pain seared through the wound, and Jake's knife jabbed into his stomach again, and again. There was pain like he'd never felt, but he could only think about the blood that coated his hands when they fumbled around and found the stab wounds.

Jake stared at him a while, nodded as if satisfied, then took his knee off Hines's chest, stood, and ran from the park.

Leaving Hines for dead. Yes. He was going to bleed out in less than half an hour. He would die without treatment. If he hesitated at all, he'd be dead for sure. His insides felt wrong amid the excruciating pain. Probably sliced up his intestines. Damaged skin, nerves, blood vessels, muscles, organs. He turned his head side to side in the wet grass, but no longer saw Jake. No one else either.

Get up.

He'd read somewhere that a stab wound could kill a guy in fifteen minutes, but someone else in fifteen hours.

Don't be that first guy.

With a painful surge, he rolled onto his unwounded side. Pins and needles everywhere now. He was almost numb to the pain, but that might not last. He brought his knees up, curling into the fetal position, then used his arm to elbow himself up. In what seemed like an eternity—*no, fifteen minutes could kill me*—he stood, hunched over, his hands now covering his stomach. Not that he could stop the blood flow. Not that it would do any good.

He felt dizzy and cold. He knew what was happening. Shock.

His dad had lost two fingers in the woods on the job once. He remembered the doc talking about shock in the ER and this was happening now. Hines's pulse rate was up, blood pressure probably down, and his skin felt cold, and not from the rain, which had started to lessen.

Quick, while he could still think. Which way?

Hobbling back the way he came, he hoped to reach a street with traffic. A street with some goddamn *light*. If he'd only just gone straight to his truck after Duffy's. The young woman had clouded his judgement.

He zeroed in on a streetlight in the distance. Blood seeped through his fingers. Cold. Very cold now.

Thoughts swirled even as he reached the light: He deserved this. Jake was right; Bill Hand was right. He hadn't got away with the theft. He had no one to blame but himself. And, well. His mother. The woman who brought him into this world and didn't stick around to help. His father's drunken stories hadn't helped much either, but Hines didn't care about him.

Where *was* everyone? The light seemed overly bright, but it didn't matter. He fell to his knees, numb and cold. He wasn't going to make it.

He crumpled to the sidewalk, and *that* hurt like hell. He lay on his back, the rain coming straight down, bathing his face. He hummed a couple of those echoed tones he'd heard earlier. Repeated them, off key. Felt tired. He tried again to get sounds out, but all that was left was his raspy breath. That was all he could do. All, that is, except close his eyes and die.

5

LET'S DANCE

IT DIDN'T RAIN.

Truman didn't dance in the street, but kept his eyes on the skies, looking for clouds, hoping the weather would turn. But the days stayed warm and dry, and he felt guilty ignoring his music.

Jacob had warned Truman about the Fourth of July traffic at the resort, but it still didn't prepare him for the onslaught of tourists and locals who rolled in for the festivities.

Andrea worked the front desk while Truman manned the side register for the little general store. By the afternoon, the crowds swarmed the store nonstop, the check-out line always two or three people deep. He hardly had a moment to think between transactions. When he did have a few moments, he ran to the back cooler to restock the beer. Even Jacob's wife Lisa came in to help for a few hours.

About four o'clock, Truman rang up a 12-pack of Schmidt beer for a local, Ben Dobbs, a logger who lived up the road in one of four cabins the locals called the Stone Cabins.

Andrea attended to a couple checking into an RV spot. They were staying a month, leaving only after the annual Northwest Championship Hobie Cat sailboat races took place on Lake Quinault in August. They had their Hobie Cat on a trailer behind their Airstream RV.

"Getting a head start, are we?" Andrea asked them.

"Our first time in Quinault," said the woman. She was about Truman's age, early thirties, brown hair tied back into a ponytail. "Since it's our first time on this lake, we wanted to get a feel for it, and have a good vacation at the same time."

Andrea handed them a card to fill out. "Spot number twenty-two. Are you going to pay nightly or by the week?"

Truman turned back to his own cash register and found Dennis Reynolds, a high school senior, waiting with some Doritos, M&Ms, and sodas. He worked across the street as a dishwasher. Jacob had hired him a few weeks back to help with the summer rush.

"Hey, Dennis." Truman's fingers flicked across the register, entering the totals.

"I hear you play guitar," Dennis said. He had blonde hair and blue eyes, but Truman didn't see much life in his dark pupils.

"That's $9.44," Truman said, smiling. "Sure, I play. You too?"

He nodded, but he didn't smile or look that excited about it. "I'm already working on the basics," he said. "I want to learn more, and there's no music teacher at the school. It's boring this summer."

"You graduated this year, right?"

"Yeah. The one thing my parents did of any use to me was buy a guitar for a graduation present."

Truman nodded, smiling politely. "Nice. Actually, I think I might have heard you playing it one night across the street, back behind the restaurant."

Dennis frowned, then remembered what Truman meant. "Right, on a break. Out in the fenced supply area. I guess sound travels."

"Sounded all right."

"I'm thinking I can improve." He handed Truman a ten-dollar bill. "Maybe you'd be willing to give me a few pointers? A lesson or two?"

The request surprised Truman. He stared at Dennis, who now looked at him expectantly. "No," he said. "I don't think so."

"I'm willing to pay some."

Truman handed back the change. "I don't really have time—"

"Maybe we can see how it goes."

Truman crossed his arms, staring Dennis down. The boy looked uncomfortable.

"Okay. We'll figure something out. Promise."

"Awesome. Thanks." He looked toward the door. "Well. I'm going across the way and get back to work. Looks like everyone's getting here early for the fireworks."

Dennis left and closed the door behind him.

Truman hardly believed he'd agreed to give the kid some guitar lessons. When would he have time? He wondered if he'd enjoy it, or resent the time it took away from composing.

Then again, what composing was he actually doing?

Perhaps teaching would lead him back to normal work habits. The July weather wasn't likely to change, and he really wanted to return to the first movement of his symphony, muse or no muse.

Kachina.

The name came to him again, and it was like before, as if it had just been implanted into his brain.

Is that your name?

His skin prickled, and he shook off the chill and forced himself to smile at the next customer.

Every Fourth of July, the Quinault Tribe put on a fireworks show at the Cedars Resort. Locals and tourists alike gathered during much of the day on the large lawn that sloped down to the lake shore, anxious to find a good viewing spot.

A beautiful evening. The lake like glass. Clear, warm, and quite without any rain.

Jacob kept the store open an hour longer to accommodate the extra traffic before and after the show, so when the first fireworks went off at 9:30, Truman was still on duty. Predictably, the customers disappeared when the first mortar thunked its payload skyward, lighting up the darkness with blooms and sparkles.

Truman stepped outside with Andrea, and they viewed the show from the front porch. Five minutes in, Truman realized they hadn't said a word to each other, preferring to admire the pyrotechnics without comment. The crowd on the lawn across the street provided plenty of commentary, however, the oohs and ahhs joining the pops and booms of the fireworks. Truman daydreamed about those firework detonations burning a hole in the sky and letting loose a torrent of rain: soaking him and drowning him and filling him up with the voice of his muse, flooding the valley with music to soothe his soul.

The fireworks ended with no such apocalyptic rapture, and Truman found the grand finale anti-climatic and disappointing. What had he expected? His dancer to swoop down from the sky on a wall of water?

Later that night the festivities continued in the lounge, more boisterous than usual with the holiday crowd enjoying the afterglow of the evening. During the off-season, the lounge closed down early, usually at nine, but the summer crowds made it worthwhile to stay open until midnight, and on the weekends, until two a.m. On the biggest weekends, Jacob hired small bands to provide live music, and tonight, Black Velvet—two guys and a drum machine—were trying to rock out with covers of '70s and '80s tunes.

Cheesy. Truman didn't say so to Jacob, who bought him two drinks before drifting off to mingle with the crowd. Truman sat at the bar flanked by strangers. A lot of locals knew him now, but none were close enough to talk to, and he frankly didn't want to give up his bar seat.

Black Velvet had just started ba ba baa-ing a pretty decent version of Abba's "Take a Chance on Me" when Truman noticed the woman on the small dance floor in front of the brick fireplace. Her feet barely moved, but she twisted and rocked back and forth to the beat, her arms held up high, head bobbing and turning side to side. Multi-colored lights flashed in her long, silky black hair, as if the ceiling spotlights were focused on her alone. Her hair whipped across her face with each bob of her head. She had on a dark halter top and wore jean shorts that were loose around her thin legs.

Much of the dance floor was in shadow, and most of the dancers did their own thing along the periphery of the spot-lit floor, but here was this thin dark-haired woman, maybe late twenties, bathed in diffused light, radiating a sexual energy that Truman found difficult to ignore. He couldn't make out her face, but imagined it was angelic.

She was dancing alone.

Several dozen people sat near Truman or leaned against the dividing wall separating the main bar from the lower level, but they didn't pay any attention to the girl. For a moment, Truman wondered if he was seeing things, but just then a couple came onto the floor and purposefully stepped around her to find a spot to dance. As Black Velvet crooned Abba's lyrics about love strong enough to last, she spun, her arms wide and head back, and he heard her yell out "It's magic" in synch with the music.

The boys in the band finished their Abba tune, said thank you, then flew into David Bowie's "Let's Dance."

She mouthed the words to the song, channeling Bowie, colored lights on her face, swaying under the moonlight, now, the serious moonlight. She smiled in his direction. He was one of many guys in her line of sight, so he most likely imagined it, but it still made him smile back and nod. Then she was spinning again, drifting out of the spotlight toward the darker edge of the dance floor and the seating area near the double doors to the deck.

"Let's Dance" ended, Black Velvet announcing a short break, and when Truman turned back to the dance floor, the girl was gone, nowhere in sight. He stood next to his chair and scanned the lounge, but he didn't spot her. A surge of panic ran through him because he hadn't had a chance to say hello. Thinking he might not see her again, he left the bar stool and weaved through the crowd, glancing in every direction until he made a full circuit of the lounge. He stationed himself for a few minutes by the old broken-down jukebox, in case she had gone into the restroom, but she didn't come out of there. She'd gone, disappearing as quickly as she had appeared to him on the dance floor.

He stepped into the warm night and searched for a sign of her, but she was nowhere in sight. He hadn't danced with her. Talked with her. Asked her name.

It was closing in on two in the morning. Someone set off a big firework somewhere that rumbled through the night. He listened to it echo off the lake for a moment before he realized it was not some retort from a loud firework.

It was thunder.

By the time he climbed the stairs to his upstairs rooms, the rain started. It was no cloudburster, that was for sure. Truman felt as disappointed as he had at the end of the fireworks show, but it *was* rain.

Usually, the rain brought the voices he couldn't tell anyone about. His dancer. This—*Kachina*. No way to know for sure if the name went with the voice, but Truman liked to think so.

He leaned out his window, listening for her, but heard only the patter of rain on the roof. It surprised him that he couldn't hear her. He'd come to expect it.

Still, and maybe because of the images he had in his head of the girl dancing in the lounge, he found himself inspired enough to sit at the piano and stare at the staff paper where he had scratched out the opening third of the first movement. The melody from the rainstorm early in the summer was transcribed there in the most delicate of pencil strokes. A simple but unforgettable melody.

Let's dance.

He needed to transform it now, after a simple restatement, and come up with his variations. He wanted the listeners to hear different permutations of the whole so their minds would work to compare the ideas. Set them up by creating tension and surprising them with the unexpected.

Something unexpected had hit him the moment he set foot into the rain of Quinault, and the lack of summer rains had caused him to stubbornly ignore his symphony. The ache in his chest tonight had pushed him to the piano. He struck a key with the pointer finger of his left hand. The B just to the left of middle C. The note sounded and lingered, unnaturally loud in the small room. B natural.

Be.

He hit the note again.

6

※※

MOSS

K AT HADN'T BEEN TO THE CEDARS RESORT TO DANCE SINCE
the previous fall, after the tourist season wound down and
their live music nights came to an end. Last week, out on the floor
dancing to Black Velvet's covers, she felt an energy she'd not felt
in a long time. She drew a lot of attention. She didn't mind a bit and
felt no shame in flirting with some of the guys—and girls—in the
lounge. Except for a few locals she knew, the tourists in the lounge
were made up of mostly blank faces.

The next day, she decided to take the evening bus into town
and spend the next week with Serena. Visit Allie for more coaching
on telos making. She wondered what extra practice she'd need to
master *those* skills. For now, she was learning what she could about
theory, and would let Allie guide her to the, um . . . final exams.

As the bus entered town, she felt once again the sizzle of uncertainty in her brain, and glanced out the window, looking for
anything amiss. The streets were dark, though punctuated with the
light of civilization. What *was* it, that feeling? It was the same feeling she'd had standing in the rain outside the ranger station before
her dad told her to get inside. Before then, she believed she'd heard
another call.

An echo.

Allie had told her about spheres of influence. Given the right
magical resonances, listening with hyper-awareness to sounds, Al-

lie claimed she could detect echoes of others in her vicinity who might wish her harm. Kat remembered laughing the first time she heard it. After spending time with Allie, though, learning what the woman could do, learning about sex magic and magicked drugs, the idea didn't seem so far-fetched.

What prickled her nerves on the bus didn't seem to be the same echoes though. What she'd heard—or imagined she'd heard—was something altogether different. She was amazed she could tell it wasn't the same. A bell sounded, and she pushed away the uncertainty and gazed toward the front of the bus. The driver slowed down, then stopped to let someone out. A kid with a skateboard under his arm walked down the aisle past her, heading for the exit.

Kat thought a moment. Serena's was a few stops away yet. She watched the kid, a heavy ski cap crammed low on his head, right until the moment he clunked down the steps to the door and left the bus. In slow motion, the driver closed the door. A second later, the bus inched forward.

"Wait!" she yelled. She was tired and she just wanted to get to Serena's and crash, but she pushed back the fatigue and stood. She stumbled down the aisle, backpack half-slung over her shoulder, while the driver looked at her in the rearview and frowned.

He stopped the bus.

"Sorry," she said. She knew this driver from many back-and-forth trips, but still didn't know his name.

"Are you sure?" he asked. He opened the doors. "This isn't your stop."

"Yes. Thank you. Good night."

She was off the bus right away. The driver might've said good night back to her, but she didn't hear it. The door closed, but only after a delay, the driver just making sure his passenger hadn't made a mistake.

She hadn't. Echo or sphere of influence—whatever the reason for her unease—this was her stop. Allie's home was a few blocks west, and right now Kat had the strong urge to go see her, late in the evening as it was.

A short walk on the quiet street, no rain falling, and she wondered if she'd imagined everything. She often thought the worst about gut reactions and signs and portents. Hadn't she felt nausea for weeks before the impending split between her parents? Maybe the anger in their voices had clued her in back then.

No. She wasn't imagining this. There was . . . *some*thing. The whisper of a breath that held both a beautiful possibility and a stern warning. The heat of it warmed her. Almost immediately, a light drizzle started; surprisingly, it only added to the warmth.

A scream.

Pause.

Then another, more anguished cry.

That, for certain, she hadn't imagined. The next scream was muffled, as if the person had been dragged indoors. Kat quickened her pace toward Allie's, because she now had a good idea where that wrenching howling was coming from.

Allie!

She broke into a run. Was this a manifestation of the echo she'd perceived earlier? It didn't seem the same, but she didn't know for certain. She covered a few blocks quickly, not slowing a second.

In the middle of the next block, Allie's two-story home blazed with light. From every window. From the porch. From the streetlight conveniently placed in front of the house. From the spotlights illuminating Allie's sign that read PSYCHIC READINGS, with a picture of a palm held upward, an eye staring out from the middle. Allie's door was wide open, and light poured from there too.

What was she seeing? The rain was more than a drizzle now, but she didn't have time to dig in her backpack for a coat. The next scream—most definitely male—confirmed that someone had entered Allie's place.

"Oh for *fuck's* sake!" someone howled. Not Allie.

"Allie!" She dashed up the sidewalk, then onto the porch. Inside the open door, Kat stopped when she saw blood on the entryway floor. Not a lot of it, but she gasped anyway, surprised as she continued into the front room.

So much light.

No one there, but blood splatters led to Allie's craft room. "Allie?" she called again.

"In here," came Allie's tired voice.

Kat turned into the craft room and found Allie, palms up, standing next to a man doubled over in a chair, hands curled around his stomach. The light was dim in here compared to the front room, and seemingly everywhere else in the house. Allie had blood on her hands and a streak of it on her face.

"I'm okay," Allie said.

The man breathed heavily, in and out, through his mouth, staving off obvious pain. He turned toward Kat and she took a step back in surprise.

Moss Man.

The guy from Duffy's who'd paid her way too much attention. He still wore that green baseball cap. His eyes were wild with pain, but he noticed her, and she thought she detected the moment he recognized her.

Allie stooped and grabbed his chin, forcing him to look at her. "It'll be better in a bit. Give in to it and let it work. Very powerful."

"What did you give me?" the man said, his voice a whisper.

"It's Moss," Allie told him. "Magicked drugs. They'll help you heal once and for all."

Kat blinked. *Moss*? Magicked drugs? Were they the ones Allie had mentioned to her before? Serena hadn't been wrong to call him mossy. Hadn't been wrong when she'd accused Allie of pushing drugs. Kat hadn't believed it, but it seemed plausible, considering the other "crafts" Allie practiced.

Allie looked at Kat and grimaced. "He was attacked, weeks ago. Someone found him on a street corner and rushed him to a hospital. He almost didn't make it. But since then, he has dealt with pain and impending infection."

Kat shook her head. "He should be back in the hospital."

"He said he can't be there. Someone told him I might be able to help."

The man groaned. Looked at Kat again. "You're the angel from the bar." He managed a smile. "You're prettier than her."

Kat frowned. "That's a stupid thing to say."

"No," he said, glancing at Allie, "not her."

"Who, then?"

"My mother. I know that because of some old pictures of her. She died."

"I'm sorry," Kat said, still not certain about this guy who'd semi-stalked her in Duffy's.

"Don't be. She was wrong to leave me after my birth."

Kat ignored that, like you ignored all crazy talk.

He smiled at Allie. "You're right, I'm already feeling better."

Allie nodded. "Very powerful, as I said."

"You gave him . . . magic *drugs*?" Kat said, disbelieving. "He's bleeding, and you do that instead of taking him to the hospital?"

"The blood is because of me," Allie said.

"You?"

"This is the third time he's been here. There are side effects to the healing." She pointed at the man's middle; he still cradled his stomach in his arms. "The pain's there, but the blood is not."

Kat realized then that the man's nose was rimmed in red. Nosebleed. A bad one.

"Moss," the man said, his voice hoarse and scratchy. "I'll remember that."

"I told you. You can't just ask around for it. It doesn't exist."

"But—"

"Only here. Only for emergencies." Allie looked sheepish. "It has—certain side effects."

The man raised his eyebrows. "Besides the nose bleeds?"

"Those will go away soon enough."

"What else then?"

"The drugs, magicked as they are, have combinations that work miraculously, but they open your mind to the possibilities of unnatural magic."

Kat shivered, hearing that. *Allie, what are you playing at?*

"I'm warning you now," Allie told him. "Now that you're in the last phase of healing, you must listen. The alterations to your consciousness could lead to unwanted and dangerous permutations in nature itself."

"Unnatural?" he asked. He'd straightened in the chair and stopped holding his gut. He rubbed a finger under his nose, then checked in the dim light for more blood. The flow had stopped a while ago.

"Unnatural," Allie said, "and . . . *enticing.*"

"So I just stop now?"

"Not yet, but soon. If you continue using Moss blatantly, you risk trading its healing powers for destructive impulses that darken your mind. You'll crave the power it gives you and be more willing to explore its limits, bending some aspect of the natural world around you. You'll ache for more of it." She shook her head. "It's best you let me monitor you for a few more weeks."

Kat listened in silence, and she had the impression that this sad, pitiful man—for she had finally decided that much was true about him—would not handle well any unnatural awakening. She stared at him with a growing sense of dread, and maybe he *did* have something to do with the echoes. Or, maybe Allie had instigated—hesitantly, but knowingly—those echoes. Giving out Moss to someone like this man on one hand, and encouraging Kat on the other, instructing her to *find your song.*

That didn't seem quite right, even still. Allie was more an inciting incident than exposition. No. Someone else had a part.

A song from a song that came from a song.

She didn't know where *that* bit of weirdness came from. The weird guy was staring at her. Staring at her the same way he'd stared at her in Duffy's. She didn't give in to him, glaring right back like a wounded animal, daring him to say something stupid. Instead, she was the one who eventually blinked.

"Who are you?" she asked him. "Who are you and why do you—"

Allie cut her off. "No! Stop. No names. This much is true: names have power. In his case, with the Moss taking root in his system, knowing his name could damage him."

Kat shook her head. "It's just a name. This is all too—"

"Until the Moss is out of his system, we risk tapping into his deeper shadow, and we could very well render him useless for controlling when we need to. Like a sudden wind, he could sweep in and blow past us."

"I do like the sound of this," the man said.

"Do not give in to it," Allie said. "It'll dissipate soon enough. Until then, you *can't* test its possibilities. Promise me."

The man held up his hands. "Promise. I don't understand half of what you're *saying*, so I'm not sure how I can *really* promise."

"Just go home and rest."

The man shrugged. "Fine." He grinned at Kat. "See you at Duffy's. I look forward to your songs."

Kat felt heat rise to her cheeks. He pulled on the brim of his cap and winked. *Leave already*, she pleaded. She wanted to bolt for the door herself. Maybe the rain had started up again. Enough so she could run outside and stare up at the sky and let its water cool her.

"I don't think you'll want to hear them," Kat said, defiant, hating this guy for mocking her, and for putting Allie in a precarious situation when the woman only tried to help him.

"We'll see about that," he said. "Won't we?" He winked, then left the room.

Kat and Allie stared at each other as the man's footsteps echoed from the front room and entry. Eventually all was quiet.

"I don't know why," Kat said to her, "but I felt compelled to come here early. Got off the bus, feeling this weird shit—what I think of as echoes—and I get here and find *this*."

Allie took Kat's elbow and pulled her farther into the craft room. "Yes. We have some work to do. I think it's more important than ever to prepare you for what could be ahead."

"I don't even *know* what's ahead."

"Nor do I, but you are definitely in tune with something. Pun intended."

Kat shook her head and grimaced. "There's someone out there," she whispered.

"Hmm?"

"Besides the Moss Man."

"Moss Man? Oh, that's good." She laughed. "But why do you say this? Someone else?"

She shrugged. "I don't know. It's just—" She stopped. Looked into the front room. Saw all that light. "I see *more* light."

Allie scoffed. "Eh. I just feel more comfortable with the lights on when that man comes in here." She dug into a small drawer filled with coins, beads, paperclips, pens, and other items Kat couldn't see. She withdrew a small silver key. She handed it to Kat.

"What do I do with this?"

"Hide it." She closed Kat's fist around it. "Anywhere. Somewhere out at the lake. Put it in a hole in the woods, or under a rock. Remember where, but do *not* tell me where."

"Why?"

"Just do it. It's—security."

Kat paused, then nodded. Right now, she felt safe inside the craft room's dimness, even though the fullness of the light from outside shone through, as if it came from another place far away.

"I feel like something has—" She wasn't sure how to explain it. "Reset?"

Allie pulled a face. "A reset of what?"

Kat didn't know.

7

꒰꒱

MUSIC LESSONS

J ULY BOASTED CONSTANT CROWDS AND WARMER DAYS, AND
the Cedars Resort, full every night, turned away many a
frustrated tourist.

Holding their ground in the campground, Sam and Cindi Werner, the young Seattle couple with the Airstream RV, sailed the lake almost every day with their Hobie Cat to "get the lay of the land." Or the lay of the lake. Practicing for the big race mid-August. The Werners, married for five years, had spent every summer in their RV looking for good sailing lakes. This was the first year the Northwest Championships had come to Lake Quinault, and they rode into town to conquer the lake and take home a trophy. Truman had no idea if they were any good at sailing. He had no knowledge of the sport himself, and he couldn't tell their aptitude by watching the Hobie with the blue and pink sails out on the lake.

Jacob had promised to take him out on his own Hobie earlier in the summer, but the long working hours made it nearly impossible. Eventually, he joined Jacob for a quick ride. Truman couldn't get into the swing of the thing. He didn't feel at ease, the wind picking up and throwing the boat around. The stupid boat hardly ever glided on two pontoons.

Truman forgot his promise to teach Dennis Reynolds some guitar lessons, but rarely saw the surly kid. Truman had no luck writing music without his muse, so when Dennis came across the street to fetch a box of lettuce, they arranged to hang out in the restaurant after hours.

Dennis Reynolds already had his guitar out, plucking away at a few chords, when Truman came in through the back service staff door.

The kid's blonde hair looked like it hadn't been combed for a few days. Sitting on a chair next to a table that hadn't been bussed, he hunched over his guitar with great concentration, humming under his breath as he worked the strings.

"Hi, Truman," he finally said.

"Call me Tip."

"Tip?"

"A nickname my friends saddled me with. But I grew into it."

"A name used by your friends."

"That's okay, you can use it."

"I thought you'd decided not to do the lessons," Dennis said.

Truman forced a smile. "Got busy, is all. I just forgot."

"Yeah. I figured."

Truman sat down in the chair next to him. He sized up Dennis's guitar. It was a nice one, actually. An Ibanez, ivory and dark brown, one with a retro look and feel. Looked like a solid spruce top.

"You like the Ibanez?" he asked Dennis.

He nodded. "It sounds good."

"You'll find it'll age well. Improve over time."

Dennis strummed a strong G chord. "You know guitars pretty well, huh? This one's okay?"

"Sure." He pointed to the Ibanez. "Look at that body shape. You could be heard well enough in a group, but man, those tones are smooth. Great for solos, too."

Dennis stopped strumming and held it out to Truman. "Try it."

Truman took the guitar from Dennis, looked at it a little closer, then started fiddling a bit, no tune in particular. Then he fingered a little "Classical Gas." He noticed Dennis smiling at him as he pushed the tune through the refrain.

"I want to get really good," Dennis said, "but I'm late getting started."

Truman told him it didn't matter. "Eric Clapton didn't touch a guitar until he was a teenager. Tom Scholz? From Boston? Even later. It's *never* too late. You've got your guitar, you're starting to play, not waiting for inspiration. That's good."

He stopped for a moment, and on a whim played the melody from his symphony. Single notes, light and airy, ascending in pitch, nothing fancy. "You've got to practice. Practice a lot. Drive your folks crazy."

Dennis grimaced. "When they're around."

Truman ignored that and threw some arpeggios in with his muse's melody. "It's all about discipline." He stopped playing and handed the guitar back to Dennis.

Dennis frowned as he grabbed the guitar by the neck. "What was that last thing you were playing?"

Truman shrugged. "Something I'm working on."

"You gave me the chills."

Truman looked up sharply, wondering what the kid meant.

"I mean, I like it," Dennis said. "It seems . . . unreal."

"Unreal."

Dennis shrugged. "I'm talking shit."

"No," Truman said. "Unreal seems a good way to describe it. I'm with you. It's like I can't even claim it as my own." And he couldn't. *It belongs to her.*

Dennis put the guitar across his lap. "It's funny, but it even seems familiar."

Truman sat forward in his chair, searching Dennis's face.

"I dunno," Dennis went on. "It's like I've heard it before. But I can't imagine how I could've, if it's yours."

Intrigued, Truman thought about pressing him a bit. When he'd quizzed Jacob about voices in the rain, Jacob hadn't a clue what he was talking about. And why should he? Stupid, crazy shit. But maybe Dennis had heard something.

"What?" Dennis asked, after Truman had stared for a while, saying nothing.

He chickened out. "Maybe you heard me playing it. I'm up late sometimes, messing with the tune."

Dennis shook his head, but he immediately picked up the guitar from his lap, and, after a deliberate pause, he plucked the seven notes of the melody from memory, and in the same key.

Now it was Truman's turn to get the chills. The kid had picked up the tune easily.

"Do you read music?" Truman asked. "Or do you play by ear?"

"I did trombone in band in 5th and 6th grade," he said. "Learned the basics, I guess. But I do pretty okay playing things back. Like I said, that tune seems familiar."

As much as Truman wanted to keep on him about it, he needed to get a lesson in for Dennis. "Okay, play that again?"

Dennis did.

Truman watched his fingers. "Stop." He leaned forward and moved Dennis's fingers. "Press closer to the fret, without touching it. Not the middle. Not the back." He moved Dennis's thumb. "Keep your thumb behind where you're pressing on the string. Right. Good."

He continued to work a bit on Dennis's form, giving pointers, explaining how his fingers would get stronger with practice. He showed him some very easy chords to work on.

Soon enough, their time was up and Truman said, "That's it for today. We'll talk about guitar tabs next time, and I might have some music I can bring."

"Okay."

"Next week?"

Dennis nodded. "Thanks—" He paused a moment. "Tip." Almost in a final salute, he played the symphony melody again, louder this time.

Truman smiled thinly and left the restaurant.

Outside, echoes of Kachina's song traveled with him. He didn't understand how the kid had picked up his melody so quickly, and he shivered thinking that somehow, Dennis had heard the seven mournful notes of his muse some other place, at some other time.

The melody was already in his blood, its emotion moving him, becoming more and more a part of him. It seemed to have moved Dennis too, even if he didn't know where he'd heard it.

But it seemed he *had* heard it.

The lessons with Dennis continued into August. The boy had some ability, mixed in there with his dour personality, but Truman didn't think he would be reaching guitar god status anytime soon. Neither of them talked about the melody again. Truman intended to, but once he settled down with Dennis, the week's lesson began—always late in the evening in the restaurant, after hours—and they both lost themselves in the music.

Then the lessons stopped.

"Why?" Truman asked after the last lesson, when Dennis told him the news.

Dennis shrugged. He'd kept pretty quiet during the lesson. "I just want to take a break. Maybe look for some job in town before the fall."

Truman thought it odd, considering the kid's earlier eagerness, but decided not to put too much stock in it. Dennis gave him cash for the last few lessons, paying more than they'd agreed upon. He mumbled his thanks and that was that.

The resort stayed busy. August wound down, and more folks arrived for the Hobie races. With just thirty RV spaces in the campground, the huge sloping lawn that led down to the water became a good place for campers to set up tents. Slowly, the resort lawn turned into an ever-growing tent city.

With the tents and the race participants came the Hobie Cats, of course. They lined up along the beach, sails sporting a rainbow of colors, seemingly no two the same color scheme or pattern. Their owners brought them in and out of the lake for rides, testing the wind. The race committee had chosen Lake Quinault because the wind came up like clockwork every day in the early afternoon.

The last Tuesday of August, four days before the races, the rain began.

Jacob stared into the sky, fretting, nervous about the races as the rain poured non-stop most of the day, and into the night. By Wednesday the lake level had risen several feet. Some campers had to pitch their tents on higher ground, and all the Hobie Cats had to be pulled up the bank.

But it was *raining*. It hadn't rained this much since the beginning of the summer, and Truman expected to hear the rain music. None came the night before. He remembered again the first encounter with his muse, listening to the words she'd sung to him: Circle. Lake. Moon. Key.

Although he'd never found any signs of a Circle Lake, another possibility was on his mind: Circle the lake.

Truman found Jacob in his office in the back of the store on his computer.

"Can I borrow your truck?" Truman asked.

"Where you going?" Jacob asked without looking up from his computer screen.

"I want to drive around the lake. There's a way around, right?"

He swiveled his chair toward Truman. "Sure, but you have to drive up the valley some distance, where it turns to gravel about six or seven miles past the east end of the lake. Cross the river bridge then head down the North Shore Road. Eventually you'll hit pavement again. Round trip about thirty miles."

Jacob rummaged around in the top drawer of his desk and found the truck keys, tossed them to Truman, and pointed to a blue Toyota pickup parked behind the office building. A Cedars Resort logo was stenciled in white on the door panel.

"Thanks. I'll gas it up."

Jacob shrugged. "If you want. Have fun."

A few minutes later, Truman headed east on the South Shore Road, windshield wipers thumping away. As he passed by the last of the residential houses, he began to see the error of his around-the-lake plan. Inside the truck, with the windows up, he couldn't hear anything in the rain. He tried cracking open the driver's side window a bit, but that didn't help, and he only succeeded in getting everything on that side damp.

He passed the trailhead for Colonel Bob Peak, then decided to stop at Merriman Falls, a forty foot falls visible right off the road. He pulled the truck over and turned off the ignition. The falls was on his right, partially obscured by three or four moss-covered trees. He didn't have an umbrella with him, and he didn't find one in Jacob's truck, so when he slid out of the truck it wasn't long before he was soaked. He ignored the discomfort and listened to the rain.

The rain pushed down even harder, but nothing musical emerged from the downpour. Merriman Falls was right there at the side of the road, and the noise of the cascading water didn't help as Truman tried to listen for singing. The air smelled pungent, and as he looked out into the moss-draped trees, among the shrubs and ferns, he caught sight of the bright yellow skunk cabbage, which often had a foul-smelling odor. Still, he found it intoxicating. The rainforest, populated with big leaf maples, Sitka spruce, western hemlock, and red cedar, often hosted plants that grew on other plants, such as moss, giving the Quinault temperate rainforest its distinct visual appeal.

He waited a few more minutes, then clambered into the truck. After wiping the water from his eyes, Truman took a deep breath and sat a few minutes with his hands on the steering wheel. He started the engine and eased out onto the road. After a few more miles, the road turned to gravel. He heard as well as felt the crunch of the gravel under the truck's tires.

He should have had no trouble hearing her in this unseasonal heavy rain. The pressure in his chest was a longing, urging him along the bumpy road at a faster clip. Long past thinking about the craziness of his obsession, barely wondering how anything so fantastical could possibly happen, Truman let that almost primal urge drive him toward the bridge that would cross the river and take him to the north shore of the lake.

The concrete bridge appeared suddenly, and he started to cross it, but decided to stop mid-span. He left the truck again, the engine running this time. While the rain drenched him, he leaned against the rust-colored railing and gazed at the upper Quinault River as it headed west toward the lake.

She wasn't here either. He started to wonder if he needed to be back at the resort, if he was somehow out of range. His impromptu lake drive had seemed like a good idea at the time, but now it felt like a waste. He couldn't even enjoy the scenery with the rain coming down so hard. Still, if she had really meant "circle the lake," maybe he had to complete the circle before he could find out anything new.

Soaked to the skin now, Truman climbed into the truck and finished crossing the bridge. He turned left onto the North Shore Road. A flash of lightning caught him by surprise, brightening the gloomy sky.

A close one. A crash of thunder followed, and he slowed down, almost as if trying to give the lightning a chance to move away from him.

He drove another eight miles or so before catching a glimpse of the lake through the trees on his left. It meant he had another four miles before he rejoined Highway 101.

The rain slapped his windshield, as if demanding he stop. Almost unwillingly, he edged the car to the side of the narrow road and stopped. He turned the engine off and emerged into the summer rain with a little less enthusiasm.

The intensity of the storm picked up, and the lightning continued to slash through the darkening sky. Truman walked off the road toward the lake, about four hundred feet away. The undergrowth and heavy moss felt spongy beneath his shoes as he picked his way through the trees, and the rain, almost as if on cue, doubled its efforts to obscure his vision and douse him. Lightning sizzled and cracks of thunder followed him, but Truman kept going, ignoring any danger. He didn't know why this felt right. Maybe he'd heard the song subliminally?

He came to a clearing, tall cedars surrounding him. He raised his head, closed his eyes, and let the rain splash his face, and listened.

Come on, where are you? Why don't you say something? He realized he'd said that aloud, and he repeated the words, practically yelling now. He really expected his dancer to say something, to make him understand all that had happened since arriving at Quinault, to explain her melody. Did any of it have any importance? Did it mean anything at all?

No words. Instead, he imagined the melody of his symphony sliding in and out of the trees, grabbing onto the raindrops and pelting him mercilessly, insisting he just pay attention.

Pay attention.

He soon knew he wasn't imagining anything.

It was *her* voice. Kachina's melody, her song, loud and clear, as if she were standing right behind him, belting out those seven notes like an anthem.

He pivoted, pointing himself back toward the road. No one there of course, but the singing continued, as loud as ever. He thrilled at it, a tingle buzzing his skin, but even as he swooned to her voice, a rumble of thunder boomed at the heart of the song. The throb of this almost dissonant sound threatened to drown her out, but between claps of thunder, Truman soaked up the words.

Moon. Key.

Like before, the words were distinct.

Magic.

Truman heard her say her name: *Kachina.*

"What do I do?" he mumbled at the sky.

The next flash of lightning came so close to him that the thunder sounded almost simultaneously. Truman felt the electricity sizzle, felt his hair stand on end. Its brightness nearly blinded him, the thunderclap pounding in his ears.

He had to get out of there.

He wanted the perceived safety of the truck. He pointed his feet in the right direction. Get in and drive home.

Another fifty feet and he'd see the road and Jacob's red truck. Another twenty feet . . .

Lightning and thunder crackled again together, and a flash of fire flared as the lightning caught one of the cedar trees in front of him, blowing it apart. A wave of heat made Truman stop, and when he looked up toward the tree he saw the heavy limb coming toward him.

Time seemed to slow as he thought of another time in his life, another tree crashing through glass at him, but the moment was lost and he ducked instinctively, taking a glancing blow on his shoulder. It flung him backward, flipping him, his legs flailing in the air as he landed hard on the ground. He grazed the side of a half-buried rock and the world spun for an instant.

Truman Starkey's world went black.

Fire. Rain. Tree. Glass. A young girl on a couch. A game board on the table in front of her. A storm. Where are his parents? What can he do? There is someone he is responsible for . . .

He awoke to black.

Night had fallen on the rainforest, and Truman sat up, disoriented. The sudden movement brought dizziness, and he fought a wave of nausea. His clothes were soaking wet, his skin cold, and his shoulder ached where the tree limb had clipped him. His head throbbed where he'd hit the exposed rock.

The rest of the day had passed him by. He shivered, aware that he could have died out here. The rain had stopped. The lightning strike had obviously not started a fire, but there seemed to be too much light in the sky. He craned his neck upward and saw the reason why.

A full moon.

He stood slowly, testing his consciousness, his mind cluttered with the words and song of his muse.

In the light of the full moon, he caught a glimpse of something near the rock where he'd hit his head. He bent down to pick it up, a glint of silver light reflecting off its surface. He grasped it and brought it close to his face. It was a small silver key that almost disappeared in his palm. It must have been under the rock. His head, when it struck the rock, had moved it enough to uncover the key.

Kachina's words suddenly made more sense.

Moon.

Key.

He realized that no matter how much of a coincidence the day's events seemed to be, no matter how crazy and unearthly, finding this key was important. He believed it symbolized some kind of struggle.

Truman slipped the key into his pocket, shuffled back to the road, and found Jacob's truck, key still in the ignition. No one had bothered it. He started the engine, pulled out onto North Shore Road, and drove west toward the main highway.

It was after midnight when he climbed the stairs to his room above the store, wet, shivering with cold, and sore from head to toe.

He went straight to the piano, thought a moment, and set to work. He'd heard enough of Kachina's song today to make headway on the first movement's development, and the additional discord of the sounds of thunder and the crack of the tree limb seemed like the instability of the dominant of the tonal key, screaming for release, for resolution. The idea of using it in his symphony seemed almost repugnant, but a wholeness in the tonality made it impossible to ignore, the tension needing to develop naturally.

In spite of everything he'd experienced today, he forced a smile, understanding that he had found his way to the recapitulation of the movement, both harmonically and thematically.

He just had to get it written down.

For that, he would need to hear Kachina sing again. Thinking back to the Fourth of July, and the mysterious girl in the lounge, he believed it might even be possible to hear it from her in person.

8

⁙

WINDFALL

NO DOUBT ABOUT IT, JOEL HINES WAS A MAN WITH POWER. Power of the unnatural, true: power enhanced by the drugs of magic.

Hines fought the consequences of the night Bill Hand tried to have him killed. He'd been lucky. Someone found him on the street and rushed him to the hospital, but after that, the wounds healed poorly, infecting, paining him, until he'd heard about a middle-aged woman in town known only as Allie who advertised her services as a psychic. At first, he wondered how the hell a psychic could help him, but someone had mentioned there might be some unusual drug remedies.

Fuck *yeah*, unusual. Allie said they had some magic in them. Like what? Like Frosty the Snowman, some kind of magic in the hat he wore? He didn't have Frosty's hat, but he had his Olympic Rainforest ballcap. But no, it had to do with drug combinations, Allie doing some magic shit with them, and they were a miracle. The more he visited the stronger he felt, all pain in his torso gone, infection gone.

There was Allie's warning about the side effects of course. He should only take what she gave him, and once the healing was done, that was it. He'd be cut off. She warned him about alterations that could lead to unwanted and dangerous permutations in nature itself. He scoffed at that. He didn't heed her warnings, taking extra doses at once, palming extra packets of the stuff she called Moss.

She suspected he'd somehow taken more than he should, but he denied it. He found the side effects unnaturally enticing. The unexpected benefit opened his mind to the possibilities of . . . well, magic. His *unnatural* magic.

Hines had power never experienced before, and it trumped his almost gloomy, obscure life. He could go where he wanted, do what he pleased, and the side effects seemed pure hyperbole.

Early in the process of rehabilitation, that girl Kat from Duffy's showed up, saw some of what was going on with him. Oh, she was a vision, that one. Her angelic voice, her fluid dancing on the nights she wasn't singing. She would never give him a second's glance, but that night at Allie's, there she was, shocked by his pain.

During the last weeks, he'd found his mind darkening, those twistings of the natural world forming a coldness within him that he despised. Still, he ached for more. If only he could draw more power, he could mold the landscape of his brain, and heal himself.

He really didn't enjoy doing the things he did when he practiced outside Allie's influence. When he left town and stayed in his fifth wheel, parked out in the middle of nowhere, he toyed with the possibilities of using his power despite her warnings and dreaming how he could win over Kat. He thought it might be the only way to be certain she wasn't an obstacle to his mother's return.

He hadn't dared show his face in Duffy's since the attack for fear of one of Bill Hand's people spotting him. Tonight, he walked the streets behind Allie's apartments, Moss jazzing his blood. The wind smelled of cedar, and the puddles from a day of rain dampened his shoes. It was a risk to practice so close to Allie. He thought her idea of a sphere of influence silly, but then again, he'd thought the possibility of magic drugs silly too.

He glanced across the street and concentrated on a light pole. The light flickered weakly. Closing his eyes, he found his center, and called up power. His magic mostly manifested as a force of nature: wind. Wind he harnessed with his will, concentrating it to whatever point on whatever vector he needed, aiming where he liked, hurl at any speed he wished.

Energy coursed through him and he channeled it, and just before he released it, he opened his eyes and glared at the light pole as if it were an enemy. The pole seemed to wobble in anticipation of his attack. When Hines had gathered enough power at his center, he needed only a flick of both hands and the force released, centered on the upper half of the light pole. It groaned, and in a few seconds, it bent noticeably, about 20 degrees. He grinned as he lowered his hands, clenching his fists when they were at his side.

Hines squinted down the block, saw someone sprawled out on a bench near a bus stop. Some bum, someone homeless, probably. Moving closer, Hines gathered up power again, and while still walking, flung his wind at a puddle inside a rather large pothole. The water rose and slashed across the street to soak the man on the bench. Hines just kept walking, whistling on the other side of the street as the man sat up groggily, examining himself.

Oh man, that felt good.

A woman who exited the alley turned and walked away from him up the street. He had to wonder where she'd been, walking out of an alley this late at night without any concern for her safety.

"Here I am," he called out.

She turned, and though he couldn't see her face, he knew she was scared now. She ran. He called a modicum of wind to chase the woman, the gusts ripping at her clothes, knocking her once off her feet. He grinned again, but he lowered his hands and let her go.

This was what Allie had warned about, though. The unnaturalness. The darkening of his mind. Here he was, tormenting a couple of innocents. The power was intoxicating, though. It was healing. The only way to full health, it seemed to him, was to wield this brand of magic, and the only way to do that was to stay enhanced with Allie's Moss. His path. His doorway to his mother.

He wanted to purge the blackness that had pooled in his heart since his youth. Dispel the heaviness in his soul that pushed him to do . . . questionable things. With the Moss, that blackness had increased ten-fold. But it would heal.

Allie had cut him off. She'd found out somehow. No more Moss. She never had extra lying around for him to sneak away with, having hidden most of it. This was the worst time imaginable to be without it.

Heal.

It's what he needed to bring back the boy who listened patiently to his father's drunken stories; bring back the mother who'd abandoned him. It didn't matter how it had happened, her leaving him. It had happened, and he didn't think it was right. He was convinced he could change it.

Now, with darkness closing in, he had to think fast how to get more Moss, because even now, after his display of power here on the streets (controlling the *wind*, for fuck's sake!), he felt tired. Weak from the effort. That wouldn't change unless he had more Moss.

The girl, Kat. She might know how to get more. Or that other girl. Kat's friend. Serena. She might be "convinced" to help if he couldn't get anything out of Kat. Follow her one night. Find out where she lived.

Kat first, though.

His own darkness insisted he do whatever he had to do to succeed.

What Hines needed was a little help. He felt a little more comfortable after his practice and decided—at least in the daylight—to chance going into Duffy's. More than ever, he thought he could expend the power he still had within him—even though it was diminishing—to handle Bill Hand and his cronies.

It didn't take long to find the perfect help.

The kid sat at a table filling out a job application. Hines strolled over and sat down opposite him. The kid stopped scribbling and looked up. "What do you want?"

"You want to work *here*?"

He shrugged. "Why not?"

Hines gave the kid his most assuring smile. "Because I can offer you something better."

"Better how?"

"Fewer hours, better pay. And—" He leaned closer to the kid. "—definitely big bonuses if things turn out well."

The kid leaned back in his chair. He spun the pen around as if it were a drumstick. "What do I have to do?"

"Be my eyes and ears. Help me find someone. Give me a hand once in a while."

"That doesn't tell me much."

"Under the table. Work for me and you'll get a piece of the magic."

"The what?"

"The *magic*." Hines tried to gauge the kids' interest. What did this kid want? What did he need? "Do some work for me, and you'll be paid richly. If it's not all you hoped it'd be, well—" He leaned back. "No hard feelings. You can come back here and finish your application."

"I don't know—"

"These are strange times, my friend, strange times. There's power for the taking."

"Is this a drug thing? Something illegal?"

"No, no. Just a search and rescue. Some odd jobs with great rewards."

"Search for what? Rescue who?"

From his pocket, Hines pulled out a glossy photo that he'd folded in quarters. He opened it and slapped it on the table. It was a promo poster for Duffy's live music, featuring the band Deluge, with dates and times they'd play. Inset underneath was a photo of a young woman. A second act to some, but a first desire for Hines

"This girl. She sings here sometimes. Hangs out here."

The kid looked at it closely. "I recognize her."

"You do?"

"Yeah. She comes in where I used to work. Likes to go into the lounge and dance. I don't know her though."

"She does love her dancing," Hines said. "Her name is Kat."

"What's with her?"

"She has something of mine. Or . . . she might know something about it. Think of her as a bit of leverage."

"Look. Duffy's is fine for me."

"If they take you on."

"They will. It's already better than my last job. Pays better, and I can do more than just wash dishes and be a gopher."

"Where was that?"

"Where was what?"

"Your last job."

"At the Cedars."

"Cedars?"

"Resort on Lake Quinault."

Hines spread his hands wide. "There, you see?"

"See what?"

"You've already earned some money."

Hines reached into his pocket and pulled out a hundred-dollar bill. He slapped it down in front of the kid, who didn't need to know that was about all he had on him right now. A hundred-dollar bill had a mesmerizing effect on someone not used to seeing one.

"Just for answering a couple questions?"

"Piece of the magic. It's a beautiful thing. We must do what we can to hold back the darkness and bring back life."

The kid grimaced. "Magic. *Really*?"

"You in?"

The kid paused. Looked down at the hundred on the table.

"Not getting any younger here."

The boy sighed. Then he scooped it up and crumpled it into his own pocket. "I can give it a whirl."

Hines clapped once, loudly. "Great. What's your name, kid?"

"Dennis."

Hines nodded. "Dennis, let's go hunting."

9

※

QUIXOTIC

THE HOBIE RACES WOULD TAKE PLACE OVER TWO DAYS, beginning on Friday. When Thursday rolled around, Truman thought the Cedars Resort looked like a three-ring circus, with nearly three dozen Hobie Cats parked along the beach. Tents covered the campground and main lawn, cars and trucks and campers jammed the parking lots, guests filled the rooms and cabins, and patrons for the restaurant and lounge kept them hopping nonstop.

A bright fluorescent green pavilion dominated the upper lawn, the race committee registering participants and selling all the accoutrements the serious racer would need. Another fluorescent yellow tent close by sold T-shirts, muscle shirts, sweatpants, and hoodies. The largest cabin became the race headquarters, and the committee's official Hobie Championship banner stretched across the railing of its cedar deck.

The driving rain from earlier in the week calmed down, seemingly willing to cooperate for the races. Clouds threatened rain, but the next few days remained dry. The sun had come out and the threat of rain passed. The local forecast called for clear skies through the weekend.

Waves of customers swamped the store. The crowds would only get worse during the race days. Keeping his cool, Truman did his best to calm customers as he worked, but he nevertheless had moments of frustration.

At 10 p.m., after twelve hours on shift, Truman and Andrea closed the store. Truman crossed the street and entered the back of the lounge to see if Jennifer, the head bartender, needed help with the beer taps. She was okay, but warned him she might need help Friday night, even with several bartenders on duty. The lounge was crowded, certainly, but not much crazier than the Fourth of July, when Truman had seen the woman on the dance floor. Contestants and their families, fans of the sport, and curious tourists, pacing themselves, waited for the insanity that would be the weekend.

By midnight, the crowd thinned, and Truman nursed his second beer, talking to a group from Portland at one of the larger tables.

Before 1:00 a.m., he was across the street and back in bed, heeding Andrea's warning about what race officials called the Friday Frenzy.

꼐

Frenzy didn't quite cover it.

Truman didn't have a break the whole day in the store. The races happened. He knew nothing about the course, or the number of heats, or who the favorites were. Occasionally he'd glance out the window and see the bright-colored sails. The restaurant brought a few burgers over late in the afternoon. The double shift passed by in a blur, the days' races ending at some point (and even more crowds pouring into the store), and when the clock finally said 10:00 p.m., he barely noticed Andrea shooing out the last customer and locking the door.

"Leave the tills," she said. "I'll come in early and do the money in the morning."

Truman raised an eyebrow, questioning her decision.

"Go." She tilted her head toward the street, the lounge, and the ongoing merriment. "Have fun."

This time when he came back to the lounge, Jennifer smiled and nodded at the beer taps.

"Okay," he said.

"Four Buds, an Alaskan, and two Stellas."

Truman got to work.

Black Velvet was back, squeezed into an even smaller space near the balcony doors, plunking out their covers of drum machine-enhanced tunes. People had been dancing for several hours by then.

It was loud, it was hot, it was claustrophobic.

Black Velvet played a few sets while Truman poured, the music mercifully cutting out for fifteen minutes each time the band took a break. Their last set started at 1:00 a.m., and they launched into ZZ Top's "Sharp Dressed Man."

As the ZZ Top song played, he spotted the woman with the long dark hair, the one who'd danced and then disappeared from the bar on the night of the fourth of July. She stood at the edge of the dance floor, surrounded by three other guys who barely gave her any room. They all seemed to be talking to her at once.

"Go," Jennifer said. He looked back at her. "We're caught up."

"Thanks," he said, slipping out from behind the bar.

A man in a black T-shirt and rainbow suspenders, a local writer who liked to put all the locals in his stories, peered over his black-rim glasses and gave Tip a bleary stare. The front of his T-shirt said I'VE BEEN KILLED OFF IN BETTER NOVELS THAN YOURS.

"Hey, Bob," Truman said.

It seemed that somehow, amid all the noise, Bob had nodded off and only now woke up. A Scrabble board sat on the counter, and many of the letters had come loose from the tile holders. The only readable word still on the board was QUIXOTIC.

Truman had read a few of Bob's stories and they were quite funny. He patted Bob on the shoulder, but the writer had already slumped back onto the table.

The path to the dance floor opened and closed at will, keeping Truman on an unsteady, meandering path. Black Velvet finished ZZ Top and eased into The Cars' "Drive," slowing things down.

Without any effort, she drew in the trio of guys, all young and about her age. They revolved around her, moons orbiting, and they were awkward in their attempts to stay in her path. The sensuality of her movements suggested she wielded power, as if she were doing ritualistic magic. She wore almost the same outfit from the night he'd first seen her: jean shorts and a black top, although this one fit loose about her, and had a detailed sketch of Kurt Cobain outlined in white.

Slow song from The Cars, but he couldn't worry about the song selection. While jockeying for position, the guys left a little path to her, and Truman squeezed through the crowd and into her line of sight.

She smiled at him, and he wondered if she *had* smiled at him the first time he'd seen her, and not at someone else nearby.

He didn't even look at the other guys, he just boldly came up to her.

"Dance?" he said.

She nodded, grabbed his hand, and pulled him to the dance floor, leaving the three guys gawking.

They didn't speak to each other for a while, dancing close, touching, but not too tight. Black Velvet's lead singer did his best to croon Benjamin Orr's lyrics. Holding loosely onto the girl's back, her long black hair in his fingers, Truman felt a chill when the lyrics told him to *pay attention to your dreams.*

The girl gazed up at him and said "who's gonna plug your ears when you scream" as she lifted her arms to his shoulders and cupped her hands around his ears. He flashed on an image of Paulina Porizkova reaching up in the song's video, scribbling on the wall above her. Playing the love interest, but battling drugs and alcohol addiction.

Now that he looked closer at the young woman, the flashing lights of the dance floor giving her some depth, he saw her face was drawn, pupils small, like tiny pinpricks, her mouth and nose dry. She was beautiful, but something about her seemed off. Something dark nested in her eyes, something far off and frightening in the way she looked at him, as if she were unsure about his reality.

For an instant she seemed to sense his attempt to read her face, her eyebrows furrowing, hands sliding back to his shoulders, but then she regained her angelic spirit, laughing, throwing her head back. Her hands clawed at his shoulders, as if worried she might fall backwards if her grip didn't hold.

"What's your name?" he asked over the music. "I'm Truman."

She lifted her head and searched his face, a smile on her lips. "Kat."

"Cat?"

"With a K."

"Well, Kat with a K," Truman said, "who's going to take you home?"

It was a horrible line, but he'd timed it perfectly with the finish of Black Velvet's rendition of "Drive," skipping the *tonight* at the very end, leaving the keyboardist holding onto the final chord.

She stopped dancing, and he thought she looked confused. Smiling warmly, she wrapped him up in a hug. Was she trembling from the exertion of the dance, or was it something else? Then she laughed and broke away just as Black Velvet pounced into Michael Jackson's "Billy Jean." It brought a cheer from the crowd, and Kat whooped as well, starting to dance like she had on the Fourth, feet nearly still, hips swaying, arms above her head.

He wasn't a great dancer, but he let go and released all the pent-up energy of the day, letting loose the hours behind the counter and the demands of difficult tourists and eager race fans wanting to blow off steam before Saturday came along. He danced with his feet and legs chewing up the dance floor, almost the exact opposite of her statue-like style.

On the chorus, though, Kat propelled herself close to him and sang along, Billie Jean, not my lover.

I am the one.

Truman was sweating now, but he didn't stop to wipe his face, focusing instead on her sinuous movements, her sensual presence.

Her voice crooned above the lyrics, but the lounge was too loud for him to make out any nuances in her voice, any inflections.

In his mind, however, he was thinking it should be his muse singing to him. For a while now, he'd entertained thoughts of this girl being his muse in the rain.

Kat.

Kachina.

Maybe?

Like a parent encouraging a puppy to dogpaddle toward her, she waved in two guys dressed in cargo shorts and Hobie T-shirts—none of them the trio of guys from earlier. Somehow, with her heavenly pull, she cleared space around her and Truman, and the four of them finished out the song.

They kept dancing.

Truman tried not to frown, wishing he had Kat to himself. He figured the guys had more than a few drinks in them and would fade out after a few dances. But they'd raced during the day, it turned out, and in between songs, as Truman became just a new moon in orbit around her, he heard that the two racers had done well in their heats and qualified for further racing on Saturday.

When Black Velvet finished the set and said good night, with twenty minutes still to go until closing, bar time, Kat left the dance floor and the Hobie guys followed her. Truman thought *what the fuck* but decided he wasn't going to lose her this time. He fell in behind them.

They left the lounge, then Kat turned and said, "Where's Truman?" She spotted him and said, "Oh, there you are."

"Still here," he said.

"Ryan," one of the guys said. His Hobie shirt was a bright neon green. He had a shock of wild brown hair and a deep tan. He raised his arm to clasp hands with Truman and nearly fell over.

"Hey," Truman said.

The other racer, shorter, with a black crewcut and a moderate tan, sported a white Hobie T-shirt from a race held somewhere in

Vancouver across the Canadian border. He reached out and shook Truman's hand. "Nate."

"Where we going?" Truman asked.

"Swimming," Kat said. She said it as if it were the most logical choice in the world. Her smile lit up the night, and it was only after he heard her laugh that he realized her powers had steadily been pulling him closer to her.

"It's close to two o'clock," he heard himself saying, even as he checked Nate and Ryan for their reactions.

"Yep," she said.

He laughed. "Well, I don't have a suit."

"Neither do I."

He could imagine several reasons why this might not be the best plan, but he didn't want to be the spoilsport, and besides, it was Kat. The voices from the lounge popped abruptly when the lounge door opened and closed. He also heard talking and laughter closer to the water, coming from the many campers on the lawn and the campground. The lounge might be closing soon, but the party might go on a long time.

Truman knew nothing about this girl, but he desperately wanted to know more, and the prospect of an early morning swim with her kept him treading water, waiting for a signal. He thought for a second about humming his symphony theme, gauging her reaction, but the moment passed.

"Awesome," Nate said, "let's swim!"

"We need more beer," Ryan said.

Kat walked across the street, and everyone followed. "Too bad. Store's closed."

He couldn't find his thoughts for a moment, but just as Kat turned to look at him he said, "I work in the store."

She smiled, her eyes bright and beautiful and playful. "Lucky for us."

Truman nodded, staring into the darkened room behind the windows. "You should probably stay out here."

"Couple six-packs should be enough." Ryan patted him on the back. "Thanks, man."

Kat hooked an arm around his and reached up and gave him a peck on the cheek. "You're sweet."

"Whatever you like," Nate said. "We'll drink anything."

Truman believed that to be true.

In a daze, Truman fumbled for the keys and let himself into the store. For a moment he panicked, believing Jacob would show up any moment and ask what he was doing. Well, he was buying beer. After hours, but it wasn't that late yet, and he would pay for the beer tomorrow.

Besides, *it was Kat*. He didn't care about Nate or Ryan. They were here for the races and would be gone in a few days. He didn't think it would be the same for Kat because he'd seen her here before in July.

He hummed his tune on his way to the cooler, only slightly worried the guys might run off with Kat and ditch him. He picked out two six-packs—he didn't take notice of the type or brand and didn't care—snagged a brown grocery bag, jammed the cartons in, and fast-walked to the door. A clean getaway.

They were still out front waiting.

"Aren't you in a mood," Kat said.

Truman stopped on the top step, hugging the bag to his chest. "What?"

"You were humming something." She threw a broad smile that seemed bright even in the dim glow of the single streetlight. "What was it?"

His pulse beat in his throat. Had she recognized the song his muse had revealed to him? Was Kat his Kachina? She wasn't the first one to show some recognition. Dennis Reynolds had recognized the tune during his first guitar lesson.

"It's . . . something I'm working on," Truman said.

"Aww, a sappy *love* ballad," Nate said, grabbing the bag of beer from Truman's arms. "Riffing off Black Velvet in there."

"No," Kat said, "it was sweet."

Sweet wasn't the adjective Truman would've chosen.

"*Sweet* sappy ballad," Nate insisted.

"No, not just sweet," she said. "It was also—" She frowned, thinking of a word. "—Mournful."

"*Mournful* sweet sappy—"

"Shut up, Nate," Truman said.

"It sounds old," she went on. "Plaintive. Like a chant. Like calling down ancient power."

He considered this description much more appropriate, if not over the top.

Nate snickered, but Ryan nudged him quiet.

Truman stepped off the porch. "I write songs." He felt awkward without the grocery bag now, not sure what to do with his hands. "This melody is something I'm hoping goes somewhere."

Kat grabbed his hand, solving that problem. "Seems to me it already is." She pulled him close and walked him across the street, Ryan and Nate in tow. The guys talked under their breaths about Black Velvet songs.

At the farthest point of the resort property, east of the main swimming area, a lonely dock jutted into the night-calm lake. It was wide enough for foot traffic, but not at all functional as an actual dock. The wooden surface floated on the lake, chunks of odd-sized foam pontoon blocks stabilizing it somehow, the whole structure tied to a metal culvert pile-driven into the lake bottom. A ramp led from the beach to the dock. To keep tourists off, Jacob had posted a sign on the beach in front of the ramp that read **NO SWIM-MING, NO DIVING**. You had to tread lightly on the slatted wooden 2 x 4s or end up tilting sideways into the shallow lake.

Despite the crowds in the campground and main lawn—their hoots and laughter a constant counterpoint to the lapping of the water against the dock—none of them had made their way to this end of the property. Truman, Kat, Nate, and Ryan had the place to themselves. Here was a seemingly secret, somewhat forbidden dock, wild clumps of brush and weeds from the beach trailing into the lake and giving them a measure of privacy.

"Be careful," Truman said as the guys edged by and clunked their way out on the dock. The surface tilted wildly, Ryan wind-milling his arms to remain upright. That pulled Nate askew, and he had no choice but to give in to gravity and pitch toward the water.

"Save the beer!" Ryan whooped when Nate held the bag high just before splashing into the lake on his back.

Kat let go of Truman's hand. She stepped onto the still gyrating dock, walking carefully down the middle. The dock seemed not to notice her as it reached a sort of trembling state of rest. Truman followed, a little less sure as he made his way toward her.

Nate declared the lake to be like bathwater and set the beer on the dock. He reached in and pulled a bottle, twisted the top, and guzzled half of it before Truman sat down in the middle of the deck. Ryan pulled his Hobie shirt off, slipped off his shoes and socks, and jumped in on top of Nate.

"Shit, man!"

The dock wobbled dangerously again, but Kat stood in the middle, perfectly balanced. She looked down at Truman, gave that bright smile again, then pulled her black Kurt Cobain shirt over her head. She soon had everything else off. In the moonlight, she was undefined, almost ghost-like. Nate and Ryan encouraged her need-lessly until she jumped in naked next to them. Nate's sopping shirt slapped onto the dock. So did his cargo shorts. Ryan's too. They wrestled beers out of the grocery bag.

Truman pulled at his shoes, socks, and pants, fumbling around, worried now that he would make a fool of himself. Fall over back-ward in a somersault into the water on the other side. Rip out his pants. Skewer himself on the beer bottles.

He worried his age and I'm-no-longer-20-something body

wouldn't measure up to these toned, younger sailboat racers. The water was shallow, and Nate was standing, his whole torso on display. Kat scrunched down to her neck, whirling around as if she were back on the dance floor. Nate and Ryan circled Kat, no longer orbiting, but caught in her current.

Truman stood, got naked, looked down into the water at Kat, and hesitated. Under the surface, the ripples hazing everything, Kat's body shimmered in curves and delicate points and sharply black geometries.

"Yeah, yeah, we see it, Truman," Ryan called out. "Jump in and spare us the sight!"

Truman came to his senses and jumped in, giving them some room. He submerged and stayed under a while, letting the cool water purge him of the day's cares. When he came up, facing them, Ryan handed him a beer.

Now they were all in a circle, crouched, water to their necks, drinking the beers—Miller Genuine Draft, it turned out—saying nothing, listening to the distant, almost comforting, sounds of the campground. Kat was on his right, Ryan on his left, Nate across from him. Truman felt a wisp of a touch of Kat's fingers along his side as she took a slow sip of the beer in her other hand. Her breasts out of the water, small and buoyant, perfect.

They took sips almost in turn.

Ryan and Nate had been tipsy before leaving the lounge. Now they stared like jackals at Kat. Truman stared too, enamored with her, mystified by her almost suffocating sensuality.

Nate belched.

"Thanks for ruining the moment," Kat said, sinking deeper again.

They laughed, and then the near-quiet fell on them again. A few minutes later, in a low growly voice, Ryan started humming the opening lines of the *Jaws* theme.

"Shut the *fuck* up!" Nate said, laughing. He slapped his hand against the water and splashed Ryan. "We're in a goddamn lake."

"Lake shark." Ryan sang on, head low, inching toward Nate, mouth half in the water. "Duh duh, duh duh, duh duh, duh duh . . ."

Nate dunked him.

They never stayed quiet long, but the noisy moments kept returning to that comfortable silence. The surface of the water reflected whirls of moonlight, half-submerged detritus captured in the dusk and gray.

"Truman," Kat said, "sing us your song."

No.

A simple request, but he didn't want to go there. This song was everything to him, beautiful and poignant, but he feared its darker side, the rumbling thunder that had soaked into it. A part in an unasked-for duet, as if someone were feeding him forgotten lines from a script.

If he refused—if he stayed still and stayed in this protective circle forever—whatever it was that was *bad* out there might stay away. He could survive because of the fleeting, almost magical, touches of Kat's fingers along his thigh, teasing him. He could survive because of the glimpses of the gentle curves of her body beneath the surface.

Kat said, "Truman?"

He stayed quiet, and Ryan began singing Abba's "S.O.S."

The tableau lost, the two racers laughed and splashed again. Nate tapped down hard on the top of Ryan's beer bottle with his own, and Ryan's beer bubbled and foamed wildly out.

While they swore at each other, Kat paddled to the dock and pulled herself out of the water. She stood a moment with her eyes closed, then she stretched her arms to the sky, her body pale in the gloom, her hair heavy against her back, her breasts barely rounded, stomach flat. The water ran in small rivulets down her arms, her sides, her thighs and legs. Under her spell, Truman wished she could hold that pose forever, the beautiful lines of her body stretched in an almost religious gesture, like a supplication, or a benediction, to god, the lake, the moon.

Truman watched, bemused, as she let go of the moment, bent, and used Ryan's shirt to dry herself before getting into her own shirt and pants. She ran fingers through her dark hair. Again, Truman was the last to move. Ryan and Nate scrambled to the dock ahead of him and rolled out onto its deck, laughing and swearing the whole time.

Kat picked up the rest of the beer as the guys dressed and Truman worked his way to the dock.

"Find us in the campground!" she said, then glided off the dock. The two racers trailed along like bulls following a lamb, still half-dressed, barely keeping their balance.

She was so sudden.

He had no way to catch up to them. They disappeared around the brush. It took him five minutes to climb onto the dock and don his clothes.

In the campground, Truman found no sense of order in the way campers had pitched their tents. It had to be past three in the morning now, but campers still talked around the campsites that had fire pits. As he wound around the tents, he stopped occasionally to ask if any of them knew or had seen Kat. Girl with long dark hair? Two guys with her?

No one knew her or had seen her.

He worked his way to the main lawn and the makeshift campsites. No fires allowed here, and it was quieter, fewer people out of their tents and talking.

He never found her.

When he finally crawled into bed, the window open and no sounds from the campground drifting through, he dared himself to hum the melody.

But he didn't dare.

10

≫⟫

GOLDEN APPLES

K AT AND THE TWO SAILBOAT RACERS FOUND A CAMPFIRE ON the resort lawn after the swim, talking it up for a while with several others from—well, she couldn't remember where they were from. Nate and Ryan sat down, but she excused herself right away to hit the porta-potty, and just kept going, walking the mile to the ranger station. She didn't give the Hobie guys another thought, but she did think about Truman. His reluctance to let loose and have fun surprised her, but at the same time, she found it a soothing contrast to Nate and Ryan. Truman was handsome, she thought. She saw dimples the few times he smiled, and that right there made her take notice. His hair was medium length, brown and soft, and his eyes were both soft and piercing. His presence hit her hard in the chest, and she wasn't sure why, because she'd decided a while back to take some time and live life just for herself. She didn't need further complications.

Something, though. Something kept pulling at her. Was it Truman? He was moody, sure. Unpredictable. He readily danced with her, but let Nate and Ryan cut in without protest. He agreed to sneak some beer but wasn't comfortable doing it. He wrote music but seemed unwilling to share his song.

Find your song.

Wasn't that what Allie had been trying to get her to do? So why had she rushed so quickly out of the lake and left him behind? It seemed awful of her now, but at the time, she thought he might do something to make her stop. Hold her up. Demand she wait. Also, she'd felt frightened. Maybe Allie's current lessons about magic and creating a telos had prompted that fear. If there was power in sex? What then? That moment on the dock when she'd stretched toward the moon: had that been a test? Had she expected to feel something between them? Instead, when she hastily dressed, all she got were two drunk Hobie Cat racers rushing after her as if she were Atalanta in Greek myth, thoughtless men racing for her hand in marriage. All they had were bottles of beer, not golden apples.

Kat's mom had found something else on her own path. Something that had distracted her from her marriage and pulled her away. Whatever it was, Kat doubted it was anything golden.

Kat had felt her own pull. Again. That echo. The sense of her own self caught up in something larger, and something dangerous. She thought she might've felt the pull of the Moss Man. Whatever it was, she needed to get out of Quinault and learn more from Allie.

When she reached the ranger station, her dad wasn't there—not a surprise—but she had a key to let herself in when the place was locked up. He said giving her the key was against the rules, so if she stayed, she had to be out early, before anyone showed up the next day, even if it meant waiting until someone opened the place up and she could walk back in, as if she'd never stayed the night. She didn't want to put her dad in a bad spot, so she never overslept.

Even this morning, after only a few hours sleep, she left early and took the bus—after waiting an hour for the first one of the day—back to Aberdeen. Once again, she experienced regret at leaving Truman behind, but she thought it best to be near Allie and Serena. For now, Truman could wait—she imagined him holding back his own golden apples—and she would continue her race toward her own song.

11

※

RECAPITULATION

THERE IS MORE TO LIFE THAN WIND.

And yet, for some—sailboat racers in particular—without wind, there was no prize. Hadn't they heard the old Latin proverb? *If the wind will not serve, take to the oars.*

Of course, oars would be against the rules for a sailboat race.

On Saturday, the Hobie Cat races stalled completely, the ever-faithful lake wind a no-show. Race officials had marked out the course for the day, but the boats stayed grounded on the shore, on-call, with the contestants hoping for a late surge of afternoon wind.

Truman had half-stumbled down the stairs to work, bleary-eyed, frustrated that Jacob wanted the store opened at 8:00 a.m., an hour earlier than normal. Truman barely registered Andrea as he began stocking the shelves and the coolers. Losing Kat to Ryan and Nate in the wee hours of the morning had been a little like a sailboat caught in a dead calm on the lake, losing ground—and losing sight—of his goal.

He didn't much like the way Kat had twice vanished from sight.

Race contestants *harrumphed* into the store all morning and afternoon: in the morning, they'd grumbled about the forecast; in the afternoon, evidence of the wind's absence made them surly as hell.

Truman told his Latin proverb to Cindi Werner when she came in to buy some orange juice, and she stared at him, seemingly unable to comprehend its complexity. Then she quoted a proverb of her own. "No wind is of service to those bound for nowhere."

"I don't think that means what you think it means," Truman said. He thought, however, that it might be apt for her and her husband Sam.

"Whatever." She stalked out of the store.

"Tempers are flying," Andrea said.

"Unlike the Hobies."

At two o'clock, still no wind. Thirty minutes later, Truman heard the first rumble of thunder.

"What the hell?" he said.

Andrea checked her phone. "Weather report says we've got a storm coming in."

"But still no wind."

"No."

But maybe rain.

Truman expected to see Ryan and Nate come into the store at some point, since they were part of the races, their boats as stalled as everyone else's, but they never did.

Where was Kat?

The whispering wind accompanying the calm, patient hours past midnight had whisked her away like a magician's trick. Truman had felt safe in the bathwater of Quinault, the full moon peeking from a blameless and perfect sky while they laughed and joked about songs and lake sharks. He had eyed Kat not as a prize but as a cipher, as mysterious as the song that had become his heavy burden and his potential deliverance from obscurity.

Kat had called his song a chant.

Truman, during a quick reprieve from pushy customers demanding his attention, found himself staring out the front door at the lake and the impending storm. He put his hand in his left pocket and fingered the silver key there. This he had kept with him since he'd found it the night he'd circled the lake.

Naïvely, he wondered if the key unlocked some ancient power

that the lightning would trigger. Or maybe, buried deep in the bark of an old growth tree trunk, a secret wooden mechanism would only turn with the key inserted during the full moon, bringing about eternal peace. Maybe it'd bring unmistakable evil.

Or perhaps it just opened some bus locker in Aberdeen.

"The beer cooler's low again," Andrea said from the registration counter.

Of course it was. And it was missing two six-packs of Miller Genuine Draft.

At four o'clock, race officials cancelled the day's heats. Since running heats or any type of final races on Sunday had not been in the plans of the committee (and most racers), the Northwest Hobie Cat Championship went to the team with the best time on Friday, two brothers from Billings, Montana. Cindi and Sam Werner finished in fourteenth place.

Truman didn't hear the race results until a little later, when one of the disgruntled race teams trudged into the store and passed on the news. Truman sighed with relief. He was ready for things to get back to normal.

Thunder and lightning rocked the resort, and had there been any wind, the lake wouldn't have been at all safe for racing. So, there was *that*.

Truman waited for rain, glancing anxiously out the windows between customers, but none came. Business died down as race contestants slowly made their escape from Quinault. They pulled their Hobies from the water and secured them on boat trailers, then checked out of rooms and cabins, collapsed tents, unhooked campers, fired up motorhomes, and one-by-one, they rolled down the lake road toward home.

Andrea left too, and when only a few hours remained in Truman's shift, a man entered the store wearing a long gray trench coat and a green Olympic Rainforest baseball cap. Truman's pulse quickened. He wore blue denims and brown hiking boots.

Then, right behind him, Dennis Reynolds entered the store.

Dennis, who'd stopped guitar lessons for no apparent reason, and quit the restaurant.

Dennis wore dark sunglasses and a ballcap of his own, a black one that had no words or designs on it. He avoided looking at the register, sliding in behind the man in the trench coat.

"Dennis?" Truman said.

"Truman," the boy mumbled back.

The man came up to the cash register and smiled.

"Do you need help finding something?" Truman asked.

"Actually," the man said, his voice raspy, like a heavy smoker's, "I do."

"Okay," Truman said, trying to recover from his surprise. "Lot of stuff here, even though it's been picked over by the craziness of the races this weekend." Truman was trying to be polite, all the while wondering what to make of this man in the trench coat that Dennis seemed to know. Or had the boy just come in behind him by accident?

"I'm sorry," the man rumbled, "I'm not interested in anything in your store . . . *Truman*."

Truman pretended to be interested in the keys of the cash register. "Then what can I help you find?"

"I'm looking for someone. A friend of mine."

"I see." He looked up. "Was your friend here for the Hobie Cat races?"

He shrugged, then reached up and adjusted his ballcap a little.

"A local then."

"I doubt it. Unless you call Aberdeen local." He smiled a twisted smile that made Truman wish Andrea were still in the store. Or that Jacob had wandered in.

"I'm sure I can't help you then—"

"Her name is Kat."

Truman stopped fussing with the register. The ensuing quiet made him uneasy. He didn't much like that this man knew Kat in some way.

A rumble of thunder outside broke his reverie.

"Sorry," Truman muttered, "I don't know her." Technically, not a lie. He really didn't know her. Or understand her. "A lot of people have been in the store this weekend. Very few offer their names."

"Long dark hair, dark eyes, slender, very attractive," the man said. "She'd seem very out of place here, I would think."

Truman shook his head. "Sorry. But did you try up the road, at the Lodge?"

The man pulled at his hat, still crooked. He raised it, more light hitting his face. His eyes were cold, almost dead as they focused on Truman. "At the moment, I'm looking here," he said, his voice louder. "Be certain of your answer."

"I'm sorry?"

The man towered over the register, blocking Truman's view of the rest of the store. "You better be telling the truth."

Truman fought the urge to back up a step. "Why wouldn't I be?" His stomach tightened. He half expected the man to reach over, grab Truman's throat, and demand an answer. The man was angry, no doubt about that.

Dennis slid out from behind the man, having been quiet all this time. "Tip," he said, "try and be sure."

"Dennis," Truman said, "you know this guy?"

"*Tip*?" The man laughed, but it didn't diminish his anger. "What kind of name is that?"

"It's a nickname," Dennis said. "Can we go? I need a ride home."

"I have a tip for *Tip*," the man said, leaning over the register again, his face red. His eyes seemed nearly black, mostly pupil. Nothing bright there. "Stay away from her, and don't get involved. That's a warning."

"I told you I don't know her."

The man smacked the top of the register with both hands before backing up, looking at Truman all the while. "You'll regret it if I find out you're lying."

"Why would I lie to you?"

"Where do you live?"

Truman said nothing. He glanced nervously in Dennis's direction and wondered if the boy would say anything.

Dennis walked in front of him. "Let's go."

"Just helping out my friend this summer," Truman said in his defense. "Now I think Dennis is right, and you should go."

The man snickered. He nodded as he backed up, never taking his eyes off Truman. He wrapped his gray trench coat tight around him. "Later on, Tipsy."

Then he left.

Dennis gave a look over his shoulder before scuttling out the door behind the man in the baseball cap. A clap of thunder. Then silence in the store. Truman was by himself. He was shaking.

Truman looked out the door at the lake again, at the deepening sky and the clouds hanging low over the water. *C'mon*, he thought. *There's rain in those clouds, I know it.*

No one else had come into the store, and he wanted to close early. The encounter with the man and Dennis had really affected him. He still shook a little.

As busy as it had been all weekend in the store, the hush of Sunday evening, the looming storm clouds, and the absence of any crowds, felt almost unnatural.

He didn't need any further coaxing. He shut the door, flipped the OPEN sign to WE'RE CLOSED, and flicked off most of the lights. Jacob wouldn't even know.

Up in his room, Truman threw open the window he'd opened that first night when he heard the song of Kachina. He watched the sun set behind the lonely mountain across the lake, and it wasn't long before he flopped onto his bed, the stress of the day evident in his achy muscles and the fuzziness behind his eyes. Staring at the ceiling and the cedar slats, he started counting knotholes. He didn't get far.

The rain intensifies, causing Tina to look up from the Clue board. She stares out the large living room window. She's about to make an accusation in the game, and the storm, as it gets worse, parallels the mounting tension.

Truman reassures her, tells her to continue. He watches as she nods and returns to her notes. "Do your worst!" he says.

"It's Colonel Mustard—"

"No, I didn't do it!"

"—in the library, with the wrench."

Truman smiles. "I'm not sure you're right . . ."

"Oh, I am."

A bright flash of light interrupts them again, and a crack of thunder follows not too long after. The heart of the storm is close.

As Tina pulls the cards out of the secret envelope, the power goes out.

Thunder woke him.

The dream faded quickly, and he was okay not remembering it, or what it reminded him of about that New Year's Eve, but even as it slipped away, he felt that something about it didn't ring true.

Thunder clapped again. Thunder, yes, but something more. His heart skittered when he recognized the patter of rain.

He jerked up from the bed and recognized her voice almost immediately. The melody was his now. She'd sung it and he'd claimed it, and his prize echoed in the rain like the countless rumbles of thunder. He still believed she was looking for him. The interplay of her song intrigued him, as if there were variations hidden within, there for him to discover.

It took a moment to realize she purposefully weaved the melody between the second countermelody he'd been working on, the one inspired by the thunder. He hadn't noticed it creep back like a countermelody out of synch and out of character with the rest.

He closed his eyes and listened, wondering if he might finally find the way to wrap up the first part of his symphony.

The key is the moon, came her voice.

He scrambled to the piano and started in, the voice still seeping through from the window of his bedroom.

Flow.

Momentum.

The pencil scratched across the staff paper as if magically enhanced. Truman gripped it tightly, afraid to let go, the notes, chords, and embellishments coming so fast that even his magic pencil couldn't keep up.

He was solo on this one—that is, if he didn't count his muse giving him a hand—and that was the way he wanted it.

Moonlight seeped into the room, but he kept his head down, his writing hand alternatively scribbling and joining his other to sound things out on the piano. But then moonlight fell on the manuscript, illuminating a strip of staff paper with Kachina's theme meandering through it like a lifeline thrown on water, waiting to be pulled taut. He hadn't realized it until just then, but the tonal structure had modulated, and he'd changed key without changing the key signature, using sharps and incidentals, and it was a key that shouldn't work here, it shouldn't *at all*, but here it was, highlighted by the moonlight, an impossibility interpolated into the structure of theory, like voices inside the perfectly natural order of rain.

It was his moon key.

Recapitulation. He had it now. The hours passed by without notice. Truman, almost feverish with the effort, fought the thunder and contained it in the chordal structure underlying the moon key, letting it out only amid the strident pounding of kettle drums, and the insistent ostinatos carried by the double basses.

The rain continued, and Truman struggled to pull everything together. He wrote passionately and with urgency, as if he were inside a dream he didn't want to end, and he pushed on, not letting up until light began to chase away the shadows in the room. He glanced at the window, the music and ethereal dances of the night fading away, and he blinked away his trance.

It was morning, and the first movement was complete.

SECOND MOVEMENT

We are the music makers,
And we are the dreamers of dreams,
Wandering by lone sea-breakers,
And sitting by desolate streams;—
World-losers and world-forsakers,
On whom the pale moon gleams:
Yet we are the movers and shakers
Of the world for ever, it seems.
            —Arthur O'Shaughnessy
            Ode

This is the light of the mind, cold and planetary
The trees of the mind are black.
            —Sylvia Plath
            The Moon and the Yew Tree

12

꙳

KARMA

Hines didn't find Kat at the Rainforest. Dennis's idea had gone nowhere. Now, if he was going to find where Allie had hidden the Moss, he'd have to resort to other means to find it. Kat was hidden from him—for now—but he felt confident that he had enough power to manipulate the ley lines about him, and even disrupt nature enough to cause some damage in his attempt to track and manipulate her. Or, failing that, manipulate someone close to her, just as he had manipulated his own clueless tagalong.

He needed help now, and he waited at the end of the pier, his fifth wheel sitting above, on the bluff. He looked down, and the tide was out. Mudflats. You wouldn't want to get stuck in that. It gave him an idea, though. Something he might be able to do if someone got out of line.

No luck with Kat, so his best chance of getting what he needed was the Moss witch, Allie. At the same time, he thought getting to Kat's friend Serena might work even better. Draw Kat out, and he'd remain out of Allie's sphere of influence. He believed, and not for the first time, that he needed his full power returned to him if he were to find—well, what should he call it?—the plane of existence his mother might be on. The Moss might be turning him inside out. Might be making him do questionable things. Might be he even liked—

No. Stay back, blackness.

Footsteps sounded on the pier behind him.

Hines turned, and the boy was there. He wore a plain black stocking cap and a gray rain slicker over a black T-shirt and jeans.

"Yeah?" the boy said. "You call for me?"

Hines had been ready to throw the boy off the pier after the second hour straight playing his damn guitar in the fifth wheel. Over and over, the same melodies, some things he learned from guitar lessons. Then the kid had switched things up. Did something to the guitar with a bar he attached to the frets, changing the key. Started strumming some chords. Then he plucked out some crystal clear notes.

Hines had listened and shivered. It was a song, or a pattern, he was sure he'd heard before. Somewhere. Someplace. Some—time?

"What is that?" Hines had asked him.

Dennis shrugged, but kept playing. "Just some notes. They're cool, though, huh?"

"Did you think them up?"

"No, I heard Truman play them."

"Who?"

"Tip. The guy at the store. You were asking him about Kat. Remember?"

He remembered, and then, much to his glee, realized that the guy at the store—and now Dennis—had heard the same melody he'd sensed himself. Oh, he could use that. He could use Dennis even more, now, if the kid had a connection to the song. This Truman was an enigma. It was almost as if he didn't really belong, just spiraled in from somewhere along the way, mucking things up. No doubt Hines would have to change the way he went about things.

Hines smiled and waved him closer. "I need your help. Kat is nowhere to be found—for now—and we have work to do."

The boy took a quick peek over the edge of the pier at the mud below.

"We will eventually go to the source and make her talk."

"You mean Allie?"

Hines smiled. "That's right. But first, time to go into town and pay Kat's friend Serena a visit."

"What're we going to do?"

"Take whatever she can give us. She won't sense us; she doesn't have the power or capability that the others do. I'm nearly drained of my power. It's the best way to proceed for now. Besides, if we find Serena, we might find Kat after all."

He pulled his knife and let Dennis see it. He ran his finger along the blade until blood dripped from his fingertip to his palm. "Are you ready to do this?"

Dennis paused a moment. "You promised me some of your power."

"I did. You keep working for me. You keep listening for that song I told you about. You'll have it."

"I don't know how you can offer me anything like that, but if you *really* can, I'll go along."

"Soon. You'll have it soon." Hines rubbed his fingers together, the blood wet and slightly sticky. Then, with his thumb, he traced lines across Dennis's forehead, marking him with the blood, wincing when he squeezed the cut finger harder to coax out more blood. Hines did this for his own pleasure, not for Dennis.

"You know where Allie lives," Dennis asked, "but how are we going to find Serena?"

Hines spread his arms and said, "It's a beautiful world we live in, Dennis." He nodded to himself, feeling the coldness warm up a little. "Everything comes back. The day, the night, the tide, a river. Like a circle. Like karma. *Bad* karma, this is. She'll show up at Duffy's. Maybe Kat, too."

"I thought you couldn't go in there. Isn't Bill Hand looking for you?"

"I won't. You will."

"I'm not old enough to be in the bar."

"Restaurant section. You can do some recon."

"Recon?"

"I know Duffy's well enough. You have a good view of the bar and stage from the restaurant area. Keep a watch for her."

"I don't know what she looks like."

"I do. Don't worry. We'll work it out."

"If Kat isn't there, what will you do with Serena?"

Hines smiled. "Well now." He wiped the blood off his knife and sheathed it.

"*Some*one has to be made into an example, don't they?"

13

THE RED FEATHER

Septemer in Quinault didn't mean the crowds disappeared, or the weather grew worse. Some of the nicest days of the year came during those first weeks of September. Sunsets across the lake reddened the water and drenched the sky with ribbons of bright yellow and orange, and it took Truman's breath away.

Eventually, though, even as the weather stayed nice, the crowds thinned. "Nice" also meant zero rain, and Truman hadn't touched the symphony since the night he finished the first movement. Frustrated, he ignored the piano and pulled extra duties and hours at the resort. The earlier optimism he'd felt that night finishing the movement and listening to Kachina had changed to despair. A storm of missed opportunities. It wasn't fair he had to wait for his inspiration. It wasn't fair he couldn't see Kat again—although he looked for her at every opportunity amid the dwindling parade of tourists. He wished Kat's energy and spirit would sweep him away.

It turned out the coach for the high school football team needed some help, and someone suggested Truman might volunteer some time. Truman had confessed to a few locals that he'd played high school football on the offensive line as a guard. He'd been small for a guard, but fast, so they'd drawn up a lot of plays with him pulling, leading the running back on end arounds. They asked if he would try his hand coaching the offensive line. Truman agreed. It might be fun, and it might keep his mind off Kat.

The Quinault Elks played 8-man football due to the small school population. When Truman arrived after school that first day, Coach Daniel Johnston greeted him with an over-the-top enthusiasm. The Elks had already won their first two games of the season, but their quarterback had endured a lot of sacks, knock-downs and hurries. The offensive line needed some help. Coach Johnston hadn't focused on it due to the almost fanatical attention he paid to the defense. Another assistant, Bryson Marshall, worked exclusively with the quarterback, Terry Milborn.

"We have a good chance of getting to the playoffs, and even to State," Johnston said, "but I'd sure feel better if we could shore up that offensive line."

"I remember a few things that might help," Truman said.

"Good, good," he said. "I'll introduce you to the team, and then have you split off with the offense. Give you time with that front line. And I hope you can work the games, too. This Friday we're home against Wishkah."

Truman worked with the players after school that week, then on Friday switched with Andrea so he could coach on the sidelines for the game against the Wishkah Loggers.

The stadium was fairly small, wooden, and built right behind the school. Painted blue and gold, the school colors, the stadium had an overhang that protected the rows of seats in the upper half. A press box perched precariously at the top of the stadium, a single attached ladder the only way to get up there.

The stands filled quickly during the pre-game warmups. This was Quinault's Friday night fall entertainment.

The night was clear, the temperature in the forties, and Coach Johnston pointed out how unusual it was that all three games so far had been played in dry weather. Before long, the team left the field and squeezed into the home dressing room on the west side of the stadium. Players adjusted equipment. Bryson Marshall re-taped some of the boys' ankles.

Almost as one—although Truman didn't see any visual cue to

do so—the boys grew silent and gathered in a circle down on one knee around their coach. When the room was completely hushed, the coach nodded, turning slowly to take in all of his players.

"Here we are," he said. He paused a full five seconds. "We can be 3-0 after tonight, boys. We've worked all week and we've learned all we need to know about Wishkah, and there's not much more I can say to you at this point about our game plan. Our strategies for sending these guys home with a loss are sound."

Truman wanted to say something, a "hell yeah" or a "that's right, that's right," but the boys kept quiet. They nodded knowingly, as if afraid to break the spell the coach had cast over them.

"I'm not going to yell and scream and whip you into a frenzy and have you run out onto that field whooping and hollering. I don't need to. You're ready. The adrenaline is coursing through you now, and damn it, I can *see* it. I can see the determination and the fortitude—hell, the *power*—pulsing inside you and jumping in the muscles of your jaws. We'll win if we believe in our ability to do so."

Johnston let that sink in a bit, then he reached into his Quinault Elks rain slicker and pulled out a red feather. He held it in front of him by the quill and raised it.

"Instead of going right to the affirmations, even though I told the story at the start of the season, I'll say it again for the benefit of Truman. He might like this story. This red eagle feather belonged to my grandfather. He lived in Tahola. He is distantly related to the chief the town was named for in 1905. Now, I know Tahola is our biggest football rival, and we have that game to look forward to, but my grandfather told a story about a young warrior who dared to go against the mighty red eagle to avenge the destruction of many of the surrounding villages. The red eagle's wings were so mighty that from them came a great wind that ravaged the land. The chief of the village offered the hand of his daughter to a great warrior from far away if he could bring down the terrible bird. But an imposter came instead, having captured and bound the real warrior.

The imposter shot his arrows, but they missed by a long distance.

"A young woman found the true warrior tied to a tree. She unbound him and rode ahead on her horse to tell the chief. The imposter was bound and mocked for a day until the avenger could come. And come he did, and the next time the red eagle appeared on the bluff overlooking the village, ruffling his feathers and flapping his huge wings, the avenger steadied himself, put his arrow on the bow, drew back, and let fly. The arrow narrowly missed, and the red eagle seemed indifferent to the threat.

"The next arrow the young avenger dipped in oil and set on fire. He drew back the bow, and he was so quick with his hand, and so sure of his aim, that no one in the village saw the arrow fly at the bird. The red eagle rose. It flapped once, twice, starting a great wind, but the arrow was true, and the wind did not affect it. The eagle plummeted from the bluff and fell lifeless to the earth.

"The avenger plucked a red eagle feather and put it in his hair, and gazing down at the dead bird, said, 'The fire always wins.' The people rejoiced. Then came a great feast, and the avenger won the hand of the chief's daughter. The daughter accepted him and told the story of the red eagle for many years, even into her old age as elder of the village, her husband having died a natural death before her. She gave the feather to her first born, and so it passed from generation to generation, until my grandfather said it came to him. He passed it on to my dad.

"And now I have it. And I pass it on to each of you."

With the story at an end, the boys stood and closed in on their coach, who gave the feather to his quarterback, Terry Milborn. Milborn said something about the team's tenacity and dedication, and passed it to the next player. Each player said something positive in turn, about the team, about a player or coach . . . even about the Wishkah Loggers, but always, they ended by saying "I am an Elk."

The last player gave the red feather to Truman. Surprised, Truman looked at it and wondered what to say. It was dead silent. Eventually he smiled and held the feather a little higher. "You guys

are a talented bunch of athletes. I'm pleased I've been able to help."
He paused, then added, "I am an Elk."

He handed it back to Coach Johnston, and the boys huddled
closer to him. They reached out and touched the red feather once
more. Or, if they couldn't, they put a hand on the coach or a player
in front of them. Truman wasn't sure how it was possible, but the
room became even quieter.

Above them in the stadium seats, as if on cue, fans started
stomping their feet. The band, which Truman noticed earlier consisted of about forty students, struggled through a rendition of "The
Hey Song." After the crowd's first shouted "Hey!" Coach Johnston
nodded and said, "Okay."

The boys reached for their helmets, put them on, and tightened
chin straps. Johnston always insisted they be snapped if their helmets were on.

It was anticlimactic, but all Johnston said was "Go get 'em,"
and they filed out in a single file line. When they had all exited
the room, the band started the fight song and the team captains up
front took off running. The team followed suit, sprinting until they
gained the field. They gathered in a tight circle once more, listening to the quarterback do what the coach would not: getting them
fired up. They clapped slowly after that, gaining speed until it all
sounded like applause, and they broke after a long, sustained yell,
ready for the national anthem and the first half.

The anthem played, but Truman barely heard it. Johnston's red
feather story stayed with him. He had no idea why the coach had
wanted him to hear it, but it didn't matter. The story had been told.
He could not pluck it from his mind.

⋙

At halftime, the Elks led 28-3, and as the fourth quarter started,
it was 42-17. Truman marveled at the way the boys played, and had
to agree this team looked strong, and they just might be unbeatable

in their league. A Wishkah touchdown made it 42-24, but Coach Johnston, not concerned at all, sent out whatever second-string players he had and replaced some starters, including the quarterback. The game was well enough in hand. After the kick-off, the sophomore quarterback couldn't get the first play from scrimmage off quickly enough, so he called time out.

During the time out, Truman did what he hadn't done the whole game: look up into the stands. He wasn't sure how he tracked them so quickly. Perhaps the ballcaps. But just two rows up on the right side of the stadium, Truman spotted the man he'd seen in the store sitting next to Dennis Reynolds.

Truman stared, standing still. He wished he knew this man's name. If Truman knew his name, maybe he'd have something. You could find out almost anything online these days.

The man seemed to be looking in Truman's direction, smiling, but that wasn't what unnerved Truman the most. Twisting it almost lovingly, The man made sure Truman saw the red feather in his right hand. That, and the memory of the coach's story, turned his skin to goosebumps. How did the man know about the red feather? He couldn't take his eyes off the scene.

Dennis looked uncomfortable. He glanced at the feather, then turned away, pulling his black cap lower. The man adjusted his own ballcap, twisted the feather some more, then extended his right arm toward Truman, offering it to him even at this distance.

He wondered what he should do, but moments later, the man nudged Dennis, making the boy look at him, and when he did, Dennis took the feather. Dennis glanced at it as if it were contagious, then dropped it on his seat, stood, and walked away. The crowd hushed, and a nervous energy filled the stadium.

The spell broken, Truman blinked and turned back to the field.

What? How much time had passed? He couldn't believe it.

The Elks led by just eight points, 42-34.

Truman whipped around and searched the stadium, but Dennis Reynolds and the man had vanished.

The horn sounded announcing the the end of the game. Truman was almost afraid to turn around to look, but when he did he saw the final score on the scoreboard.

42-41. A two-point conversion had failed with just seconds left. The Elks had held on to the win. Barely.

The fight song. The team in a circle in the middle of the field, singing. Helmets off and held high. The Wishkah Loggers walking dejectedly toward the visitor locker room. The stadium emptying. Students on the field joining their team. Scoreboard going dark.

Truman looked down and saw a red feather in the patchy grass at his feet. Somehow, he wasn't surprised. He wondered if it was the coach's or the one the man had given to Dennis. It didn't seem far-fetched that it could be that one.

He joined the coaches near the circle of players.

He left the feather behind.

14

֍

ADAGIO

THE NEXT TWO WEEKS, THE FOOTBALL TEAM PLAYED AWAY games. Truman continued to spend his Mondays and Tuesdays at practice, but he didn't travel with the team. The Elks won both games handily.

During those two Friday nights, a little rain fell. Truman heard little of Kachina's voice, barely registering the whisperings he might be confusing with his own internal awareness of the melody. It was enough to get him to the piano, though, to sketch out the first ideas of the second movement.

Before anything else, he labeled it *adagio*.

Slow.

He'd decided this early on, even before he'd finished the first movement.

From the Italian *Ad agio*. At ease.

He was also very aware of its meaning in the world of dance, this iteration coming to him as he thought of Kat on the dance floor, a dancer who had left him aching for her. The adagio denoted a controlled, sequence of skilled, graceful movements.

A vocal *adagio* was also a duet by a man and a woman, or a mixed trio that showed off highly technical feats. He thought of the man with the ballcap somehow in a morbid duet with Kachina—Kat?—and Truman making up the rest of the triangle. The mixed trio.

In ballet, the adagio was a love duet sequence, a pa de deux, a step of two, two dancers stuck together until, in the climax of the ballet, they were peeled apart by some mysterious force. It was more than a love dance. It carried the dancers' emotions of joy and longing, but also fear and grief.

Truman didn't need to hear Kachina's melody to find inspiration for the second movement. He decided to play off a four-note section from the middle of her melody, but take it elsewhere, a musical development before moving to the dominant and lingering there, holding longer than expected, then resolving to the tonal center. It was a musical phenomenon that the dominant existed *only* in the listener's ear, creating a desperate need to return to the tonal center and release the tension.

All humans experienced tonality. Some animals, too.

The adagio was slow and haunting, yet seemed to capture the complex and unresolved relationship between Truman and Kachina. Or Truman and Kat. Tension, release. It was a love song.

At ease.

He didn't feel that at all.

The middle of October brought the Elks back to Quinault for Homecoming against the Tahola Chitwins.

"Chitwins?" Truman had asked when he'd first heard the team's nickname.

"Chitwin is Quinault for bear," Johnston explained.

This was the big game of the year. Not only because it was Homecoming. Not only because it was Tahola. It would possibly decide the Pac-8 league championship, even though a few games remained on the schedule.

As big a rivalry as it was, Truman found out it wasn't a vicious rivalry. Opposing fans often got together for pre-game dinners. Players knew players from the other team well. Quinault team members, however, ate a team breakfast alone. Tahola had a late lunch of elk steaks.

When Truman arrived at the field, the stadium had started to fill up. Some road signs had been "borrowed' for the game that said "Elk Crossing." Tahola players had painted their faces to express their Quinault heritage and the idea of preparing for war.

The game started well for the Elks. Quinault's premier running back Daniel Hobucket found a rhythm as the Elks pounded the Chitwin's defense, and soon led 16-0 in the first quarter.

When the second quarter began, the rain came down. It started as a drizzle, but a few minutes later, the clouds opened, and the downpour soaked the fans sitting on the lower rows of seats. The stadium's overhanging roof kept most of the fans sitting higher dry enough.

Before halftime, players started complaining of burning sensations, which seemed odd, considering the rain should be washing away any sweat or fluids that might cause irritation.

In the locker room at halftime, the players were hurting. An inspection revealed many of the boys had some type of rash across their arms and lower backs—basically anywhere skin had been exposed, but no one had a clue what was going on, and the second half began.

The Elks' offense could do nothing. They gave away two safeties to Tahola, but luckily, Tahola couldn't move the ball either. The players felt the burning even stronger now, and they knew something was wrong. Daniel Hobucket gained just three yards in the second half.

When the game ended, the Elks had held on for the win, 22-10, but a total of seventeen players from both schools were transported to Aberdeen Community Hospital to be treated for first-, second- and third-degree burns. By the middle of the week school officials discovered the source of the burns. A hydrated lime substance had been inadvertently mixed with the non-chemical chalk substance normally used to line the field. Hydrated lime, mixed with water, causes a chemical reaction. What the school had ordered was line marker, but what they'd received was *lime* marker. The bags were mixed together.

Truman was convinced the man in the ballcap had something to do with the lime incident, even though locals pointed to a similar incident happening forty years earlier at a neighboring town. Plus, he hadn't spotted the man or Dennis in the crowded stands. Increasingly, events unusual and strange had become real, dangerous, and almost commonplace. In a two-week span, there were four alcohol-related traffic deaths, and a 15-year-old had a heart attack. There were four deaths by natural causes, and an 18-year-old involved in a murder. A drug bust, a rape, and one suicide. A woman tourist, just twenty-three years old, left a big tip at a restaurant on the other side of the lake, then shot herself in her rental cabin. Truman already half-believed in his heart that the man hanging around Dennis Reynolds had something to do with all of it.

The man had warned Truman in the store about being involved.

For the last home game—a formality for the Pac-8 league champions—the Elks took on the South Bend Indians. Once again, the game was played in a torrential downpour. Johnston called the coaches together early on and discussed the game, including the details of the lime incident and the strategy to make sure it wouldn't happen again. The replacement line marker had been checked and double-checked before the game.

"The last thing we need," Johnston said, "is another damn Lime Bowl."

The first half went Quinault's way, and the Elks led 28-0. During the third quarter, Truman took a quick, almost nervous glance at the stadium, but he didn't see the man or Dennis Reynolds. Five minutes later, though, when he looked again, he saw them. They sat two rows up, as they had during the Wishkah game, but on the other side of the stadium. Truman expected to see the man twirling his red feather, but instead, his eyes were closed, and he seemed to be mumbling to himself. Dennis kept his head down, looking at his knees.

Truman did not make eye contact and returned his attention to the game. The Indians mustered no points in the second half either, and the game ended with Quinault victorious, 35-0.

As the teams filed off the field, Truman chanced another look in the stands. The man was back in his spot, but not Dennis. This time it was a young woman next to him . . .

It was Kat.

Almost instantly, he remembered her dancing in the lounge, then the curves of her pale body from the moonlight skinny dipping. They were the only real things he had of her. But because of the association with Kachina, the mysterious melody of his symphony came almost unbidden to his mind.

But no. He was mistaken. It was a young woman with black hair, rail thin, but it wasn't Kat after all. Truman was relieved and anxious at the same time. How would he have reacted if she'd been there sitting next to the man?

Truman made a decision. He rushed toward the stadium, weaving between the exiting fans, heading for that row of seats before the man could run off. The rain hadn't let up since it started earlier in the game, but now it seemed to push ahead in waves. Truman lost sight of him, and he panicked, but as he reached the steps leading up into the stands, he saw the man was still there.

The woman he thought had been Kat frowned at him, then she picked up her empty popcorn bag and left.

"Where's Kat?" Truman asked.

"Ah, you *do* know her." He smiled, and it made Truman feel small and insignificant. The man adjusted his ballcap and leaned toward Truman. "Do not help her," he said, his voice gravellier than when he'd spoken to him in the store.

"Help who?" Truman asked, feigning ignorance.

"If you do," he said, "there will be consequences."

As if in response, the rain surged, pounding the roof of the stadium. In the store, the man had told him to stay away from her. He'd said there'd be consequences even then.

"I can't help you," Truman said. "I don't know who she is, or where she is."

Coach Johnston yelled up at Truman to come down to the coach's post-game circle. Truman turned to acknowledge him just as the man growled loudly in his ear, "Fucking liar!"

Startled, Truman spun back, but he found himself alone on the first row. The man was gone. He stood in awe, a shiver shaking his shoulders.

Do not help her.

This threat echoed in the rain; it was a strident warning even more disturbing than the actual voice of the man.

There was a power here that defied the natural order of things—Truman had been subjected to it from the day he'd arrived—but now it had the reality of whoever-his-name-was, and, if his suspicions were correct, Kat with a K. Kachina.

Johnston called up at him a second time. When Truman heard, he gladly fled the stadium, joined the coaches circling near the sideline, and tried to forget what he'd seen.

Johnston dropped Truman off at the store, and Truman dashed to the door, the rain coming down harder than it had during the game. He was soaked from the evening, but the short rush to the door—now that he didn't have the school's team rain gear—drenched him even more.

Worse, the voice of Kachina bombarded him the entire trip back. Truman couldn't make out the words, but it was obvious she was not singing but . . . *arguing*, oblivious to anything else.

"Do you hear anything strange?" he asked Johnston casually during the drive. He didn't want to be the whacko asking about ghost people in the rain.

"Strange, how?" Johnston asked. "Do you mean the rain? It's amazing, isn't it, how heavy it can get? Have you not seen it rain like this before?"

He had. It had rained just as fervently the day he walked down the road with his guitar case and first heard her voice. "Once," Truman said. "I guess I was just hearing the sound of it on the roof."

Why did no one else hear her voice? What was so special about Truman? Perhaps the music connection? Perhaps it had to do with his symphony, his personal brand of magic slowly coming to life the past four months.

He had no doubt that his second movement—his adagio— made him uneasy.

Not at ease at all.

15

DUFFY'S TAVERN

I 'LL DRINK TO THAT," SERENA SAID, AND SLOSHED HER SHOT glass of Jameson's drunkenly as she attempted to clink glasses with Kat.

Kat sighed. Serena was shit-faced and getting a little too loud. For once, there was no music, so everything Serena said seemed to echo through the room.

"What?" Serena tried to clink her glass again.

"How'd you get that many drinks ahead of me?"

"Sleight of hand," she slurred.

"Magic, is it?"

Serena pointed out a bartender, her drink spilling some more. "That one. Didn't you notice him?"

"Ned? Of course I noticed him."

"Come by the table?"

"Yeah, to check on us, take our orders."

"But the other times. Just walking by."

It dawned on her now. "You mean walking by, *behind* you."

Serena grinned. "Yup."

"He slipped you some extra drinks."

"Sleight. Of. Hand."

"You're toasted."

"Pleasantly *polluted*." Serena lifted the shot glass, then downed it. She exhaled loudly, then waved at the bartender making rounds.

"Probably enough for both of us," Kat said.

"C'mon, Kat, we're *celebrating*."

"It doesn't feel like it. I'm tired. Aren't you?" She paused, then let herself smile. "Well, I guess not now. I guess right now you feel no pain."

"But we did it. Did what Allie told us and got the box out of her place."

The Moss. Kat knew the key she'd hidden for Allie in the rain forest was for the box. Now they needed to take it somewhere safe where the asshole couldn't find it. She was nervous enough leaving it locked in Serena's car. At least she had Serena's car keys. She'd insisted after Serena started getting tipsy. No way was she going to let her friend drive in that condition, at night, with cops out and about on patrols.

"There's that guy," Serena mumbled, as if she'd been reading her thoughts.

Kat froze. The ballcap guy? She craned her neck, scanning the bar. "Where?"

Serena grabbed Kat's chin and pointed it toward the restaurant area past the railing that designated the bar. "*That* guy. You know? From the resort?

Kat squinted. He looked familiar, but he had no idea who it was. At least it wasn't the Moss Man.

"Dishwasher or something," Serena said. "Busser. I swear I saw him before."

"I'll take your word for it." She looked at the kid again. "He's too young to be in here."

Serena pouted. "It's too quiet in the bar section."

"Have you *heard* yourself this evening?"

"I want to dance. Where's Rand? Where's Deluge?" She stood and nearly fell over. Kat reached out and steadied her from across the table. Serena recovered, then wavered. "I don't—" She frowned. Put a hand to her mouth. "Oh fuck."

Kat waved her off frantically. "Jesus, go!"

And Serena was off toward the restrooms, barely holding everything back. Kat sighed and took a sip of her own glass of Jameson's. She stared at the guy in the restaurant, and he smiled at her. He raised a glass with dark liquid—probably a Coke or something. She smiled back. Maybe he did look a little familiar. To be honest, she never paid much attention to employees at the resort, her attention usually on music and dancing. Well, except for Truman, even though she'd only noticed him that last time during the sailboat races.

The guy looked at his phone, and Kat watched as he stood up quickly. He fumbled with some cash, left it on the table, and hurried out. Giving her a backward glance, he almost ran into the hostess.

That made her nervous. She looked back to the restrooms where Serena was puking her guts out, then made a decision. She stood. That box of Moss was in her car, and she wished she'd not let Serena talk her into this pit stop at Duffy's before hiding that box somewhere. *Just a few drinks. It's safe in the car. C'mon.*

She didn't know why, but sometimes it felt as if she could fast forward or rewind her life: send herself back to try a different path or skip ahead to discover something better down the road. This felt like one of those moments. There'd been a lot of those moments lately, wrapped up in bizarre echoes and song and Allie's lessons about—

Follow that kid.

One more glance at the restroom doors in the back, and Serena wasn't coming out. Fine. Serena would be okay. Kat made a beeline for the door.

"Hey, your bill?" Ned yelled after her.

"Serena's still here. I'll be back."

She reached into her pocket to grab Serena's car keys and stepped out into the cool evening. After a pause, she looked to her right down the block.

Kat's heart lurched when she spotted the boy who'd left the restaurant next to Serena's car, a black Honda Civic.

"Hey!" she yelled, heading his way. "Get away from my car."

It wasn't her car, but he didn't know that. Did he?

He only stared at her.

"Did you hear what I said?" She threw herself forward, expecting him to pull away. He was just a kid, maybe in high school, maybe out, and he had toasted her with a Coke, maybe not expecting her to move toward him so abruptly.

He did step back, but someone else came around from the other side of the car, hopping up on the curb.

Moss Man.

"Well lookee, lookee," he said, and gave her a hard look, his brows knit with menace. "My angel from the bar has not been very angelic."

Kat sneered. "You're a fucking lunatic. Get away from me."

His voice dropped to a guttural rasp. "Where's the key, Angel?"

He was so close, and now she couldn't see the younger guy. She willed herself to hold still.

"I've got the box already," he said. He scrunched down and pointed at the car. "Sorry about the window on the other side." He tsked at her. "You should never leave valuables in the back seat of the car. It's just inviting a break-in."

Kat felt her legs weaken. The bastard had the box and would do anything to open it. It wasn't very big, maybe the size of a small microwave, but heavy in its construction of metal and wood and heavy-duty hinges and brass locking mechanism. He couldn't open it, though. Not without the key. The key that only she could use to navigate the box's interlocking system, and only if she practiced what Allie had taught her.

Transmute the shape of the key through Allie's magic and not Moss-induced magic. Magic that Kat would have to channel, although she hadn't found her song yet. She wondered how she'd be able to accomplish any magical feats without it.

She crossed her arms. "I don't have the key," she said. "It's somewhere you'll never find it. *Never*. Never find it, never *use* it."

"Never?" The man laughed. "That's *bold*. I think," he added as he drew closer to her, "that I might have some power left to figure it out. At least the *finding* part." He nodded at the kid.

The kid sidled over and behind her and grabbed her by the crooks of her elbows, forcing her arms back. Holding her.

Kat didn't even try to resist. There wasn't any point worrying about the kid. She had to worry about the man in front of her. He had some Moss in his system still? How much? He couldn't do too much, could he? As cut off from it as he'd been?

The man smiled, then narrowed his eyes, lids slightly open, and he let his arms dangle at his side loosely. Then he brought them up slightly.

Kat felt the pull in her head, which suddenly throbbed.

He was pulling information from her head! How did he do that? She had to think fast.

The man's eyes were completely closed now. A slight breeze tugged at her that hadn't been before. The kid gripped her tighter.

She had to subdue her thoughts somehow. Think not of the key—she didn't even think of the place she'd ditched it—but something else.

Some *place* else.

Where would it be harmless? Not where people might be. Even farther out in the woods. Yes, that was it.

Are you listening, asshole?

Much farther away than where he thought she might have hidden it. Almost no one around. Hard to get to. Fool's errand to go traipsing up *there*. A safe bet.

Safe as she could think of, anyway.

Up valley.

Keep going, keep going. Oh, don't give it away to him (give it away, give it away but not the other place she was *not* thinking of), it was this place, this place only, miles and miles away, and much of it on foot, and everything locked. Secure. He could believe her because she knew how it was with the Forest Service and knew the whole lay of the land, thanks to—well, the *Forest*

Service. Her dad. She clamped down on that thought. Don't lead him that way . . .

Let him try and find the key up there and—

"Enchanted Valley," the man whispered, opening his eyes almost immediately afterward. The breeze died.

Kat's eyes widened in surprise. Surprise because he had figured it out so quickly from her thinking about the place. No, not surprise. It was more a feeling of fear that he'd done it so easily, even in a presumably weakened state.

"No," Kat said, struggling a little against the kid's grip, giving a bit of a show, still thinking of the valley. "How did—? No, you can't go up there. You *can't.*"

The man came up until he was just inches from her face. His breath was stale and dead. "Just think what I can do when I have all that back in my system, hmm?" He poked her in the forehead. "You are a piece of driftwood, my dear. I can see the holes, sense the smooth lines."

"You can't get up there," she said. "You won't find the key. Even if you do, you have to have the box with you or it won't work. You going to carry it all the way up there?"

"I have help," he said.

The kid. "Sure. Both of you. See how long that takes you."

"*Both* of us?" the man said, laughing. "There'll be three of us."

Three?

"You're coming with us."

Her stomach knotted and she almost lost the few drinks she'd had at Duffy's. That made her think of—

Serena. Oh god, stay in the bar. Stay in the rest room, puke your guts out. The man wasn't reading her mind with his magic now, so he didn't know, did he? The *kid* knew she was in there. Would he say anything?

"You'll help carry the box," Moss Man said, "and you'll lead us to the exact location."

She could buy some time. Lead them away, take them on a

wild goose chase. Better for all of them. Serena, Allie. Maybe even Truman.

Truman. She wished he could help. Help get this asshole out of the way.

"You don't have a choice," the man said. He jerked his head to the left. "We'll put her in my truck. We keep her until we're ready. Then, she'll help us."

She shook her head. "No."

"You will," he said, grabbing her chin. She avoided looking into his eyes. "You'll take us up valley, and you'll show us where the key is."

"I won't," Kat said. "You can take me, and figure out where it is, but by the time you get up there, your power will be gone. You won't be able to read anyone."

"If you don't help us up there," the man said, "then we won't have any choice. We'll just kill you, or—hmm, maybe—something worse. And then we'll do something else. Come back for your friend Serena, see what *she* knows."

"No. She knows nothing—"

"Blame that guy up at the lake. Truman. I'm losing patience. By the time I get to Serena, though? I will not be in a forgiving mood. And if not her, then I'll figure out how to get past Allie's sphere of influence."

He shoved her away by her chin and the kid grabbed on more tightly.

"Please," she whispered.

"No one will find you up there until it's way too late."

16

THE GHOST

IN HIS ROOM ON A RAINY NIGHT, TRUMAN SAT DOWN AT THE piano, closed his eyes, and tried to listen to Kachina, but her song seemed muddied, as if she were bickering with someone else. He leaned into the piano, his forehead on the music stand. This would just not *do*, this channeling of—an argument?—into his *adagio*. He couldn't concentrate. The thunderous clatter of rain on the roof grated at his nerves.

God*damn* it. How long could he deal with this? Ten minutes later, he straightened, dropped his hands to his lap, and opened his eyes. He stared at his staff paper; at the *adagio* marking; at the introduction of the movement in the opening staves; at the faint scratchings of the new theme: four notes of Kachina's song and the hint of something else. A strident voice, transitioning seamlessly to the dominant.

Tension. Release.

It was obvious he would have to run with this new direction, even though his whole being balked at it. Although marked *adagio*, the second movement would have to evolve into something more dissonant. Into something heavier and darker.

Slowly, painstakingly, he set up the movement with the new theme and let it rumble at the lowest, darkest notes he could get away with, including a smattering of tritones, which added more dissonance. A tritone pushed toward resolution, so Truman de-

fied convention and let it linger, restlessly, without a return to the
movement's established tonality. In fact, he ended the phrase there,
poised on the tritone.

In the Middle Ages, the tritone was called *Diabolus in musica.*
The Devil in music.

Truman was certain something devilish hovered around the
man in the ballcap who was so interested in finding Kat and so
insistent with his warnings. Truman found himself afraid for Kat.
Afraid for Kachina, whose voice had changed, so it seemed all she
did was rain-argue with someone else. Truman wanted to help Kat,
but he didn't know how. He had seen her during the Hobie Cat
races, but since then she had become more of a mystery than a reality. Even so, he feared losing her.

Truman wrote for another hour, then noticed the rain had lessened. Kat's melody simplified, which overlay the next portion of
the movement with a calmness.

The moon was back, shining through the window, and this time
it found the top of the piano and illuminated the silver key sitting
there. He swallowed hard, finding the moment almost too conve-
nient. Perhaps this, too, was his moon key. He wondered if it fit
somehow with the end of the first movement, when the moon had
shone on Kachina's theme that had modulated almost by accident.
The key is the moon.

As the rain disappeared altogether, and even Kachina's soft
song dissipated, Truman stood and peered out the window at the
full moon.

Perhaps it was time to return to the spot he found the key. Perhaps, under the light of this fall moon, he might understand and
know this woman he was afraid to lose, before he'd even found
her. She was looking for him. This he had believed for a while, but
maybe he needed to find *her*. Maybe she needed him to come to her.

He scooped up the silver key, thumped down the stairs, and
stole back into Jacob's office. In the top drawer of Jacob's desk,
Truman found the key to the blue resort truck. In minutes, he was

outside, sliding behind the wheel. He hoped he could find the spot again. He remembered driving about eight miles west after crossing the bridge, spotting the lake through a clearing.

If Kachina wanted to be found—if she was somehow stuck there in the spot he'd found the key—then he would find her, most definitely. Maybe the key would unlock something holding her there. Or maybe he was delusional, and this trip would be all in vain.

He didn't think so.

Truman started the truck, which grumbled and came to life and sounded too loud in the quiet of the night.

He pulled away and made his way to the lake road, and soon he was speeding east toward the river bridge. The rain had stopped, but this time he didn't need its guidance.

When he crossed the river bridge, Truman checked his speedometer. Eight miles from here, he would find the spot, and he didn't want to pass it by. The river paced him, although he could barely see it in the dark, and the trees, shadowy and still, lined the riverbank like sentinels. The wind had picked up, coming down from the east, causing the Toyota truck to buffet around on the gravel road.

Truman held tight to the key in his left hand, driving with his right. He didn't miss the spot. When he found it, he angled the truck to shine the headlights into the trees, then turned off the engine and put the key in his pocket. He climbed out and left the road, tracing the memory of the steps he took in late July, passing over the moss and undergrowth, and into the clearing with the tall cedar trees.

A moment later he mustered up enough courage to yell loudly into the clearing. "Kat!"

The vegetation deadened the sound of his voice, and a moment later he felt silly for even thinking that he could drive out here on a whim to this particular spot on this particular night and time and find her waiting here.

But he yelled her name again.

And again.

The more he did it the more the word felt dead and meaningless. If anyone else had been out here, they'd probably be wondering why a man was out here in the dark looking for his cat.

Cat. Kat.

Two words the same, two words so different.

That was it. Different. *Unique.*

"Kachina!" he yelled, certain this was what he needed to do.

He peered forward, the glow from the headlights creating a ghostly path, but he saw nothing, still. He thought for sure that might have brought her out from hiding—if she was even here at all. No, this was ridiculous. He had no business being out here, searching for someone who hadn't cared enough about him to say goodbye at the end of the summer.

He turned to go, but he paused, chilled as he listened to the forest. It was deathly quiet, seemingly quieter than it had been moments before. If he said something now—if he made *any* kind of noise now—he felt sure everyone on the north side of the lake would hear it.

There was only one kind of noise he thought to make.

He hummed. Soft and delicate, the melody came forth. He knew the song so well now, it felt as intimate as a loving caress. Kachina's melody from his symphony vibrated in his throat, and when he hummed louder, it sounded strong in his ears.

When he opened his mouth and sang it, the beauty of it swept through the clearing and passed into the forest. He almost believed he could track its path.

Near a tree in front of him, a larger one layered heavily with green moss, she appeared, side-stepping from behind it. Had she heard him all along and simply waited for him to sing that song? *So sudden.* But he couldn't believe she would do that, as forward as she'd been during the sailboat races.

She almost glided as she came forward, a long flowing white dress—the fabric barely substantial—hiding her feet. The outline of her body, visible under the dress, curved like an ancient vase. Her face furrowed with confusion as she stopped in front of him. She frowned, then stared.

Truman tried to hide his discomfort. He offered a reassuring smile, then said, simply, "Hi."

She just stared at him.

"Aren't you going to say something?" He almost said *Cat got your tongue?* but he held back. "It's been a while since the Hobie races, but not *that* long."

Finally, she said, "I heard your song."

He nodded. "Yeah. The one you asked about before. I'm Truman. You danced with me."

"I—was on the pier. I—wait. Danced?"

Truman looked more closely at her. No question: it was her. Kat with a K, the girl he'd danced with, the girl he'd skinny-dipped with, the girl he'd gone searching for in the campground afterwards.

"Something's happened to you," he said. "Hasn't it? It's that man, isn't it? What'd he do to you?"

She paled. He noticed even in the dim light of the headlights. When she dropped her gaze and stared at the spongy ground, he knew he was right. She *did* know the guy.

"I know him." She looked up at him again.

"I called your name. Kachina. That's your name, right? Or is it Kat?"

"Kachina is my name."

"I heard the name in the rain. I heard *you* in the rain. That song. That song was yours, not mine. I only took it for my symphony."

"Your symphony. Yes, of course."

"What does it mean? Your name, I mean?"

"It means sacred dancer."

That certainly fit.

She sighed. "I know you, but in a way I can't begin to explain to you. It's—complicated."

Truman believed it too, whatever it was she was trying to get across to him. "I think—I mean, maybe?—I heard you arguing with the man. His voice was in the rain too."

The light dimmed, and he realized the battery on the truck was running down.

"Wait right here? The lights. I need to turn off the lights."

She nodded, and he half believed she would disappear when he left for the truck. But after running to the road and clicking off the lights, he looked back and she still stood in the clearing, in profile, her face to the sky, illuminated only by the moonlight. She mumbled some undecipherable words. He felt his heart thump a little faster, and he felt an unbidden stirring in his groin.

Okay, what the hell was *that*? He'd already felt the magic of her song, felt the sexual pull of it, but still. It wasn't normal, these stirrings.

He approached her cautiously, and the words she uttered took on more form, but not any more meaning. He came closer to her than before. She radiated beauty beyond what he remembered, and for a handful of heartbeats he forgot to breathe. His pulse was in his ears, and that sensual ache in him nearly doubled.

For the first time in the silvery light, he noticed something not quite right about her face. A heavy bruise marred her right cheek, and a scratch lined her forehead. She gazed at the moon as she whispered words he couldn't hear, and he couldn't help but look up as well.

"What is that?" he asked. "What are you chanting?"

She intoned a few more words, then stopped.

"I—I'm sorry," he said. "I shouldn't have—"

"There's a Native American myth that names the sun and moon as a chieftain and his wife, and the stars are their children. Do you know this myth?"

He shook his head.

"Well, the sun isn't very nice, and likes to snatch his children and eat them. So whenever he appears in the sky, they flee."

Truman had the next part figured out. "The wife—the moon—plays with the children in the dark sky when the sun is gone."

"Yes, when the sun is sleeping." Kachina turned away from him, toward the tree where she'd appeared, her features losing the light of the moon. "Once each month, she turns her face to one side and darkens it to mourn the children that the sun succeeded in catching."

He was guessing the story had a point, but he wasn't sure what, other than that the moon, like the rain, had played a pivotal role in much of what had happened since he'd come to Quinault.

"Into each life some rain must fall," she said. "Some days must be dark and dreary."

Truman thought: *But certainly, there are more days like that here in Quinault.* What he said was: "Why are you here?"

She smiled as she faced him, but it was a sad smile. "Darkness has overtaken me."

"The man in the ballcap."

"Yes."

"He's been looking for you."

"He found me."

"What?"

"Yes, but it wasn't me *then*."

He began to understand that maybe this sacred dancer had appeared in the forest for a reason, even if it made no sense. "Are you—even here at all?"

"I'm here, but not for long. I can't stay."

He had started to figure it out. He drew his words out slowly. "Because—you're already here. Kat is here. It's you, but *not* you."

"I am what Kat becomes."

"You're a ghost." There. He said it. A *ghost*. He said it, and meant it, believing it the same way he accepted voices in the rain.

"I am—" She brought her hand to her face, rubbing at her bruised cheek. "I'm like the moon in the story, turning her face to mourn. In a way, yes. I'm a ghost. And eventually I'll go away and the sun will return."

"This guy looking for you," he said. "I mean, who found you. He has her—damn it, I mean *you*—right now, doesn't he?"

"He's a mage," she said, the words uttered with the same assurance he'd felt calling her a ghost. "He has done evil magic. He has murdered people, and he will again. Less than a year from now, I will be dead, and so will my friend and mentor Allie."

"*Dead*?"

"Yes, it's inevitable."

"How can you be dead, but not dead *yet*, and be here talking to me?"

"The song," she said. "Elements of music are magical and can do wondrous things. It's a song you taught me."

"No, the song came from *you*. To *me*."

Magic had become a part of his symphony for a while now. The magic was inside Kachina's song and, out of necessity, it was also in the man's voice that had, for some reason, seeped through. Probably because he was with her now. "Somehow, you came back here. Earlier in time?" He repeated what she'd said earlier: "You're what Kat becomes."

"We have to stop him. *You* have to stop him."

"Me?" He laughed. "How can I stop an evil mage?"

"You know me—that is, you know Kat in *this* time. Find her, rescue her—"

"*Rescue* her?" His head was swimming; this was all going too fast.

"Get her to trust you. She now knows about him. And—" She looked shyly at the ground. "She knows you. She cares for you."

Truman smiled. *That* was good to know.

"I can't say more about that," she said.

"But you can help. Right?"

"I can't remain here long. I can help, but not physically. I'm anchored to this spot. Before long, I'll return to my own plane. When I do, I'll have to face him, and I won't have the strength. I wish I could say you could change my future. Or my friend's future. But I don't know if it's possible."

And, Truman thought, perhaps the future of Dennis Reynolds. "So how can *I* help? Against—a *mage*."

"He uses Moss to enhance his power."

"Moss? He eats *moss*?"

"It's what Allie calls it. It's a drug. The kind that can't be sold or found anywhere. Only someone who knows how to synthesize it with her own brand of magic has access to them."

"Your friend. Allie."

"Allie knew the Moss could enhance my own magic, if used sparingly. She made it to heal him following a vicious knife attack. Allie warned him about the drug use, but he didn't listen. The drugs have given him considerable power, but they have warped him. He exhausted his supply. He demanded more, and she refused. Another good friend, Serena, she knew about Moss, too. She wouldn't tell him anything either. And she—" She broke off.

"What?"

She shook her head sadly. "She—kept quiet. I did too. We needed to keep the Moss from him, but available for me, just in case. I took the Moss from Allie, as we expected a future struggle with the mage. We locked it in a box—with a very secure, interlocked mechanism and a key that won't fit until the time and situation is right—and Serena and I took the box."

Magic. Truman shivered. "You hid it, and left the key here."

"We were *not* able to hide the box in time, but I actually hid the key before I knew anything about the box."

Truman dug in his pocket and pulled out the silver key. "This one."

Her eyes sparkled in the moonlight. "You *did* find it."

"The first time I came out here."

She reached for it, and Truman thrust it her way. Immediately she drew back her hand. "No. I can't."

"Why not? Are you unable to interact with objects here?"

"I can interact." She whisked her fingers across his face, and he felt them. Real. Substantial. "But if I have the key and leave this plane, it returns with me, and I'll be right there where I was, beside him on a pier in the mudflats. I can't take that chance. You keep it."

"So where's the box?"

"In the Enchanted Valley."

Truman knew where this was, but he'd not had a chance to hike there during the busy summer. It was a popular destination for backpackers and hikers, further east beyond the upper river bridge, but it wasn't a simple trip. It was October, and he doubted if it would even be open.

"I know the place, but I don't think I can get there this time of year."

Kachina looked a little sheepish as she came closer to Truman. "You can't go now."

"It seems waiting until the spring will be too late, won't it?"

"Yes."

"Then when—?"

"The full moon."

"That *soon*?"

She nodded.

"That's crazy. There's no way I can get up there."

"Sure you can. The man has the box. He knows about the power of the full moon. He's looking for the key, and he'll have help."

"Dennis. I know him. I gave him guitar lessons."

"The mage will use him against you."

Truman fumed. "Don't you know the mage's last name?"

She shook her head. "I never figured it out. Perhaps you will."

"Damn it. What can I do?"

"The planes, and the times between them, are not fixed. There's a fluidity to time that makes it malleable. It makes it dangerous, too; when I leave here, I will have to face him again."

"How long will you be away?"

"If he doesn't kill me, you mean." She lifted her head and set her sights on the moon again. "Until you can call me back."

"In the Enchanted Valley."

"No. Maybe." She shook her head. "I don't know. After this moment, everything is a blur. Nothing will be the same because you were not with us when this happened. You asked what you can do? You can keep doing what you've been doing. You must keep working on your symphony. It's your magic."

"But it's your song. It's *your* magic."

"It's *our* magic. We'll need it."

"I can't rush it. I can't finish it that soon."

"I know. You only need to keep making progress on it."

He thought of something important then. "Enchanted Valley. It's a big place. Where am I going specifically?"

"The shelter."

"Shelter?"

"It's an old, historic chalet on the Quinault River. You'll find the box in the chalet. You must come alone. Full moon. Near midnight."

He nodded. "Where in the shelter?"

But she backed up, gasping.

He came forward. "What?"

She stuck out her hand, warning him back. "No. Stay away. I'm leaving. He—"

He still reached toward her.

"Please, you can't touch me."

"But—"

A slight breeze blew her dark hair, and her outline shimmered, as if she were dancing. "The chalet."

"Yes, I know! But where in the chalet? How big's the box—?"

"You can't tell Kat about me. Promise."

"I promise. But—"

"And the key, it must—"

But she was fading, and her words disappearing with her. He willed her to stay. The key. What about it? Bring it with him? He didn't know. Maybe he could sing her melody. In a moment of panic, he realized he couldn't remember it. Didn't know how to start it.

Then, like a mirage disappearing upon closer look, Kachina was gone.

The light dimmed as a cloud inched across the moon's face. The silence was complete. Truman closed his eyes and let out a breath, drawing the memory of Kachina into his heart.

Come alone.

He couldn't remember the last time he had hiked or camped. He didn't know the trail, the terrain, or anything about the chalet. Well. He had a month to learn.

In his head, her song came back to him, but it was far too late to sing it.

17

⁂

THE TRAIL

IT RAINED A LOT NOW, ALMOST EVERY DAY. THE VOICES OF Kachina and the man—the mage—meandered through the precipitation. He did as she had suggested and kept writing. He would have anyway, considering that the rain and the singing pushed him forward, but also because the resort continued to be quiet. Beyond his tireless pursuit of knowledge about the Enchanted Valley, he sat and reviewed his symphony in his head, making connections and discovering directions he could take on his quest to finish the second movement.

It's your magic, she'd said.

But no, it was *their* magic.

When he wasn't working a shift in the store, he composed music, and when he wasn't doing that, he did his best to look for Kat. He still had a little trouble believing that the Kat he'd met that summer was a slightly younger version of Kachina. Kachina, the girl who heightened some of her vocal magic with mysteriously synthesized Moss—the same drug the mage had abused to increase his own power beyond what it should be.

That summer, Kat had taken notice of the symphony melody when he hummed it. She wanted to hear more of it. He'd refused, and afterward, she'd run off with the Hobie boys and disappeared.

Truman worried about the kid, Dennis. The man had seemed utterly in control of him. Dennis had recognized Truman's song, too, during that first guitar lesson. Recognized it, called it unreal, and played it back to him. Truman wondered what the man had offered Dennis.

Truman borrowed the resort truck when he could—traveling the main roads and the back roads—inching guiltily down longer driveways, even, to maximize his search. He asked workers at the businesses around the lake if they'd seen anyone like her. He roamed the grounds of the Forest Lodge. He hiked all the nature trails more than once, braving rain and mud.

Once, he drove up beyond the upper river bridge as far as he could to the lower Graves Creek campground, a usual staging area for hikers heading into the Enchanted Valley. The rain pelted him as he studied the trail with some skepticism, worried about his upcoming trek to the chalet at the far end of this trail. A wooden sign showed the various hikes out from Graves Creek. Thirteen and a half miles to Enchanted Valley, although Jacob had said the distance was closer to fifteen miles.

Foolhardy.

There were longer trails. Eighteen miles to Anderson Pass. Thirty-four miles to the Dosewallips Trailhead. He'd thought initially, if he'd had some of his gear, to say fuck it and head up the trail right then, totally unprepared for it. But Kachina's directions were clear. During the full moon. Bring the key. *Come alone.*

The good news was that he'd heard the hike itself wasn't too strenuous, for all its length. No switchbacks, not a lot of steep terrain.

After he'd stared down the trail for another ten minutes, enduring the weather, he headed back to the resort.

He even returned to the clearing where he'd spoken with her, but neither version of her was there. He worried for the younger Kat's safety. If the mage did something now that harmed her, or he killed her, what would happen to Kachina? The whole fluidity of time thing drove him crazy when he thought about it. If only he could find the girl he'd fallen for that first night in the lounge.

True, if he found her, now, he would run into the mage. Most likely. Would Truman be ready for him?

The football season petered out, and the earlier hope Quinault's fans held onto gave way to disappointment after a playoff loss to the Pateros Billygoats kept them from the state tournament. At least the season ended better than the previous year. They hadn't had enough players to field a team to even *start* the season.

The day of the full moon, with what knowledge he had gleaned from references and locals, Truman set out for Enchanted Valley. He packed his backpack the night before, having bought a tent and other needful supplies from the mercantile, and some of the more difficult to find items at an outdoor store in Aberdeen.

"This isn't very advisable, Tip," Jacob told him, even as he helped with the pack. "It's not fun up there in November. Rain and mud of course. Snow, likely. There's no cell service."

"There's barely cell service *here*," he said. "I'm prepared for it."

"The park service isn't maintaining a regular schedule, the trail might be dicey, and—well, you'll really be on your own, and you *shouldn't* be. Are you sure you want to do this?"

"It's Kat," Truman said. He'd told Jacob as much as he dared about her. Jacob remembered her from the lounge.

"I hope she's worth it."

"There's a chance she's in danger."

"And Dennis?"

"There's no point arguing with me. I have to do this. I'll be fine. I'm as prepared as I can be, thanks in part to you."

"And the Enchanted Valley guidebooks."

"Maybe that more than you."

Jacob smiled. "All right then. We have the 'if I don't hear from you in such-a-such-a-time' plan in place. Rest assured, we'll be looking for you if time runs out."

"You sure you'll be okay without the resort truck?"

"I've got another at the house. You're fine."

There was a brief hug, and then Truman was on his way.

Up the south shore road, to the bridge, and from there to Graves Creek Campground. He parked, grabbed his gear, and left the truck. As anticipated, Truman found the campground wet and muddy. The trailhead signs warned of adverse conditions. No shit.

He shouldered on his pack, grabbed the walking stick Jacob had given him, and placed himself at the Enchanted Valley trailhead and the wide-open section of the Quinault River. In the summer months, the Enchanted Valley was one of the easiest backpacking destinations. But now the weather evened things out. The hard rain from the night before had at least diminished to a drizzle. The gained elevation would be manageable, Truman believed. He had a bear canister for his food, for although bears might be slow, and in a torpor, they could be troublesome if hungry. The bear canister was heavy, a couple pounds, but he could get all his food, toiletries, and trash inside, and he could also use it as a stool.

Fifteen miles. *Here we go.* His first steps took him in the direction of the chalet, and a meeting—he hoped—with Kachina. He wasn't going to overdo it. He had the whole day, and Kachina said to meet her on the night of the full moon. He could arrive early and wait, but what would he find? With his left hand, he touched his jeans pocket and traced the outline of the key for the tenth time that day, making sure it was still there.

The trail crossed the river, and Truman marveled at the beauty of the old growth trees—close to a thousand years old. Hundreds of feet tall. Left alone, the trees displayed the Earth's natural order, the moss dripping from the branches and clinging to the trunks. He climbed steadily for the first few miles, cresting a hill. The trail then dropped to a rustic wooden bridge that crossed a deep gorge to the north bank of the river. From here, Truman would follow the north bank nearly the whole way to Enchanted Valley.

He had stunning views of the gorge below as he made his way further east, the drizzle of rain turning misty. In a few places, he could lean off the trail and look straight down into the cold river. Several steeper hills made him work for the next few miles. Back-country campsites were right off the trail. Several times, Truman stepped off the trail into the lush understory of the rainforest, the ground carpeted with moss, ferns, and nurse logs.

Eventually he endured a steep climb to O'Neil Creek. The trail leveled out and he found himself in meadows filled with bigleaf maple trees and cedar. About ten miles into his hike, he reached Pyrites Creek. Having made good time, Truman rested at a camp-site just over the creek on a flat by the river. The scenery here was breathtaking, with lovely views of Mount Anderson's jagged west peak. Fallen moss-covered branches arched across the forest floor.

He spotted a small herd of elk in the distance. Word was, they were more likely to attack a human than a bear was, so he kept his distance. He ate some turkey and cheese sandwiches he'd made in advance and chomped on an apple.

He began again. A bridge crossed Pyrites Creek. Jacob told him the National Park Service built bridges across this creek to help hikers many times, but heavy rains would wash them away. This bridge had been damaged, but it was crossable. Confused for a few moments, he studied the various trails snaking out from here, but soon spotted the main trail on the north side of the meadow. He'd read in his guidebooks that bear sightings were more likely in this section, but he saw no signs.

The light of the day dimmed, and the misty rain let up. He half expected the rain to increase and be a conduit to Kachina's song guiding him into the valley.

A few miles later, he reached an old fence that had been part of a gate, and he became anxious, knowing he was closing in on the chalet. Frustration set in as he faced many downed trees. Logs, too. He picked his way through dozens of them, keeping the trail in sight. When he'd finally navigated the maze of trees, the trail bent back toward the river. One more crossing, and one more bridge. It was long, a single I-beam with a wooden handrail on one side. A bit nervous, Truman started across. Many hikers crossed this bridge. It was solid and passable. He willed himself to take it easy, slow down, and reach the other side without mishap, knowing that the Enchanted Valley and the chalet were minutes away, a quarter mile at most.

He caught his first glimpse of the wooden shelter in the distance as he picked his way through more fallen logs, but he also fell victim to the beauty of the surrounding valley, its meadows, and the rocky alpine slopes of the Olympic Mountains. Behind the chalet, but seeming to tower over it, Chimney Peak rose blue and brown and white with snow into the gloom of high clouds. Along the peak's steep cliffs, waterfalls cascaded majestically down rock chutes thousands of feet long. Truman shook his head in appreciation, understanding why the Enchanted Valley's nickname was "The Valley of 10,000 Waterfalls." Enchanted, indeed. Magical, idyllic, almost unreal, as if snagged from the pages of fairy lore.

This late in the season, the river had swelled, and it meandered the valley, its course never the same one season to the next. As Truman approached the chalet, a small avalanche started on one of Chimney Peak's rocky cliffs and roared down the side as if it were a pure white waterfall.

The chalet itself, sitting dangerously close to the Quinault River, looked to be several stories tall, its windows locked up with yellow shutters. The famous chalet had sat here since 1930 and was now a national landmark. The park service took over in 1943, and they closed it to hikers and backpackers, using it only as a ranger station and as an emergency shelter.

It wasn't dark yet, but Truman saw the full moon bright in the sky. He didn't see Kachina, however. Would she even be here? Thinking back, he realized she hadn't said as much. *Come alone,*

she'd told him. *Bring the key*. The box was somewhere in the chalet. She hadn't been able to tell him where, but the chalet wasn't
that big.

He worried about the mage, too. Kachina had said he knew
about the locked box and would also be looking for it. And if he
had Kat, perhaps she would be helpless to keep him from finding
out about this location in the Enchanted Valley. He spent a few anxious moments glancing around the valley, wondering if the mage
was here somewhere.

He reached the chalet, circled it nervously, and saw no way to
get inside. There was a heavy front door, but it was shut and locked
with a heavy-duty padlock and chain.

The rain had started up again, but it had also thickened, and it
looked like it might be turning to snow. Best to set up camp. Close
by, to the northern side of the valley, would be a good place.

He trekked on, spotting even more cascading falls. Camping
spots appeared along the way. About five minutes from the chalet,
he found a good spot near an erected outhouse at the top of a small
rise. Food lines were draped like vines in the trees, so campers
could lift food containers off the ground. In the distance he spotted Mount Anderson again. During the summer, many backpackers
continued from here to Anderson Pass.

He set up his tent, made a fire, and prepared for dark. Snow had
started, but the flakes were wet, and Truman didn't expect to get
snowed in here. While he rummaged through his pack and his gear
to make something to eat, the snow turned to rain and intensified.
He put on more rain gear and pitched a tarp over his eating area.

He heated a can of chicken soup, and in another pan cooked
some beans, tossing them into the soup a little later. He grilled
chicken he'd pre-sliced, then put that in the pan too. Almost forget-
ting, he toasted some crostini on the hot fire pit grate, and when
ready, he ate the soup meal from the pan, using the crostini to sop
up every bite. Hearty and pretty easy meal, and it made him forget
the discomfort of the increasing rain.

Complete darkness took over before he finished eating. After he'd cleaned up and made sure he'd packed everything safely in the bear canister, he entered his tent, stripped off the rain gear, and checked the time. There was no service up here, but he could still use the phone as an alarm. He had an extra battery if he needed it. He set the alarm for 11:30. Kachina had said near midnight. Okay. A little rest, and then he'd walk back to the chalet and find some way inside. Look for the box.

Tucked inside a sleeping bag, he shivered. What was he doing up here? Taking the word of a ghost. A *ghost*.

During a month when he shouldn't be up here. At a time—midnight—associated with all things foul. The witching hour. *Now o'er the one half world, nature seems dead.*

He didn't know what to expect. The prospect of facing the chalet and starting his search for the locked box in the dark frightened him.

18

THE CHALET

I N THE MIDDLE OF THE ROOM, AWASH IN THE GLOW OF THE
WOOD stove, Truman and his sister Tina sit close together on
the couch at the coffee table, the howls of the storm threatening the
peace and quiet of their home. Rain spits against the windows. The
power has been out for an hour. Once in a while, lightning lights up
the darkness. Lightning, a rare occurrence in Seattle.

Their parents are out for New Year's at the Space Needle, and
Truman, old enough at fifteen to stay at home and watch his younger sister, has done his best to comfort her during this unexpected
windstorm. Tina, six years old, has her warm terry robe on. The
Clue game board is forgotten on the coffee table.

"We're safe here, Tina," Truman says. "Nice and cozy, okay?
Mom and Dad will be home soon."

Tina has pale skin and brown eyes, light brown hair, and her
state of fright makes her look younger. She nods, but she doesn't
seem convinced. The wind gusts, and the evergreen tree outside the
front window lashes out with its branches against the house and the
picture window. Mom has said they should take out that old tree.
Someday it might be a problem.

He recalls the giant tree that comes to life in the movie Pol-
tergeist and threatens Robbie and Carol Anne. He hopes there are
no secret burial grounds under their housing development. He
shouldn't have thought about that movie, because now he is freaked

out. The storm seems more of a presence than earlier, something that might do them harm.

Tina shies away from him, tucking herself into the corner of the couch and burying her face into a pillow. He glances at the window again. The dark makes it difficult to see the tree, and the space beyond its vague outlines is shrouded from view.

Where are his parents?

He disentangles himself from Tina's feet and stands, the picture window a forbidden portal to the storm raging outside. He approaches it anyway. Slowly. His socks slide a little on the wooden floor.

He tells himself he is safe inside.

Nothing outside can hurt him or Tina.

His hand shakes when he puts it on the glass, but he keeps his eyes on the tree. Rain splatters the window, and the branches scratch the glass with an increased urgency, as if alive. Reaching for them.

Hurry, Dad.

Hurry, Mom.

He has the most horrible feeling. His heart thuds in his chest, and he takes his hand off the glass and glances back at Tina. Her eyes are wide. She makes a move toward him.

"Stay there!"

A flash from outside lights her face. It is a flash as bright as the high beams of a semi-truck slashing through the windshield of a car; Truman snaps back to a memory of a time in his dad's car, head pushed back hard against the passenger seat, his dad panicking at a sudden blinding light from an oncoming vehicle. Time slowing down.

He turns back to the window.

A crack sounds, and it isn't thunder. The tree falls. Glass explodes inward and shards come at him like daggers. Truman cries out, scrambles backward, and falls.

Time slows down.

"Truman!"

She is right behind him.

The tree comes through then, as he had known it would, and attacks them.

⁂

Truman woke with a start. The rain pounded the tent canvas so hard, it sounded like the continuous roar of a jet engine. He sat up as a wave of lightning made the tent glow. The shadows of the surrounding trees crisscrossed the canvas like veins, and Truman scrunched back out of the way.

Tina!

No. Who?

It wasn't right, that dream. Why this dream now? This fragment of a larger dream, it seemed.

He gathered his wits about him and made sense of where he was, and why. He checked his phone, and the soft glow of the digital numbers surprised him.

11:45.

Fifteen minutes later than he'd set it. Had he made a mistake? Had he not heard it? Maybe it had gone off at the height of his nightmare, during the time the tree crashed through the window.

A flicker of light. It was more lightning, something less intense, an afterthought. He bolted from the sleeping bag then, determined to make up lost time to work his way back to the chalet before midnight.

He found his flashlight, turned it on, and swung it wildly, trying to remember where he'd put his rain gear. Near the tent flap. Jacket and hood. Rain pants. Quickly, he crawled to them. He checked reflexively for the key in his pocket again, and it was there. He tackled the rain gear. As if in a dream with his feet slipping in mud, or hands fumbling for keys, or knees suddenly giving way, he fought hard to get rain gear on.

The rain backed off, and the lightning flashes dwindled. Perhaps it had been good timing after all. The alarm had gone off, and although he hadn't heard it, the extra fifteen minutes had allowed the weather to settle toward something a little more endurable. He zipped the mesh door, pulled the flap, and left the tent.

11:50.

One minute more to secure the tent.

One minute to catch his bearings and remember which direction to go.

Rain slicked his jacket. After a deep breath, he headed toward the chalet.

He'd almost forgotten about the full moon. The weather had obscured it. He looked for it, but couldn't see it as he half-walked, half-ran past the other campsites. A hint of an ethereal glow meant that some moonlight made it through the shield of the storm.

He should see the chalet soon.

He squinted his eyes, but it wasn't the sight of the wooden chalet with the yellow shutters that stopped him. Not sight. *Sound*.

The rain had ceased.

Standing still on the path, the sound that reached him now was a sound he'd become acquainted with over the last six months. But hearing this sound denied completely its natural progression.

It was a song.

"Kachina," he said. It was her song, though not quite the same, not exactly. It could've been Kat's voice, here and now, if she actually *knew* his song. He took it as a sign, though. She had to be nearby.

Inside the chalet.

The chalet shimmered fifty feet in front of him, its form half shrouded in the dark, half illuminated by the full moon, and bathed in music.

How could the song be so beautiful, and yet be tainted with such fear?

Was Kat here? His late start from his tent and his hesitation in this very spot might have doomed her. Was the fear in her voice because of the mage? Was she trapped in there with him? Truman had hoped this would be a safe place. Half expected to see Kachina here, or some sign of her that might lead him to the locked box she desperately sought. He'd hoped not to see the mage. He'd hoped to get inside.

He had a vision of reaching for the key, watching it light up like a beacon, a shaft of light from the full moon enveloping it, silver-laced tendrils showing the way to the box.

The chalet, however, seemed the same as before, with no visible way inside. He wondered what he would've done if he'd seen the main door flung wide to the elements.

The next sound was soft and subtle. *Rustle*. Then hurried. *Footsteps*.

Truman turned and yelled out in surprise as he stared into the man's face. The man's eyes smiled, but his lips were drawn back in a grimace. He still wore his Olympic Rainforest baseball cap, the brim tilted up unnaturally. In his hand he held a walking stick.

"Why don't you join us, Tip-wad?"

Truman had only a second to register the sudden movement of the walking stick, now a club as it swung around toward his head. He knew he wouldn't be able to avoid it.

The moon threw down all its light.

Then nothing remained but darkness.

Truman felt the hard wooden floor before he opened his eyes. Waves of pain immediately made him close them again. The left side of his face throbbed where he'd been hit with the heavy walking stick. After a moment, he made a second effort and opened his eyes enough to see a blurry light. Opened a little more, his eyes focused on the wooden rafters above. He was inside the chalet. No skylight, no un-shuttered windows. Looked like there'd be no chance for his moonlight-streaming-in-to-light-the-way scenario. Everything was dim, even with the single plastic lantern—a plastic battery-powered one—throwing out its light. It hung from a cord in the ceiling, swaying slightly.

He rolled his head to the right, and the plastic of his rain gear rustled like wadded up wrapping paper. Someone was standing there, but Truman only saw legs. Another set of legs strode into view, and without seeing the entire room, he knew it was the mage and Dennis Reynolds.

"Tippy boy, you're awake!"

It was *his* raspy voice, but it was tinged with relief. Why? Because Truman was finally awake? Not sure he liked that idea.

Knocked out and thrown inside the chalet. Not sure how he would get out of this.

Truman wheezed as he sat up, gingerly rubbing his head where the stick had smacked him. He fought back dizziness for a moment, then allowed himself to see the mage staring down at him with that idiotic grin. He wasn't wearing the baseball cap, so it seemed more broad than usual. The hair on top of his head was stringy and patchy. Dennis, passive as ever, did not look at him at all.

Yes, but where was Kat?

"Tip?" the man said. "Tiiip?" He said it the second time with the vowel stretched out, as if he were a mother questioning a child who had told a lie.

Truman rubbed his head again and fought back the pain.

"Stop me if you've heard this before, but—" He crouched down low and patted Truman's cheek. Truman turned it away. "Looks to me like you've got some *'splaining* to do."

Truman forced words to his lips. "About what?"

Still crouching, the man lifted his hand and held it out. The silver key was there, held tight between thumb and forefinger. They had searched him and found the key. The main door was ajar, too, so they'd managed to get past the chain and padlock somehow. "About this."

"What?" Truman asked. He faked a shrug. "You want me to lock up after you leave?"

He slapped him with the other hand. "I *want*—" He took a moment and regained his composure. "I want a little respect. A little respect, too, for young Dennis here."

"I don't know what that's for," Truman said, nodding his head at the key. *It opens a locked box.*

"I *know* what it's for," the mage said, tangling his fingers in Truman's hair. Then he grabbed it and snapped it backwards. He reached back with the hand he'd slapped Truman with and snapped his fingers at Dennis.

Dennis said, "He said he doesn't know."

The man growled, "What am I paying you for, Guitar Boy?"

Dennis turned and left Truman's sight for a moment. Truman felt a little better since the blow to his head, but he didn't feel any better about what the man was up to.

Where was Kat? He'd heard *Kachina's* voice, clearly. He thought the mage and Dennis must've heard her too. Had he imagined it?

The floorboards creaked, and Dennis came back in sight holding an ornate metal and wood box. Around it on all sides was a set of interlocking bars that Truman couldn't understand. The box was big enough—shoulder-width—to hide something significant. Big enough to hide the Moss.

Kachina had been right about the mage having the box in his possession.

Truman tried to focus on the box. Yes, that looked to be a slot for a key. The interconnected bars that wrapped looked complicated, like every mysterious horror movie device ever devised.

"Pretty," Truman said.

The mage sneered, then took the key and inserted it into the keyhole. It seemed to fit, but the key wouldn't turn. Hines's face suddenly furrowed with confusion, and even Truman looked on with surprise.

It didn't work.

It wasn't the key to the box?

The mage kept trying. He did everything he could to make the key turn, swearing all the while, but it just wasn't the right key.

Then Truman remembered. Kachina had said it wouldn't work until the key was ready. A certain place and time. He thought: here the place, the full moon the time.

The mage shoved the key to within an inch of Truman's nose. "What the *fuck* is this?"

Okay, fine. He would play the man the best he could. "How should I know? I found it the other day on a walk on the rainforest trail. I liked the way it looked. Put it in my pocket—"

"You're a goddamn liar," he said, his voice lower. Serious, with a menacing undertone. "If it's not for this box, if this wasn't why you're here, then what the fuck, Tip for Tat?"

Truman shrugged, doing his best to be nonchalant. "I was afraid for Kat. I've searched everywhere for her—" He pointed at the mage. "—which means I was looking for you, since I knew you were looking for her. I tell you, I searched *every*where. Except here. The trail, the chalet. I thought I heard her voice. I heard her *here*. So where is she?"

The mage's face grew slack a moment, and without his cap, there was way too much of his ugly head too look at. Truman had struck a nerve telling him he'd heard Kat. "Why would she be here?" the man asked. "You're hearing things."

"You're lying."

"I'm not. *You're* lying." With four fingers he tapped his own temple rapidly. "I can read you. I can find out. You know where the real key is."

"I don't." Truman tried not to look at the key in the mage's hand. He didn't want him to think it was important in any way, and he doubted the man could read his mind.

It's just a key I found, Truman thought. Give it back. It means nothing to you.

Dennis spoke up, his voice timid. "I don't think he knows anything. Let's just go back."

"Shut *up*."

Truman watched the mage reach into his pocket and snick open a heavy blade. In an instant, he tucked the blade point under Truman's chin. Truman froze.

"Last. Chance. Where is the key to the box?"

More pressure from the knife. The knife dug into Truman's skin, and a trickle of blood dribbled down his neck.

Dennis, despite the man telling him to shut up, said, "He can't help us. Just leave him."

Truman felt the critical moment sliding past. Moments later, the pressure under Truman's chin went away, and the mage showed Truman the knife, holding it as if it were a torch, point up toward the ceiling.

Truman sighed in relief, and he calmed himself the best he could. Difficult, because almost a full minute passed as the mage stared Truman down. In the silence the breathing of the three of them was pronounced and disquieting. At the same time, outside the chalet, the rain intensified, and the wind picked up, too. It whistled as it found its way through the cracks and crannies of the chalet.

"Fine," the mage said. "Looks like Dennis has saved your life, Tip Trip. For now." He put the knife away and kicked the locked box toward Dennis.

"Are we taking the box?" Dennis asked.

"Of course we are," the mage said. "It has what we want." He took one last look at Truman's key, huffed, and threw it across the common room. "That key means nothing. We'll find the way to open the box."

Truman kept silent, taking it all in, hoping for a clue about what they'd do next. It turned out he didn't need a clue.

"Her friend," the mage said. "We'll bleed it out of her. And if not her, we'll work past the Moss witch."

"And the box?" Dennis asked.

"It mustn't be found or brought anywhere close to any of. It certainly won't be safe at my place. We'll hide it where no one will ever think to look for it. Then, we'll take a trip into Aberdeen and have some fun."

Truman took this all in, filing it away for later. If there'd even be a later.

Dennis nodded, seemingly convinced this was a good plan. At the same time, Truman thought the boy looked relieved. Why was that? Relieved that the mage wasn't going to kill his guitar teacher? Or relief that they had any kind of plan at all?

Kat's friends. The man hadn't said their names, but Kachina had in the forest. Serena. Allie.

The mage waved the knife at Truman. "You. On the floor."

Truman stared him down, but eventually sat.

"Stay there, you understand? We're leaving now, and we'll not have you following us. You can die here, as *she* will die."

"She's here? Where? Why don't you just kill me now?"

The mage lightly punched Dennis's shoulder. "This young man here thinks it'll be too cruel. Personally, I think it would be an easier death, and not as cruel as leaving you here to waste away."

"Please tell me where Kat is."

"Wherever she is, she's in the same predicament as you. I wouldn't look for her."

The mage and the boy exited quickly through the main door, then shut it tight. Truman stood up right away, ready to follow them after they'd had a head start. They hadn't seemed to have any weapons. *Only drug magic.* He waited, and after a few seconds, a grating sound made the hairs on his neck stand straight up.

The sound of a chain. Metal rattling as it passed through the handles of the outer door. Truman had seen the chain and padlock when he first came upon the chalet.

No. *No!* He rushed the door.

The chain rattled some more. It stopped as Truman reached the door and pulled on the inner door handle, but there was an unmistakable thunk of the heavy padlock as it engaged and locked.

Truman turned the doorknob, and it turned, but the door didn't move more than a few inches. He rattled the door. He threw himself at it. Rattled it some more. Despair washed over him. He backed up a step, staring at his side of the door, aghast at what had happened.

Trapped in the shelter.

In the meantime, a new storm had brewed. The wind outside howled, and the rain fell heavy. Although he couldn't see it, he imagined the rain thrumming against the chalet at an odd angle, as if trying to reach its soggy fingers inside in search of him.

He almost welcomed it. He thought it could be a blessing in disguise if it brought the healing power of song. Kachina's melody. The similar but slightly skewed version of it he'd heard when he first approached the chalet.

Safe from the storm for now, but trapped, nonetheless. The windows shut tight. The outside shutters solid and locked. Truman tried all the windows, testing the shutters, but none of them budged.

The battery-powered lantern hanging on the cord buzzed reassuringly. He wasn't sure if it had been in the chalet to start with, or if the mage had brought it. It emitted an almost magical light. If it had been the mage's lantern, why had he left it? Still, Truman was glad he did. Glad to have the light and not be paralyzed by darkness.

Truman checked the rest of the chalet, first in the direction the mage had thrown the key. He found it easily enough, near one corner of the room, close to a double bed that had no mattress or box spring. Putting the key back in his pocket, he continued his circuit of the room. Once in a while, the floorboards would creak with his weight. Needed some work, this old chalet.

In another corner, next to a sink and small stove, a fridge sat crookedly, scrunched out from the wall, not plugged in. He opened the door and found nothing inside. Behind the fridge was a dark recess, and he decided it was worth investigating. He bent low for leverage and pushed aside the fridge. He found a cubby behind it, but it was empty. He also noted a boarded-up hole. Probably some-one had pushed the fridge too far and its compressor had punched through at some point. He opened boxes in the large living space and found most of them empty as well. One had a can opener and several green plastic cups. Another had several dish rags and towels.

Close by, what he had thought was a wall was a divider that jut-ted out from the back. An opening, equipped with a sliding pocket door, led to a small bathroom.

He froze when he saw the door in the back of the bathroom, hope rising. A back door! But despair came back when he noticed that *this* door was padlocked too, from the inside. He took the time to rattle the chain, but it was wrapped around as tight as the one outside must have been.

He left the bathroom, dejected, and sat down on one of the few chairs left in the chalet, an overstuffed cushioned chair of brown leather that swallowed him up and held onto him.

He stared up at the lantern. Now that he could do nothing else but wait for morning, he should turn it off and save its battery. If his captivity continued beyond the next day, he'd want it available. The chair, however, refused to give him up.

Fatigue pulled at the inside corners of his eyes. He was tired, for sure, and horrified at the prospect of being locked in. He still had his phone—they hadn't taken that—but he had no signal to make a connection to call anyone. He checked it, and—fuck. It was dead. *Damn* it. His other battery was in his tent.

He didn't know how long he'd been out cold. Not long, maybe. He gazed up at the lantern again. That too. He should get up and turn that off.

Was he really stuck here? For how long? Would any more hik-ers come up here this winter? Maybe not. If any comfort came to him, it was Jacob's "if I don't hear from you in such-a-such-a-time' plan, a safety valve that should, in time, send someone up to the valley to search for him. Rescue him.

He had almost died here. The memory of the knife point under his chin made him sink deeper into the chair cushions. He could die here anyway. He wondered if Kat knew about all this. *Kachina* had known. Did she lead him here to die? Had she wanted him to confront the mage to help her in some way?

The rain pummeled the chalet. A gust of wind rattled the shutters. He wanted those shutters gone. Maybe with them gone, if he could even manage to do that, after the night passed, and after a night's rest, he might be able to break the windows and go home.

But he also didn't want to see out those windows. Not right now. Not at the height of a howling storm, with the unknown lying in wait for him out there. Tree limbs reaching for him. Dark magic waiting.

It was another storm in his life.

He woke suddenly and forgot where he was. But it came back to him when he saw the lantern. It still glowed, but it seemed dimmer. He wondered how many hours that thing could last. He had no way of knowing how long he'd been unconscious again. He stood and stretched. He made a circle of the common room, then sat down again.

Nothing had changed from his last conscious moment, except that his head ached where the mage had hit him, and he felt rather nauseous. He needed more sleep.

The storm still raged outside, and it had a certain rhythm to it. The thrum of the rain intensified for a short while before backing off, intensifying again, then lessening, like the rise and fall of a drum roll. The scattered howls and whispers of the wind had their own patterns, and sometimes the seemingly random tones harmonized with each other, sometimes not . . .

Truman sat straighter in the chair.

Random tones.

The crescendo and decrescendo of percussion.

He'd always had a good memory for sounds, and for melodies. He would hear the music in his head, know the notes intimately, and fill in the blanks. He could build stacks of chords and weave in melodies and countermelodies. Beethoven was nearly deaf when he wrote his Ninth Symphony. When he conducted its premier, he didn't hear that the orchestra had finished, and he still thought he had more measures to conduct. Someone had to turn him around to see the crowd applauding.

Although not a musician, the poet John Milton was blind when he wrote his greatest work, *Paradise Lost*, writing in his head each night, then dictating from memory to someone the next morning.

The music he'd heard just before the confrontation with the mage sounded in his head. It was easy enough to recall, for its musical structure almost perfectly matched the melody he'd been working with all this time. Almost. He closed his eyes and tried to remember where the melody had diverged. It took five times humming through it before he found the intersection of the two songs.

Right there. An extra note, an extra interval, and a move toward melancholy, almost a lament. He took that note, and the ones on either side of it, repeated them in his mind twice, transposed them, repeated them, and threw them out into the storm. Folded them into the breathy tones of the wind and the swells of rain.

He knew he had it. A perfect way to end his second movement, and completely true to the rest of it. The mage's presence had forced the *adagio* in a darker direction, and it was only fitting that the ending of the movement—although it continued to degrade into atonality with a hint of sadness overlaying all of it—pushed the darkness toward a random decay . . . into . . . nothing. The second movement would pull the listener toward darkness until the concept of anything resembling a real melody was lost. It would fade. It would trick the listener into believing the end of the symphony— a tragic one at that—was at hand.

A death.

But what about that last note? He puzzled over it for a moment, but soon enough, the answer was obvious. The last note, perhaps played by a single flute in its lowest register, would not sound for two—no, *five*—full seconds, creating that tension he hoped for. Silence. Then the note would play, and he'd let it linger long enough to give the listener a smidgen of hope.

After all, the third movement *had* to play. And play it would. The inevitable celebration would begin with a sustained, bold unison of the same note the second movement had ended on.

And then they could dance.

A minuet? A scherzo? The memory of Kat in the lounge whirled in his head. Her black hair wild in the lights. Arms raised above her head. Feet moving, barely. The sexual energy of her movements.

Let's dance.

Before the storm could change dramatically, he ran the ending of the second movement through his head a dozen times until he had it memorized. When he returned to the resort—if he returned—he would write it down.

Confident he had it tied together correctly, he managed a small smile. A lot had happened today, almost none of it good, but he had *this*. Anything *else* that happened now, he felt he just might be able to endure it.

The lantern flickered. The dark between flickers lengthened steadily, until the last flicker came almost unexpectedly.

The lantern died, and his hope dwindled.

Still . . .

He closed his eyes and didn't move.

The last note of rain—the last remnant of *adagio*—whispered in his head just before he gave in and drifted off to sleep.

19

※

A MAGICAL CHILD

H E HALF EXPECTED TO WAKE TO SUNLIGHT. THEN HE REMEM-
bered the shuttered windows. Automatically, he went for
his phone, but then remembered. No battery.

He didn't know what time it was, but he felt as if it were still
dark out there. Still, he felt oddly rested. His head still throbbed,
but the nausea had gone away. The rain had stopped. The world
outside made no noise that he could hear. He stood, stretched again,
and wondered how his eyes could've adjusted to the darkness as
well as they had.

No, not adjusted. Light. Somewhere, light filtered through.
Was it daylight after all? He made a circle of the room and found it:
a tiny window no bigger than a small picture frame high up on the
wall closest to the bed, way out of reach.

Moonlight.

A tiny shaft of light hit the slats of the wooden floor. Kachina
had said it was important to be up here during the full moon, but
nothing so far had depended on one.

He thought about what to do. The windows seemed to be his
best option. Sliding over to one of the windows, he tapped on the
glass. He could break one. Then, somehow, get through the shutters. He knew he had to get free of the chalet soon, while the weather cooperated.

At that moment, unbidden, the changed melody of the second

movement came to him. He still remembered it. Surprisingly, the memory was strong, and it sounded like Kachina's voice. As always, there were no words, only the musical tones drifting through his mind.

Enough. He needed to get out of here. He willed himself to stop thinking about it, but . . .

The melody persisted like a seduction, reaching for him with the intent of hanging on and never letting go. Now that Truman thought of it, the singing voice, as loud as it was, as *insistent* as it was, seemed muffled.

Kachina. The altered melody. Louder. He didn't know how, but he believed that somehow, some way, Kachina—no, *Kat*—was inside the chalet.

"Kat?" he asked the room.

The song continued. He listened intently, attempting to pinpoint the location, but it stopped. During the silence, Truman closed his eyes and turned his head, leaning an ear in the direction he thought he'd heard the song.

A weak thumping made him jump. "*Je*sus," he said.

A pause, then more thumps.

Truman stared at the floor where the moonlight touched it. With the next thumps, the floorboards shuddered ever so slightly.

You have *got* to be kidding.

He dropped to his knees and crawled over to the spot, putting his palm on the board. His rain suit rustled with every movement.

Another thump. The vibrations came closer toward the kitchen area. "Kat!" he cried. "Kat, can you hear me?"

If she *could* hear him, could she answer him? Was it her pounding on the floorboards? How had she ended up under the floor of the chalet?

The fucking mage, that's how.

The thumping came again, and Truman's hand registered the vibrations. "Kat, I'm coming!"

The spaces between the slatted boards were small, and he

wasn't sure he could get his fingers in deep enough to grab hold underneath and yank out the board. It didn't make any sense. Had the mage taken out these boards, put Kat inside—perhaps in an unconscious state—and taken the time to *replace* them?

No, there was another way. That boarded up hole behind the fridge. It made more sense, if that had been an entrance, to board *that* up.

He ran back to the kitchen, to the fridge—still pulled out from the wall—and looked behind it again. The patched hole. No, it was a goddamn entrance to the crawlspace. It seemed obvious now that this had to be the way down. It was secure, though. Tight as a drum. He had no finger holds, and no means of prying it open.

"Kat, still with me?" he yelled back behind him. He heard no more thumps, no noises, no song, and he hoped she was okay. Perhaps passed out, perhaps awake, but saving energy now that he knew where she was.

If he could get to her.

He stood quickly and pulled off his rain gear, throwing its pieces aside as if getting naked for a secret lover. He got on his knees again and did his best to wedge the tips of his fingers behind the board blocking the entrance to the crawlspace. Barely. He pulled on it, but it wouldn't budge. If he had a pry bar, he'd have that off there in no time, but his earlier search of the chalet had yielded nothing. He pulled harder, but no luck. He slammed his fists on it, frustrated, then stood. There had to be a way, if he could just *think*.

Back in the main chalet, he listened for Kat. No sounds. The wood creaked as he paced back and forth. Where was she? When he reached the board lit up by the moonlight, he stepped heavily on it.

And fell through.

He cried out in surprise, but the gap between the floor and the bottom of the crawlspace was not large. For an instant he thought—illogically—that the moonlight had pointed out the weak board.

Now, with some leverage, he could pull up some other boards around him. "Kat?"

More boards. The space wider.

"Kat!"

He had enough room to get on his knees and inch his head through the space to look in all directions. Pitch black, except his own spot where the moonlight shone down. If he had battery, he could've used his phone's flashlight.

Then he saw her.

She'd crawled closer to him while he'd made all the noise to widen the hole. She was on her belly, inching toward the light.

"Kat! That's it. Can you get to me?"

He thought she nodded, and he saw her black hair and black T-shirt—at least he thought it was black—as she crawled ever so slowly his way.

He worked feverishly then and managed to pull a few more boards from the floor. When Kat's face became visible, he was relieved to see her eyes. She was gagged with a red cloth. The moonlight caught the shine of adhesive on her cheeks.

"Kat," he said, working on another board. "Keep coming. You'll be out soon."

After another board pried loose, he had enough room to reach her and, with some difficulty, take out the gag. When it came free, she coughed uncontrollably until she could catch her breath.

"Truman," she whispered.

"Shhh. No need to talk right now. Let's get you out of there."

"Please," she said. "Help me."

"I am, I am. Hang on."

"Do you . . . have the key? How—how did you find it? Oh, you should never have brought it with you. But—thank you. Did—did he take it?"

He patted his pocket. "I have it, but—"

A smile came to her lips, but that slid away. "Please."

"Just hang on."

"You have to . . . there's little time . . . please hurry . . ."

He wasn't sure what she was trying to say. He couldn't come to her, he had to get her *out* of there. Just a little farther and he could get his arms under hers and pull her up. She'd endured a lot during her time with the mage, he figured, and perhaps some physical pain, and it was dirty and claustrophic down here, so she might not be aware of her surroundings. She wasn't making much sense right now; Truman smiled reassuringly and rested his hand on her forehead.

"A little more, Kat."

She slid closer.

"That's it."

The frantic look in her eyes worried him, but when he wrenched another board away, her arms shot out to him, causing him more surprise. This wasn't the girl he'd danced with. This wasn't the self-assured young woman who'd casually removed her clothes and swam with him.

Truman, sing us your song.

She grabbed his shoulder. "Come," she said. "Come *here*."

"Kat, I've got you, so—"

Her eyes focused. That improbable shaft of moonlight, which hit this very spot so conveniently, bathed her face in a glow so unearthly, she looked ready to grant a prayer request.

"I'm right here," he said.

His grip tight, he pulled her toward his chest and slowly drew her to her knees next to him.

"I'm fine," she said. "I'm—fine.

"Yeah, maybe." His next pull, using their weight against each other, got them both standing, but as soon as he did, the sudden freedom upset his balance, and he fell backward. He had enough presence of mind to reach out with his hand. It hit the floor behind him—an unbroken piece of it—and he cushioned his fall. She fell next to him.

He pushed up onto one elbow and studied her. Her black T-shirt, in heavy white block letters, said *Musick Magick*. Her chest heaved up and down and her breath was raspy. Her blue jeans had ripped down one seam.

"Kat, *Jesus.*"

She didn't look at him. She closed her eyes and struggled to breathe, and it was several minutes before she stopped gasping for air. She turned her head away from him and coughed so much he thought she might never stop. When she finally seemed to take control of her breathing, she turned her head again, opened her eyes, and stared at the ceiling. No, she stared into the light. The moonlight. Earlier, it had led to the weakened floorboard—by chance of course. Right? But now the path of light had crawled across the floor enough that it bathed them in its glow.

"Kat?"

She blinked at the little window letting in the moonlight. "What time is it?"

"I don't know. My phone died."

She reached out and pulled him to her with a strength he didn't think she could muster after this ordeal.

"What—"

Their lips met. Surprised, Truman jerked back, but Kat tightened her grip around his head and held him fast. He lost himself in the softness of her, and the earthy taste of her breath. He didn't understand what was happening—well, he understood what was *happening*—and wasn't sure he should fight it. She was surprisingly strong, and as he thought that, she rolled enough so he was on top of her.

She smiled weakly, then gazed up at the window again.

A memory of the swim in the lake; a memory of her hand's fleeting touch against his thigh; a memory of her naked on the dock, stretching to the sky, as if trying to tickle the moon.

He had wanted her, it was true. And she had run off with the sailboat racers. Now she had him far away from there, locked away in the heart of the Enchanted Valley, and at her insistence, he had broken her own prison and found himself trapped with her. But oh, what a trap.

His passion rose, and he returned her urgent kiss. She reached for his belt and he lifted his hips to give her room to awkwardly pull down his pants, and Kat arched her back so he could roll up her T-shirt. Truman had the heat of her skin—chest to chest, stomach to stomach—to warm him as they fumbled for each other. The wash of moonlight, almost otherworldly, silvered her face like glitter paint.

So very quickly, he was inside her. She exhaled, and her breath was a whisper of a song. Even in the cold, sweat beaded on her forehead, and a drop slid down her neck. She held him tight against her so he couldn't thrust. Whispered his name. She didn't try to grind against him, and she didn't allow him to move. If this had happened with anyone else, he would've wondered if he'd done something wrong.

With closed eyes, she tilted her head back, offering her neck. Body relaxed and unmoving, she hummed, the vibrations visible in her throat. He kissed her there and flicked his tongue upward along her neck. The vibrations buzzed his tongue like an electric current.

"Truman," she hummed. "Sing me your song."

He was still inside her and still aroused, but even though she seemed distracted and he was puzzled about her intentions, the connection between them hadn't lessened. The electricity he'd felt along her neck had traveled through him like a shiver.

"Kat, what—?"

She held up his silver key, which she'd somehow fished out of his pocket. She said, "Magic." One hand tight around his waist, she repeated her request. "Sing me your song."

Magic. *Sex* magic?

"How—?"

"You're channeling the thoughts and emotions of the night, and I can feel them. And now, we feel it *here*." She put a hand on his chest. "And *here*." Her hand moved under his stomach, toward his groin. "Now, we go slow, maintain our balance. Let the sexual energy build. The release of its energy can change your world. Sing your song, Truman."

He was with her now, even though he had no understanding of it.

"What for? What's all this for?"

"The key. It's all about this key. Now, Truman. The song I heard that night. It's your song, and I think it's mine, too. *Sing it*."

Truman did. He hummed softly at first, but soon set the melody loose, the seven upward mournful notes rising in pitch and volume. He sang the variations of it memorized from the first half of the symphony. He even let loose the darker thread of the *adagio*, even though he wasn't sure he should.

"Keep going," she said. He did, and she put the key on her chest, between her breasts, a pendant without a chain. "Sex magic requires an objective."

He paused.

"No, keep singing. Soft, now. And listen. We must decide before we go much further. I'll guide you the best I can."

Still chanting, still listening to her, he wondered if "moving on" meant finding an easy way to escape the chalet or discovering what to do next about the mage. Kat knew less than Kachina, and it had been the ghostly Kachina who'd sent him here in the first place. He had sensed something "magical" about Kat the few times he'd seen her but had no chance to get close to her. Well, he was close to her now, no question.

"Western New Age practitioners would call it a telos," she said in time to his music. "An objective. We must have the same objective. Native Americans might call it a charm, or a dream fetish. My choice was to either leave you in the dark about what I was doing, or let you in. If you're not in fully, then this won't work. Do you agree?"

He nodded without missing a beat of his song.

"This key *does* open the box the mage took. But not until it's infused with magic. That's why it didn't work for him. He only knows of drug-induced magics."

Truman felt good about that. Maybe this was an edge over the mage, who used the stuff that Kachina had called Moss.

"Transmuting the key is our objective," she said, "our *charm*. I'll tell you, I'm very new at this. Allie was teaching me all the precepts without the—well, you know. The contact. Keep an image of the key in your mind. A key that can unlock the box, not this key here. It doesn't matter what it looks like."

She brushed the key with her fingertips, then drew her fingers across the slight swell of her breast, grazing the nipple. He was so close to her mouth his singing breath was almost a resuscitation.

"If we have the same *dream*, our combined sexual energy has the power to bring us our desire. Life is chaotic, but we can find balance. Truth." Without warning, she raised her hips into him. Hold. Then down. "Truth is a balance point that evolves. Multi-layered. Changing all the time."

If it was a magic spell they were casting, then what Kat called their sexual energy was a spring coiled and aimed with purpose. It scared him, his willingness to have Kat guide him. Did he trust her? He must if he'd gone this far. He kept singing. He knew he had to succumb to the sexual energy, the *life* energy, thoughts and emotions composing art out of nothing. Reality from the rawness of the world. The power to *transcend* reality. Even music born from the scribbles of pencil on staff paper.

He had to surrender himself to the power, but he also had to claim it.

She put a finger to his lips and said, "Shhh."

He stopped singing, and the last notes trailed off.

"Sexual energy is neutral, but it's powerful." She picked up the pace of her movements against him. Rise and fall. Slower and faster. Faster and slower, just on the edge.

The arousal, the waiting, the anticipation: it all seemed likely to bring him to orgasm too soon, but no—the heaviness in his limbs suggested an almost unbearable exhaustion.

"Reality," she said, "is not straight ahead, go left, go right. No. Everything in nature is a circle, a *curve*. That's how we should approach life. It's how we should express ourselves in love."

Orgasm would be the most powerful aspect of sexual energy, he realized, and they were building toward it now. They were moving faster, but Truman's essence barely seemed present. He hoped that was supposed to happen. He couldn't speak to his unconscious—he understood that much—because unfortunately, his unconscious did not speak his language. It spoke in symbols, which is why he loved music. Music was a tool for change. That was *his* power. He could only imagine the altered states music and magic could unleash together.

"Breathe," she said.

He did. She moved slower, and he followed. His eyes bore into hers, and once or twice she closed them, the arousal heavy there, lids gorged with blood. Her black hair framed her face and draped over her collarbones, which rose and fell with her even breaths. The wetness of her parted lips reflected the moonlight. They had not kissed since she pulled him on top of her.

But always, Truman came back to her brown eyes.

Although increasingly difficult to do, he trusted her and did as she asked, visualizing the key that would open the box. The charm. He matched her movements and the heightened awareness of their union, and soon they reached the pinnacle of the magic. His orgasm washed through him the same time it took hold of her. She didn't hold back. She practically screamed their mutual song of power, poised like the gigantic wave pushing a boat along its violent crest.

Riding that crest themselves, the energy subsided, expelled. His imagination might have got the best of him, but Truman thought for a moment the key between Kat's breasts shimmered with extra light. Perhaps it had been a chance angle of the moonlight.

Kat panted heavily, her stomach moving up and down rapidly

against his own. She kissed him tenderly, smiled, and wrapped her hand around the key.

"I like this kind of magic," Truman said.

She laughed, her arm across her breasts, the key still in her fist. "We made a child, you and me."

He felt an ache in his chest, the wind knocked out of him. "Um. *What?*"

She laughed again, this time with such genuine emotion that he never wanted to forget what it sounded like. "A *magical* child."

That didn't help him one bit. "It's not—a real child?"

"No." A smile this time, as genuine as her laugh. "All that energy is life energy," she added. "Altered states bring stronger connections to the spirit world, and it wants to *create*. The union of sex creates the idea of a child on the spiritual plane."

"That was my next guess."

"Uh huh." She ran a fingertip lightly across his cheek. "A great man once said, 'With our thoughts, we create the world.'"

"Some great sex magician, I assume?"

"Shit, Truman, no. The *Buddha*."

"Oh."

"Our dream is a part of the universe now."

"And our key?"

She opened her palm and revealed it to him. "We can hope. To the eye it would look identical. We won't know until we can get to the box."

A few things troubled him about this whole encounter. "I—" He thought back to his conversation with Kachina in the woods, remembering not to say anything directly to Kat. "Earlier you said this guy used drugs for magic. I take it this box contains something like that. What happens if he gets hold of them? And have you used them yourself?"

"I've not used them. I can't unless absolutely necessary."

He wondered what the Moss would do to Kat. She already exuded a magical presence hard to ignore. If forced to augment her magic with these dangerous drugs, how would Kat channel that power so nothing horrible happened?

"You left with Ryan and Nate that night, and I looked for you in the campground . . ."

Her face darkened. "I'm sorry. We were there around some-one's fire, but I had to leave. I know it's hard to accept, but I sensed a darkness, and I thought maybe this man had come to the resort."

"He came into the store the next day, with the boy, Dennis. He was looking for you. He scared the shit out of me."

She nodded knowingly. "I ran from the campground to the Quinault Ranger Station. My father works for the Forest Service, and even though I don't see him often, once in a while he's there. A day or two at most. He doesn't turn me away if I show up."

When Truman arrived at Quinault that first day, after the rain-storm had let up, he'd spotted the ranger station just past the Forest Lodge. *Another sanctuary where he could've waited out the storm.*

Truman was cold now, partly clothed, having just invoked sex magic with someone he barely knew. Slowly, he worked his way to a position that allowed him some leverage and got his feet back on the floor without tripping over his pants. He held out his hand and helped Kat up. Without any sense of embarrassment or regret, she pulled her T-shirt back down and tried to smooth it out. They both finished dressing just a few feet from one another.

"He can't get those drugs," she said, answering his earlier question. "We've already seen what he's like with them."

"Your friend Allie. Serena."

She raised her eyebrows. "I can't even begin to understand how you know about them."

He had learned about them from *her*. "It's a long story, but I know who you are." *Who you become.* "I was told to find you. To bring that key here on the full moon."

"*Who* told you? Allie? Serena? How do you know them?"

"It's a long—"

"Truman. I can't imagine them telling you to bring the key with you to the same place the box might be, even if you did manage to—"

She stopped. He couldn't tell her about her ghost self unless it became necessary.

"How the hell did you find that key?"

For now, a "chance meeting" with her friends would be far more believable than ghost-Kat. "One of them told me. I forget which one."

"Only Serena knew."

"Serena. Right."

"Not believing you."

"You'll just have to trust me."

"*Trust* you?"

"Like I trusted you just now."

"That was different." She let loose that smile again. "It's easier to trust someone when you're stuck in a chalet having sex in the moonlight."

He was putting that on a T-shirt someday. "I don't know. I mean . . . I trusted you and look what that got me. A magical baby."

They'd finished dressing. Arms crossed over her chest, Kat searched his face, suddenly serious. "I trust you."

His eyes had adjusted to the darkness, and the room seemed lighter. The moonlight had dissipated, and it seemed as if pockets of light existed throughout the common room. Some cracks and crannies let in some of the early morning light. No rain or wind out there, as far as he could tell.

"Well." He sighed, running a hand through his hair. "We won't know about the key until we find the box, and to find the box we have to find the mage."

"You even call him the mage. Who have you been talking to?"

"Your friends."

"Serena and Allie, who you know, but can't tell me how you met them."

"And before we can do that," he continued, ignoring her, trying to change the subject, "we have to find a way out of here."

"Oh," she said. "That part will be easy."

He stared at her in confusion. "*Easy*? How?"

She reached into her pocket, pulled something out, and held it up so he could see. "I have a key."

Sure enough. A bronze key on a keychain with the Olympic National Forest logo encased in the acrylic fob.

"Kat, you're kidding. A key to what? The back door in the bathroom?"

"Opens both the door and the padlock."

"Did you sneak this request in during our . . . magical baby-making ceremony?"

"No. I stole it from the ranger station when I spent the night there. I thought it might be fun sometime to have access—" She smiled and shook her head. "Well. This time of year, my dad and the other rangers won't even miss it." She could barely hold back her glee. "The man searched me, but I had it in my shoe. I had a natural limp as he dragged me up here. He kept complaining I was slowing him down."

He hugged her tight, barely containing his relief. Still, he was afraid. The threat of the mage had frightened him for sure, but he'd also been afraid of giving in to Kat's power. Her magic. He had done so, though, and somewhere buried within, he thought he sensed his own power, whatever it was. He was not entirely Kat's creature. He had his own magic, he was certain.

He grabbed his rain gear, taking the lead. "Let's get out of here before it rains again. I have to pack my tent and gather my stuff."

"I'll help." She rubbed her arms briskly. "I hope you have an extra sweater or jacket."

He did. Kat and Truman left the chalet and found his camp trashed. They'd taken out all the clothes in his pack and strewn them around the campsite and beyond. The tent had collapsed, and Truman noticed a number of long gashes in the fabric, probably from the mage's knife. They hadn't opened up the bear canister and thrown food everywhere, but they'd rolled it from the top of the small rise down to where it had lodged against a scraggly bush—the only thing that had kept the canister from going into the nearby river.

Truman first found a sweatshirt for Kat, and a jacket. Truman put on the raincoat. It hadn't rained since they'd left the chalet, and a check of the sky bode well for a dry trek back to Quinault.

Ruined or not, everything they found they stuffed back into his pack. The tent took some time; poles were bent and fabric out of shape, which made it difficult to put away.

Once they cleaned up the camp, Truman shouldered the pack and they headed down the trail. The hike was uneventful, and they made it safely to the truck in the campground. The tires weren't slashed, the distributor cap not missing. They saw no sign of the mage, and they hadn't expected to. During the hike, and the drive back to the resort, Truman and Kat barely spoke. Although they'd come to the same conclusion about what had to happen next, they didn't talk about what had occurred in the chalet.

The task ahead of them, though, burned into Truman's mind like the sexual charm. The mage had taken the box. They had to find it.

20

COME AS YOU ARE

THE TOWN OF ABERDEEN WAS A DEPRESSED TOWN OUT ON the Olympic Peninsula, just half an hour from the ocean, and about forty minutes south of Quinault.

Aberdeen, Gateway to the Olympics. Doorway to the Rainforest. Home of Kurt Cobain, where the music all started, practicing with Krist Novoselic in his parents' garage in the '80s. A sign leading into town told tourists to "Come as You Are." A drawbridge passed over the Chehalis River that once, a long time ago, used to be choked with logs destined for the mills. A rare early afternoon swath of sun streamed through the car windows. Joel Hines sat in the driver's seat of his truck, and Dennis Reynolds sat shotgun. They didn't speak. Hines thought about the town and what he had to do there, and Dennis—well, who knew what he was thinking about. His fuckup dad, maybe. Something about his mom, an affair or something. Kid needed to work that shit out, just like he was. Get it out of his hair early. Don't wait so fucking long to take care of things.

He had that sense, though, that Dennis could help. Work a way around Allie's sphere of influence using that same unearthly song. Hines had been aware of that little ditty for a while now, its melody an irritant, and he thought: could it be used against him?

Not if we can use it first.

Keep practicing that fucking guitar, kid.

Hines hated Aberdeen. The slow entrance into town—a boring stretch of road taken at a reduced highway speed that seemed to drag on forever—and the constant twists and turns took nearly thirty minutes to drive through.

He also hated it because of his experiences there and the events that had darkened his life. He had forgiven many of his father's failings, but maybe not his disregard of his mother. His mother who'd left him. His mother who, regardless of her abandonment of him, deserved to be found again. That would happen, he was certain, when he released his darkness and found the path to her. Wherever she was, Hines believed he could attain a type of enlightenment that would help him reach into the void and find her. He had started his journey. He just had to open the gate and walk through.

He blamed much of his hatred toward the bitch Allie, the witch who first introduced him to the Moss that saved his life. But then, when he'd needed it most, she took it away.

What did it matter that he and Dennis had found the box of Moss? He couldn't open it, even after the shit that went down in the Enchanted Valley. That got him nowhere except saying goodbye and good riddance to Kat and Tiptoe. He still didn't know how that young man had found them at the chalet. Maybe he and Kat had been working together somehow from the start. Maybe Serena had told him to go look for her. The key wasn't at the chalet, and the key Tippy had didn't work, so maybe Serena had kept it after all.

Some protective spell kept him out of the box. For now, he'd hid it where no one would think to look for it, because he hadn't dared bring the box anywhere close to Aberdeen. Anywhere close to Allie.

He knew how to get to Serena though. Dennis had found the address in Serena's car. Hello, registration card.

"Here's the turn," Dennis said abruptly from the passenger seat.

Hines braked hard, spun the wheel left. The tires squealed. "A little more warning next time?"

Dennis nodded, eyes down. "Sorry."

"You should be."

Now that he'd made the turn, Hines recognized the road. Serena lived in the Westpointe Apartments, two blocks down, apartment A-1. *Everything's A-1.*

"Taking no chances," Hines said. It was unlikely Serena would spot it from an apartment window since the "A" building sat back a ways from the road, but you never knew. "We'll park here and walk the last block."

They left the truck parked on the street and headed down the road to the apartment complex. Hines passed apartment building "A" on purpose, telling Dennis to shut up, he knew it, just casing the place. He turned back to the building and spotted the stairwell to the upper floors. A-1 was on the ground floor next to the stairwell.

"What're you going to do?" Dennis asked. He ran a hand through his close-cropped blonde hair, and he looked nervous.

"What needs to be done," Hines said. "You understand, don't you?"

"Sure. I guess."

"You *guess*?" He smacked the boy alongside the head. "Do you want a piece of the magic, or don't you?"

Dennis nodded.

"Get away from your dad? Get a place of your own?"

"Yeah," he mumbled.

Hines cupped a hand to his ear. "Sorry?"

"*Yes.*"

"Very well, then."

Each apartment had an exterior entrance. Flower boxes hung from the windows, and planters were near each door, filled with cedar bark, but no flowers. Tall hedges made a line in the inner courtyard. The afternoon sun was slowly giving way to evening, and the chill in the air heightened his senses. Hines stopped in front of Serena's door and breathed deep. One step closer to his salvation. A step toward wholeness.

He knocked. Dennis took a position in front of the door and

peephole, and Hines stayed to the boy's far left a few steps back. Dennis held up some brochures about the rainforest they'd taken from the information racks at the Cedars Resort and smiled the best he could. During the short wait, cars hummed down the street behind them, and a slight breeze swished the branches of the trees.

The door opened, and there was Serena. She seemed a bit drained from the recent stress. Awww, poor thing.

She opened it a little wider and managed a weak smile. "Yes?" She spotted the brochures. "I'll tell you right now I'm not buying anything, so—"

Hines made his presence known then, one, two, three steps toward Dennis. He raised his arms above his head and grinned like a little kid. "Serena!"

She saw him and gasped. "No—!" She stepped back in a rush and shut the door. Or tried to.

Hines jammed his foot in the opening and stopped it, then he pushed the door open wide. Serena stumbled backward as Hines invited himself in. Dennis followed.

Hines politely latched the door as Serena looked on in fright.

"What do you want? I don't know anything. I don't *have* anything."

"Serena, of *course* you know something, and I'm going to find out."

She shook her head emphatically.

Hines said, "It's 2:00 in the afternoon. We've come to see you, Serena. We're here, and it's time to relax."

He practically threw himself into an overstuffed comfy chair. It was a shitty color, a drab green, but he immediately liked the way it felt as it pulled him in. The upholstery wrapped around him like a mother's loving arms. He took his time taking off his shoes and his socks. He propped his bare feet on the matching ottoman in front of the chair.

"I do believe it's time for tea," Hines said. "Earl Grey. Hot."

She didn't seem to get the *Star Trek* reference. He waved his arm over his head with nonchalance, as if he were a Victorian man of letters, unconcerned with the rest of the world around him. Serena stood nearby, arms folded around her midsection. Give her credit: she hadn't fallen apart and lost it. He didn't like the look in her eyes, glaring at him as if he were the devil himself, but he appreciated her spunk. It would get her killed, but still . . .

He raised an eyebrow. "Tea?" He narrowed his eyes to slits. "*Now.*"

She glared with even more contempt, but eventually she turned and disappeared into the kitchen.

Dennis still stood, but once Serena left, he chose a heavy oak chair from the dining table and sat.

Hines nodded, content. "Beautiful," he said, sinking even deeper into the chair. "It's a beautiful world we live in. At least it is *outside* this shitty apartment."

"It's not that bad," Dennis said. "Better than my own folks' double wide."

Hines laughed. "Aren't *you* the connoisseur of good taste."

"Not really."

Hines pointed at him. "Remember. No names."

Dennis nodded.

"Serena!" Hines yelled without warning. "Where's my fucking tea?"

She appeared in the doorway, arms around her middle again. "Maybe you should get your own tea."

"Maybe I will. After you tell me what I need to know. Or maybe after you're dead I'll brew my own tea. A good blood tea."

"That's not even a thing," she said, showing no fear.

Gutsy gal. "You've got a lot of nerve. You don't know anything about magic, do you? But there's *Allie*, the great magician of Aberdeen, holding the secrets of science and substance, offering me a Mossy Nirvana, synthesizing my salvation!" He threw his head back and laughed at the ceiling, proud of his alliteration.

"Karma's a bitch, either way," Serena said, "whether you believe in it or not."

She was being dangerously glib for someone in such a precarious position. "You know what?" He pulled himself out of the chair and marched right to her. At the last moment he stopped, his face inches from hers. "Maybe I *will* get my own tea." He remained glued to that spot, his eyes searching hers. She didn't back up.

He hissed in her face, and that, at least, got a reaction. She tilted back her head and closed her eyes. He continued to the kitchen. He found the tea she'd started to steep. Before returning with it, he spotted a knife block. He altered his path and retrieved the biggest of the knives.

Tea in one hand and knife in the other, he came back into the main room. He stopped by the dining table and gave the knife to Dennis. "Hold on to that for me, will you?"

Dennis took it from him, but he didn't look very happy about it.

"Whatever needs to be done," Hines said. "Right?"

Dennis gulped, but said, "Joel, whatever you think—"

"Shut *up*," Hines said. Hadn't he just reminded the kid about names? "Didn't I just tell you—"

Dennis shook his head. "Yeah, sorry."

Then, to Serena, Hines said, "Don't say anything else unless it's to answer my next few questions. Understood?"

She was silent.

"I'll take that as a yes."

Her eyes had that look in them again, that look he didn't like. Only his father had looked at him that way, registering his disappointment in him.

"Sit down," he said.

She headed for the couch at the front of the room.

"No, stop," he commanded. He pointed to an area of the carpet in the middle of the room. "On the floor, right there."

She was reluctant, so he sighed and looked Dennis's way. Dennis stood up with the knife. It was enough. She pulled away from the couch and sat cross-legged on the floor.

"You don't have many choices here," Hines said. "I hope you'll consider the severity of the situation as I ask you these questions. Are you ready?"

She said nothing.

"I'll take that as *another* yes," he said. He leaned farther back in the chair. "Where is the key?"

"I don't know."

"You and your girlfriend Kat were going to hide the box. You know that. You found your car window broken, the box gone. How do you think I found out you lived here?"

He saw her work her lips around her anger. She was trembling. "Where's Kat?" she finally asked. "What have you done with her?"

"Kat wouldn't tell me either. I'm sorry, but I left her to die in a place far enough away that no one will find her for a long, long time."

Serena whimpered now. She was having trouble holding back tears.

Well *now* they were getting somewhere.

"So I'm back to square one, without a key to open the box. I tried a sledgehammer. Can you believe that? It did shit. Dented things a little, but the lock didn't break. I can't find any seams to work. It's a beautiful box, Serena. Why don't you tell me where you hid the key. Or, better yet, tell me where else I can find Allie's Moss. She can't have boxed up *all* of it."

"That's all it," she said, her voice and posture exuding a confidence Hines hated seeing.

"You're *lying*, Serena."

"You said I wasn't part of the magical world. What do I know? I didn't glom onto Allie the way Kat did. Allie took Kat in and was teaching her that stuff. I didn't care, I just wanted to help my friend."

"You can help me by—"

"I don't know anything!" she screamed. "You can't get past Allie's mumbo jumbo shield, whatever she calls it, and she didn't dare make any more because of you. *You*, you freak. Kat told me about your mommy fetish, you sicko. Bringing her back? Really? And you wonder why Allie won't give any more to you. Not with you out there abusing it. Not with you out there *looking* for it. Looking for power and looking for acceptance. Poor baby who misses his mommy. You—"

Hines stood up abruptly. "She showed me their power and saved my life! But just as I realized my full potential? When I realized I might have a way to find and bring back my mother? She took them away from me."

"She had to. You couldn't control them, and you can't possibly believe you can bring her back."

"I didn't get a chance to try."

"You hated her, and you didn't even know her. Allie said your mother died giving birth to you."

"But I can make it better now."

"I don't know much about Moss, or magic, or any of that, but I know what my friends told me. They saw what you became. You tried and failed. It can't work." She shook her head. "Until you are gone—she will not make more. She may *never* make any more."

"Gone?"

"Very far away, or dead. Do you have a preference?"

"You bitch!" He was so tired of her. He would punish her for talking back.

"I'll take that as a vote for *dead*," she said, spitting in his direction.

Hines growled and launched himself at her, angrier than ever. She fell back to avoid him, hitting her head on the floor even as he landed on top of her and slid right up her torso, knees on either side of her shoulders, his crotch pushed up against the underside of her chin.

"Please," she whispered.

"You should've been nicer to me," Hines said. "You're all riled up. If you'd been nicer, maybe I'd just have taken you far from here, out to the bay, and thrown you into the mudflats. Let the tide come up. Drown you *slow*."

"Oh my god—"

"Dennis," he said. He grabbed her arms, held them over her head, and pinned them on the carpet. He turned around and sat on her arms, crotch near the top of her head. Dennis took two steps toward her but paused.

"Dennis!"

Dennis jumped a little.

Hines waited until the boy looked back at him. "Whatever it takes," he reminded him. He pointed to Allie's legs. "Sit."

Dennis nodded vigorously, then awkwardly sat down on her thighs and hips, the large knife still in his hand. She struggled beneath them, but they had her well pinned.

Hines bent down and hissed softly into her ear before reaching out for Dennis's knife. The boy was more than willing to get rid of it.

"Where's the key? I know you and Kat hid it. She didn't tell me—led me far astray, actually—so that leaves you." He lowered the knife and traced a line from her chin to her forehead.

"I wouldn't tell you even if I knew," she said, her voice steady and low, almost oblivious to the knife.

"*Still* with the attitude!" Hines said. He bent over her, pulled her chin with one hand, and with the other, placed the knife at her throat. "What would your darling Kat say about that?"

"Please . . ." A small tear rolled down the side of her face.

Finally. *Finally*, a reaction he'd waited for. "Okay, okay," he said, "since you said please. Kat's dead by now, stuffed unceremoniously under a *floor*."

"Fuck you," she said. More tears fell.

Hines raised the knife. She turned her head away. He was too far into this now to back down now. He plunged the knife into her stomach.

She cried out, or tried to, a breathy exhale that followed the harsh *twhick* of the knife. She struggled to move, but he and Dennis had her pinned.

"Joel," Dennis said.

"No. Fucking. *Names*."

In a quick motion, Hines pulled the knife out and jammed it in again in a new spot, but a little deeper. She cried out again, louder. Unable to control herself, she whimpered, then started to cry.

He pulled the knife out and plunged it in again. Out. In. She couldn't even scream, probably trying to wrap her mind around what was happening to her. He handed the knife to Dennis.

Dennis held it and asked, "Should I search the house?"

"No, I'll do that." He pointed at the knife. "Take a turn, kid. See how it feels. This bitch is not long for this beautiful world. Her fight is almost over."

"Joel," she said, shaking her head side to side. Pain in her voice. Pain in her eyes, her lips. Tight muscles in her neck. "I'll help you if you'll just let me go."

"Dennis, did you hear her just use my name?"

"You just used mine."

He ignored him. To her, he said, "It's too late, you. It's too late."

"It's—not. No, it's not, it's not."

"Oh, Serena."

She looked at him in horror, and he saw she understood he had no intention of letting her go. She screamed.

"*Dennis*?" he yelled over her.

Dennis shook his head.

Hines frowned at him, and what he saw surprised him. Or maybe it didn't. Was that a tear in the boy's eye?

"I can't do it," Dennis said. "We shouldn't do it."

"If you don't do it? Even if I stop now and leave her here, she'll still die. She'll bleed out."

"It's not too bad," Dennis said. "We can get her help."

"You ignorant little pussy. Take a turn!"

"No."

Hines reached for the knife, but Dennis pulled his hand away. He scrambled backward from Serena's legs and stood. Her legs free, Serena tried to kick at him. Hines got up a moment after Dennis.

Let her be free. It wouldn't be for long.

Hines snatched the knife from the kid before he could back away. Serena was wounded, but Dennis was right. Fatally wounded but holding on.

Finally, Allie screamed as loud as she could. Hines pointed the knife menacingly at Dennis. "Search the house," he said. "Tear this place apart and leave no cupboard, drawer, or hiding place unchecked. It's a fucking one-bedroom apartment, one floor. Look for a key. Hell, maybe even Moss. She could've lied about that. Do that, or I'll kill you too."

Dennis, his eyes wide, nodded slowly, then backed away. He disappeared into the kitchen, and drawers started rattling and crashing to the floor as he searched.

Serena struggled to a sitting position and looked around frantically, her hands clutching at her stomach.

Hines smiled, and in a few awkward movements, tore off his blood-streaked shirt. He was still barefoot. Here was more darkness to purge from his soul. He could still gain his power, still experience what he had experienced before. He could untwist the unnaturalness lodged inside him. The darkness that clashed with the light. Find that spot and release himself into whatever plane kept his poor, misguided mother safe. Bring her back and start again.

Allie had regained her feet, but she wobbled precariously. She bent over in pain. She looked to escape, but there was only one door, and Hines stood near it. Weak and disoriented, she sat by a down again.

Hines would have to get to Allie. Get to her before she managed to widen her sphere of influence. He knew, also, that he would have to keep a low profile for a while, after what happened here today. Slink into unwanted obscurity and hide in the shadows.

Oh, he so wanted to be high on magic! It was his day to heal. It was *his*.

Hines came at her and extended the knife in his hand, pointing it as if it were a gun. She tried to scream as he came at her, but it came out as a squeak.

The knife was a blur as he jammed it into her gut, and he flashed back to the knife attack he endured when Bill Hand tried to have him killed. How cold he'd been as he struggled to the hospital.

But there *she* was, all warm and red. Leave as you are. *Like a friend. Like an old enemy*. He placed his free hand on her stomach and pushed in, coating the skin, and she let out a muffled moan. Cupping his hand, he brought it to his mouth and drank what he could.

"Practice," he said, grinning ear to ear. Then, using his hand as a brush, he painted streaks of red on his chest. "Magician," he said, "heal thyself."

THIRD MOVEMENT

*Who is the happier man, he who braved the
storm of life or he who has stayed securely
on shore and merely existed?*
—Hunter S. Thompson

21

THE METRONOME

TRUMAN STARKEY TOOK ON THE COLDER, DREARIER DAYS in Quinault with the added bonus of Kat's company. She hadn't gone back to Aberdeen. Instead, she spent her time split between his rooms above the store and the occasional night at the ranger station. She'd put the chalet keys back without anyone knowing they were missing, and she tried to spend more time with her dad. His name was Andy Gregory.

Truman and Kat fell into an uneasy routine in the weeks after the incidents at the chalet, but circumstances were even more dire for Kat.

Serena was dead.

"The police found her in her apartment," Kat said on one of her visits. She was—" She couldn't finish, and Truman held her, waiting for her sobs to subside.

"I'm sorry," he whispered.

"There's a detective on the case. Name's Frank Medina." She wiped her eyes with her sleeve. "I was a person of interest and had to go in for questioning."

Of course she would be. It was no secret they'd been friends. "What did you tell him?"

"Only the facts from the last night I saw her. She'd been drinking with me, and I left her puking in the bathroom. But nothing about the box or us hoping to hide it, or about Moss guy."

"Why not say something? He's a nutcase, and dangerous. You know it was him who killed—" He didn't finish.

"I'm certain of it. But Allie said not to."

"Isn't she afraid he'll come for her? What about you? Or me? He left us to die, and then he killed Serena. Do you think he knows we escaped the chalet?"

"Maybe. He will eventually, I guess. But I'm laying low. Not going anywhere. Allie sent a text saying Medina questioned her too. She could get into serious trouble if they found out about her— side business."

"A small crime to confess to if it got her some protection and took that guy off the street. Kat, it's *murder*, now."

She nodded. "Allie's protected by her sphere of influence. She says as long as the guy is free there's a chance we can locate the locked box of Moss. It's unlikely, but think what would happen if he got into it somehow?"

Over a period of time, they continued to weigh the pros and cons, and argued about whether to say anything to the detective.

Truman's schedule working at the resort, Kat's back and forth living arrangement, and her tendency to leave without warning, made it nearly impossible to focus on the most urgent matter: finding the box. He still hadn't told her about the visit with her ghost-self, but he knew they shouldn't delay any serious attempt to locate the box.

But where to look? Quinault was a large place, and although Kat said they had no reason to believe the mage had taken the box further away, a search might include scouring the national forest and the national park on either side of the lake. Kat was certain the man wouldn't risk taking the box anywhere close to Aberdeen for fear of running into Allie's sphere of influence.

Talking about the sex remained problematic. It wasn't only about that morning in the chalet, it was also about Kat's return to Quinault, the occasional questions from Medina, and the inability to focus on the missing box. When Truman pressured Kat about it, she said they should start looking soon, but her heart never seemed in it. She missed Serena, she missed Allie. She seemed lost.

To alleviate the tension, Truman did what Kachina had told him he needed to do in the first place, and that was to finish the symphony. He started in on the third movement. When he'd returned from the chalet, he wrote down the end of the second movement he'd memorized. It didn't surprise him that he remembered it in detail. Transcribing it onto the staff paper didn't take that long at all, and he was ready to pick up that note of hope darkening the end of the second movement and repeat it at the start of the third movement. The scherzo.

The rain that fell came as often as it had the previous few months. He still heard Kachina when it did rain. Part of him hadn't been sure he'd be able to, now that she had left her own time to warn him. When she sang, her voice had the same vibrancy as always, even as she added new musical ideas he hoped to form into some kind of overlaying theme for the scherzo.

In the days of Ludwig van Beethoven and Franz Schubert, the scherzo became widely used, replacing the older minuet. Beethoven took the scherzo away from the polite minuet toward a more spirited dance. Truman had decided to take that first note of the movement, hold it with a steady crescendo, then run with it full tilt into the playful strains of the scherzo and its triple meter. Traditionally, the scherzo took on a light-hearted approach, but he didn't think his version would be that way. Scherzo meant "to joke," but Truman knew the movement wouldn't have a humorous tone. Rather, he would take the dance more quickly than usual, and more intensely, mirroring his and Kat's own hectic search for the box.

Truman's symphony was a modern composition, and the scherzo didn't appear as often in present-day works, but he believed he could make it work. He also knew he would do as some composers did and rely on a repeated phrase. Something unique to the movement, but still tied to Kachina's theme. He imagined that first note leading to the first bars of the movement in a dominant key.

He'd transpose it, perhaps up to the tonic key, creating an illusion of starting in the wrong key. Beethoven had done this very thing in one of his piano sonatas, although Truman couldn't remember which one. It seemed fitting to lead the listener astray, considering what had happened at the end of the second movement: the disintegration, then hope. The hope would be fleeting, as it led to an unexpected, almost savage dance.

At first, he worried that he'd be unable to write the urgency into it. Recalling the ordeal with the mage helped. He also followed his gut, which said: not *too* heavy.

Kat learned the melodies and countermelodies of the first two movements, and before long, she could sing them to him. He cringed at first because her voice was Kachina's voice. Was this how Kachina learned the music? Learned from him in his rooms above the store, internalizing them so that she could later sing them back to him in the rain when he arrived last summer? The thought made his head hurt.

The month wore on, and the resort stayed mostly quiet. One night, when Kat came back after spending time with her dad, he took notice of the dark circles under her eyes and the way she dragged her feet as they climbed the stairs.

She had brought him an unexpected gift, though, tightly wrapped in metallic green paper. He tore into it and found a Wittner mechanical metronome, one of the best ones available and, he knew, expensive. It had to have cost her a hundred dollars or more. It had a beautiful walnut case, good volume, and kept excellent time. It had a bell that rang on whatever clicks he wanted.

Back and forth.

Symmetrical motion, ticking equal parts, a constant pattern, keeping a tune on track.

"How do you think Dennis knew your song?" she asked suddenly. "When he recognized it during that first guitar lesson you gave him?"

Truman sat at the piano bench, still admiring the metronome.

Before she'd arrived, he'd sat plunking out notes, trying them on for size. He hadn't made much progress on his scherzo. Kat sat on the end of the bench to his right.

Kat's question wasn't something he'd thought about. "I don't know. Maybe because Dennis had already met the mage? Maybe he heard it in the rain like I did?"

"You said no one else can hear it. Even now on the days I'm here, when it rains and you run to the piano, I hear nothing. It'd be like you turning on that metronome and seeing it go back and forth, but not hearing the clicks."

"Perhaps you're not meant to. You know—hearing it could destroy all of space and time."

She punched him playfully on the arm. "Perhaps it's the only thing holding the universe together."

"Like duct tape."

"Look. Dennis is tied to this guy somehow, but the boy knows that song. I don't know what it means, but maybe it leads somewhere. Maybe a weakness that can be exploited."

Truman played the original seven note theme on the piano, his touch so light on the keys that the tones were barely audible. "I don't like that kid mixed up in all this. I'm afraid for him."

"His own fault."

"I think he was manipulated."

"That much is true."

"I mean in a way counterproductive to the man's own desires. Dennis seems a liability, and it also seems the mage sees him—and treats him—in a negative way."

"Because Dennis has some knowledge he doesn't."

"The song."

"Maybe?"

Truman sighed, played the melody again, and leaned his head on her shoulder. He took his hand from the keyboard and rested it on her thigh, and he felt her stiffen. Right afterward, she repeated his sigh and left the bench.

"What?" he asked.

She found her coat and shrugged into it. "I'm tired, and I think I need some air."

"Okay."

"I'm going to walk down to the ranger station."

"It's ten o'clock at night. You're going to walk a mile down there now?"

She shrugged. "Think I just need to stay there tonight. I've got all these thoughts bouncing around. I've got to get them straight."

"You could do that here, couldn't you?"

The silence lasted a few beats as she looked at him, but that also turned into a sigh. "Not tonight."

Or any night, Truman thought. Even when she spent the night at the resort, she'd keep her distance in the bed, or she'd move to the couch in the TV room.

He stood and pointed to his coat on the bed. "Do you want me to walk with you?"

"No, Truman. I'm fine. I'll see you tomorrow."

She left the room and hurried down the stairs, anxious to get away. It hurt him to think she wanted to escape him. His desire for her in the chalet had been overwhelming. It was a feeling he'd not had in a long time, dating back to his early years with Melissa. He loved Kat, he knew, even though he had only known her a little while.

The sex in the chalet had happened because Kat needed it to happen. A specific dream fetish, a charm, a purpose suited to the needs of them both. He understood that. It hadn't been a means to an end with her. Still, he had a hard time believing she hadn't felt something similar for him. Something tangible had risen from that coupling, her longing like a song's counter melody: different from his own need but tied to him in spirit.

What had happened since then to bring her to this restlessness? Was it simply the stress of dealing with the mage? He could believe that. Jesus, the guy had tried to kill her, stuffing her underneath the floor, leaving her in a deserted chalet in the middle of nowhere.

He left me to die, too.

Now the mage had disappeared. Kat was distant. Her friend Serena dead. Once again, he wasn't writing enough. He wasn't getting any exercise, and he was eating too often in the restaurant.

What else could go wrong?

Truman eyed the piano. The best thing to do would be to focus on the work Kachina had tasked him with. Finish the symphony. It would be needed, she'd said. *It's your magic. It's our magic.*

Working downstairs in the store cost him hours of composing time, but he had more than enough hours off to settle in and write if he kept distractions at bay.

Craft the weapon. The four movements honed like precision-machined parts designed to fit together for a larger purpose.

He still didn't know how to slide further into the third movement.

He turned on his new metronome. Tick tock, tick tock. Focus and forget about Kat, the mage, Dennis, the resort. Make music.

Again, what else could go wrong?

22

THE UNHOLY TRINITY

Hurricane Melissa arrived at the Cedars Resort two days later.

"Hello, Truman," she said.

She stood just inside the store doorway wearing a raincoat, her hands tucked inside the large pockets, brown hair loose, wet, and tangled from the rain. She must've walked from farther away than the parking lot. Maybe she'd parked down by the motel, not sure where to go.

Truman stared at her with his mouth open, his skin tingling, his whole body numb. He never would've expected this. He hadn't told her anything about his whereabouts. Where he had gone, or when he had left, or how he had arrived. Somehow, she'd found him, and that seemed more magical in some ways than the music in the rain. This just wasn't possible.

The open door let in a gust of wind that swirled in behind her. Well *that* was appropriate.

"Melissa. What the hell are you doing here?"

Noticing the cold breeze at last, Melissa turned and shut the door slowly until it latched with a *snick*, as if she were entering a church.

She hadn't completely turned around when she said, "I called Andrew, and he told me to try Elsa. She told me you'd mentioned this resort, and I remembered your friend Jacob. I called here on a whim."

"What are you *doing* here?"

"Here to see you," she said meekly, facing him now, her eyes looking at the gift shop, the grocery store, the souvenirs on the counter—everywhere but at him.

He laughed out loud, and she finally looked at him. "That's bullshit, Melissa. You don't give a fuck about me."

"That's not true. I—"

"It's always been true." He held onto the counter and gripped it so tightly his hand hurt. "You've always been for yourself. Not for me or anyone else. Just you. And—" He paused and couldn't continue, not wanting to say it. Not wanting to bring all this dead weight back into his life. He was never within Melissa's gravity well for long before his life came crashing back at him.

"And? And what, Truman Starkey? Your music? You think that's all I wanted from you?"

"My music. Yes. My *music*."

"You're pathetic. I never wanted your music. I wanted my own."

"You stole it from me and *made* it your own."

She shook her head and looked at him with such pity that he felt like a schoolboy. "Oh, Truman. Is that what you think?"

"That's what I think. Tell me I'm wrong."

"You're wrong. We worked on that music together."

"It doesn't matter. You took it as your own."

"Because you weren't working on it. You *quit*, Truman."

"I didn't quit."

She rolled her eyes. "Oh, that's right. You were taking a break." He shrugged. "Maybe I was."

"I ran with it because your break had lasted two years. Two *years*, Truman."

"You ran with it because we broke up, and you didn't want to wait for me anymore. You told me the only reason the symphony had promise was because of *your* work. Do you remember that? Remember calling me an amateur?"

"You *are* an amateur. You've never made a dime off your music."

"Not true."

"Your guitar gigs don't count."

"Then you're an amateur too."

She stopped, and he didn't know if he'd struck a nerve with that comeback, or if she had something else to tell him. Her face colored and she glanced away sheepishly.

It was something else.

"Truman, I—" She struggled to say it.

"What?" He held out his arms. "If you're here to rub it in my face, then just do it."

"I'm sorry."

He nodded knowingly, the truth coming to him in a rush. He felt a little light-headed. "You sold it, didn't you?"

She looked ready to deny it. "It's complicated—"

"It always is."

Crossing her arms, the rain jacket rustling, she looked him in the eye. "The Seattle Symphony premiered it three weeks ago."

He didn't move for nearly ten seconds, holding her gaze. "And then you sold it."

She was silent.

"How much?"

"It doesn't matter. Not that much." She took a tentative step toward him. "It's . . . dedicated to you."

"Oh, that's just great. Dedicated to the ex-husband you stole it from."

"Damn it, Truman, I didn't steal it!"

"Tell yourself that every day if it makes you feel better."

"Can we talk about this later?" she asked. "In private?"

"There's no one else here, Melissa."

But right then, the door behind Melissa opened, and Truman thought: thank God, Andrea's here. His shift was nearly over; he'd tell Melissa to go home and she could sleep with their symphony, for all he cared.

The door closed, and Truman looked around Melissa to find Kat shaking off rainwater.

"Kat," he said.

She looked up. "Truman?" She came behind the counter and gave him a small hug. Then, surprisingly, a light kiss on the cheek.

Melissa pulled her arms even tighter around her chest. "And who's this?"

"Melissa, Kat. Kat, my ex-wife, Melissa."

"Oh," Kat said. "Hello."

"I'm sure he's told you all about me," Melissa said.

Kat glanced upward, thinking a little. A slow head shake. "No, actually, he didn't." To Truman, she said, "I didn't even know you were married."

"Not for a while now. Can't say I've missed the experience."

"Look," Melissa said, "say all you want, but I only came to find you because you disappeared so abruptly, and I was worried."

"Again, bullshit."

"And to tell you the news about the Seattle Symphony."

"That I can believe."

She smiled, her face exuding a calm that belied their earlier argument. "There was a standing ovation."

"Oh, *Jesus*, Melissa."

Kat waved her hands in front of her. "You know, I'm just going to leave you two alone. Truman, I have some good news to tell you, when you have a moment."

Truman so wanted to hear that rather than stand here and listen to Melissa crow about the symphony. Kat, though, had already left for the back room and the stairs.

Melissa started up where she left off. "That applause could've been for you, too."

"Not likely, considering the music ended up in your hands." He gave her little room to argue.

"If it meant that much to you, why didn't you say more? Fight for it, maybe?"

"What? Sue you in court, you mean?"

"What if you had? Maybe then we might've worked something out."

"We never could work things out, and you know it."

"Then I don't know why you're arguing with me. Maybe you could be gracious for once and congratulate me."

He left the counter and sat at the chair behind the desk. "Maybe you should just go home. I don't know why you came out here. You must've known this would go badly."

She leaned across the counter. "Come on, Truman. We'll go across the street and have dinner and talk more sensibly." She pointed in the direction of the door to the back room. "You can bring your friend."

"My friend?"

"Is she a composer? A musician? She looks a little crunchy granola to me. Are you sleeping with her?"

"It's none of your business."

"C'mon, have dinner with me. We'll work things out."

"It's too late to work things out. That's why I left. I needed to get away from you. I needed to do something for myself."

Andrea finally came in the front door. She smiled at Melissa and disappeared into the back room.

"Is she here to spell you? No excuse now. Come to dinner."

"For the last time, no." He picked up a pencil and tapped it on the desk. "I have some work to do."

She raised an eyebrow. "Are you writing?"

"Some." He sneered. "But it's amateurish." He didn't believe that, of course. He believed it to be the best work he'd ever done.

But Kachina's helping *you*. Once again, he had let someone else into his music. Was it okay to allow his muse to collaborate with him? Maybe. She wasn't likely to "run with it" on her own while hiding in whatever moon plane she'd disappeared to.

He'd told himself he only needed inspiration. Apply swift kick to the seat of the pants. The Kachina-kick had thrown him into his work like no other incentive had, including Melissa. It wasn't as if the entire symphonic structure was being fed to him note by note.

It was still his symphony.

"Okay, Truman, whatever you want to believe. Your problem is that although you're a wonderful musician and quite the technician when it comes to ordering and structuring your music, you're missing something important."

"And what's that?"

She looked at him sadly. "Heart."

He wanted to throw that back in her face, but he found that he couldn't. Was she right? Maybe she was; he was having a hard time admitting it to himself.

"If you want to know what really drove us away from one another," she said, "it's that."

"Because I'm missing a heart?"

She shrugged. "Maybe." She knocked on his chest as if he were the Tinman from Oz. "You've never found that emotional center. There's been something missing there. There's a wound that has kept you from taking that musical genius and turning it into something magical."

Magical. Truman didn't speak; he waited for her to go on, even though he knew where she would take this.

"You've never forgiven yourself for giving up on *us*. On this symphony. You can see the music, but you can't hear it. You can't *feel* it—"

That was all he could take. "Just stop, Melissa. You can't give me that song and dance and chastise me—"

"The usual refrain."

In the silence, the two of them faced each other as if brought together on a playground, and they didn't quite know how to play with one another. Self-conscious, Truman felt the tug of a healthy relationship: the one they'd had for a while before music pulled them apart. He missed it. There was no going back to this old storm, but he almost appreciated the calm of these last echoing rumbles of thunder.

She readied her coat by pulling it tighter. "I'm going to eat before I go." She reached inside the raincoat pocket and pulled out a CD. "Symphony No. 1, The Memoria." She slid it across the counter toward him. "If you're interested."

He didn't move.

She stood there looking at him another moment, then turned for the door. "Goodbye, Truman."

He couldn't imagine ever picking up that CD. A part of Truman's soul was on that disk. He was afraid to hear his music interpolated into her now successful symphony.

In the long run, he *had* left The Memoria behind. It was hers now, and not his. Hadn't he just lent her a theme, scribbled out a few bars here, a few melodies there? He'd suggested the title, too.

Hadn't Kachina done the same for him by offering him her song?

He still had to make this Kachina-inspired symphony his own. Kachina had pleaded with him to finish it, and this was all he needed to know right now. Few people understood the true pull of creativity and the artist's way of striving to reach that lifelong dream. No one, not even the most prolific, musical genius, could do it without a little help.

Andrea came back in and waited by the store cash register. She didn't look at them, probably sensing the tension in the room.

He stood.

"Melissa, wait."

Her hand on the doorknob, she turned and regarded him with that raised eyebrow of hers.

He came around the counter and stood beside her. "Dinner would be fine."

"Good. Does your friend want to come?"

"I don't know, but I'm not going to ask her."

"Just us, then."

"Sure. I could use a little help on my third movement."

"A dance, I bet, knowing you." A smile came to her lips. "A scherzo?"

"Yes, and it's kicking my ass."

⋙

When Truman got back from dinner, Kat was gone. He wondered what her good news had been. She hadn't left a note lying around, so how good could it be?

Truman had suggested Melissa stay at the resort for the night, but she wouldn't have it. She wanted to be back home, and she figured to get there before eleven o'clock if she didn't make too many stops. When they said their goodbyes, she looked quite sad, but she held it together, and so did he.

He did pick up the CD on his way upstairs. He wasn't sure when he'd listen to it. Maybe never. But he had picked it up. That was saying something.

At the piano he paused, thinking back to his dinner with Melissa. It didn't take her long to tackle his delinquent scherzo. Simply, she suggested staying away from the triple rhythm in favor of a duple one. Change the 3/4 to 2/4, she offered, and because he'd already decided to pick up the tempo beyond the range of the typical scherzo, he could get across the feel of 3/4 in the 2/4 measures by writing out the notes in shorter bars and trying some grand pauses.

"It'll play like 6/8," she said, "but then you're not stuck with it. Literally, you want to take your dance and push it forward at an almost unrelenting pace."

He heard Kat's metronome ticking in his head. "Maybe at 116?"

"Whoa. *That* would do it. You'd gain a lot of momentum with that."

"And then interspersed with grand pauses. You think I should have stretches of silence in my dance music?"

"Beethoven did it in his most famous scherzo ever."

"From the Ninth Symphony."

She nodded, twirling her fork around the giant portion of pasta on her plate. "*Essential*," she insisted. "Who was it who said that blank bars are as necessary to planning good symphonies as parks are to planning good towns?"

He'd never heard the quote before.

Blank bars. Grand pauses. Silence. Parks and open spaces. Perhaps somewhere in there the silent voice of the mage lay in wait.

And now to work.

He still had the variation of Kachina's song in his head and knew exactly how to shape it into the scherzo's first section. He had Beethoven's scherzo on his mind, and he had to get past that simple opening statement of open octaves and grand pauses before he could concentrate on his own.

Punctuate the dance but preserve the continuous flow of the movement.

Like rain.

⁂

At eleven o'clock, about the time Melissa might be getting back to Seattle, Kat came upstairs. She lay on her stomach on the bed and, chin in her hands, watched Truman at the piano.

He hadn't expected to work this long, but a heavy squall of rain had started an hour earlier, and Kachina's voice had helped him plan a sequence that could end the first section of the scherzo and prepare for the contrasting second section. Then he could repeat the first section again in true ternary form, and not much else would be left to do.

Stretching his back, he swung his feet around on the bench and faced Kat. She wore a gray T-shirt with a halftone image of Jim Morrison of The Doors on the front.

She smiled at him. "Dinner go okay?"

"Better than expected."

"So you were married to her, and she was your collaborator on a piece of music."

"Sort of." He pushed back the earlier negative idea of stealing the music, not collaborating.

"But not this one you're working on now."

"No. At dinner, she gave a little help on my scherzo. I forget sometimes— she's an extremely talented composer."

"Are you going to listen to her symphony?"

"How did you know about that?"

She chuckled, and he liked hearing this more cheerful Kat. She stretched her left hand toward him, and he reached out and took it, surprised at her decision to initiate contact. Her fingers were cold. "I saw the CD sitting on the counter as I went out."

"I've not decided. I think not until mine's finished."

She squeezed his hand. "That sounds like a good plan."

"What about the good news you were talking about?"

The bed creaked when she sat up and leaned forward eagerly. "Do you remember anything unusual about the mage when you were stuck in the chalet with him?"

He frowned as he thought back. Anything different? Maybe more crazy than usual, but she didn't mean that, he was sure. He searched his memory for something, but nothing came to mind. He shook his head.

"He wasn't wearing his Olympic Rainforest baseball cap," she said. She stated it in a way that made it seem the most obvious— and most important—revelation ever.

"I remember now," he said. "What about it? Why wasn't he wearing it?"

"I'm guessing he took it off there and forgot about it. Or it fell off at some point and somehow he didn't notice."

"Assuming he had it there at all."

"He did."

"How do you know?"

She grinned and practically bounced off the bed to her day

pack. The day pack rustled as she rummaged around inside, and when she pulled out her hand, she held a green Olympic Rainforest ballcap, its brim shaped purposefully into an inverted wide "U."

"Is that—*his*?" It certainly looked like the same cap. Same color, logo, bent brim.

"It has to be."

"But where did you find it? You didn't snag it when we were up there, did you? Keep it hidden until now?"

She shook her head. "It was at the ranger station, on the desk my dad sits at when he works there."

When Truman gave her a look of confusion, she smiled and handed over the cap. He held it by the brim and inspected it from all angles. "Okay, so it was on your dad's desk—why?"

"A ranger went up there a few days ago to walk the trail and check out the chalet. I think doing maintenance, that sort of thing. Dad said he found it inside."

Truman visualized the scene of the ranger entering the locked-up chalet and finding that solitary out-of-place ballcap sitting inside somewhere. "Why is this good news?"

"We can locate him."

"Because of this ballcap?" Still holding it by the brim, he waggled it rhythmically. "How so? Because it's something of his? You have some sort of spell or charm that will locate him because he's touched this cap?"

"Magic?" She laughed. He didn't know if he'd guessed correctly, or she was humoring his clichéd answer. With exaggerated aplomb, she took the cap back and flipped it over. Across the back of the brim was something written in uncertain block letters, faint but seemingly legible from close up.

He leaned in. "What is that?"

"It's an address."

"You're kidding."

"Not a full one, but maybe enough."

"Maybe enough to find him?"

She handed him the cap. "I don't know. But there it is."

The block letters said RR#2, Bay Port. He shrugged. "Where's Bay Port?"

"About thirty minutes west of Aberdeen."

"Jesus, you think he lives out there?"

"I'd be more certain if 'Moss Man' was written across the brim."

"Doesn't it seem a stupid thing to do, writing where you live in your cap if you don't want to be found?"

"It does. But maybe it's because he *is* stupid. Or distracted. Maybe he just found the hat, and it's not his address. Perhaps it's some other reason we don't know about."

"RR#2. I'm guessing that means Rural Route 2. That doesn't narrow things down much. It could be an awfully long stretch of road."

"Maybe we *do* need a locator spell."

"I'm game if you are."

"I'm kidding, Truman. I don't have that ability."

"You knew the sex magic. Was that different?"

She reddened, perhaps in response to the building tension since the Enchanted Valley. "Very different."

"Regardless, we can't face him until we're ready. And you were certain he wouldn't take the box close to Aberdeen. Would you say Bay Port is within Allie's sphere of influence?"

"I wouldn't think so. But to get there he'd have to go *through* her sphere of influence."

"A lot of time's passed and we've not had any hints about the box. We need help."

She looked down, and her body language hinted again at her earlier distance.

"Kat." He reached and grabbed her other hand. "I don't understand why you pulled away from me. It's obvious. Please. Tell me."

It took a while for her to collect her thoughts, and then she let them all out in a rush. "The sex magic. Some of the spells I wove in there? We established a connection."

"What kind of connection?"

"A powerful one, and a dangerous one."

Truman shook his head, confused.

"It's not a connection between just you and me," she explained. "I didn't sense the presence until much later."

"The mage."

"Yeah, somehow he became a part of our link, and for any number of reasons. He was at the chalet earlier. He put me under the floor. He touched the key. The box. There's a strange—echo. One I've felt a while, as if a part of him is somewhere else, not entirely here, somehow searching."

He wondered if it was similar to what he heard from Kachina. Her future self. Was this a future version of the mage trying to manifest here as Kachina had? "He's used the drugs before, too, so maybe his awareness is still heightened."

"I'm afraid we've created a mismatched trio."

Truman thought about the trio in his scherzo. The earlier adagio and the feeling that he was part of some unnatural triangle. "A trinity of sorts."

"That's a good way to put it. In religious terms, probably an unholy one. To me it seems not only dangerous, but necessary. All three of us have power that emanates from beyond our own natural world. Whatever happens, we'll be tied together for it."

Kat had the magic that would lead to her Kachina persona. The mage had a sensitivity to magic, and synthesized Moss that enhanced it, overly so. And Truman? He had his music. A symphony tied to all three of them, even if much of it had come about because of the other two.

A wonderful musician; a technician; but missing heart.

As inspired as he had felt composing this piece, as breathtaking as his melodies from the rain had become, he had to fuse all of that with his own magic, or he would be right back where he started.

He'd be better off letting Melissa take that symphony too. Take it and run with it. Melissa had called his lack of emotion a wound that needed healing. He had to figure out the emotional center at the heart of his symphony, and he had to figure it out soon.

All he knew was: he wanted Kat alone, without the mage, and he wanted her to want *him*, too.

She held his hands and rubbed them as if she were blind, trying to understand by feel what she held onto. "I couldn't get close to you, Truman. The connection concerned me. I can't be certain whether the mage is aware of the connection or not. Any physical contact like what we experienced up valley—I just didn't know what it might do. I didn't risk it."

"You could've told me."

"Perhaps I should have."

"Now you have, so what can we do?"

"We still have to locate the box."

"With a locator spell you don't know how to do."

"No, with magic I didn't *want* to do because of the danger to you."

"Sex magic."

"We have to take the risk. No other options. Honestly, I have no idea what will happen with the mage tethered to us. I have to believe he would've come back for us by now if he thought we were still alive, so although the connection is there, perhaps he hasn't sorted out what it means."

"His magic from the Moss is different."

"It means there's a chance we can do this without him tethered to us. But I won't do it—I *can't* do it—if you aren't willing to take the chance."

He sat on the bed, close to her, hands still in hers. "Of course I'm willing."

She sat up and kissed him. The kiss lingered. She pulled back and her eyes were wet with tears. "I'm sorry, Truman. I was never more in tune with my body, and with someone else, then that morning in the chalet with you. The magic had a purpose, but so did the sex. I know it's hard to believe, considering how long we've known each other, but that morning I understood you. I sensed a shimmer of it that night in the lounge, and in the lake, during our swim. But that morning . . . I've felt vulnerable for a long time, but I felt as safe as I've ever been. Overcoming that helplessness made me fall in love with you."

He smiled. "I was kind of hoping that might be the case."

"Then—?"

"Love you? Yes. Maybe even from the moment I saw you on the dance floor."

"Love at first sight? Very Shakespearean."

"More like *Les Miserables*. Cossette and Marius fall in love even before they exchange names."

She smiled shyly, her black hair falling loose. She tucked one side back behind her ear. "You're willing to try this?"

"Yes."

"It will be quite different than before."

"I figured. When do we start? The mage isn't going to wait long."

"We still need the full moon."

The disappointment thrummed inside him. He counted in his head. "That's still weeks away."

"I know. But there's a positive side to this."

"There is?" He knew there *was*. She loved him. The earlier distance between them had been a way to keep them both safe.

"Of course." In one smooth motion, she removed her Jim Morrison shirt and sat back on her heels. "Without the full moon, without sex *magic*, we have the ability to love one another and show it in the most romantic way possible. And—" She grabbed his hand. "—we have lots of time to practice the sex part."

23

※

MOONLIGHT SONATA

T HE TREE CRACKS, CRASHES THROUGH THE WINDOW, AND *Truman falls backward. Tina has come up from behind and stands over him as the tree falls. The sound of shattered glass is so loud, it drowns out his screams to get her to move, and he reaches out to swipe at her, to push her aside, but she has no time, and the heavy trunk looms. The living room window is obliterated. The window frame is there, though, and he hears a heavy thud as the tree pounds into the house. It stops the tree from falling through completely. But a limb of the tree catches Tina on her chest, knocking her to the floor. A few limbs and branches immobilize him in an intricate trap. Another massive limb smashes against the wood stove, and the sound of wrenched metal is loud in his ears; burning logs from the grate are thrown against the dislodged door of the stove. A log rolls out onto the hearth, and then the rug, and it stops near Tina's outstretched arm and her robe that has fallen open, but she's unconscious—or dead—and can't move out of the way. The crackling and pops of the fire seem louder than the outside storm. The smell of wood smoke. Somehow, he's able to remember that wood smoke, even though it can have a pleasant smell, can be harmful. Particles measured in microns, getting past the body's defenses. Gases. Chemicals.*

This wood is dry, so there's that. Dad said it helped. Burns faster. Burns hotter.

Hotter. His heartbeat is loud in his ears, keeping a macabre rhythm completely out of sync with the mournful whispering of flames.

Something in the room has caught fire.

He woke from the dream and once again he puzzled over it. *It's not right, that dream.*

It faded away, Truman grasping at it. The windstorm had happened. The tree. The fire. But—

Tina.

The name came to him, and he rolled it over in his mind, on the verge of something.

Memories of that night had dimmed over the years. Out of sight, out of mind. On the night he pitched his tent in Enchanted Valley, he'd slept and had a dream he believed had been as vivid as anything he'd ever dreamt, but the memory of it had left him quickly, as most of his dreams did. Still, he remembered it being a powerful dream, something on the outer periphery of his memory.

His alarm went off, and his brain finally registered daylight. It was early, before 7 a.m., and the store wasn't open until later.

He had the day off. Why not get right back to the piano and compose? Three movements nearly done. He'd had very few problems with the structure of the scherzo and felt confident he'd finish the movement earlier than expected. The quiet, cool, rainy weather had something to do with it.

Grabbing his robe from the bedpost, Truman headed downstairs. He had the robe on by the time he padded into the store area. He nuked up a few breakfast burritos, grabbed some water, and trudged back upstairs.

Today, the third part of the Scherzo would receive his full attention.

〰️

As the days passed, the night of the full moon still to come, Truman "practiced" often with Kat. He called it—sarcastically—a minor sacrifice, but practice was not just an invitation to have sex. They really *did* practice. Testing endurance, finding their rhythms, tuning their patterns of slowing down and speeding up, and timing their paths to arousal and release. Truman had never been so tired after sex than after his times with Kat.

And yet—

He felt the tenderness between them that had been missing before. They practiced, but the *passion* was not mechanical. They had that now. Truman reveled in the understanding that Kat experienced their lovemaking *as* lovemaking the same way he did.

He had kept his promise to Kachina and not told Kat about the ghostly meeting. He couldn't, maybe, because of something related to the different planes of time. *Tear a hole in space and time.*

Nothing could make him believe that.

He believed in what Kachina had told him, though. The most important thing he believed in was the symphony. He had to finish, and he had to finish before facing the mage. Wield a symphony of rain—infused with magic from his bright muse—against the dark voice seeking chaos and destruction.

Truman would bring balance. That is, once he figured out how a symphony could do that in the real world. Or the other-world of Kachina.

Trinity.

Nothing to do until that full moon, other than working on the symphony and practicing with Kat. After the harrowing encounter at the chalet, the time since seemed tense in a completely different way. Something ominous and dangerous should be happening, shouldn't it? What was the mage doing? Truman thought he might be keeping quiet and out of sight while the detective, Medina, and the police department were investigating Serena's death. Where was he and the boy?

He thought of Melissa and her visit. She'd reminded him about the truth of their symphony and helped him understand he needed to finish his own. Hurricane Melissa. She'd been here, and now she was gone, and he was waiting.

The calm before the storm.

The day of the full moon came even as the light brightened in Quinault and the weather improved. There'd been a freak snowstorm, then a few days of rain that washed it all away, followed by several bright, sunny days. Truman had the day off, and Kat stayed in his room. He wrote at the piano, working his way through the third section of the scherzo. The absence of rain meant he worked without his muse. He felt distracted by Kat, even though she did what she always did when lounging in his room. Reading, mostly. Sometimes she'd help with his music. Nibble on Wheat Thins and string cheese. Lay on the bed with her eyes closed.

They saved their energy for the evening at moonrise, when dark, when sex would mean so much more. Truman moved the piano to the back wall, remembering how the moonlight shown down on his manuscript paper the night he discovered his moon key. Now, the exact spot and the time would be different. Moonrise would be around five o'clock. The sky was clear. They maneuvered the bed to that estimated spot, knowing both of them would need to be bathed in the light; in the last few days, moonlight had poured in as the moon phased closer and closer to full, rising an hour later each night.

They ate a light dinner brought over from the restaurant— salmon for her and chicken for him, no potatoes or bread, or even salad—and they ate in silence. Diet didn't necessarily have an impact on the magic, but being overly full might make things uncomfortable, and that could distract them.

As darkness fell, they lay down on the bed, fully clothed, silent. They both knew what to do and didn't have to review. He knew things would be different this time trying to locate the box. Locating something, Kat said, required a different charm than the kind needed to infuse an object with power.

They also knew that the unknown factor in all of this was the connection they now had to the mage, or the mage's echo. Would he sense them? Would he understand what they were trying to do? If he suspected they'd found the hiding place of the box, might he try and intervene? And how would that happen? Through their connection during the magic, or in person?

Kat said that however uncomfortable, however harrowing the experience might be, they had to endure him, for the magic would be more powerful, even if the mage discovered something about their plans. They had to honor the link. Honor the trinity.

Moonlight streamed through the window, hit the mattress exactly. Moonlight was really *sunlight*, reflected off the moon— less than 10 percent of it. This still made the moon shine very brightly indeed. The light reached Earth in just one second. Hello, moonlight.

Hello, sunlight and fire.

This time they wouldn't be on a cedar plank floor, disoriented in some unfamiliar place. This time Truman wouldn't need instruction. This time they wouldn't fumble around. As if on cue, Kat sat up and removed her T-shirt. They'd start the session without having to fight clothing. Truman sat up too, shedding his own shirt. They lay back and pulled off pants and underwear, and soon they were naked in the moonlight, on their sides, facing one another.

Time stood still. It seemed they needed to hold this position for a while. The key had remained around Kat's neck since they'd returned from the chalet; a brown leather thong borrowed from a leather journal from the gift shop made it into a crude pendant. The key pendant hung down toward the mattress, the thong rest-ing at the top curve of her breast.

Kat spoke, barely above a whisper, as she rested the palm of her hand on his cheek. "This is for you, Truman. Do you understand? For your symphony. Hearing what you've already written and listening to what you've told me about your muse, I believe this spell is more important than anything."

He was taken aback, but he kept his emotions centered. Sure, this magical search for her box of drugs was important. But not just to him. "It's for all of us, Kat. Even the mage, unfortunately."

"Truman, don't be modest. If whole, this symphony is yours. And no matter what you do the rest of your life, it could be your greatest work."

"My magnum opus, huh?"

"*Magic* opus."

He chuckled softly. "Nothing great to look forward to after that?"

"We need to get through this, or there won't *be* anything to look forward to. There's no telling what damage the mage could do if he succeeds. I don't know what his real desire is, what he thinks the magic can do for him, but it can't happen."

"I know."

Kat scrunched closer to him. Her skin was almost silver in the light. "Did you know that magnum opus is actually an alchemical term?"

"No."

"It's Latin for 'The Great Work.' It's the process of working with matter to create a transmutation."

"Like us, transmuting the key."

"Yes, but this is a larger goal, creating something ultimately more powerful than imaginable. Turning solids to gold. Producing the Philosopher's Stone."

"You mean like Harry Potter. Magic."

She smiled. "Well. There *are* those connections in art and literature, and yes, even modern fiction like Harry Potter."

He nodded but didn't know what else to say. It seemed that they shouldn't be saying anything right now. He believed she sensed that, too. He was ready, physically, almost achingly so. She was ready, too; the heat between her legs already exuded an arousing scent of sweat, ocean, and wine.

She kissed him lightly on the lips. "It's time."

He was inside her quickly. They stayed on their sides, the movements natural, the pace unhurried. If they maintained contact and remained coupled, Kat believed having sex on their sides would take away the distraction of one another's weight.

Their earlier sessions had led them to this point, to this intersection of passion and practicality. He loved her, and these moments would naturally express that, but he knew the goal was beyond the boundary of love, erotic or otherwise.

They had known their goal intimately for months now and had practiced visualizing it. Their objective. Their *charm*. It was simple: Find the box.

But he had to concentrate.

They visualized the same dream, the sexual energy the nectar of their desire. Life energy. His reality, his magnum opus, the great work, the need to bring it forth.

As they'd practiced, they gained momentum, their movements more urgent, seeking that line between potentiality and release. He felt the connection between them now, and the heaviness of his muscles and bones.

Faster now, building from start to finish, exposition to recapitulation.

This time, the two of them together had the song. It might keep the mage contained if he turned up. Weeks of practice had convinced them they could focus their energy without the song being audible, which meant they could keep the mage in the dark about that power. Keep it hidden as their ace in the hole. Their grand finale. An unexpected coda. They'd agreed it was best to start the song as a hum, then turn it into a round so the music was continuous.

Once that was going, they could subvocalize it, the music sounding only in their heads.

With their concentration centered, they lost track of anything but themselves and the building energy. Kat said the mage was connected to them, perhaps poised to invade their magic, but Truman barely believed it, even though they had come up with strategies to contain him if he did. Perhaps even *use* him if he did.

He did. The echo of the mage slammed into his awareness like an unexpected fall that momentarily paralyzed muscles, limbs thrumming. Kat drew in a breath, feeling the presence too. She gripped his upper arm tighter but didn't stop her movements. Neither did he.

We knew this could happen. Remember the song.

Had she said that aloud? Or was their connection such that he'd simply heard her thought? If she spoke aloud now, would it break the spell? In the chalet, she had spoken to him—and he had responded—as they worked their way to transmuting the key. Was this time different? Her eyes locked onto his, forcing him to fight through his uncertainty.

Where? Where?

The mage. His voice sounded gravely in Truman's ears, but distant. Christ! The mage sensed them. Truman was certain of it, and that realization made his skin crawl.

"Breathe," Kat said aloud. "Hear your song."

She had told him similar in the chalet. He lost sight of the goal. He pushed hard, hoping to cast the mage from his mind. He took a deep breath.

Alive? came mage's voice. There was a long, lingering exhale. *Ah, yes, alive.*

"Don't listen." Kat's voice.

Two shall become one. Two shall become three! The mage's laugh, although still far away, jangled his nerves.

Truman kept his eyes on hers, bringing himself back to the edge, and her own heightened arousal bunched up in the muscles of her legs and the grinding of her hips.

What do you want? Hmmm?

"Like we practiced," Kat whispered. "Visualize."

Although difficult to do while keeping the song in his head and dealing with the voice of the mage, he thought of the box and put it in the center of his forehead. He held it there and waited for her to pin it to her own brow, and in the space between them the box took shape as if they had entered a virtual world, a three-dimensional reality, the prized object floating and rotating like a video game treasure that would—if you could only avoid the demon protecting it—open with a simple touch. But it would take the key around Kat's neck to open it.

The box!

They hadn't planned and practiced avoiding the mage; they had planned to *include* him. The box was visualized, the magic hummed, but it had the potential to be even more potent with the mage involved, if not more dangerous.

The song was her magic: the song she'd learned from him that her Kachina-self sang in the rain. They did not sing aloud. They both knew the music well, and Truman continued the song in his head. Truman ordered it into a complex stack of melody and harmony. *His* magic. The box, filled with Moss: The mage's magic.

Little love birds.

Truman tried to push the voice away. That was not the sound he needed to hear, and he didn't want to imagine him looking in on what they were—well, doing, physically. What *did* he need to hear? Well, the sounds since coming to Quinault. Music, yes. Wind and rain. What else? The peaceful imperative of Kachina, the love of Kat. The storm of Melissa. The sound of breaking glass—the dream of New Year's, the tree coming through the window, fire blazing in the damaged wood stove. The sounds of life.

Kat moved urgently, her muscles tightening in anticipation of climax and magic, but the memory of these sounds of life meant something to him. They were important to his symphony, he was sure, but was he losing focus for the task at hand? Was he staying in synch? The box was still there in his mind's eye, but now surrounded by green.

Green. What did that mean? It wasn't a garden, it wasn't a forest. It was a state of mind. It was a state connected to nature and innocence. Children playing. The buds of May. The incipience of sexuality. Strong feeling, strong emotion. A special kind of beauty.

He remembered that sense of arousal when he first met Kachina in the clearing. He wished again he could tell Kat everything.

You will not find it. The mage's voice, low and grim, seemed hesitant, as if he were not sure that was true.

Kat moaned. Then, almost a whisper: "Green."

She saw it too. A special kind of beauty. Green was Paradise. Green was Happiness.

Truman believed all of this would help in his symphonic deliberations. What had Melissa said?

You're a wonderful musician, and technician, but you're missing heart. You've never found that emotional center.

She'd said there was a wound keeping him from turning music into something magical, even if she hadn't meant *actual* magic. He could hear it, he could even *see* it, but he couldn't *feel* it.

Breaking glass. And yes, he remembered the dream, and the tree bursting into the room. Truman feeling so helpless, hoping to protect his sister from the storm. The sounds didn't *mesh*, though. They were out of synch with the events unfolding in the dream, the same way he felt out of touch with the heart of his symphony. He remembered the emotions associated with the dream, experiencing them there. Could he open those emotions and transcribe them into his symphony? Emotions, not the events. He needed to associate emotions with the sounds of the wind outside the chalet, or the breath of passion.

I'm feeling helpless: storm, wind, rain . . .

I'm feeling trapped: tree, glass, mage . . .

The mage chattered endlessly now, on about something, but

Truman didn't care. It didn't matter what the mage said. It didn't matter what Kat said either, and she had said little during this window of passion—this window he could look out, visualizing his way to magic, as if gazing out from his room overlooking the resort and taking in the lake, the cabins, and the *green*. The trees. Even the top spire of the largest tree, the spruce tree on the corner of the property.

He thought about the tree, but an instant later, as Kat moved beneath him, he realized his own control had to give in. The music—only in his head—grew weak and stopped.

The end was intense as a blinding light, their aching muscles jumping, and the sensation sent shivers along his skin.

He didn't move for several minutes, but eventually he rolled onto his back and stared at the ceiling, letting the energy of the session dissipate. He was more prepared for this feeling, with the practice, than he had been the first time they had invoked the magic.

But wait. Had it worked? With all his musings about his symphony—sounds, emotions, the worries about the mage—had he contributed enough to the magic for it to be successful? What had they learned about the box's location? He felt as if they'd failed.

Kat sighed, and it seemed she, too, was admitting failure. When he felt her eyes on him, he rolled his head to look at her.

She smiled. "Better than practice?"

"Different than."

"Of course it is." She reached and kissed him lightly on the lips. "So. What do you think?"

It was his turn to sigh. He returned his gaze to the ceiling. "It seems we didn't get the location."

"But we *did*."

He didn't know how, but as soon as she said they'd been successful, the images came together.

"The tree."

"A very specific tree."

Not the tree in his dreams crashing through the window. "A spruce tree."

"A *Sitka* spruce."

The tree had sprung from a nurse log, which made its base exceptionally large. In fact, according to the sign Jacob had made for tourists, it had the largest base ever, over fifty-eight feet. Nearly two-hundred feet tall. There'd been another tree in Oregon considered a co-champion, until it fell during a winter storm years back. Another one up north in the rainforest was larger in volume of wood but didn't have enough points from the forest service to be champion.

Jacob had the reining champ on his property, amidst the forest, amidst the green—

His thought startled him. Had the mage truly hid the box under their very noses?

"It's pretty audacious," Kat said, echoing his thoughts, "that he would hide it here."

"He didn't think we were alive, so it would've made sense to him."

"But not now," she said.

"Because he was there with us. He knows we know."

Kat pushed up on one elbow and shook her head. "I'm not so sure. We projected a lot of images, including the tree from a distance, but we didn't confirm anything while connected."

"Is that why the sudden change? You pushed us to finish. I felt the music inside diminish."

She nodded. "Before he could catch that we knew anything specific. *You* didn't know, at first."

"Jesus, that's right."

The moonlight no longer bathed the bed in light, having moved along its path. Kat's face was more shadowed, but he saw her smile, her face softening at the sound of his voice.

"What we know," she said, "is that he was with us and he saw us. Likely, the connection strengthened the magic, but ironically, it gave us the location."

"Yeah, but *he* doesn't need the location. No doubt, he'll come for it. He'll come back to the resort. Won't he?"

"He might, but not right away if he doesn't suspect we know."

"It doesn't matter. We have to get the box as soon as we can."

"Yes."

"And open it."

"No."

"No?"

"Last resort."

"Then where do we hide it? Where do we go? We can't stay here, can we?"

"Truman, you have a job here. What's he going to do? Walk into the store, buy a carton of milk, then shoot you dead? And me if I'm around?"

"Why not?"

"He'd be crazy to do something like that. It would put him in the sight of witnesses and the police in the middle of an ongoing investigation. He has to approach us his own way."

"What way is that?" He asked it, but he knew the answer. He'd done it once already.

"By putting someone else in danger."

"A hostage," he said with a sincerity that didn't match the actual threat.

"I've got a feeling he might."

"Allie?"

"More likely. She had the Moss originally."

"And she's the one who synthesized them, right?"

Kat nodded. "It's time I go and see if she's okay. See what she knows."

Truman thought a moment, suddenly conscious of his nakedness, and Kat's. He wasn't sure what to say to her. Allie was her friend and mentor, in danger. *But so are we.*

"I'm cold," she said, and she scrambled to get under the covers.

He let her cover him, too, and they snuggled close. She might have said she was cold, but her skin was warm and comforting.

"We have to help," he whispered.

"We do."

"So what happens next?"

"I can't stay here. I'll go—"

"No!"

"You can stay and watch for him."

"But the box—"

"If it's where we think it is, then we'll get it, and I'll take it with me. It can't stay here. If the mage gets to it and moves it? No. I'll look for Allie."

He shook his head. "It's too dangerous."

"Allie will know what to do. There's no reason for you to go. The mage is connected to both of us, but if you and I are apart, we might be better off."

"Maybe. That's a big risk."

"We have to take it. *I* have to take it. You have to finish that symphony."

"To stop him."

"We hope."

"But we separate the key and the box."

"No."

"No?"

"I have to have the option to open it in an emergency."

"So, the box?"

She breathed deep, and before she exhaled, in the silence, Truman thought he heard splashing in the lake far away. He wondered what might have made that noise. When Kat breathed out, a long sigh, he felt it on his neck.

"Tomorrow," she said. She blinked as if coming out of a trance. "Tomorrow, we dig it up."

24

ECHOES

THE ECHOES WERE REAL, JOEL HINES REALIZED.

He sensed them as if they were just outside his fifth wheel. He'd done almost nothing, gone nowhere, since his visit to Serena's. Maybe not the smartest thing he'd ever done, killing her, but *god* it had felt good.

Now more than ever he sensed these strange, ethereal echoes, and it didn't take him long to understand he had picked up on the two he'd left to die in the chalet. If they'd escaped, where had they gone?

Where? Where?

"Fuck!" he yelled.

That woke Dennis, who was sitting in a chair up front. "Joel?"

"Get your guitar."

"Now? I'm tired. Do we have anything to eat—"

"Yes, *now*. It's right there. Just pick it up."

Dennis did. He started strumming a simple melody Hines didn't recognize.

"No, play the notes. The ones you heard Tip play."

And then there they were. The notes from the guitar, and then the notes among the echoes.

"Again. Keep playing, you idiot!"

Alive. Ah, yes, alive.

How did they escape the chalet? And how the *fuck* was this

happening? What kind of fucked up magic was this? There must be a reason. Hines wondered: was there Moss still in his system that he was tied to these two thorns in his side?

Two shall become one. "Goddamn. You're making up for your cowardice earlier, Dennis. Keep playing." *Two shall become* three!

What were they doing? He couldn't tell. Oh, he knew he'd waited too long avoiding contact with the outside world. Police poured over Serena's apartment for days. Hines had watched the endless TV reports about it, but he couldn't. Too weak to attempt a confrontation.

What do you want? Hmmm?

He wondered what kind of magic these two were weaving. Nothing kept still. It was like a fencing match. Parry, thrust. Parry, thrust. Parry—

Thrust. Ohhh.

The box!

He closed his eyes hoping to clarify their purpose, but it was hard focusing with—extracurricular activities going on.

Little love birds.

What brought him back to the underlying meaning of the echoes was the now strong sense of a search for the box he'd hidden. He grumbled about the possibility, but he felt confident at first that they wouldn't.

You will not find it.

Their songs dimmed even as Dennis's strumming became louder. What was happening? The love birds lost focus on their task. Why? Had they discovered something? He couldn't sense it. They were *good.* They'd worked on this, knowing he might hear them—join them—but they were doing everything they could to keep him out. Keep him in the dark.

A bit of light peeked through.

Green.

They'd figured it out, he was certain. He squinched his eyes tighter, but the echoes were fading now.

"Fuck's sake, *stop!*" he yelled at Dennis.

"You said—"

"No more. It's done."

"What did you see?" the kid asked.

Hines swallowed, and there was a bitter taste in his mouth. Not from the knowledge gained just now, but because he knew he was powerless to stop them getting to the box if they'd truly discovered its whereabouts.

"Trouble," he answered.

Well now, hold up a minute.

He might have a second chance with Kat. They wouldn't dare keep the box there at the resort. Kat must know about Serena, and Hines bet she'd want to do something for her friend. Revenge her. Get back to Allie. There was more than a good chance he could intercept her and the Moss somewhere along the way. And if he had power back, he could deal with Allie's sphere of influence. Wipe it away like an annoying mosquito.

What to do about Truman, though. He was a wild card. Dennis said his one-time guitar teacher believed he could put the song onto paper in an ordered coherence, and maybe load it up with magic powerful enough to—

Hogwash.

Nothing would match Hines' power at full strength from the Moss. He knew it, and Allie knew it. He'd be unstoppable. He could do anything. Change the fabric of the veil that covered the phases of the world. Silence the echoes and conjure wind to blow it all away.

I could see her. Meet her for the first time. See her at this moment with mature eyes.

"Dennis, get yourself ready. We're heading into town."

"What for?"

"Stuff to do. People to see."

Dennis frowned. "Who?"

Who indeed? The Truman echo had mentioned something unusual near the end. Something the music man had in his head he didn't expect would be heard. A name. Hines had heard it, and he wondered mightily about the name that briefly braided itself between the other echoes.

Kachina.

Now who the hell was Kachina?

"For me to know and you to find out," Hines said, not giving Dennis any specifics.

That was all the coaxing he had to do. Dennis sighed and headed to the back to change.

Hines beamed like a groom seeing his bride for the first time on wedding day. *Mother, I'm coming for you.*

But now.

Now?

There was someone else to meet. Let me show you my beautiful world, Kachina.

25

_⁂_

THE TREE

T HEY ARGUED A LITTLE LONGER THAT NIGHT ABOUT THE
danger she would face going into Aberdeen without him.
She was adamant, and at some point he gave up and went to work
on the third movement.

It now seemed to write itself, the music coming to Truman with
ease and a flow almost mesmerizing in its simplicity. The last third
of the movement, following the trio, repeated the first third: classic
ABA format. He was pleased at how everything progressed, fitting
like carefully tailored clothes around his scherzo, with the echoes
of Kachina's main melody fitting in elegantly like the finest fabrics.

In the overall scheme of things, although critical to the symphony's success, the third movement wasn't as important to him.
The "dance" was a necessary break from the previous movement,
true, but he couldn't wait to reach the end and work his way to the
last movement. He'd have Kat's help for that movement, of course,
and she would, by then, have an even better understanding of the
music and its structure.

But she was leaving.

They picked up the argument early the next morning, Truman
pleaded to go with her, but eventually, though Truman hated the
idea, they decided Kat would head for Aberdeen alone.

At seven in the morning, they walked down to the spruce tree.
The sky was gray, the air cool, but the rain held off. Truman car-

ried a small shovel in one hand and held Kat's hand with the other. The air was cool and crisp and dry. They walked close, bumping shoulders, walking between the lower cabins without a word, not wanting to disturb any guests.

Once they reached the lower loop and the mostly deserted campground, an unmistakable silence settled over them. The tree rested at the far end of the property, surrounded by foliage and other trees, but the tree's towering spire rose impressively over the canopy of green. Kat squeezed his hand a little tighter.

Not until they left the asphalt of the loop road did the blue information sign come into view. After a dozen steps toward the sign, they saw the tree beyond it, dazzling in its height and girth. To their right, a pedestrian bridge crossed the creek and led to the short nature trail that ended up back on the lake road.

Truman had been down to see the tree several times since coming to Quinault, and every time, just like now, he felt awed by it.

A thousand years old.

Tourists took time to climb a short distance up the wide base and settle in one of several hollows suitable for the obligatory photographs. Those photos revealed the immense scale of the tree. Truman and Kat, as they stepped lightly toward the tree in the morning light, thought only about the box's location, remembering the echoes of the magic, and the memory of green.

They didn't ponder this long. The front of the tree was what most tourists saw, and the path leading to it was devoid of any vegetation, the ground worn from a million footsteps all the way to the base and the tangled roots. But rich foliage ringed the tree otherwise. Was it in one of these areas the mage had buried the box? In several spots, the green encroached upon some of the roots, and one spot felt right to Truman. Kat felt it, too, and started toward that position.

This was it. Truman examined the ground carefully until he found an unnatural mound: a relatively fresh dig with less ground cover. Visible when the person knew what to look for, but still hidden from view. Something someone like Jacob would never see unless he came down for some reason to weed around the tree. He looked up and saw Kat glance at him, eyes widened a little. He nodded.

They didn't say a word; he just started digging. He felt a little guilty for thrusting his shovel into the earth so close to the giant thousand-year-old tree, but only a little. They needed this leverage over the mage. Kat had said opening the box and accessing the Moss was a last resort. He assumed that meant Kat would suffer the resulting negative side effects if she used them. But would it be worth it if that meant overcoming the mage?

He dug in the still-loose dirt, and after just a handful of shovel-fuls, the blade clanked against something solid. A few more times with the shovel, then they both fell to their knees and scrabbled in the dirt until they saw the box.

It seemed unthinkable that it had been hidden here. Without the connection created by the sex magic, though, they never would have found it.

Although caked with dirt and loam, the box revealed its distinctive interlocking bronze bars and intricate lock. Kat shuffled backwards on her knees, hands to her chest. She had the key around her neck, hidden under the layers of her warm clothes. At first Truman wondered if she might be tempted to open the box right there, but he knew she wouldn't. She had instinctively sought to protect it.

Those drugs were powerful enough to scare her. If they had warped the mage so much—someone who had not been aware of magic to begin with—what might they do to Kat, who had practiced forms of magic before?

She lifted the box from the hole until it sat on the ground at her feet.

"And now you'll go," he said, these being the first words either of them had said to one another since walking down to the tree. They seemed too loud.

"Yes."

"You'll take the next bus?" Lighter and less bulky, even, than a large suitcase, the locked box wouldn't be difficult to carry on the bus with her.

She nodded. "It'll drop me off on the north end of Aberdeen. I can transfer or call a cab and make my way to Allie's from there."

"I can drive you to the bus stop."

"It's only a mile to the ranger station. I'll walk, and I can catch a lift from my dad to the bus on the main road."

"You'll text me? You have to talk to me, tell me what's happening."

"I'll text you. So do you."

Truman nodded. "I will."

"And you know what else you need to do."

"Work on the symphony, sure. But I can only write so fast. The last movement is coming up, but you'll be back long before I finish it, and you'll help."

She lowered her head, staring at the box. "If things turn out that way."

He frowned, not liking the doubt in her voice. He put his hands on her shoulders and waited for her to look at him again. "A few days. You'll be back."

A second or two passed. She smiled. "Of course I'll be back."

Truman felt a twinge of relief. "Good."

"I have several hours before the next bus. It'll take me about twenty minutes to walk to the ranger station."

"Yeah?"

"Yeah. So I wonder what we can do for the next hour or so." She smiled at him mischievously.

26

A DARKLING PLAIN

AND THEN SHE WAS GONE, AND WORRY BURIED ITSELF DEEP inside Truman's stomach. He kept telling himself nothing would happen on her bus ride over there. She'd work her way to Allie's, where he knew there'd be protection.

She had both box and key now, so he hoped Allie could keep her safe.

He returned to writing.

The scherzo—and the third movement—were all but finished. During the rest of the day, which had become drearier by the hour, punctuated by a light but steady rain, Truman heard Kachina offer up the newest variations on the musical development of the scherzo. Truman reached the recapitulation with a repetition of the theme from the first section of the scherzo and settled back—after dallying in Kachina's moon key—into the dominant home key of the movement. He pulled in his knowledge of the form and did what he could to keep the transitions smooth and uneventful, preserving the flow of the scherzo.

He would let the movement sit for a few days, then come back to it with a fresh eye. There was *composing*, but then came *composting*. By giving it some time away from his eye, he'd let the scherzo generate more fodder for the last movement. Besides, he expected to hear from Kat soon enough about her visit to Aberdeen, and when she returned, he'd feel more confident about throwing himself into the final movement.

Her texts were frequent as she rode the bus in. At the north end of town she got off as planned, but she'd missed a connection with a city bus. She wanted to go to Allie's, but she didn't think it wise without more information, which she believed Serena would have. Entering her sphere of influence might also trigger a warning to the mage. He could even *be* there, waiting.

I'm at the Stoked Motel for the night, she texted. *Don't worry about me. I'm fine.*

Seriously? The Stoked Motel?

It's a crappy motel. The people who named it must've been high. I don't think many rooms are rented.

Has Allie texted you?

No.

The box is safe?

Safe as it can be.

Truman asked if Kat might chance going to Allie's.

I might have a way to connect to her sphere of influence without endangering anyone else.

You can do that how?

The box.

The box? You mean the Moss?

Yes. Maybe, but of course it's not my first choice. It would be dangerous. It could expose me.

How?

If he's within the sphere, the mage could sense the change.

Then don't do it.

Also, I've never taken Moss. Allie said they should not be ingested without guidance. Without focusing.

How long can you wait?

I don't know.

He told her he wanted to go down to Aberdeen.

No, stay.

Later that night she called him. She sounded so distant that it seemed impossible she was just forty miles away.

"Are you sure you shouldn't just come back?" he asked.

"Why?"

He didn't answer at first, tapping the phone against his ear. "It's been quiet here. He's not come for the box, not come to threaten me. Maybe this is all blowing over." Like a storm. A storm that had passed through, but it lingered along the edges.

"You have to finish, Truman."

"I need you here."

"I'm your muse. I'm not the voice you hear."

"Maybe you are."

"Truman, you've said this before. It's *your* muse. It's not my voice."

Yes, it is. And no.

"Finish," she said, and after reassuring him she was okay, she hung up.

It was the last phone call.

She texted a few times afterwards, the next morning. They were sound bites, short and devoid of emotion, save for the few times she texted *I love you.* Those words kept him sane, at least until the second day wound down. Her occasional queries about the fourth movement only heightened his sense of foreboding.

He called her later, but she didn't answer.

He texted.

He called again.

He texted again.

No response, even when he tried a few hours later.

That was it. He would borrow Jacob's truck and drive into town. But she finally texted.

Stay. Finish.

Have you chanced looking for Allie?

Stay. Finish.

Is this really you, Kat?

He wasn't certain about who texted him back, particularly because she hadn't answered calls.

Just stay, please. I'm okay.

He called the Forest Service and talked to Kat's father, Andy Gregory. Her father hadn't heard from her, but he hadn't expected to hear from her, either.

"Can you text her?" Truman asked. "Call her? See if she's okay. She went to Aberdeen a few days ago." He wasn't sure how much to say to him.

"Sure. I'll call. If I have any concerns, I'll call you back. Otherwise, I wouldn't worry about her. You should know that about her by now, if you're seeing her. You know. A relationship? She's like this. She's always been like this."

Truman thanked him and hung up. After he finished his shift that evening, he lay down on his bed, opened up his symphony score, and played through the third movement in his head. He still liked it a lot, but it didn't give him any insight into the riddle of Kat. He didn't know what to expect. Did he think his scherzo would already contain the roots of the magic formed by their new-found Unholy Trinity? Did he think that somehow, the answers would suddenly become clear?

No. Not until he finished the last movement. Balance. He would achieve it as he strode between the green growth of his muse Kachina and the black destructiveness of the mage.

His own magic wouldn't be complete until he found the heart of this piece. He had to understand the past. He had to understand it, yes, but if he was to connect the music—the sounds—to his emotions, he would have to find the way to unlock them.

Unlock his dreams.

But first, he had to find Kat. It was time to go look for her.

The burning log from the wood stove has fallen out and ignited the rug. The fire has spread and creeps ever closer to Tina's out-stretched arm, toward the fabric of her robe. The chair to the left of the stove is also on fire; smoke is rising, and soon that's going to be a problem. He stretches out, but for some reason he can't extract himself from the trap of branches.

He is responsible for her. He's been left in charge. The two of them started this night together on their own, their parents out for New Year's, and the job to protect her has fallen to him.

The sounds of the night still reverberate in his ear. The wail of the storm. The crash of broken glass. The scratches and thumps of the falling tree . . .

It's helplessness.

He can't reach her. "Tina!" He yells at her in vain. He's rooted to his spot. Helpless.

He is responsible for her.

He is responsible.

He woke suddenly, and the emotions of the dream were in his throat, choking him, then in the burning sensation in his eyes. Tears welled there. The dream was frequent now, enough so that he had started to remember the earlier parts of it. It helped him hold on to the new revelations.

It was 9:00 in the evening. He hadn't planned on falling asleep, and he cursed as he went to look for Jacob. He found him in the lounge, asked for the keys, and soon sat in the truck, the engine warming up. He remembered Jacob mentioning a Spring-field pistol hidden under the driver's seat, and he searched for it now. When he found it, he pulled it out from under the seat and placed it on the passenger seat. He climbed in, picked up the gun from the seat, checked it carefully, and found that the single stack magazine was loaded. Five rounds, and an extra round in the chamber. He felt a little safer knowing he had it close by if things went awry. He rubbed a hand over its surface and stared at it a moment before popping open the glove box and placing the Springfield inside.

It was late to be starting a search, but he could no longer ignore Kat's absence. In forty-five minutes, he'd be in Aberdeen. He googled up the Stoked Motel. The north end of town, just off the main road. He'd start there and keep looking until he found her.

His symphony could wait. Kat was his muse—in the form of Kachina, anyway—but without her at his side, even if it wasn't *her* voice he heard—although it was, really—he didn't think he could succeed. Stay, she'd said. Finish. But he couldn't do that until he knew she was safe.

He felt responsible for her.

⁕

The clerk at the desk of the Stoked Motel remembered Kat. Probably in his fifties, he had several days of stubble on his face, and wore a like-new velour track suit that seemed better suited to the '70s. A TV monitor mounted in the corner of the lobby—if it could actually called a lobby—was tuned to a sports channel. Strange buggy-like vehicles zoomed around a muddy track, and the drivers had minimal success trying to steer them. While Truman waited for the clerk to check his register, several of the buggies flipped, and another one flew off the track. But the race kept going.

"So she *was* here."

"Yeah," the clerk said. He put on some reading glasses that had to be someone else's. They had horned rims and decorative rhinestones along the black plastic, and a silver chain kept them around his neck when he wasn't using them. He peered at the computer screen, head at an awkward angle so he could get the most out of his reading glasses. "Kat Truman, checked in two nights ago."

"Truman?" He smiled at her use of his first name as her last name. An alias. Perhaps a wise precaution. "Two nights ago. Right, that's when she said she arrived. What room is she in?"

The clerk diminished the registry window, and the Stoked Motel logo popped up and started bouncing around the screen. He pulled off the glasses and let them dangle on his chest. "She's not in a room."

"What do you mean, not in a room?"

"She checked out the next day."

"Checked out?" His pulse beat a little faster. "She paid the bill and left? Or did she run out? Luggage with her, by chance? Or a box, maybe? Did you see a box?"

The clerk frowned, obviously annoyed at the barrage of questions. "I didn't work that day. She checked in with a credit card when she arrived, so it charged once she left. I don't know if she came down here to drop off keys, or check for messages, or if she just up and left the room."

"She didn't put down anything for a car make and model, or a license number, did she?" Truman knew she wouldn't have, having come in on the bus.

"Name and address. Pretty much it."

"What address?"

The clerk just looked at him.

Truman nodded. "Okay, I get it." He tapped the counter with one hand for a moment, thinking.

"You need a room?"

Truman stopped tapping. He looked up at the clerk. The glasses around his neck looked even more ridiculous there. "No. Thanks for your help."

"Okay, have a good one." The clerk sat back down in front of his computer, and Truman left the lobby.

Dread seeped in as Truman frantically wrapped his brain around possible scenarios. Kat must've found her way to Allie. Or—

She was in trouble.

Truman searched his phone for any mention of an Allie in Aberdeen. There was actually an old phone booth outside the motel, and a battered phone book hung from inside. He looked through it for a few minutes, but he didn't know her last name. He dialed information on his own phone. No listing remotely close.

He climbed into Jacob's truck and tried calling Kat again. He sent more texts, but nothing came back from her. Truman didn't know what to do, completely taken aback. He longed for those *I love you* texts. Anything she said now would be better than a blank text screen.

He looked up and found Rural Route #2, Bay Port, west of Aberdeen. He could drive that way, see what he could find. Search for the mage's whereabouts. Finding him in the dark without any further knowledge was unlikely. Rural Route #2 stretched for miles. Besides, should he be heading into the mage's territory on his own, without Kat, without his symphony? Hell, he didn't even know how a symphony could possibly stop an evil mage. What was he going to do? Sing it to him? Whap him alongside the head with the manuscript?

He could go to the police. That detective who'd talked to Kat about Serena. Medina. Tell him about the missing girl. Bring Kat's father into it. Start a search. How would he explain everything that had gone on up to this point?

Though it was a long shot, he decided to drive out to Bay Port. Perhaps he'd get lucky.

He left the Stoked Motel, drove through town, then found the state highway that led out toward Bay Port. The weather was good, no wind or rain. Maybe he should wish for rain. Maybe Kachina could guide him somehow.

He drove west of town, and a handful of miles before coming up on Bay Port, a sign for Rural Route #2 appeared in his headlights. Two more miles and a left turn put Truman on a small black top road south. Eventually, though, the road wound back around, and after the first mile, he once again drove west.

Truman rolled the window down. He smelled salt. He was near

the ocean, close to the actual bay that made up the western boundary of Bay Port. He passed a few homes, but he didn't give them
much thought: they were well-lit, well-kept, and quite expensive.
They were definitely not homes Truman believed the mage would
live in. Another voice inside him, however, asked: Why not?

He shrugged it off and kept driving. The lack of homes along
the road seemed an advantage in trying to pinpoint a possible location. A few miles later, the road intersected another road at a
"V." He stopped in his lane, since no other cars were around, and
looked things over. This new road looked to be gravel, although he
couldn't be certain in the dark with the truck headlights aimed at
the main road. There were no road signs marking it. Was it part of
Rural Route #2? An extension of it? Or was it a private driveway
heading toward someone's beach house?

It seemed promising to Truman.

Besides, the main black top road, which disappeared into the
gloom, couldn't go much further. A yellow warning sign announced
it was a dead end.

He checked his phone, needlessly. He knew he'd be without a
signal out here, and he was. No service. Silence. Blank bars.

He turned onto the gravel road. The car bumped down it,
rocking a bit, passing over ruts and potholes, the headlights saw-
ing through the night air. Truman's heart beat faster as the truck
rumbled down the road. The tension in his chest was almost painful
as he thought again about Kat. He continued to second guess his
decision to go on his own into what might possibly be the mage's
domain, but another part of him believed it the right thing to do.

He reached into the glove box, pulled out Jacob's Springfield,
and placed it on the passenger seat.

A homemade sign, black paint on a white board, said CAUTION
. . . DANGEROUS BLUFF AHEAD KEEP AWAY.

Truman slowed down, and soon enough he reached the
end of the road, the terminus marked with a makeshift barrier
someone had made with several concrete pillars about shin high.

They'd been formed with some type of mold, perhaps a square water bucket. There'd been no dead end sign on that road, but here it was.

No house, no other roads or trails, no streetlights, no vehicles. Just a lonely scenic view that he couldn't even enjoy here in the dark.

He left the headlights on and climbed out of the car, Jacob's pistol in one hand, a flashlight in the other. He crept toward the barrier, but again, saw little. The bay stretched before him as a dark plain, and he wasn't sure how much of it was beach front. No lights down below either.

Nothing.

Perhaps he'd missed something. He shone the flashlight on the ground at his feet, then swept it around the bluff and the pillars of the barrier.

Nothing at all. Some tire tracks, but that seemed an obvious find, considering tourists could've come out here for the view.

"Kat!"

He yelled it at the top of his voice, but the word seemed flat and meaningless. The bay sucked it up like a sponge. He silently recalled a poem Matthew Arnold wrote about two lovers remaining true to one another while looking across the Straits of Dover. But here? No metaphorical sea, no grating roar, no retreating roar. Just Truman's land of dreams: no peace, no light, no certainty.

Here he was, motionless on this bluff, gazing out over land and sea, silently recalling a poem.

Jesus, what was he *doing* here?

He answered that question immediately: looking for Kat. She was alive. He believed it. He *felt* it. He didn't much care about finding the mage. He just wanted to find Kat. If finding the mage meant finding Kat, then fine, but the more he thought about it, the more he found it unlikely she had looked for him on her own. What seemed more plausible was that she had somehow found Allie. Found her, but fell into the mage's trap.

He swung the flashlight around and to his right. He figured the bay wrapped around the bluff, and the dead-end road led to a similar destination: another scenic view.

The tension in his chest from earlier had lessened, but not the fear he felt in his throat, or the vertigo aching in his head. The bluff was deserted, but he felt an almost palpable dread, unable to shake the feeling that the mage should be here. Or that he *had* been here, or very near this place.

Whether he liked it or not, he had a passenger tethered to him. This hadn't happened simply because sex magic had revealed their dark trinity. He'd been in tune with the mage's essence from the moment he stepped off the bus the first day in Quinault.

A voice in the rain.

The feeling he'd had about a presence in the mirror in his room when the lights had gone out.

The presence in real life, too, each meeting setting the tone for later confrontations. Seeing the man in his ballcap the first time in the store, Dennis there with him. The time at the football game sitting in the stands with Dennis. And of course, at the chalet in Enchanted Valley.

The moment he remembered these connections, Kat's final texts seemed a strong command: *Stay. Finish.* He believed now that their tethering was to his advantage. He felt it. The mage was associated with this place, or someplace very like it. He could find it again. Kat might be in trouble, but he had his part to do.

Stay.

Finish.

He would keep searching, somehow, but he also had to return to his symphony. Wrap up the third movement, which shouldn't take too long, then begin the fourth. Finish his music and find the center of the mage's influence, and, with Kat, wield his symphony like a sacred text. He'd release it on the mage—as if he were Lucifer banished from the plains of heaven—and send the son of a bitch to hell.

FOURTH MOVEMENT

And we are here as on a darkling plain
Swept with confused alarms of struggle and flight,
Where ignorant armies clash by night.
　　　　　　　—Matthew Arnold
　　　　　　Dover Beach

27

※

PRESTO

TIME SPED UP. KAT WAS MISSING, AND HER DAD FINALLY understood and started an urgent search. The local authorities took an interest, and everything related to her case—and Serena's—ramped up dramatically. The best clue Truman and Kat had come across had been the ballcap with the partial address: Rural Route #2. It had come to nothing, however, Truman's search fruitless.

But not completely. Truman had tethered to the mage. He'd sensed a place remarkably like that bluff, perhaps somewhere else along Rural Route #2. He'd tried the other fork, and found nothing.

Truman texted, but had no luck. He tried to call Kat, but the calls always forwarded to her voicemail after the first ring. Kat's disappearance weighed heavily, but he had to channel his restless energy into the fourth and final movement of the symphony. He hated the idea it might even be more important than Kat and her own safety. Truman wrote, but barely functioned when he thought too much about Kat. He kept telling himself, *Finish*.

He completed the scherzo the day after he returned from his search for Kat. He hit a point near the end when everything came together, and he started to believe he could find the missing element Melissa had told him he must rediscover in his music: heart. He felt certain the emotional impact of the third movement, a conclusion to the smaller symphony that included the first two movements, magnified the essence of the entire piece. *That* might be the heart. It had Kachina's melody, it had the discord based on the mage's echoes, and it had the built-in nostalgia of his own past. Even if he didn't completely trust that past, he believed it could carry the movement.

The three elements firmly in place, and the scherzo still echoing in the listener's ears, the fourth movement would be its own entity, concluding the symphony as it recalled all the other movements. He could start those first bars of the fourth and allow the chaotic to alternate with the sublime, because heart could balance it. The fourth could resolve the entire piece and bring it to its resulting emotional climax.

A finale.

Fast-moving. Hurried. *Allegro*, maybe, or *allegro molto*. Or even faster: *Presto*. He would work it into the fourth, this last movement its own symphony of sorts, embedded at the tail end of the larger piece. It would still echo Kachina's melody, even as it recalled the first three movements and introduced new themes tied to all of them.

He understood Kat's plea to finish the symphony. With Kachina's song as its backbone and the threat of the mage—who might even now be keeping Kat prisoner, if he hadn't killed her as he had Serena—he would be writing the most complicated movement yet, if not the most powerful. *If* he could find its heart.

Truman launched into the exposition of the fourth movement, staying with the classic sonata form, but taking liberties as he saw fit to match his vision. He thought to himself, *symphony: agreement or concord of sound*. The other movements had the sounds of the rainforest and its magical whispers embedded in the lines and staves of its structure. They were not all coherent, those sounds. He felt something slightly askew, something not quite right as he worked these sounds into his score. Once he found the correct patterns, and once he understood the underlying emotions . . .

He kept coming back to his dream of the storm at New Year's, and the tree crashing through their window. The event puzzled him greatly, and he wasn't sure why. He believed now that the most important aspect of the dream was not the event, but the emotions tied to the event. If he could translate them into his music, he believed he would unlock the symphony's magic.

Okay then.

Finale.

28

A SECOND DOSE

WHEN KAT WOKE, SHE FORGOT WHERE SHE WAS AT FIRST. The headache pounding her skull brought it all back, and the cheap, thread-bare carpet she lay on confirmed it.

The Stoked Motel.

She sat up and winced. Automatically, she reached for the key around her neck, but it was gone. The mage had taken it. He'd surprised her outside her ground floor room, and she'd only had a moment to panic and run. He caught her though, and then something wet covered her face and she knew this was it as she breathed the fumes from the cloth and weakened. What was that stuff? Chloroform, she guessed. It wasn't like in the movies, because she struggled for several minutes while the mage kept saying "There, there" and "Easy, don't fight." She wasn't sure how long before she lost consciousness, but she remembered him guiding her back inside her room as she struggled. While unconscious he must've taken the key.

Oh, god. What about the box?

She'd opened it. Taken out a few packets of Moss. Took one. *God help me.*

The window shades were down, and it was dark in the room, but some light leaked through the edges of the shades. What time was it? She had planned on checking out the morning after she arrived.

Her head continued to throb. Not all the pain came from the

mage conking her on the head. She leaned a little so she could get into the pocket of her jeans. She'd stuffed the extra Moss packet in there.

As she struggled with the pocket, she stared at the door. It locked from the inside. She could just take off. Get far away from here.

"You're not going anywhere," a low voice said behind her, "and you won't find anything in your pocket."

Kat lowered her head, and she was on the verge of tears. But she held them back as a chair creaked behind her. Footsteps. Then the mage—the Moss Man—was in front of her. He crouched down.

In his hand he dangled the key. "Looking for this?"

She wasn't. She already knew it was gone. She'd been looking for the Moss. "Fuck you," she said. The same moment, she confirmed her pocket was empty. She'd taken the one packet just before all this happened, but there should've been one more. The mage had found that, too. She had no idea what the Moss would do to her or how she'd react, but so far, it had only caused her some extra head pain and made her feel a little drunk. She *knew* how it might affect the mage, though, and that worried her.

The man didn't react to her obscenity. He ran a finger through his stringy hair. "I lost my lucky cap at the chalet, thanks to you and Trip."

She looked at him with bleary eyes.

The ballcap. He hadn't found it. Good. Then she silently chastised herself. She didn't know if he had any Moss in his system. It had been too easy for him to deduce the Enchanted Valley location when he used the minimal power he had in his system out in front of Duffy's.

Don't think about things that could give you away.

"We found it," she said. "We saw the address in Bay Port," she said. Her words slurred a little.

"So you know the area. Big deal. I come and I go." He laughed. "Besides, it's okay if you know. Big place. Did you know the cops have even been out that way searching? But as I said, I can come and go. In fact, we're going there soon. Might not be as comfortable as this fine establishment, but it'll do in a pinch."

"You won't find—"

"What surprises me the most is why you thought you'd be able to come into my town and stay hidden. Didn't Allie tell you about spheres of influence? Hell, I had to track around the far side roads to avoid her own sphere to get here."

"I don't understand."

"Seems you took a little of the Moss, Kachina." He reached into his own pocket and pulled the Moss packet he'd taken from her. "Another gift for me, but I think you had at least one other packet you took yourself."

Kat barely followed the last sentence. Confused, she blinked. "Kachina?" she asked. "Who's Kachina?"

The mage grinned widely. "That's *you*. I heard you two love birds. I know you found the box and you were going to bring it to Allie. But your boyfriend said this strange name, and all the echoes made sense after that. Have *you* been hearing the echoes?"

"I have no idea what you're talking about." She did. She'd felt them more than once.

"There's been this sense of wrongness for a while now, ever since I first saw you sing at Duffy's Tavern." He shook a finger at her. "I think you did something. I think maybe your song and the Moss started us all over when I was about to successfully power up and breach the very planes of existence." He measured a half-inch with his pointer finger and thumb. "I was as-close-as-this to meeting my mother, I *know* it. Your name, which I heard during our little—*threesome*—finally clicked. Kachina. Ah, man, you fucked me *up*."

It was scary how much sense this made to her. It would explain a lot about everything that had happened with her and Truman. The muse he heard could've been the echoes of her own singing. His symphony a loop, a melody he heard that came from a version of her, which she had to learn from him all over again so she could echo it to him later. It made her head hurt even more just thinking about it.

"Where is the box? Hmmm? C'mon, I know you hoped to bring it to Allie. So where is it?"

Kat made up the first lie she could think of. "Destroyed. No one deserves to have that vile stuff."

He squinted at her, then shook his head slowly and deliberately. "No, not possible. I think you might've hidden it again. Maybe Allie came and retrieved it when you first arrived at this fleabag motel. But it's not destroyed."

Kat shrugged. "Believe whatever you want. I obviously don't have it. You searched me and my room, and you found nothing but a Moss packet and a key that no longer matters."

"I think it *does* matter, because you were still wearing it around your neck."

Kat showed no emotion. Said nothing.

The mage stood, knees creaking. "No matter. If it's at Allie's now, I can get to it. Your little present of Moss will help a lot."

"It won't be enough."

"Maybe not." He leaned down and pressed a finger to her temple. "But what you have here I can get at." He then caressed her throat. "And here. Your blood has power now. As does your song. It's not Truman I have to worry about."

"You should."

The mage scoffed. "A symphony. What a stupid idea, thinking the power of song can be caged in some abstract way. Your blood and your song's *vocality* does. My assistant proved that when he played something on his guitar other than fucking power chords."

"You can't take it from me."

"Oh, but I *can*, beautiful Kachina. Your blood sings with the real power of song and Moss. I'll take both from you when I'm ready." He held up the Moss packet he'd found in her pocket. "The two doses will be enough. After that, I'll no longer need to concern myself with Allie's puny sphere of influence."

"My—blood?"

"Don't worry. I've had a little practice at blood extraction. Your friend Serena gave her life for it."

"You bastard," Kat whispered. Her eyes watered. "She didn't deserve to die. She didn't deserve to deal with your evil *shit*."

"Were you really her friend?" he asked. He cocked his head as if waiting for an answer. "Did you even show up for her funeral?"

"You know I couldn't. It doesn't mean I didn't want to."

"When I was in middle school, I missed a lot of school. There was this big test coming up, see? My teacher said I couldn't miss it, or I'd fail. He said, 'The only excuse I'll accept is a funeral.' Then my teacher narrowed his eyes and said, 'Your *own*.'"

Kat had nothing to say back. She struggled with many emotions, and she fought back the tears associated with many of them. Mostly, though, she felt a sad resignation.

The mage reached, and with a hand under her arm, pulled her from her sitting position. "Well," he said. "Let's get ready for yours."

29

THE INTERROGATION

O N TRUMAN'S DAY OFF, A LIGHT KNOCK ON THE DOOR OF his bedroom interrupted him. He thought for a moment it might be Kat. No, she would've just walked in. He left the piano and opened the door.

Andrea stood there, looking grim.

"Hey," Truman said.

"You're needed downstairs," she said.

Truman shrugged. "What for? Is it Jacob?"

"No, it's someone else. An Aberdeen police detective is at the front desk and wants to talk to you." She left as soon as she delivered the news, leaving the door open. Truman stood still against the door jamb.

With the search ongoing, Truman knew it would be a matter of time before the police came to him. The day before, that detective, Medina, talked to Truman on the phone: How long have you known her? When was the last time you saw her? Where had she been going? Has she contacted you since?

Truman mentioned Aberdeen and her plan to meet a friend, but he didn't bring up Bay Port and Rural Route #2. Was it wrong of him to think the best thing he could do was keep the police from running into something they couldn't handle? He couldn't risk them breaking the magical connection the three of them had formed. Not yet.

He wondered what else he would say to the detective. He wondered if Medina was here to talk to him because of something they'd discovered. Had they found Kat, perhaps? Found her dead? Maybe he was a suspect. He shuddered, hating his line of thinking. He didn't want to believe she could be dead. She wasn't dead. *Couldn't* be dead. Would he be able to tell if something *did* happen to her?

He was nervous, but he couldn't keep the detective waiting. He took a deep breath and headed downstairs.

He hadn't met Medina, but he knew it was him. The detective stood on the other side of the front desk, wearing plain street clothes: jeans and a collared shirt, and a heavy jacket. The moment Truman came close to the desk, he smelled the cigarette smoke on the detective's clothes.

"Frank Medina," the detective said.

"Detective," Truman said from behind the desk, nodding. "I'm Truman." He hoped his voice didn't betray his nervousness.

"Hope it's okay to come out here like this," Medina said.

"Sure. Any luck finding Kat?"

He shook his head.

Truman waited for Medina to say something. The detective remained silent, so Truman said, "What can I help you with?"

Medina pulled a small notebook from his coat pocket and flipped a few of the pages. He put on some reading glasses, scanned the pages, read for a little bit, turned to another page, and read some more. He still didn't answer.

Any time, Truman thought, anxious for the man to speak. "I've still not heard from her," he said. "Is there something—"

"Where were you on Tuesday?" Medina said.

"Sorry?"

"The twenty-fourth. It was a Tuesday." He looked up from his notebook and peered at Truman over his glasses.

In the awkwardness of the moment, Truman honestly couldn't think of the date and failed to attach any significance to it. Truman shrugged. "I'm trying to remember. I guess I would've been here. I don't stray too far from the resort. I'm working on—"

"It was your day off, am I right?"

"Day off?"

"It was," Medina said.

Truman let out a nervous laugh. "Okay, if you say so."

Medina flipped back a page. "I talked to Jacob Platt, the owner of this place. Your boss, I guess you'd say."

"He's my friend."

"And your boss."

"Sure."

"On your day off, on the twenty-fourth, he says you asked him for his truck, and you went into Aberdeen."

Truman thought, Oh, *that* day off. He nodded, widening his eyes. "You're right. Yes, I did."

Medina stared at Truman, waiting for more.

Truman said, "Why did I go into town?"

Medina might have nodded.

Nothing to lose by telling the truth. Sort of. "I went looking for her."

"For Miss Gregory."

Truman nodded.

"This was the day after you phoned Andy Gregory asking about his daughter. You hadn't heard from her, and you asked him if *he* had heard from her. If he would try and touch base with her."

"I did."

"So naturally you went into town to look." Medina nodded as if he were answering for Truman. "You were worried about her."

"I was."

Medina scribbled a few notes. He frowned as he wrote them.

"I didn't find her," Truman said. "I didn't even know where to look."

"But you did look."

"Yes."

Did you know her friend? This Allie you mentioned on the phone last time?"

"No," he said truthfully.

"Her last name? Where she lived?"

"No. None of those."

"But you still drove into town to look. Aberdeen isn't a particularly large town, but it's still too big to just wander around town hoping to spot someone if you don't know where to look."

"That's fair."

Medina narrowed his eyes. Truman could tell he wasn't buying it. The detective had been way too fond of silences and odd looks. Straightening his back and his coat, Medina collected himself and made a quick glance around the room. Andrea sat at the desk behind the counter, pretending not to listen in on the detective's interrogation.

"So where did you go?"

"Go?"

"To look for her. Where'd you look?"

Truman shrugged again. "Around. Around town, driving the streets. You know. Hoping to get lucky and spot her. Like you said, it was unlikely I'd find her that way, but I thought I had to try."

"Any places you stopped at? Went inside to check? Ask anyone if they knew her? Or her friend?"

"A few. Nothing came out of any of those stops."

"How about outside the city limits? Did you search toward Ocean Shores? Or Elma? Bay Port?"

Truman tried to be as truthful as he could without giving the detective too much. "A little bit, but not far."

"A little bit."

"Yeah, a handful of miles each way."

Medina pursed his lips as he stared hard at Truman. Finally he waved the notebook as if acknowledging someone who had just waved to him. "All right," he said.

"Is that it?"

"That's almost it." He dove back into his notebook as if it were a lifeline. "Just . . . let me find . . ." He paused on a page a moment, then pointed at it, deliberately. "Oh yes."

Truman waited while the detective did his awkward silence thing again.

"What about the Stoked Motel? Did you search there?"

Truman swallowed, his skin tingling at the mention of the motel. He didn't know what to say, and Medina filled in the silence. He was apparently good at that too.

"Routine," Medina said. "Case like this, we check all the motels. At the Stoked Hotel—geez, you gotta love that name, don't you?" He mimicked smoking a joint, then shrugged. "We found out Kat stayed there."

"Of course. That much I knew. It was after that, when she didn't return calls or texts, that I came looking."

"She registered with your last name. That's surprising. You're not married. Yet, right?" He winked. "So an alias—your name—written down as if she didn't want anyone to know where she was or who she was. But it turns out she checked out before you arrived."

"Yes."

"Arrived at the Stoked Hotel on that Tuesday. You were there. Guy at the desk confirmed it. Identified your picture."

"You have my picture?"

Medina gave him a pained look.

Of course he did.

"Okay, so I searched there. So? She wasn't there. I moved on."

"Clerk remembered you asking a lot of questions about her."

"Why wouldn't I?"

Medina nodded sympathetically. "Of course."

Truman couldn't stand this push and pull any more. "Am I being accused of something?"

"You mean, did we find her dead, and the clues point to you?"

Truman just stared at Medina in answer.

"We're just trying to figure out what happened to her, that's all.

We're covering our bases." He held up his hands and managed the first smile Truman had seen from him. "It's what we do."

"Sure. I understand."

"Her friend was murdered before this, and, you know, we want to get to the bottom of things."

"Of course, detective. Of course."

"You got to know her pretty well, I understand."

Truman let out his own smile. "Yes. I care about her a lot."

"Love her?"

"I don't know if I know what love is anymore, but I think I do."

"You were married before."

"For a few years. In Seattle."

"Ex-wife's name?"

"Melissa." He did not say Hurricane Melissa.

"Melissa who?"

"Melissa Webb."

"She was out here not too long ago, wasn't she?"

Truman smiled. "You're pretty good, Medina. Yes, she was."

"It's what I do. Did she meet Kat?"

"Briefly."

"And why was your ex-wife here?"

"To tell me about her work."

"And what is her work?"

"Like me, she's a musician. She'd had some recent luck with a new symphony." He said that without any regret. If nothing else, Melissa had made him see that their stormy relationship had grown out of his own insecurities.

Medina inclined his head and smiled. "You're a musician?"

"Yes, and a composer. I'm writing my own symphony. I was working on it when you called me down."

"Any good?"

"I hope so. It's almost done."

"Well. Good luck with it."

"Thanks."

Medina sighed and put his notebook away. He took off his reading glasses and shoved those in his pocket too. "Thank you, Mr. Starkey."

"Truman, please."

Medina extended his hand and held out a business card. "Truman, thank you. If you think of anything, let me know."

Truman took the card. "Of course. I want to help if I can."

Medina stared hard into Truman's eyes, maintaining an uncomfortable silence. The little smile again, and he turned to go. He was halfway to the door when he started to rummage around in his pocket.

Considering how strong the odor of cigarette smoke was on the detective's clothes, Truman figured he was looking for his cigarettes so he could light up once he got outside. Truman wondered how long the detective could go without one.

Medina turned around, pulled his hands from his pockets, and snapped his fingers. "Ah. Now I remember." He came back to the desk, reaching inside his heavy jacket.

What he pulled out and showed Truman took him aback. He couldn't hide his reaction, a quick widening of his eyes and a single step back.

It was the mage's ballcap. The cap with RR#2 Bay Port written inside. The cap Kat had found on her father's desk, and the cap the ranger had found up at the chalet. Truman couldn't begin to understand how Medina could have it in his possession.

"Yeah," Medina said, the word drawn out. "You recognize this, don't you?"

Truman could deny it, but he figured Medina knew something about it, and would see through the lie. Better to play along and be as truthful as the situation would allow. Perhaps he could in turn find out more about the investigation. About Medina.

"I do," Truman said, ready to play detective himself. "Kat had it. How did you get it? Where did you find it? In Aberdeen?" He raised his eyebrows, for suddenly he realized that Kat could've taken it with her, and that was *exactly* how Medina had found it. "Aw, fuck. Do you think—"

Medina interrupted. "Did you see this partial address on the hat? Do you know where Bay Port is?"

"I do know. But a rural route is a fairly lengthy road."

"Did you go out there? Were you looking for her out there? Or did you take her out there? Is this *your* hat?"

Truman frowned, holding back the anger that bubbled up inside him. "So I *am* a suspect."

"I'm just asking questions, Truman. We haven't found Kat. We don't know if she is alive or dead."

He told the truth. "It's not my cap. Yes, I looked out there. I found nothing along the stretch of road I searched."

"Neither did we." Medina fiddled with the cap, holding it by the bill and turning it over and over. "So," he said, once again pointing the hat toward Truman, "you must know my obvious question."

"Whose cap is it?"

Medina smiled. "Whose cap, indeed."

Truth again: "We don't know his name. Kat found it on her dad's desk. A ranger found it up at the Enchanted Valley chalet and brought it down."

The cap landed right side up on the counter when Medina flipped it there. "Well now we're getting somewhere, aren't we?"

Truman could still stay close to the truth. "Listen. We don't know who he is. We hiked to the chalet and he was up there, and he threatened us. He had this ballcap on." A lie. "We got out of there, and later, Kat found it at the ranger station, as I said. The guy must've dropped it there. You still haven't told me where you found it."

Medina puzzled over the new information, scratching his head and rubbing his face. "When were you up at the chalet?" he asked, ignoring Truman's question.

"November."

"Awful late in the year to go up there."

"It was."

"Can you give me a description of this man?"

Truman did, the best he could.

"If need be, could you come to the station and work with a police artist?"

"Certainly."

"All that stuff at the chalet, and this hat. Is there any connection to Kat's disappearance?"

"I think it might be possible."

Medina picked up the hat and put it back in his jacket. "If this isn't yours, you won't mind if I hang onto it for a while."

Truman shrugged.

"To answer your question, we found it at the motel. Kat left it there. Why she did that, we don't know."

"Did she just forget it by accident, or was there foul play? The man from the chalet, perhaps."

"As a matter of fact, she brought it to the front desk the first night. Said she found it out in the hall and was turning it in to lost and found."

"That's strange."

"Maybe Kat left you a sign. A bread crumb or something."

"I honestly don't know."

Medina did his awkward silence thing again, then he smiled. "I've taken up too much of your time. I'll be heading out now. Call me if you think of anything, or if anything happens, or she contacts you."

"Of course."

The detective turned without any more pleasantries and left the store. When the door closed, Truman let out an audible sigh.

"That was interesting," Jacob said from behind him.

Truman turned. He hadn't known Jacob was there, in the back room, listening in. He nodded, then looked out the window, tracking Medina as he climbed into his car. "Just a little."

"I figured it was okay to tell him you went into town that day. He asked, and I just—"

"I know. It's okay. I'm still here, aren't I? I'm not handcuffed and in the back of his car."

"Small favors."

Truman nodded grimly. "I've got a lot of work to do upstairs."

"Symphony?"

Ideas arced across his brain, powering his thoughts like spark plugs. Truman expected the musical notation of his fourth movement to spread across the manuscript pages like oil on water. "Yeah. The big finale."

Jacob patted his shoulder. "Do your best, man. Before you know it, you'll be aching for that beer cooler next summer."

Honestly, he didn't know what he'd be doing a week from now, let alone next summer.

Kachina just had to sing her song and share her melody. Truman would listen more closely than ever, and in the magic of his muse and the uncertainty of the Unholy Trinity, he would find his music's heart.

30

TINA'S FIRE

RAINS CAME WITH A FURY.

On some days, the downpour matched Truman's first day in Quinault, when he escaped the deluge by huddling against the side of the gas station. That day when he first heard Kachina and the voice of the mage. Or rather, the *other* version of the mage.

He'd wondered if Kachina's voice would stay strong during Truman's newest composing sessions, and not be drowned out by the rain's intensity. He also didn't have the reassuring physical presence of Kat, who had learned the melody of her own ghost, and she'd even managed to help Truman with some of the instrument voicings.

That reminded him of his loss. Kat an integral part of his music magic was missing. He didn't dare wait any longer to finish his symphony.

Yes, the rains came down.

But there were no voices.

It was hard to believe. He panicked almost immediately. Kachina's voice was missing from the rain just as sure as Kat was missing in Aberdeen.

He needed to tackle the fourth movement, but he had lost his muse. With her voice completely absent from the rain, he wouldn't be able to depend on her.

He would have to finish on his own.

Melissa was right; emotion in music usually trumped structure. *You've never found that emotional center.*

Heart.

She'd called it a wound. Heal, she implied, and turn genius into magic. He'd felt the start of this as his scherzo took shape. He'd breathed some of that magic into the music by piggybacking off Kachina.

Now Truman would have to find that magic without her. Kat had hinted that he should be able to do it on his own when she talked about Truman's magic balancing hers and the mage's. It meant he was just as powerful as the other two. On the other hand, if he was the balance between the two, was his magic potentially greater than each of theirs?

He had to realize that potential now, with Kat gone, Kachina gone . . . even the mage was gone.

The fourth movement—the finale—was his alone to discover. He would pull from his past. His life, his tragedies, his hopes and fears—

He already had a good start on all that.

The timing was perfect, for he had a few days off. He stayed upstairs at the piano. He didn't let himself get distracted, working on the symphony nearly non-stop. He didn't sleep much. Jacob warned him about overdoing it and suggested he back off a little. But he didn't. He kept up his frenzied pace, and when he became stuck, he pushed even harder. After months with his muse by his side, he fumed about her absence now.

During a difficult day, struggling to move forward with the fourth movement, he borrowed Jacob's truck. He couldn't look for Kat, but that didn't mean he couldn't look for *Kachina*.

He drove to the far side of the lake to the spot where she'd first appeared, back before he understood any of this, when she insisted he finish his symphony and hike to Enchanted Valley during the full moon.

He left the truck and made his way to the clearing. It was raining lightly, for now. During their conversation, Kachina had explained how she was anchored to this place and couldn't leave. She avoided his touch and wouldn't take things from him. In the end, she disappeared, but he believed she remained in some way.

Truman frowned as he searched the area anxiously. What if she had stopped singing because she had vanished from this plane? Had she been pulled back unwillingly, or had she simply run out of time?

He called out to her, but he heard only the rain on the foliage. Singing her melody didn't bring her out, either. After a half hour his gut told him she had left this plane.

The walk back to the truck was agonizingly slow, because he still hoped she'd show up and say "Sorry I'm late!" But she didn't, and he climbed into the driver's seat and shut the door on her anchor spot for good. He didn't start the truck. He sat unmoving, staring out the windshield into the darkness. After a while, as he gave in to fatigue, he thought he might just wait, maybe even spend the night here. He didn't know why.

He fell asleep.

The fire is big enough now that he fears the smoke will choke him. The flames threaten to engulf the living room as they gather fuel and burn brighter.

But Tina is closer to the fire than he is. Long before the fire comes to Truman, she will be die from the flames that even now lick at her skin. He's surprised the heat and smoke haven't woken her.

Her robe catches fire.

"Tina!" he cries. He can't reach her, and she's still out cold.

The fabric in the robe burns slowly. Probably it is made of a fire-resistant material. It only delays the inevitable. The fire has jumped easily enough to the fallen tree and the crackle of fire spreads among its branches.

It is too late for Tina.

The fire has wrapped her in deadly orange and red, choked her with heat and smoke. Truman looks on in horror. He believes he can hear skin charring. It's a blessing, he thinks, that she's unconscious and can't feel what's happening to her.

But then she wakes up.

He expects screams, but that doesn't happen. Tina calmly rises to a sitting position and peers out at Truman, a halo of fire all around her.

"You should probably get out of here now," she says in her young, innocent voice.

Truman makes a last-ditch effort to stretch and reach her, but nothing helps him get any closer. And what if he did? She is a torch now, more dangerous than the tree that fell on him.

That thought is soon tempered by what Tina does next. She gets to her feet and comes to him. *She reaches out with a fire hand and touches his arm. Somehow, he can see her sweet smile through the flames, and somehow, the fire does not catch on his own clothes. He can feel the heat of the fire elsewhere in the room, but Tina's fire is different. It is cold, and the color has shifted to a brighter white.*

"Leave," Tina says. "Save yourself."

Truman's heart aches for her. "I was responsible for you."

She shakes her head. Sparks spit. "You were never responsible for me. I've only been an impossibility. It's someone else you're responsible for."

"No. It's you." He shivers, even in the ever-increasing heat of the fire around him. Standing this close to Tina, though, her white fire protects him.

She laughs, a response so opposite to the emotion she should have, he shrinks back from her.

"Tina?"

"You silly," she says in a child-like voice, as if chastising him for being in this situation in the first place. "You're on your own now. Find your way."

She pauses, suddenly serious. Her face is angelic even in the hellish flames that nearly obscure the rest of her from view.

"I can't," Truman says. "Not without you."

"Truman, it's okay! If you love her, you'll find her."

"Her?"

"It's not me. It never has been."

She is dazzling in her white coat of flames. After a moment, she crouches and wraps her arms around her legs until she's a little ball, cold light making her shimmer like the moon.

The moon turns away from the sun.

She disappears, and he begins to weep.

Truman hesitates only a moment. His cage of branches gives way, allowing him to flee the fire, and he runs from the house and casts himself into the storm. Jagged light slashes across his face. The headlights of a car. Have his parents finally come home? Soon, they would open the doors and run to him, yelling his name, asking if he's all right, Oh Truman, my god, we should've never left you alone, what happened, are you sure you're okay? Are you sure?

Alone?

He looks back at the house, wondering what happened to . . . to . . . who else had been in there? Only now, he realizes the smoke has caught up to him. He hasn't taken a full breath for a while, and he coughs, hacking loudly, bent over.

"Son? Are you Truman? Truman Starkey?"

Truman straightens. A police officer looks him over, frowning.

"There's someone—" Truman points at the house.

"There's been an accident," the officer says.

The house is whole. There's no fire, no tree crashed through the window.

"It's your parents."

But . . . he had seen everything. *And he has managed to save—*
Himself.

꧁

Truman woke up in the truck to the roar of rain. Sheets of water obscured his windshield and hammered at the roof of the cab. It was all oddly soothing, but he still found himself crying, his body aching with emotion.

The dream solidified into a memory, which rewired his brain to match this reality. Well, of *course*. He knew the reality:

He didn't have a sister.

He was an only child.

The emotions from that stormy day caught up to him. They had locked themselves away after that, leaving only the sounds associated with them. He'd locked away the helplessness. Put aside the visceral feeling of being trapped.

Then who was Tina? In the dream she'd been a young girl, and now that he thought about it, he didn't know how he'd missed it. The girl was a young version of Kat, he was sure. He'd tried to pull her from the fire to protect her.

There hadn't been a fire.

Truman had transplanted Kat, and Melissa, and even his mom, into the dream, creating Tina to cope with his loss. He met Kat, felt so strongly for her, felt so *responsible* for her safety, that it perpetuated the sister dream. He had never lost a sister.

He had lost his mother.

His father had sustained minor injuries in the car accident, but his mother had not been so lucky. He'd been alone. His mother passed away, and he refused to believe it. He tucked the memory away. People knew about his mother, of course. It's not like he didn't tell people a little if the topic came up, but he wouldn't say *much* to them. Even Jacob knew about his mom. And Melissa. He'd awkwardly excuse himself. Push talk of his mother away. Early trips to therapists and psychologists his dad took him to failed to break repressed feelings he'd buried. He may have understood it in his youth at its basest level, but for whatever reason now, the dream manifested in his subconscious as protection against the loss.

At least that's what he guessed the dream to be. It could've been a warning. It could've been a plea. Or a reminder of how alone he'd been while his parents were away on New Year's. It was his past, but it was also his future. Perhaps in some other plane of existence, he *did* have a Tina.

He now felt certain of the emotions he needed to bring heart to his music. To finish the symphony and power it with magic. He had never found a way to express his grief for his mom. He needed to find the way. Needed to find his way to her.

He sat in the truck cab and took this all in. He had endured a lot during his childhood, his young adult years, and his adult life. The New Year's Eve storm. Hurricane Melissa. The Quinault rains that insisted he listen to them when he first arrived. The mage, and Kat, and Kachina, and his symphony.

His life had been a series of storms. He had weathered them all, and now, after a fresh start, after nearly four movements, he had to endure the biggest storm of all.

Meaning filtered through, and suddenly he knew what the dream really was. The dream was a message.

You're on your own now. Find your way.

If you love her, you will find her.

31

≫

THE SKETCH

W HEN TRUMAN HAD HIS NEXT CHANCE TO SIT DOWN AND compose, he did so for six hours straight, fueled by the dream and its message, pushed to his limits by Kat and Kachina, who were not even there.

Staying up late, he wrote deliberately, sometimes slowly, sometimes feverishly. He had to be at the front desk in the morning, but he found the zone and kept plugging away. A few times during the session, he nodded off at the piano, but every time he shook off sleep and returned to the music score, he made a little more progress.

By one o'clock in the morning, the overall shape of the fourth movement came to him, as did the ending, and he stayed wide awake until four o'clock. Freed now from the dream he'd dreamt since meeting Kat, he gathered up all its bits and pieces and threw it at the symphony. Even when he climbed into bed, he couldn't sleep. The music insisted he listen, and as he did, more elements of the recapitulation and the coda revealed themselves.

The next morning, he felt obliged to bore Andrea about his breakthrough on the fourth movement. He elaborated on specific details about his fight with fatigue, glorifying the creative process along the way. When Jacob came in a bit later, he repeated the whole story.

Jacob told him to take it easy.

But he didn't. After his shift, Truman went right back to the symphony and did nothing else until he passed out from exhaustion.

He was well into the development of the movement. No sign of Kat. No music from Kachina. No contact with the mage. He thought about going into town again to look for Kat, but her unspoken words insisted he think of nothing else but the music.

Truman had no idea if he'd be able to tell, when the time came, how the magical potential of his symphony would kick in. When the last notes were written? Or sometime before then?

He worried, too, about the way to initiate the magic. That detail had completely stymied him. It wasn't a laughing matter, but he had this funny scene in his head about strapping the mage in a chair and surrounding him with musicians of the Grays Harbor Symphony Orchestra, Truman directing the performance of the symphony live in front of him. Releasing a wall of sound over the mage, mocking him, and telling him: "Silence *that*, you piece of shit."

He couldn't picture how an actual performance of the piece could slow down the mage. He'd expected Kachina would tell him when the time came, but she was gone. For now. He'd been optimistic that she would show up, prepared to help. What if she didn't? What could he do?

Find your way.

A hell of a lot easier to say than do.

In the end, he'd do everything he could think of to wrap up the symphony.

※

Truman ended up going into Aberdeen after all, the next day.

Not to look for Kat—although he'd keep his eyes open as he cruised the road through town—but because Detective Frank Medina finally asked him to come in to help with the police sketch. Truman wondered why Medina had waited so long to call him in. Perhaps the investigation had stalled. What had prompted the detective to get the sketch done now? Maybe they could find the mage, although it made Truman nervous to think so. What could the police do to the mage? Shoot him, he guessed. Shoot him down before he brought his magic into play. *If* he had captured Kat and had the box of Moss.

Truman pulled into the police station parking lot close to noon.

The next hour he gave details of the mage to the police artist. The artist, a middle-aged woman with light red hair, dressed neatly in police uniform, politely asked questions about the man she needed to draw. At the same time, she answered Truman's own questions about her job, her drawing ability, her family, and what she knew about the case. Very little, it turned out. She continued to edit the drawing, working it until Truman said she had it down pretty well. It was realistic, and looked quite a lot like him, right down to the ballcap. She smiled, thanked him, and left the room with the drawing.

"Thanks for coming in and doing this," Medina said when he walked into the interview room ten minutes after she'd left. Medina wore the same clothes he'd worn at the resort. The same heavy coat, wearing it even inside the station. He had the sketch in one hand, and a manila folder in the other.

"She's pretty good," Truman said.

Medina looked up. "Hmmm? Good?"

"Your artist. Colleen."

Medina slapped the manila folder down on the table and kept the sketch in hand. He scrutinized it through half-lidded eyes. "Yeah, she sure is." He dropped it on the table and pulled his cigarettes from his coat. "Do you mind?"

"They let people smoke in here?"

"They let *me* smoke in here."

Truman shrugged his go-ahead.

Medina lit his cigarette and picked up the sketch again. He blew out smoke from the side of his mouth. "So this comes pretty close to the man in the chalet."

"Very close."

"He was wearing the hat while he was there?"

"Most of the time."

"And you said he threatened you. You actually never said how he did that."

"He was up there at the chalet. We came upon him, and he came after us."

Medina took out a tiny cup from his coat and placed it on the table. He flicked his cigarette ashes in there and took another puff.

What the hell *didn't* he have in that coat?

"Came after you, how?"

And now Truman had to make up some details. He obviously couldn't tell Medina the whole truth. "He saw us, swore at us, and swung this big walking stick over his head, as if he were winding up to throw it at us or come at us with it. He said we were trespassing on his property—"

"It's a National Park."

"Yeah, I know. I mean, he seemed like a crazy street person, to be honest. We were a little nervous about him, but not overly frightened." *That* was a lie. "We decided to turn around and go back to our base camp down the trail."

"And he didn't follow you."

"No."

Medina put down the sketch and stared at the ceiling, frowning. "Let me get this straight. This guy threatens you, yells at you, whatever. This was outside the chalet?"

Truman nodded a moment before he realized where Medina was going with this.

"The hat was found inside the chalet. How did it get in there? You didn't go inside?"

Yeah, he was good. "No. It was locked up, I think. And after we saw him—"

"You just boogied out of there."

"Yeah. So maybe he found a way in?"

"Maybe so, maybe so."

Truman fidgeted in his chair, and he realized he'd sat there a long time.

Medina noticed. "You need to stand? You need a coffee or something?"

"No, I'm okay." He willed himself to get through this newest interrogation.

Medina nodded and found his little notebook in his coat pocket. Reading glasses next, forced on with one hand. He worked his routine, taking his time with multiple page flips, pauses, silence, even *more* flipped pages, a few grunts and pursed lips—the whole almost-clichéd brooding cop thing—and made Truman stew a bit longer.

"Honestly, Truman," he said, blowing out more smoke. He stubbed out his cigarette in the little cup. "I'm really at a loss with this case. As good as the information you gave us is, as much help as I've received from Kat's dad, and others, things aren't adding up." He leaned back in his chair and—continuing the cliché—put his feet up on the desk.

Truman said, "It's puzzling—"

"You're lying to me."

Truman stopped, surprised by the interruption, surprised by the accusation. "What?"

"You're not telling the truth. Hell, you might be making this whole thing up."

"Not true." *Only some of it.*

Medina pulled his feet off the desk and stood abruptly. Once again, his big coat of holding revealed another wrinkle, a photograph. He put it on the table and slid it over to Truman. "Recognize this kid?"

Jesus Christ. Truman did, and he was certain his surprised expression and body language told Medina he did, too. It was a photograph of Dennis Reynolds. Pretty clean cut in this picture, smiling, looking like a happy kid.

"Truman?"

Truman eyed the photo another few seconds, then nodded. "Yeah."

"Dennis Reynolds. You know him how?"

"I'm guessing you already know."

Medina was silent.

"I gave him lessons. Guitar lessons. But he stopped abruptly."

"That was that, but that was *when*?"

Truman had to think back a moment. "Early August."

"Quite a while ago, then."

Truman nodded.

"His dad called us," Medina announced. "Said Dennis had taken some time off from playing guitar, thinking he might get some work in town. But one night he didn't come home. He showed up a few days later, but then a few days after that he left again. And now he's not been home for several months. This started right around the time he took those guitar lessons."

"And then my name came up."

"Your name came up." Medina sat back down. "In fact, I was the one who brought it up. During our last visit you said you were a musician, so I gave your name a try."

"Certainly not out of the ordinary. I didn't lie to you about it."

"Mr. Starkey. Truman. You're obstructing justice here."

"I just gave him lessons—"

"Stop."

Truman stopped.

"Your co-worker Andrea Moore said Dennis came into the store one day when you were there. He was accompanied by another man. A man she said gave both of you the willies."

"I remember Dennis in the store."

"With this man. A man that, according to Andrea's description of him, looks an awful lot like this character sketch here." He tapped the paper with a forefinger. "Right down to the Olympic Rainforest ballcap."

Truman didn't know what to say. Medina had shit on him now.

What *could* he say? He had to come clean, didn't he?

"You didn't just see this man at the chalet. You've seen him at least one other time. Maybe more."

Truman squeaked out, "Once at a football game. Briefly."

"Was Dennis Reynolds with him then, too?"

"He was."

"And at the chalet?"

"Yeah."

Medina leaned way back in the chair, the front legs danger-ously leaving the floor. "How about Kat Gregory?"

Truman shot a glance at Medina. "What about her?"

"Was she with them, too? Is she involved with one of those two? Are you all involved in something? Jesus, Truman, you've got to help me out here."

Truman couldn't tell Medina more. Not about the evil mage, or the voices in the rain, the synthesized magical drugs, sex magic, enchanted boxes, and magic-infused symphonies. The detective would call him insane and lock him up.

How much *could* he tell Medina? The detective kept pushing for more, and the closer he got to the truth about Kat, the more it kept Truman from finishing the symphony. It might help the detec-tive find her, but that wouldn't end well if the mage had his power back. What could he say that would help Medina, but allow him to stay true to his vision and his efforts to destroy the mage and rescue Kat? What truths would keep Medina, Kat, and himself safe?

"Honestly?" Truman finally said.

"That would be nice for a change."

"I really don't know his name. But he's looking for some drugs he was promised. He thinks Kat has them, or her friend has them."

"Allie."

"I've never met Allie, and I don't know where she is. I know that Dennis Reynolds is with this guy, helping him out. He might even be trapped himself, unable to find a way to flee that situation. My guess is that this guy found Kat and is holding her. Looking for

Allie, wanting his drugs. That's why I went into town. Try to find her. She's in a lot of danger, but I don't know what to do."

"Not lying would've been a good thing to do."

"I didn't tell you about it because he threatened me once about her. At the football game. He told me not to help her. That there would be consequences."

What Truman told him these last few minutes was true. He held back what he could, for now. Having the Aberdeen police involved seemed like a good thing on the surface, but not if Kat, or Dennis, or any innocent bystander was killed in the process.

After a long pause, Medina sighed. He sighed as if he'd just made up his mind about something. He had. "There was an incident a while back. A man was brought into the hospital ER bleeding from the gut. He woke, feverish, and rambled on and on about crazy shit no one could figure out. He mentioned a name, though, pretty clearly. Bill Hand."

Truman shrugged. "Who's Bill Hand?"

"Pretty dangerous guy in town. He's the head of the local drug trade."

"Shit."

"No ID on the guy who came into the ER, and at some point, he snuck out. Or maybe someone snuck him out." Medina tapped the sketch. "This could be that guy. I'm taking the sketch over to the hospital and show it to the ER staff who were on duty that night. If it's the same guy—and I bet it is—then we at least know his name."

Truman almost missed that. "I'm sorry. His name?"

"Plenty of files on Bill Hand's crew. Known associates and all that. Plus, plenty of time for quick-thinking docs to get his prints when he came up as a John Doe."

"So who is he?"

"Name's Joel Hines. That may be a false name, but as far as Bill Hand's organization goes, that's how he's known."

Joel Hines. *Evil mage Joel Hines.* Truman's blood ran cold. "So then they have an address for him, right?"

"Nope."

"And what about that Bay Port address?"

"Didn't find anything. He may have a motorhome or something. We've checked trailer parks and the like, but nothing."

Hines. Joel Hines. Truman let that name roll around in his brain. He wanted to feel it on his tongue. "Joel Hines."

"Ring any bells?"

"Not a one, I'm afraid."

Medina nodded, slowly. "Well, it's more than we had when I first talked to you. Your answers then actually helped."

"Glad I could. I need Kat found, but this Hines guy worries me. No one should face him."

"What?"

"Alone, I mean. Not face him alone."

Medina waved a hand. "Maybe. But guys like him are probably bottom feeders in an organization like Hand's. He probably fucked up somehow and Hand set up an ambush for him. If found out, or cornered, guys like Hines will fall to pieces."

If Hines really was the mage, that was not true at all.

"So," Medina said, "you work in Quinault, write your sonata—"

"Symphony."

"—symphony, as if nothing ever happened."

"What? No. I *searched* for her. I'm fucking forty minutes away from Aberdeen. I work at the resort, and I can't go in every day. You said it yourself: it was unlikely I'd find someone in the city just wandering around."

"Is the music . . . I don't know. Cathartic for you?"

Saying it *was* cathartic seemed as good an answer as any. "Yes, it is. I lose myself in the music. In fact, it's based on a melody that Kat sang when I first met her."

"Interesting. What kind of song?"

The detective was thorough, Truman gave him that. "A short melody, very dream-like. She never said where it came from."

Medina did his staring thing again.

Truman raised an eyebrow. "What?"

"About Hines," Medina answered. "Nurse said when he woke he kept trying to hum a song. Same notes over and over."

Truman felt ice run up his spine.

Medina leaned forward and thunked his chair back onto four legs. He snagged the drawing again, looked at it, then dropped it into the manila folder. When he stood, the chair legs squeaked against the floor.

"Am I done?" Truman asked.

"You mean, are you free to go?"

"Instead of being held and locked up for 48 hours."

Medina smiled. "No need for that. You weren't completely truthful, but you didn't try and hide the matter either. I believe what you've said, and I know where you live."

"I know. Don't leave town."

"Too late. You're here in Aberdeen, aren't you?"

"Aberdeen, Quinault, and in between, okay?"

It was Medina's turn to say, "Fair enough." He lit up another cigarette and said goodbye.

And that was it. Truman left the station, tooled around Aberdeen for a while, surveyed the side streets and sidewalks, and eventually drove back to the resort.

His shift was over. Andrea glared at him, probably expecting he would be back earlier. He offered to take the rest of her shift, but she softened and said no, he should go and write.

He tried. Nothing gelled for him, the voices of the various instruments having a hard time competing with Medina's voice, which continued to ask, over and over, pointed, erudite questions about Kat's disappearance. But what came through the most was the name of the mage. *Joel Hines*.

Little by little, Detective Frank Medina's understanding of the case had grown, as if aided with the whispers of magic of the others. In a way, he had worked his own brand of magic.

Where are you, Joel Hines?

32

THE MIRROR

*F**INALE**.*
  This was it.

He'd started the fourth movement by taking Kachina's theme from the first movement and fitting it into the mosaic of the exposition, sliding back and forth with different tones and different dynamics.

Each time he heard Kachina's music, sadness overwhelmed him, and he'd return to his thoughts of Kat and where she might be. This also dredged up the echoes of the fragmented dream. Somehow, he knew this last movement had to incorporate the tragedy of his mother's death and the sorrow he felt when he came out of the dream. This emotion was also at the heart of his music. It was a search for the memories of his mother and Kat both.

If you love her, you will find her.

In the second part of the movement, the development, he recalled the *adagio*. Slower. Hesitant and somewhat grating due to the larger presence of the mage. He still thought of him as the mage instead of Joel Hines. He did not conjure up his name willingly.

The third part, the recapitulation, pulled the dance rhythms of his scherzo seamlessly, and the hypnotic beat drove the movement toward its conclusion.

And now all hell broke loose.

The fourth movement's structure as its own mini symphony

reached a wild, chaotic climax. Pushed inexorably forward, an acceleration to a sudden yet fitful full stop. Started again with a sudden explosion of sound in an ordered progression that contained all the emotions he could gather, but in stages, so it wouldn't collapse under its own weight.

He slashed with his pencil and dropped the final notes of the fourth onto his staff paper. He sighed, smiled, and blinked away tears misting his eyes. It could've been his imagination, but the air itself seemed to pause, as if during his last scribbling it had been sucked out of the room. His ears popped.

A low rumble of thunder.

"Whoa," Truman whispered. *That* was cool.

The final note of the movement's—and therefore the symphony's—momentum needed resolution. It needed to find its way home. He'd write a coda to do that. A coda—the word meant "tail"—singled out a passage that brought the piece to its conclusion. Truman's coda would look back on the rest of the piece, allowing the listener to take it all in and, hopefully, experience the real magic of the symphony:

Balance.

Later that night, Truman was awakened by a storm.

The thunder that rumbled when he finished the fourth movement gave way to a louder, more powerful force. The rain slashed at his window and pounded on the roof. The noise of it was impressive, the feeling of it ominous. He left his bed, and as he made his way to the window, he glanced briefly at the mirror on the wall, half expecting he'd see something unusual. He didn't. He stared out the window at a safe distance, feeling certain the intensity of the rain could crack the glass. Only once had he seen it rain this hard, and it hadn't been from any storm in Quinault.

It had been the New Year's Eve storm, waiting at home for

his parents, learning of his mother's death. Later, he dreamed the dream of the sister he did not have.

He was tempted to open the double-hung window, but the rain would see that as an invitation and blow in and invade the room. He stared out at the street and the lounge beyond, barely visible, camouflaged by the heavy rain.

It was then that Truman heard the music.

He closed his eyes and smiled as the music flowed into the room, unconcerned with the double-hung window or the rain that brought it.

Kachina.

Oh, it was good to hear her voice. He listened, eyes still closed, and within her simple but exotic melody, he heard all its permutations. All the subtleties and variations that he'd worried over and placed in his symphony were there, layered atop each other, but distinct enough for anyone to hear, if they'd only listen.

The thing was, he didn't need them anymore.

He had hastened forward on his own, his muse's contribution complete. He'd pulled from his life, his tragedies, his heart.

He leaned into the window, but he didn't need to do that to hear better. The song—and then he realized there were also *words*—were coming through loud and clear.

Truman, she sang. *Truman, are you there?*

It had been quite some time since he'd recognized words in her music, so when he heard them now, he was surprised at their clarity.

"I hear you!"

Listen. My power is weak, the drugs are wearing off, and I will be pulled back.

What kind of power now allowed her to speak so fully to him? So intensely? "Back to where? The mage?"

A gust of wind pushed more rain against the window and rattled the pane of glass.

Back to me. Back to—

Joel Hines.

Of course. Somewhere in Aberdeen, Hines had found Kat, but Kat had somehow taken Moss. But when? Kat had decided to risk taking them. Why?

To communicate with him. Truman clutched his chest; his heart was beating too fast. Dear god, it wasn't Kachina speaking to him. It was *Kat*.

"Where are you?" he asked, raising his voice needlessly. "Kat, where *are* you?"

Come prepared.

"I'm done, Kat. The symphony is done. Just the coda and some quick rewriting to do. I can hurry and—"

Don't rush the magic.

"—when it's done, I'm coming for you."

You know where I am, Truman.

She paused, and her silence seemed to tell him the answer. "You're out on Rural Route #2, aren't you?

Somewhere, yes. You know it's a long stretch of road. You must face him alone. There's nothing any of the authorities could do. They wouldn't last long if they were within his sphere of influence. They would only muddy the magic.

"If they came in full force—"

They can't come out there at all, Truman. He's taken some of the Moss I took from the box, just in case. That alone will make him strong against any cops. They were out there once, but the mage was absent from the place.

"I've already been out there. I couldn't find you."

You weren't supposed to look. He's going to get more of the Moss from me.

His heart sank. "Did he find the box? Is it open?"

He didn't find it. He'll get the Moss from my blood. And then my song.

Truman closed his eyes, fighting back the tears. "No, Kat. Oh, no." He opened his eyes and clenched his teeth hard. "Fight him."

I'll try, but it won't work without you.

"I know I can find you. I've already been there, I'm sure. The exact location. I was there but didn't know it."

I shouldn't have taken the drugs. I wanted to talk to you, but I shouldn't have taken the risk.

"Yes, you should have. I'm glad you did."

It's taking all my concentration to reach out to you. I must keep myself away from the darkness, though, and it's taking a toll on me. This will be the last time I talk to you.

Truman thought, no, she would talk to him again.

"Kat, listen. Medina figured out his name. It's Hines. Joel Hines. Maybe knowing that helps somehow."

Hines. Yes, that's good, Truman.

"The symphony. I don't know how to use it. How do I wield it against him? It doesn't make a lot of sense, no matter what method I consider."

I don't know. You'll discover its magic on your own.

Truman thought he'd already done that. It still didn't help him understand how to access its magic.

"Help me, Kat. I don't know what to do with it. It's practically finished, but will that make a difference? I know what's infused within, now. But how will I unlock it?

Find your way.

"I don't think I can."

If you love her, you will find her.

"That's you, Kat. I love *you*, Kat."

And I love you. But you know who you've really been looking for. The tragedy and the sorrow you have to purge. The music in your soul is worth nothing if locked away, cold and unyielding. Choose the right path. Find her, and in the process, you'll keep the mage from finding himself. You'll destroy him.

"And save you."

She didn't answer, and he panicked, wondering if she knew something he didn't about surviving this ordeal.

Goodbye, Truman.

The music stopped abruptly, and even the storm died a little. Kat had used the power of the drugs to send her ghost, as it were, to talk to him in the same plane. She hadn't crossed over into another plane to communicate. She'd probably been able to do that because Kachina, her future self, had come back from her plane to merge again with Kat, perhaps when Hines had captured her.

He looked at his hands, and they were shaking. When he turned away from the window, he looked into his mirror and his skin crawled. He backed up a step.

The mage had ghosted into the mirror.

For a long time, the man didn't speak. He stared out at Truman. Truman sidled to the left, but Hines' eyes stayed focused on one spot. Hines couldn't *actually* see him. The mage's mouth moved, but it was as if Truman watched a video with the sound turned down.

Hines didn't have enough power to break through completely, Truman guessed. What was he saying with those unintelligible words? Were they instructions? A warning? A challenge?

Even this weaker display of power had to have come from the mage's own magic, enhanced by Moss. He had taken some, as Kat had said.

A wave of helplessness washed over him. Was he too late?

My power builds and you can't stop me.

The words, barely audible, were weak and halting, but they belonged to Hines. Truman stepped closer to the mirror, but still couldn't be sure Hines could see him.

Do you think your music will do me in . . . Tip-enade?

Did he know about the symphony? Or was he just referring to Kachina's song and didn't have a clue about the symphony? The mage answered that question with his next words.

That music you're writing won't hold up, and you know it. You have no clue how to unleash that kind of magic, and your muse can't help you, even if you managed to put magic in there in the first place.

Truman thought about staying quiet, not sure Hines could hear him anyway. Let the bastard wonder about him. But he couldn't do it. He had to talk to him. He spoke forcefully, keeping his voice low. As menacing as he could make it. He'd made the conscious choice to go look for Kat, as dangerous as it had been. When he came back, defeated, he focused on finishing the music, and he'd promised to send the mage to hell, in whatever way he could. Perhaps it was false bravado, but he didn't think so. Everything he'd done since then had been a step toward a certain bravery he never knew he'd had.

"I'll find you and take Kat from you," he said aloud, "and you won't have a chance against my music, you son of a bitch."

The mirror was silent for a few seconds, and the figure of the mage turned slightly in Truman's direction, as if he'd suddenly spotted him. It was unnerving to watch, but Truman held his ground, standing tall.

Come on, then, Tip-orwhill. He grinned unnaturally. *I have Kat—or should I say Kachina, my sacred dancer? I've got some plans for her.*

"If you harm her, I'll kill you, Joel Hines."

There was a pause as the mage raised both eyebrows and slowly released a smile. *Oh, big man. Found out my name, did you? Did that cop tell you? Hmm? Medina?*

"I don't care if you're Joel Hines the mage, or ugly fuck with the stupid ballcap."

You'll try to kill me even if I don't *harm her, won't you? Don't worry, Tip Top. She's just going to go for a swim. That depends on the tide, of course.*

Hines laughed and his face zoomed as his mirror image leaned toward Truman's space.

You can bring your music, Tippy Toes. We can have some pleasant tunes, and we'll play in the mud until the tide comes in. What do you think?

"You're underestimating me."

I don't think so. I've known about your pathetic symphony since you and Kat bumped uglies during the full moon and you guessed the location of the Moss box. I was confused at first, but Kat is right. We're connected now. You can't do anything without me knowing what's going on.

"You can't know everything we're thinking. You can't simply read our minds."

Can't I?

"You have no idea what I can do. Yeah, we're connected, and because of that, I know how to use your strength against you and ignore your bullshit."

Well come on, then, Mr. True Man.

"You inviting me over?"

Do you need the address? Service is weak out here and I'm not sure the GPS is very accurate, so if you need directions, just say the word.

"You son of a bitch."

That's four words, Tipster.

"Rural Route #2," Truman said, thinking he'd get a reaction.

Oh, Hines said without pause, *you found my hat, did you?*

"See, you *don't* know everything. Want to be more specific than a rural route that's miles long?"

You know where I am, Tippie Canoe. Think hard. You were here once already.

Truman had guessed right when his gut told him he'd been close. "I didn't see anything."

Next time, Hines said, his wide grin back, *you will.*

There was a grand pause. Then:

See you out here, Tip & Dip. And beware the speed trap outside Aberdeen. He laughed, and soon after, his shape misted away in the mirror. *I look forward to our reunion.*

33

THE FIFTH WHEEL

THE CODA PRACTICALLY WROTE ITSELF. AT THIS POINT, TRU-man had all he needed musically to end the symphony. The main body of his symphony reached its climax, and after a great deal of effort to work it to an obvious structural conclusion, the coda simply pulled those beats from each movement. He kept right on composing after his conversations with Kat and the mage.

The conversations still lingered in his memory; here they were again, the three of them together, the three of them playing out their own structural dance. The Unholy Trinity at work. Hines had invited Truman to face him. Kat had told him she wouldn't have enough power to stop the mage. He didn't know how much time he had, but it couldn't be long. He might already be too late.

It was midnight when he finished the coda. He scanned his room, and the pages of staff paper lay around the room in small piles: on the floor, the piano, the bed. He knew where each page fit. Even if they fell accidentally and scattered, he could easily collect them up again in the right order.

Truman's life was in these pages. His love, his hate, his successes, his failures. His victories, his tragedies. Most important of all, he had acknowledged the tragedy of his mother and added a musical eulogy of sorts into the last movement.

He remembered himself alone. He remembered his mother's coffin, and remembered throwing the first handful of dirt into her grave. He tried to remember her face. The stump of the old tree in front of the house seemed more vivid in his memory.

And then he wept.

Soundlessly at first, the emotion of the music released decades of repressed grief. He did get a clear picture of her in his mind then, and he couldn't hold back—he knew he shouldn't—and heavy sobs filled the room. If anyone had been outside his door, they'd have heard him in anguish.

He let it all loose, heaving uncontrollably, tears soaking his face. A long time later, the grief for his mom finally subsided to random hitched breaths.

Emotion. That, structured around Kachina's song, and tempered with the mage's discord, made him certain the magic lay within. But—how to draw from it when he faced Hines?

Drained, he puttered around the room and pulled the symphony together, pile by pile, until it sat on top of the piano in one stack. He stared at it, and euphoria set in. So many emotions from one writing session.

Finally, his mind quiet for the first time in a long time, he plodded to his bed and fell asleep.

꒰꒱

A knock on his door woke him. He looked at his phone. One o'clock in the afternoon. "Shit," he mumbled.

Jacob's voice: "Hey, you busy?"

"No. Come in."

"You just wake up?" Jacob asked, when he opened the door and crossed into the room.

"Yeah."

"Daylight in the swamp."

"I'm sorry, I think I'm late for my shift."

"A little."

"I've not been the best employee these last few months," Truman said. He forced himself out of bed, found his T-shirt from yesterday on the floor, and put it on. He walked over and sat on the piano stool.

Jacob waved a hand. "We're fine, Tip. I know what you've been going through."

Truman smiled. "I'm done." He pointed at the manuscript. "The symphony is done."

Jacob beamed. "Right on, man. A lot of work, and a *hell* of an accomplishment."

"It feels like it."

"By the looks of it, a fairly long piece."

"Eh. It's sitting there in bits and pieces now, but in order. My old school work ethic makes it look like a lot more than it is, maybe. Staff paper, for Christ's sake."

Jacob stood next to the piano, rifling carefully through some of the pages. "I've wondered if you're going to stay on. I knew you were about finished. Now that it's done—well, what do you think?"

"I've not made up my mind, actually."

"Sure."

"This could lead somewhere, and if that happened, I'd probably need to be in Seattle. But if not? I'd love to stay out here."

Jacob nodded, but Truman could tell something else was on his mind.

"What is it?" Truman asked.

"We've considered selling the resort. We've had a few offers."

Truman hadn't heard a whisper about this. "Is that what you want?"

Jacob shrugged. "I'm like you. Mind's not made up."

"You'd probably get a great price on it."

"I would."

"Then what would you do?"

"Something else." His face gained a seriousness Truman hadn't seen in a long time. "Are you still looking for Kat?"

Truman nodded.

"Are you taking things into your own hands?"

"Naw," Truman said. "I've been in touch with Medina."

"That cop?"

"Yeah. You know. He's involved now."

Jacob shrugged. "You're sure you're okay?"

"Why wouldn't I be?"

"Because of Kat."

"I just—miss her, is all."

"There've been strange things going on, and I think you're into something that's not safe. I hope you're right, and that detective has your back."

Truman just nodded. It pained him not to confess everything to his friend. Jacob was just doing what he'd always done since their high school days: looking out for him.

Jacob pointed to the symphony pages. "What about your symphony?"

"What about it?"

"I know you've drawn inspiration from Kat. It seems she's greatly involved in how you put it together."

"It's important to me."

"Of course it is."

"She contributed some ideas. For that matter, so did my ex-wife, Melissa. Nothing unusual about that."

"Well, I'm glad you're taking precautions. Medina seemed like a good cop."

"Pretty smart, actually."

"You'll want to borrow my truck, won't you?"

"If it's okay."

"No reason to stop loaning to you now." He grinned and clapped Truman on the shoulder. "We'll talk later about those other decisions we both need to make."

"Thanks."

Jacob left the room and Truman swiveled back to the piano. For old time's sake, he played the seven ascending notes that had become the framework of his symphony.

With the sustained pedal pressed, the notes lingered in the room. He let the music completely die before releasing the pedal.

He was ready as he'd ever be. If he was going to do this, he had to go full tilt. He'd bring the symphony, even though he didn't know what to do with it.

Today, he would go find Kat and bring the symphony to Joel Hines.

He saw Andrea at the desk when he came down, and they nodded to each other. Jacob had gone out on the resort somewhere, she said. She didn't seem angry, so Jacob must've said something to her. Jacob's truck was outside, and Truman went outside to check it. The key was in the ignition. A sticky note on the key said, *Good Luck. –Jacob.*

He returned to his room, and he paused, looking for the symphony pages. For a moment, he forgot where he'd left them, but they were there, on the piano, slightly askew. With a trembling hand, he rifled through the score, page by page. He didn't have time to change anything now. Still, as he turned the pages, nothing seemed out of place. Had he managed to write it all down without error? His hands shook, his nerve shaken at the thought of pulling off that kind of miracle. If he had truly written the perfect symphony . . . well, what good would it be against the mage?

A part of him still believed it was just notes. Music written down by a musician, nothing magical about it. But he'd seen what he'd seen and experienced what he'd experienced, and he couldn't deny the power of magic.

The last of the coda whispered in his mind, the notes giving way to the vocal tricks of the orchestra to mimic wind and rain.

Finis.

He still didn't know how to use the symphony against Joel, but he felt certain he needed the physical music score. All he had to do was think back to the sex magic, the ultimate physical manifestation of magic, and he realized this. He was out of time. He had to go.

He tidied up the pages, put them under his arm, and headed for the truck.

⋙

Before he left, Truman consulted an online map to get a better look at the area around Bay Port. He traced the monitor with his finger, zooming in on the rural route, the bluff, the actual bay. He switched to Google Maps and closed in. The satellite pictures had been taken during a low tide, and as he kept pulling in, he saw the automatic caption for Bay Port pop into view, followed by the caption for West Bay. He pinched in a little more, and a caption in parenthesis ghosted in: Morrison Mudflats.

We'll play in the mud until the tide comes in.

The Other's ragged voice confirmed Truman's suspicions. Goddamn it, Truman had been *right there* at the edge of that darkling plain.

The forty-five minute drive into town seemed an eternity. Truman's nerves jangled, and dread seeped into his heart. His mouth was dry. He started on a second bottle of water as he arrived in Aberdeen, trying to keep himself hydrated.

He turned onto the road to Bay Port and drove the twenty miles west to the turn-off for Rural Route #2. Everything looked different in the daylight. More alive, but also more desolate. Would the light be to his advantage in his fight against the dark mage?

Truman didn't take the left turn onto the road toward the bay until late afternoon. He drove past the few homes alongside the road until he came upon the V. As before, he stopped. The first time, he'd taken the left turn down the gravel road, ignoring the black top and dead-end sign. Every fiber of his being ordered him down the black top, down to the dead end, but he held to the mage's ghostly words: *You were here once already.*

Light shimmered in his rear-view mirror. Because the afternoon was wearing on, he spotted the headlights of the car far behind him easily. A local, probably, who lived in one of these houses along the road. Truman stared at the lefthand fork, gathering his nerve. He closed his eyes a second, then took one more glance at his rear-view. The car had disappeared.

Truman took his foot off the brake and the truck inched down the gravel road. He gave it a little gas and kept his speed at 15 miles per hour, not remembering how far he'd crawled down the road the first time. Perhaps Hines would come up first.

After a few miles, he knew it was farther down than he'd expected. Hines wanted to stay hidden, so it would make sense to live as far off the beaten path as he could. Medina had said the cops had also searched along Rural Route #2, so wouldn't they have come out this way, too? Why hadn't they found him?

He may have a motorhome, Medina had said.

He accelerated, rolling along now at 30 miles per hour. The landscape slowly gave way to scrub brush. The truck rumbled down the loose gravel road, and he slowed a little.

The sign came into view, the same one he'd encountered down this road the first time. Hand painted, black paint on white, the message the same. The person who'd made the sign would rather tourists not come down the road any farther. Not that it would keep curiosity seekers away. It could have said **KEEP OUT** or **PRIVATE PROPERTY**, and some diehards would chance a look. So how could Hines remain hidden? Was Medina right about the motorhome?

The answer came as he rounded a curve and drove up the last rise toward the top of the bluff. A blue and white fifth wheel and a red rusted pickup truck sat at a right angle to the road and the dead end.

It was true. Hines came and went. He didn't *live* here, he squatted here from time to time. It was the only explanation. The only reason the Aberdeen police hadn't found him here when they first looked.

Truman pulled off the road and stopped the truck a hundred yards from the fifth wheel. He turned off the engine and stared out the front window, his heart beating fast. He self-consciously put out his right hand and placed it flat on the symphony score on the passenger seat. The music flooded his mind as if he were sucking it up from the pages, like ink soaking into tissue paper.

Now he was here, at the end of the last movement, and as he had done for his own symphony, he had to face the ending with skill and heart. All those measures, jammed with notes and chords, all those sounds, all those emotions. The magic was in the sounds themselves, the sounds he'd pulled from around him (rain, wind, Kachina) and the sounds of his past (storm, tree, breaking glass, fire) to compose the thing.

Perhaps getting close to Hines would trigger something. Perhaps, but the mage had invited him out here and told him to go ahead, bring the music, it was worthless, even if Truman had somehow managed to jam magic within. Hines had been confident. He'd joked about it.

Truman grabbed the symphony and paused. Although he didn't think it would do him any good in this case, he believed the pistol couldn't hurt, either. Hines was a mage, but he was still mortal, wasn't he? He jammed the Springfield pistol into his coat pocket, tightened his grip on the music pages, and left the truck. He closed the door as silently as he could.

The music tight in one hand, he curled his other hand around the pistol. The fifth wheel seemed to bob in front of him as he walked deliberately down the road, but off to the side in the scrub brush so as not to crunch gravel under his feet. He was only halfway there. There was something eerie in the idea that the mage was here. Truman could be walking into a trap. Probably was. Anxiety pulled at him as he closed the distance.

He was within ten yards when the fifth wheel's door clicked loudly. Truman stopped in his tracks. The door creaked open, and all instinct now, he drew the pistol and aimed it at the door. So what if it didn't do any good? He certainly felt better pointing it that way.

Dennis Reynolds poked his head out, looked at him, then stepped onto a metal grate hooked onto the fifth wheel below the door. His next step brought him to the road.

"Hey, Tip," he said. He gave a little wave.

"Well," Truman said, looking into the kid's eyes. He spun in a quick circle to make sure Hines hadn't snuck behind him somehow. He brought the pistol back around and pointed it again, even though it wasn't Hines standing there. "Wasn't expecting to see you come out that door."

Dennis only shrugged.

Truman moved left, making a wide circle until he came close enough to the edge of the bluff to see down to the bay. Yes, the tide was out, and he saw the mudflats. Along a rock formation was a small pier. It was deserted.

He stared Dennis down. "Where is he?"

Dennis shrugged again. "He's not here."

"You know he invited me out here, right?"

"I'm not sure how you're still alive if he came close enough to invite you."

"It's complicated."

"Magic, I assume."

"Where *is* he? And where is Kat?"

"He'll be here. He had to move her, but he's bringing her back." He pointed at Truman. "Is that it? Is that your symphony?"

Truman didn't look at it. "None of your business."

"You can come in. It's okay." Dennis stepped up onto the grate and disappeared into the fifth wheel.

Truman took another look at the pier, moved closer to the edge, and saw the steep rocky path that led down there. He continued walking, continuing the sweep around the bluff until he'd completed a full circle around the fifth wheel. He paused at the door.

Dennis's voice said, "Don't worry, he's not in here. I promise."

Just inside the fifth wheel door, Truman waited and took in his surroundings, letting his eyes adjust to the dimmer light. Sleeping area to the back, small galley, restroom. Near the front, Dennis sat on a low chair, his guitar on his lap.

"You can put away the gun," Dennis said. "You know it's not going to do any good against him."

"Could be a good persuader."

Dennis laughed.

Truman looked at the pistol a second, then slid it into his coat pocket. He sat down in the matching low chair across from Dennis and put his music score across his own lap.

"Pretty impressive," Dennis said.

"What?"

He pointed at the score. "That you wrote most of that after you met me."

"I had lots more time when I wasn't bothered with guitar lessons for stupid ass kids."

Dennis snorted. "Wow. That's cold."

"You don't have any right to call that cold. You've been with him most of the time I wrote this. You were there at the store with him, at the stadium, the chalet. You left with him, left me locked in the chalet to die."

"You look fine."

"No thanks to you."

Dennis glanced down, and Truman thought he saw regret on the kid's face. Dennis plucked the G string, and it rang out true.

"Why did you stop?"

Dennis plucked the E string. "By then I was caught up with Joel. He made me stop."

"Joel Hines," Truman said.

He looked up. "Of course. I'm not surprised you learned his name." He hit the E string again. "What you taught me in those few lessons was amazing."

"Nothing out of the ordinary."

"I told Joel about you after the first lesson. I told him you'd played something I recognized."

Kachina's song. "You played it back to me."

"Joel recognized it. He knew it was hers. He made me play it for him, and he said it helped him connect to the three of you. Somehow. Weird shit, if you ask me. But that's why he knew you could be a problem." He waved his hand at Truman. "And there it is. It's miraculous, to create something like that out of nothing but sound. To anyone not schooled at all in music, it's a foreign language. It's an undecipherable map. It could be the plans to an even greater work of art. The plan for world peace."

"Or a weapon."

Dennis raised an eyebrow and leaned back in the chair. He folded his arms above the guitar. Truman couldn't tell what he was thinking, until he said, "It's—I don't know—a *miracle*. Really. You have a gift."

"Yeah. Yeah right. Like any of that matters now. I'm likely to die here, and these flimsy pages of staff paper would be worthless."

"I'll publish them after you die," Dennis said with a laugh.

Truman didn't laugh, and that made the kid stop.

Dennis leaned forward with purpose, situated the guitar again, and strummed a minor chord. Then he played the seven notes of the melody.

"You still remember it," Truman said.

Dennis dampened the strings with his palm. "Teach me more of it."

"What, another lesson?"

"Why not?"

Truman looked around the fifth wheel. Being brave was one thing, but he didn't dare drop his guard. He was still nervous, still on edge.

Dennis held out the guitar.

"Yeah," Truman said. "I don't think so."

34

GRAND PAUSE

TRUMAN WOKE FROM A FITFUL SLEEP AND SAT UP QUICKLY, confused. The interior of the fifth wheel was mostly dark, with only a few lights on, one above the mini stove and one over the bed in the back.

Dennis was on the bed, asleep.

What the hell?

It wasn't dark outside, but the light had deepened, and he wondered how long he'd been asleep. How the hell *had* he fallen asleep? He checked his phone. Seven o'clock. He had no signal out here, as before.

He frowned, thinking back. Dennis asking for a guitar lesson. His refusal. And then?

Oh no.

He remembered: Dennis offered him a beer, but there were none left in the fridge. He only had the one he'd opened before Truman arrived. There was some open wine, though. Truman drank half a glass, and Dennis drank from his semi-warm beer, and they sat there and said nothing.

In fact, they were silent a long time. Truman thought of the calm before the storm. *Just relax, Tip.* He wanted to mentally prepare. The grand pause before the finale.

He didn't remember Dennis wandering off to the back, to the bed. He didn't remember falling asleep. Rubbing his eyes, he stood and took in everything around him, slightly unsteady on his feet. A half glass of wine couldn't have made him this wobbly.

He wondered if it had all been a lie. Was Hines even here? Had Hines drawn him out and used Dennis as a distraction so the mage could do what he wanted in town against Kat and Allie?

Suddenly frightened, he remembered to check his coat pocket. The gun was not there. "Shit!" he whispered.

Wait.

He searched the fifth wheel frantically, his eyes hoping to see the telltale white of the music score. He couldn't find it.

No! *Where was it?*

He tiptoed to the back and leaned over the bed, gazing down at Dennis. He jumped back when he saw the boy's eyes were open. "Jesus!"

"You're awake," Dennis said.

"Where is it? Where's my symphony?"

"I was going to kill him."

"What? You mean Hines?"

"Yeah."

"What happened?"

"I took your gun when you fell asleep. I'm sorry. I . . . I don't really want to be here, you know. Not anymore. He told me I had to make you drink. He didn't trust you."

"You—*what?*"

"The wine. He drugged it. I'm afraid of him. I'm afraid, and I don't know what to do. I had to do it. He would've found out."

Truman saw the tears in the boys' eyes now, and his hands trembled. "Dennis—"

"I was going to kill him. All his bullshit about sharing his power with me. And then he killed that girl. He—" Dennis's eyes misted.

Truman gulped, waiting for the rest of the boy's story.

"When he came, though, I couldn't even the lift the gun. He found the girl in Aberdeen, at that motel, but she didn't have the box. She had some of the Moss on her and he took some. It gave him enough power to widen his—well, whatever he calls it."

"Sphere of influence."

"Yeah."

"Dennis. *Where is my symphony?*"

Dennis sat up. Looked blearily at Truman through his tears. "He has it." He paused only to catch a breath. "Joel took it. And the gun."

"Jesus. Where is he?"

"He's waiting for you. I'm sorry. I tried, I really did. He's down at the pier. He's going to do something awful to your friend."

35

GRAND FINALE

F ROM ATOP THE BLUFF, TRUMAN SAW JOEL HINES STANDING on the pier. Hines gazed out at the bay, and in his left hand, tucked in at his side, was the symphony. Huddled next to him in a ball was Kat. She wasn't moving. At that moment, he didn't care about the symphony. He only wanted Kat to be alive. He could live without the symphony if he had to, but he didn't want to live without Kat.

It was likely he wouldn't live at all.

Truman picked his way down the rocky trail that wound down to the pier, slipping only once. Rocks sprayed out from his feet and tumbled down the slope of the bluff, but Hines didn't hear it. Or likely he chose to ignore it. The mage could hear him coming, and he wasn't concerned. What could Truman do? He'd been stripped of all his weapons: gun and music.

Hines pulled Kat to her knees. *She was alive.*

At the bottom of the bluff, Truman paused. Where the pier began, scattered in pieces on the wood deck and on the rocks, Dennis's guitar lay ruined. Hines had smashed it against one of the pier posts. Maybe he'd been worried Truman would use it to perform the symphony or something. Or, more likely, smashed it in anger because Dennis had tried to kill him.

Hines still hadn't turned around, surveying the bay and the impending sunset. So much for facing Hines in the light. There was nothing else Truman could do. He walked out onto the pier. He was halfway there when he heard Hines speak.

"My God, it's a beautiful world we live in, Kachina. Too beautiful even for the likes of you."

Hines turned toward her. "If you lie to me—" But he must've seen Truman out of the corner of his eye, for he stopped, turned, and gazed down the pier.

Truman continued forward. An old rusty metal chair was overturned on the pier deck. He slid around it.

Hines smiled widely. "Tiparoo!" He stayed close to Kat, as if afraid he could lose her, although Truman could see there wasn't anywhere she could go.

Her mouth was duct taped. Hines had tied her with duct tape, too, hands behind, feet together. She had on a white cotton dress he'd seen before. It took him a moment, and realized it was the same dress Kachina had been in when they talked in the forest.

"Gotta hand it to you, Tip-a-lot." He pointed at Kat. "And to her. You two really fucked things up for me, getting this far."

"You invited me."

Hines shrugged. "Yeah, well. You already knew where I was."

"I had a guess."

"More than a guess." His voice had laughter in it. "But really, I anticipated it, knowing you'd be weak and overconfident."

Truman took a menacing step toward Hines.

"I still have the gun," Hines said. Truman stopped. "I mean, if I have to kill you fast, I will. No point in letting you suffer if all you're going to do is try and take me down physically."

"I've been told that'd be a fairly worthless strategy."

"Dennis tell you, did he?"

"And others."

Hines leaned down and patted Kat's head. "You mean her? She warned you, but she ignored her own advice and came into my sphere unprepared. I found her, and now here you are. Soon, I'll face Allie and get what she's kept from me. I'll soon be strong enough to get close to her without her knowing, thanks to a little Moss Kat shared with me, and the Moss I'll get from her blood soon. I'll have even more once Allie is dying and I can infuse some of her magic-tinged blood into my own. If the box isn't there, I'll have plenty of Sight to find it."

Kat looked at Truman, her eyes calm, but sad too.

"I'm pretty amazed by this," Hines said. He waved the symphony, and all the page ends flapped like a fan. "I'll admit, I don't have an ounce of musical talent. I can't carry a tune. In fact, music tends to piss me off." He reached down and thumped Kat's head. "You can *imagine* how difficult it's been to hear the echoes of this one's voice in the rain from time to time."

Truman said nothing. He dared to inch closer to Hines.

Hines waved the symphony again. "This is gibberish. It means nothing to me. Do you know how upsetting it's been to hear your own music coming through all these months? Holy *fuck*. Can you blame me for how angry I've been, having to listen to all this shit I can't even read?"

Truman put out his hand. "Give me the symphony, and I'll give you a quick lesson."

"Truman." It surprised Truman to hear Hines call him by his real name. The mage regarded the staff paper with bemusement. "It's just pencil and paper. That's all it is. The song is in *here*." He patted Kat again. "Meow, kitty."

He reached out with his arm and held the symphony pages over the end of the pier.

Truman, startled, said, "If that's all it is, why worry so much about it? You're right, I've always been a failure as a musician. I never had the heart. Never understood what drove it. Give it to me, and I'll get rid of it."

Hines tilted his head and looked down his nose at Truman. "Are you serious? You wouldn't dare."

"I just want Kat. I'll take her and leave you alone."

"And how about Dennis? Going to leave him here with me?"

"Yes. If I have to. I don't care."

"How about Allie? And don't forget Serena. I think she was your fault, too, although it seems to me a better death might have been throwing her off this pier into the mud. You going to let these people die for one fucking witch?"

It wasn't Truman's plan at all, but what else could he tell Hines?

"There's nothing in this music," Hines spat. He did what Truman had only jokingly thought to himself when he wondered how to get magic from it. Hines used it like a fly swatter, slapping it against Kat's head. Her hair flew wildly.

"Is your magic in here, sacred dancer?" He slapped her again with it. "Where is it?"

Truman leaned forward.

"No, Truman," Hines ordered, "*stop*. In a second we'll throw this shit to the wind. You'll never get the pages back. Mud, rain, salt water—all of your precious work ruined." He shook the pages. "Who the fuck still writes music on paper? Huh? No photocopy machine, Tipadoodle?"

There'd been no time.

"Well," Hines said. "This symphony is dead to you and me." He threatened the symphony again, thrusting his arm upward.

He didn't let go.

His eyes glazed over, and he frowned. He turned his head slightly and paused as if listening to something. Bringing the symphony down to his side again, he took a step away from Kat, toward the bluff, and looked up.

Truman looked too, but he didn't see anything.

"Ah," Hines said. "There he is."

Truman didn't say anything.

Hines retreated, returning to his place next to Kat. "Your cop friend. Frank Medina."

Medina? Truman groaned inwardly. Shit, he'd followed him out here.

"Shame, shame, Tippo. You shouldn't have brought him."

"I didn't. I swear, I came alone."

Hines pulled his gaze away from the bluff and looked sidelong at Truman. "Strangely enough, I believe you."

It wasn't long before Truman saw Medina at the bluff's edge. He had a weapon, and Dennis was near him. The detective waved the gun at Dennis, and the boy started down the trail. Medina followed.

"Well, here he comes," Hines said.

On the pier it was silent, and no one moved, as if they were actors in a tableau, waiting for the scene to play out above them.

Medina stayed behind Dennis, his gun aimed at the boy's legs, his other arm slightly outstretched to gauge his distance as they worked their way down the trail. When they reached the bottom, Hines pulled Kat up by the hair to a standing position. He dropped the symphony to the deck, stepped on it, and curled that arm around her neck. In the other hand was Jacob's pistol, and he jammed it against her head.

"Just keeping up appearances," Hines said. "So he doesn't think he can get close enough to shoot me. Let him come." He grinned. "Let him come."

Dennis was on the pier. Medina behind.

"Just a little closer," Hines said.

Truman didn't think Hines would harm Kat now, before he got from her what he needed. "Medina, stay back!"

Medina reached out and grabbed Dennis's shoulder, pulling him back a step. They stopped a quarter of the way down the pier. The boy still had tears in his eyes, and he visibly shook with fright.

"Can't do that, Truman," Medina called out. "What've you got going on down here? This is the man you talked about. Hines. I recognize him from that police sketch. Kat? Is that you?"

She managed a nod before Hines could tighten his grip around her neck.

"You can't win this, Medina," Truman said. "Just stay back. He's not what you think. He doesn't need that gun to hurt you."

"Without the gun, he's nothing," Medina said, "so you keep out of this."

"He's more than that." Truman was surprised Hines wasn't doing anything. "He's powerful. He's . . . well, he's a mage."

"A mage."

"Magician. A dark one."

Medina actually snickered. "Really, Truman? After our other chats, this is where you want to go?"

"It's the truth."

Hines sighed dramatically and loudly so that everyone on the pier could hear. "Truman Starkey, are you going to give away *all* my secrets?"

Medina kept going, slower now, forcing Dennis next to him almost the same way Hines had Kat. Medina extended his arm and pointed his gun in their direction, but he aimed at their feet.

"I do hope your aim is good, Medina," Hines said. "Probably a lousy shot."

Medina huffed. "Like you know."

Hines looked hurt. "No partner, Medina? Why in fuck would you come out here alone? Where's your backup?"

"Cutbacks," Medina said.

"Doesn't that just beat all?" Hines said.

"Don't worry about it. I have backup. Several other Aberdeen police vehicles on their way."

"Bad timing, probably," Hines said.

"You're just a lackey, Hines. One of Bill Hand's failures. You don't have it in you to do this."

"Well fuck, you know about Bill, too? Bravo, Medina."

"Let the girl go." Medina shuffled forward, closing the distance between them. "Let her go and drop your weapon. Let's end this without any bloodshed."

"Bloodshed. Really?" Hines laughed so loud, Medina stopped. "Who said anything about bloodshed?"

"I did. I'll shoot if I have to."

"Not with Kat up sweet and tight against me." He kissed her cheek and she tried to turn away. "But I tell you what, sir. I'll make a deal with you. I'll do *one* of the things you asked. Your choice. I'll let go of the girl or drop the weapon."

Medina looked confused, and Truman sensed a trick. Truman had experienced Hines's power, but only from a distance. In space, in dream, in shadow. He had no idea what the mage could do this close, particularly if he'd taken some of the drugs.

"What'll it be, Medina?" Hines was almost choking Kat now.

Medina decided, and the moment he chose, Truman believed it was the wrong one. Either choice would've been the wrong one.

"Drop the gun. Behind you. Pitch it into the mud."

Hines grinned. "Of course, detective. I'm a man of my word."

Truman tensed, ready for Hines's betrayal.

"I see you, Tippapotamus," Hines said without taking his eyes off Medina. "You stay where you are."

"Do it now!" Medina yelled.

To Truman's surprise, Hines did as he was asked. He took the gun from Kat's head and flung it behind him. It sailed in a long arc and fell from sight. A second later, Truman heard it plop in the mud.

Medina nodded, somewhat relieved. "Any more weapons?"

"Me?" Hines said. "That was Truman's gun, actually. *He's* the one with the weapons."

"Truman?"

"You should stay back," Hines said. "Looks super dangerous to me. I'm just a lackey."

"He have any other weapons?" Medina looked at Truman. "Do you have a weapon?"

"Not anymore. He's right. He took it from me, and now it's in the mud."

Hines ground his heel into Truman's symphony, twisting it. He kept his grip tight around Kat. "No weapons?" He looked down at the symphony pages on the deck. "What a liar you are, Truman."

"Truman," Medina said. "I'm warning you."

Truman came to his senses. This was Hines's magic. Or some of it. He was worming his way into Medina somehow. "You're turning him against me."

"I'm sorry, what?" With an indignant look, Hines said, "He's crazy, detective. You should watch out for him."

"You were the one with the gun. Hines, was it?"

Hines shrugged. "Eh. It's a name. I've gotten used to it." He pointed a finger toward Medina. "You should let my friend Dennis go. It's only fair."

"You're right," Medina agreed. "It's only fair." He pulled Dennis back, turned him around and said to his face, "Go back up there. Don't come back down."

Dennis nodded, but didn't move.

"You hear me? Don't come back down. Go."

With a look behind him at Hines, then at Truman, Dennis ran off, heading for the bluff.

"Now what, detective?" Hines said.

Medina had relaxed quite a bit, more so than Truman thought he should. He walked up the pier until he stood within a few feet of Hines and Kat. He looked them over as if he had all the time in the world. He looked at Truman and narrowed his eyes.

"Medina," Truman said softly, almost a whisper. He gained a step in Kat's direction, although he was sure Hines had seen him.

"Now what?" Medina asked. "Well hell, I think I'll have a smoke." He reached into his pocket and pulled out his pack of cigarettes. Tapped one out and put it between his lips. Found and snapped open his lighter. Lit the tip of the cigarette. Drew in a breath until the paper smoldered and caught, mercilessly slow.

It was a moment stuck in time, with the sun going down, the cop leisurely smoking a cigarette, the smoke rising and curling into the night air, the villain waiting to make a move, the damsel helpless and in distress. A classic image, but Truman knew Kat was no damsel, that there were hardly any damsels left in this day and age, and if she hadn't been bound and gagged, she'd have already fucked Hines up and kicked his ass from here to Quinault. Truman wasn't sure what he was himself. Was he the cop's partner, or the villain's sidekick?

"What about *your* weapon, detective?" Hines asked.

"As long as you're holding Kat, I'm holding the weapon." He smiled. "It's only fair."

Hines said, "So be it."

The air swirled on the pier, and Truman felt, more than heard, Hines's nearly silent invocation. Medina shook his head, then turned the gun toward Truman.

"You're the real problem here, Starkey," Medina said, and his face looked as if he didn't believe a word of it. The detective sighted down the barrel, but Truman took that instant to leap out of the way, driving himself headlong toward Hines, not caring where he ended up. If he could distract Hines somehow, maybe . . .

Medina's gun fired, and it sounded more like a pop gun with an added *whump*. The shot missed Truman; he didn't feel pain, anyway. That is, until his shoulder clipped Hines and he landed near the mage's feet, thumping his head on the pier.

Truman raised his head, disoriented, and caught a glimpse of Kat scooching away from Hines the best she could. Away from Truman. He rolled to his back and lashed out hard, his forearm connecting with Hines's leg.

"Goddamn it!" Medina yelled from somewhere.

"That's it!" Hines kicked out at Truman's arm. "That's it!"

Truman felt utterly helpless now as he tried to get up, failed, then rolled again and wrapped his arms—or tried to—around Hines's legs.

He could barely make out Kat's shape, and she was kicking too, trying to get at Hines.

"What the fuck's going on?" Medina said. "What—How can this be?"

Truman couldn't see the detective behind him. "Medina?" Hines continued to lash out at him with his legs. A foot thudded into his side, knocking the wind out of him.

Another shot rang out, and Medina screamed. "God*damn* it, in my fucking *leg*? Truman, what's he *doing* to me?"

Truman craned his neck so he could see over his shoulder, but Hines's foot came down at his head, and Truman tucked it down in time to save a strike to the chin. The foot glanced off his temple, but it was heavy and painful, and blackness crept in at the corners of his eyes. He shook it off, but Hines continued to kick at him. Maybe it was all the mage could do while he concentrated on Medina.

There was another gunshot, and then another.

"Medina!" Truman yelled between kicks. "Drop the gun, throw it away!"

Hines stopped kicking. Kat was trying to say something, loudly, through her duct tape.

Medina, however, said nothing.

Free of Hines's barrage of kicks, Truman rolled and faced Medina. He had a bemused look on his face. Truman frowned, wondering what was wrong, but then he noticed Medina's gun, smoking slightly. Medina had it pointed at his own head. Blood already seeped from two bullet wounds in his chest and shoulder.

Medina coughed once, exhaling bubbles of blood, then his eyes rolled up into his head.

"No," Truman said, his aches and pains forgotten. His words were barely a whisper. "Medina, no."

Medina pulled the trigger, and Truman shut his eyes as the gunshot popped loudly in his ears. He opened them again in time to watch Medina fall to the deck. The gun skidded away. The cuffs clattered to the pier, and Medina's body fell on top of them. He dropped his cigarette lighter too, which landed in a crack near Truman. It stuck out at an awkward angle, the flint wheel keeping it from falling through to the mud below. The detective's last cigarette lay beside his mouth, smoldering.

Truman rolled to his back again, barely holding back an anguished cry. Hines's footsteps were loud as he walked over to Medina and kicked at the body.

A sense of peace washed over Truman, and he didn't understand why, because it was so wrong. Hines' voice sounded wrong too. The thuds from Hines's foot kicking at the body? Surreal. The sounds of Kat trying to speak? Almost musical, but off key.

"I guess," Hines said, "he wasn't such a bad shot after all."

Even Hines's voice seemed extra loud and wildly modulated.

Truman remembered the trouble he had lining up the sounds from his dream of the New Year's Day storm. The cracking of the tree. The crashing of the glass. The crackling of the fire and the conflagration of the tree engulfed in flames. They were off just a little. Just out of synch. He'd associated emotions with the sounds. Helplessness. Loss. Entrapment. Love. Shame.

Passion.

Joel Hines was saying something again. He was kicking again, lightly, at Truman. Truman thought he heard Hines say, "Get up. Get up and watch her die."

Passion.

More than that. Compassion. In the evening air, he wept soundlessly for Medina. The feeling was hot, like a raging fire. As he internalized this, the sounds made more sense. They came into line. Found their place on the staff paper.

Get up. Get up and watch her die.

The sky dark now. Truman spotted the full moon and thought: what is the moon except darkness engulfed by the light of the sun? Lit by fire.

Oh, *that* was it.

Truman had one hand over his heart. He let gravity pull at his arm, and it slipped down. When his hand flopped on the deck, it touched the very edge of paper.

The symphony.

"What?" he mumbled.

Hines sighed. "I said, get *up*. Get up and watch the paper fly. I'm going to conjure more wind to blow your music to oblivion.

I'm going to release it to the wind, page by page. And then I'll finish you."

Truman wasn't sure when he had reached over and grabbed it, wresting it from the crack in the pier, but Medina's cigarette lighter was in his left hand. Truman turned to his right side, pulling the hand with the lighter to him, working his way to the symphony pages that had miraculously stayed on the pier.

"I'll finish you," Hines said above him, "and I'll kill Kachina and take her power. Then, when I'm done with Allie, I'll see what real power feels like again. More than has ever been taken on. I'll jump from this place to the place where my mother awaits me. Jump across the lines of force and be reunited."

Lines of force. Staff lines and measure lines. One symphonic movement leading to another.

Truman snagged the symphony pages as he struggled to his feet. Hines didn't seem to care Truman had them.

"You lost your mother?" Truman asked. It was a real question, for Truman had only just mourned his own mother, and he'd not had any time to think about this man having a mother or father or any kind of life that counted for anything.

Hines seemed surprised at the question. He stood stock still, letting the words sink in. He frowned. "She lost *me*. She left. She was a bitch, I'm sure, but I was only a few days old."

"She died? During childbirth?"

"I don't want to do these bad things, Truman. If I can draw enough power, I can fix my brain. Be healed and find the one who abandoned me."

"What about your father?"

"He was nobody."

Truman kept him talking. At the same time, he took almost imperceptible steps back, slowly gaining some distance from Hines. Kat was listening, her eyes showing her own surprise at Hines's story. Her mother had left their family too. Truman caught her gaze and nodded ever so slightly. He inclined his head just a tick to the right. She caught his meaning and, like him, worked her way farther away from Hines. Little by little.

"He—was nobody." Hines's face fell, and he suddenly looked very human, a pained look creasing his forehead with lines. That didn't last long. He shook his head and his darkness returned. "No more stalling, Truman. I see you backing up. It doesn't matter, you're not leaving this pier alive."

Hines regained the distance Truman had won, moving forward. It did take him further away from Kat, though. Hines stopped, bent over, and picked up Medina's gun.

Hines snarled. "Throw the paper away, music man."

"So you need a gun after all."

"Just keeping up appearances. I don't want you to get a false sense of security. Throw it. Away."

Truman shook his head. "No."

Hines raised both eyebrows, but he straightened his arm, pointing the gun more insistently.

Truman raised the pages of staff paper and yelled, causing Hines to pause. "You know who's in here, don't you?"

Hines laughed. "The witch's song is in there, but that's it. You can't do anything about it."

Truman shook his head. "Her song may be in here, but you're in here too. Your anger, your hatred, your evil. I was just the messenger. Not really blessed with magic of nature, only the magic of music, and once I understood its heart, I had the way to bind both of you."

"Very pretty, Truman, but this ends now."

Hines pulled the hammer back.

"You want to shoot? Go ahead. You said you didn't need anything but your magic. Where's your magic, *Joel*? I don't see it. You know where it is? It's here." He waved the symphony, letting the pages fan out.

"Throw the damned thing away, or I'll kill Kat right now." Without looking behind him, Hines turned sideways and pointed the gun at Kat, who somehow, even now, with hands tied and feet taped together, tried to get to her feet.

"You're the wind, Hines. Kachina is the rain. If you really want to stretch the metaphor? You've already buried Serena and Medina in the earth. Except it does take away from the whole Unholy Trinity thing."

Truman was saying all this, but he now feared for Kat. He was certain Hines would shoot her.

"You're fucking crazy," Hines said. He put pressure on the trigger just as Kat stood as straight as she could. "Say goodbye to your rain."

Hines pulled the trigger, and Truman twitched.

The hammer clicked on an empty chamber.

"Someone wasn't counting shots," Truman said. He said this, but he knew there'd only been five shots. Medina must have started with only five.

Hines pulled the trigger repeatedly. No bullets in Medina's gun.

"You know what I am, Hines?" Truman opened his right hand enough to bring out Medina's lighter, and with one quick motion, flicked it to life. "I'm the fucking fire."

Hines's eyes widened. "No!" He dropped the gun and concentrated, arms outstretched, the fingers of his hands fanning out.

A swirl of wind pushed at the mage, gaining momentum so fast, Truman was worried the lighter's flame might go out.

"Release it! Let go of it!" The anger in Hines's voice seethed. "Throw it away!"

"I've got a better idea," Truman said. "I'm going to burn it."

He touched flame to paper.

Truman had only decided to do it once he had the lighter and understood the passion—the fire—within him demanding the music's sacrifice. As the scene played out, the inevitability of the fire's need to cleanse his soul and wipe away the dust from his eyes became clear. The fire reunited him with his past and his mother, and it was all pure anguish. The sorrow of it crushed him.

Reality isn't a straight line, go left here or go right there. It circles, it curves.

To work so long on the symphony, only to lose it now!

But fire was the only way to release the magic. The only way to defeat the blowhard that was Joel Hines. The last part of the dream played out in Truman's mind: Tina engulfed by fire, telling him he was on his own. Melissa telling him to find his heart and the fire within. Coach Johnston's red feather story: the avenger's arrow, engulfed with fire, flying toward the red eagle, which flapped and started a great wind, but the wind didn't affect the arrow. The eagle fell.

The fire always wins.

Wind eddied about Truman now, but the fire had caught, and the pages sucked up the flames. Ashes curled and separated from the staff paper, and in Hines's wind, they twirled, and they twisted, and they danced, and—

They sang.

The music started low, humming as if someone were playing an instrument from far away, a supple hand brushing lightly against guitar strings.

Hines's Moss-induced wind was blowing louder now, but it did nothing to diminish the power of music and fire. The pages burned brighter than they should burn, almost blinding Truman, but each flash of light that separated into wings of ash carried the sounds aloft.

Seven notes.

The song of his muse. Truman made out the strains of his music. He recognized the full melody embedded in chords, countermelodies, and ostinatos. There, the *adagio*. There, the first movement inversion he had fretted over for days. There, the scherzo. First part, second part, trio. There, the *presto*.

At the same time, the seven notes blared with Wagnerian boldness, ascending note by note, all different, in intervals, timed so perfectly, it was as if the gift from Kat, the Wittner metronome, was on the pier keeping perfect time.

B

Flames crawled along the underside of the symphony, heating his hands. He didn't let go.

F#

Higher and higher, the flames reached for the moon, and the ashes sang. Lines of force snaked through the ash in bright orange, like the capillaries of leaves.

D

Kat was free of her gag. He didn't know how she'd removed the duct tape, and he didn't see it anywhere on the pier. Perhaps magic had melted it and it had blown away like ashes.

E

Hines screamed as his wind faltered. He became more desperate and whipped up mud and rocks from below the pier, heaving them at Truman, and at Kat, but they landed harmlessly on the pier as the wind died. The flames rose toward him, seeking him, and although it was more fire than should be possible if fueled only by those pages, Truman believed it to be the most natural thing in the world.

G

Kat sang. It was her own magic now, like a resolution, and Truman found her voice comforting amid the maelstrom. Rain began to fall. Hines was yelling for it all to stop, his wind failing him, yelling at her and telling her to *stop, stop it now.*

A

The sky opened up and the rain poured down. Truman released the pages, and they floated now, the magic burned away, trapped momentarily in the ascending ashes. In the rain, they slowly disintegrated. Hines fell to his knees and patted angrily at his clothes. The fire was gone, but he still felt its effects. He whimpered, distracted by false fire.

C#

There, the high point. The climax, the finale.

There, the grand pause.

In the resulting silence, Truman breathed out. Hines had stopped flapping wildly at his flames, collecting himself, but he was unable to stand. The rain music had drenched him.

The footsteps Truman heard coming down the pier a moment later belonged to Dennis Reynolds.

Truman picked up the empty gun.

Kat put a hand to her mouth and said, "Oh, Truman. Your symphony. Your poor symphony."

Yes. His symphony. Gone. Used up to invoke the magic. He didn't have time to feel the sadness, or worry about it.

Dennis reached him. The boy's eyes were puffy and red, but Truman saw a determination in his face he hadn't seen before. Dennis held out his hand, and in the palm was the missing bullet from Medina's gun.

Truman stared at it, wondering what to do. *The only thing you can do*, he thought. He took it from Dennis and carefully loaded it into the gun.

Kat walked to Dennis and turned him away.

Truman aimed at Hines. The mage looked up, confused. He babbled on about something, as if he were trying to remember where he was, or maybe how to come up with a last gust of magic, but it wasn't an invocation.

It was a benediction.

Any last words? Truman thought to himself. He didn't want to actually say them aloud, but Hines had a last word anyway.

"Mother?"

Truman said, "Go join her."

He fired.

CODA

Chords of earth awakened,
Notes of greening spring
Rise and fall triumphant
Over every thing.
                    —Joseph S. Cotter, Jr.
                    Rain Music

BREATH

WHEN TRUMAN CLIMBED BACK UP THE BLUFF WITH KAT and Dennis to the fifth wheel, he threw himself into the same chair he'd fallen asleep in. He thought he might fall asleep again, or pass out, the heaviness of the ordeal with Hines and the loss of his symphony pressing down on him.

"Something I don't understand," Truman said. "How did you get the box of Moss to Allie?"

"I didn't."

Her words confused him. "If Allie doesn't have the box, then where is it?"

"At the Stoked Motel."

"What? How did you—you said Hines searched your room thoroughly. He took the key and your Moss packet. Took all your luggage with them so the motel would know you'd checked out."

Kat smiled, the light of pride suffusing them. "You remember I told you the place was dead, and almost no one there? I checked in but went right back down and asked for a room change. I'd decided I wanted to be on the ground floor."

Truman realized what she'd done. "You left it in that first room."

"Under the bed. Didn't disturb anything else. Even if someone had rented the room later, they would never have seen it. I bet housekeeping might miss it if they had to clean the room at some point. I turned in the ballcap I said I'd found on the stairs, they took my key and programmed it to the new room, and that was that. I knew I could go back later for it if I explained."

"Genius," Truman said. He leaned over and hugged her tight. "I was so frightened for you out there on the pier, but Jesus, you got in Hines' way every chance you got." He let her go, then turned to Dennis. "Thank you, too, for coming to your senses."

Dennis nodded. He took a deep breath. "Medina gave me that bullet. Said if anything happened to him, there might be a moment when the bullet could turn the tide. I didn't know what he meant at the time."

"It meant Medina beat Hines after all, in a fashion," Truman said.

Dennis pulled out his phone and started looking something up. There wasn't any cell service, so Truman wondered what he was looking for. "When you fell asleep, I was worried what Joel would do to you."

"Well, you had a right to be worried."

"And what he might do to your symphony. Plus—" He shrugged. "I was curious about how you did it."

Truman perked up. "What?"

"While you were sleeping, I used my phone and took pics of all the pages." He held out his phone. "They're all right here. The symphony's here, every note."

Kat put her hand to her mouth again and let out a squeak of joy.

Truman fumbled at the phone and gazed at the screen, bewildered. "What the hell?"

"I can send the files to you. It'll probably still be a bitch to read them."

Truman jumped up and wrapped his arms around Dennis. "You're a miracle!"

The phone fell to the floor.

"Oh *shit!*"

Dennis laughed and picked it up. "It's okay, it's okay."

"Are you sure? Double check. God, if I broke—"

"It's fine. The files are fine. Look." He showed the screen to Truman, and there was symphony one, movement one, page one.

The symphony had died in the flames at Bay Port, but it was reborn in the magic of the digital age.

～

Out of all the possible days of the year, Truman Starkey sold his symphony on the summer solstice in June.

Melissa helped him prepare the file in proper format and made a list of music publishers to send it to. Kat had helped him transcribe it, and helped Melissa type up the business letters they would send as well.

Truman needn't have worried. The first publisher who saw it, took it, and offered him a lot of money for it. It wasn't quit-the-day-job kind of money, but for a first offering, the money was more than decent.

Later that summer, Truman was ready to leave Quinault. He was driving back to Seattle to stay. The music publisher had arranged a read-through of the symphony in August, and they'd invited him to come listen to it. He and Kat found an apartment thirty minutes south of the city, and they made several trips on Truman's days off from the resort to haul their possessions there.

Dennis had left home for good, deciding to push his guitar skills to the limit at Cornish, a music school near downtown Seattle. His parents would be poor for a while. Dennis did get a small scholarship, and Jacob lent him some money, interest free, to pay back when he was rich and famous.

On the last day of July, in front of the store in the parking lot, they said goodbye to Jacob.

"Thanks for everything," Truman said. It sounded so lame.

"You're welcome, of course."

"I mean it. I couldn't have pulled this off if you hadn't given me the chance."

"It was your choice, and you made a good one, turns out."

Truman nodded, looking down at the asphalt.

"I've made a decision," Jacob said.

Truman looked up. "You did? You're going to sell? You are, aren't you? Are you sure?"

"Oh, that?" Jacob laughed. "No. I've not yet made up my mind."

"Oh?"

"No. I've made a decision about the *piano*. I talked to Lisa about it, and she agreed. I want you to have it."

Truman was speechless.

Kat said, "That is *amazing*, Jacob!"

"Yes," Truman said. "My god. Thank you."

"You'll have to figure out how to get it out of here. I guess that means I'll see you back at Quinault at some point, right?"

The last week of August, as summer was winding down, Truman sat with Kat in Benaroya Hall, the home of the Seattle Symphony, anxiously awaiting to hear the read-through of Truman's piece. Nothing was finalized yet, and the musicians read from printouts of their parts from the score proofs. Melissa was in the audience too, but she gave them plenty of space.

The orchestra was on stage, doing its last warmups. The conductor stood near the left wing in blue jeans and a black T-shirt, drinking a bottle of water, his baton tucked under his arm.

Kat leaned into Truman. "Hey, I never asked you. What's your symphony called?"

Truman turned and narrowed his eyes, all serious. He had told Kat a lot about the past year, including her future self giving him the melody, how it helped him defeat Hines, but he hadn't said anything about this. "You really don't know?"

She shook her head.

"Symphony No. 1."

She punched him in the shoulder. "Shit. How boring is *that*?"

"It's what all the great composers have done. Haven't you ever heard of Beethoven's Ninth Symphony? Shoskatovich's Symphony No. 1?"

"Nothing else?"

"How about Symphony No. 1—in B Flat?"

"Is that what key it's in?"

"No, but it sounds neat."

"No opus or anything?

"What, Magic Opus No. 1?"

"Oh shut *up*. A subtitle at least? Come on, composers love their nicknames. Beethoven's Eroica symphony? Mozart's Toy Symphony."

Truman laughed. "Okay, you got me. There is a nickname."

"I knew it."

They were silent a while as the orchestra finished its warmup. The instruments began dropping out, and the cacophonous sound dwindled next to nothing.

"So are you going to tell me?" she asked.

He was going to say it. Almost told her the two-word title. Then he thought better of it. "You'll see it when it's in its final form. You'll like it. It's all about you." He looked at Kat and she raised her eyebrows. Then she smiled.

"A good choice," she said.

The conductor stepped up on the podium and the orchestra fell silent. He looked left and right, taking in his musicians. Then he turned. The house lights were down, the stage lights up, so he put a hand over his eyes and squinted out at the audience.

"I hope you're out there, Truman. I've studied it in preparation, and it's quite remarkable. Hope we do it proud."

The orchestra members all shuffled their feet on the stage. It was an acknowledgement of him. Musicians applauding another musician for a job well done.

The conductor said, "Are you ready?"

Truman reached for Kat and found her hand. It was soft and warm.

The conductor turned back quickly and stood at attention, surveying his musicians.

He raised his baton.

A grand pause.

"I'm ready," Truman whispered.

The baton swooped up, and the entire orchestra breathed in the rain.

ACKNOWLEDGMENTS

I owe thanks to literally hundreds of people for the creation of this long-gestating novel, and it started early in my teaching career, many moons ago, teaching at the K-12 school at Lake Quinault in a single building with a total population of about 350 students. (These days, that number has been cut in half, mostly due to the changes in the timber industry). During those three years I taught all the music from kindergarten to twelfth grade, plus some English and speech. I coached JV girls basketball. I coached the track team. (A dozen kids at most, grades 7-12, both boys *and* girls. We'd travel to away meets in a van. And yes, that included Forks, Washington, long before it became famous for sparkly vampires.)

The superintendent's secretary, Michelle, who also played piano accompaniment for my choirs and for the elementary kids for concerts, was the wife of Dave Morrison, one of three brothers who owned the Rain Forest Resort Village on the lake. One day as my first summer approached, Michelle asked, "So, do you want to work?" Meaning at the resort. Yes, I did.

The rest is history, so to speak. I worked those cash registers all summer long and greeted travelers and gave them room and cabin keys—that summer and the next two. Later, when I moved on to a new teaching job in the Seattle area, they told me I'd always be welcomed back if I wanted to work in the summer, or—if it ever became a possibility or necessity—even longer. And that did happen in the early '90s, when I left teaching for a couple years. I was, for all intents and purposes, Truman Starkey, living in a space above the store for room and board and minimum wage, just writing, heading to Seattle once a week to meet with my writers group. I *lived* that life of tourism and rain.

I started a writers retreat there in 2007, with about 20 or so writers coming to the Rainforest to do nothing but relax, write, and network. That retreat is now fourteen years old and boasts three separate sessions, and caters to over a hundred writers each year. They've been pleading for a fourth session. (When I retire, folks!) So, here's a special hello and a *humongous* thank you to the hundreds of writers who've spent time with me in the Rainforest!

All that is to explain my debt to the Morrisons for the friendships, the fun times, even the not-so-wonderful times, and, of course, for providing many of the memories and details that appear in this novel. Suggesting having the retreat there was a way to pay them back for *everything*. They love my writers, and they especially don't mind us filling up their resort for almost three straight weeks in February and March, a typically *very* slow time for them.

There's a slice of my life in this story. So much so, that I cobbled together the Cedars Resort and Quinault from a cross-section of events over the years. Some events happened in the background, some in the foreground, from my first years there, to my later years, and into the present. There *were* championship Hobie Cat races on the lake, and the scenes described are pretty much how I remember them. There *was* 8-man football in that small stadium in back of the school, and there really *was* a Lime Bowl. The World's Largest Spruce Tree *does* reside on the resort's property. The Enchanted Valley and its trail *is* real. (But would you believe in all these years I've never made that hike myself? Thank you to Google and all those informative hiking websites!)

I'm indebted to my longtime friend Mark Teppo, who, when I declared the book done, offered to do the edit on it, then suggested crucial character and structural work, brainstorming ideas with me. This book is so much the better for it, and I can't thank him enough.

A big thank you also goes to Louise Marley, once a professional opera singer, who read the book and made sure my music details hummed along and were relatively accessible for the non-musician. A thank you to Randy Henderson who spent an hour with me during a break at the writing retreat to hear my ideas on the book and played the role of "writer's advocate," which consisted of question after question, forcing me to solve some of the story problems I was having. A thank you to James Van Pelt and to Brenda Cooper, also Rainforesters, who read various drafts of the book and also provided publicity blurbs. A thank you to Honna Swenson for encouragement and support. A thank you to Bob Brown, Old Man of the Rainforest. (You're in here! I know your game is chess, but I needed the device for a chapter title.) A big but sad posthumous thank you to my friends and longtime Rainforesters Jay Lake and John Pitts, who left this world too damn soon. A thank you to Evelyn Nicholas, who has one of the best hometown book stores in the Pacific Northwest (A Good Book Bookstore), who always provides a safe and cozy spot for me at the store and at her home. A thank you to Tod McCoy for his enduring friendship, enduring those long convention road trips, and putting up with my snoring. He also read an early draft of the book and contributed valuable notes.

And then there's Nikki Rossignol, who deserves a *gigantic* thank you for *her* friendship, and for providing the art that not only graces this cover, but also hangs on display in its original watercolor format in my home. I can never repay her enough for those gifts!

As always, a big thank you to my family.

Lastly, thanks to the one constant in my life, my talented and wildly special kid Artemis. They *rock*. They're in college now and doing well, learning a career and gathering life lessons. My own life would be so much worse without them in it. My next cover is yours, Artemis!

—*Patrick Swenson*
Bonney Lake, WA
August 2021

OTHER TITLES FROM FAIRWOOD PRESS

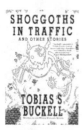

*How to Get to Apocalypse
and Other Disasters*
by Erica L. Satifka
trade paper $17.99
ISBN: 978-1-933846-17-0

*A Few Last Words
for the Late Immortals*
by Michael Bishop
trade paper $17.99
ISBN: 978-1-933846-12-5

Shoggoths in Traffic
by Tobias S. Buckell
trade paper $17.99
ISBN: 978-1-933846-18-7

Dare
by Ken Rand
trade paper $18.99
ISBN: 978-1-933846-15-6

Fantastic Americana
by Josh Rountree
trade paperback $17.99
ISBN: 978-1-933846-16-3

*Living Forever
and Other Terrible Ideas*
by Emily C. Skaftun
trade paper $17.99
ISBN: 978-1-933846-98-9

McDowell's Ghost
by Jack Cady
trade paper $17.99
ISBN: 978-1-933846-11-8

The Best of James Van Pelt
by James Van Pelt
signed ltd. hardcover $40.00
ISBN: 978-1-933846-95-8

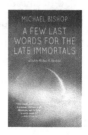

Find us at:
www.fairwoodpress.com
Bonney Lake, Washington

ABOUT THE AUTHOR

Patrick Swenson, a graduate of Clarion West, is the author of *The Ultra Thin Man* and its sequel *The Ultra Big Sleep*. He has sold stories to the anthologies *Unfettered III*, *Seasons Between Us*, *Gunfight at Europa Station*, *Like Water for Quarks*, and a handful of magazines. He is currently at work on the third in the Ultra series, *The Ultra Long Goodbye*. He runs the Rainforest Writers Village retreat every spring at Lake Quinault, Washington, and has taught high school English for the past 36 years. He lives in the beautiful Pacific Northwest with his only child Artemis, who currently attends DigiPen Insitute Technology.

CPSIA information can be obtained
at www.ICGtesting.com
Printed in the USA
BVHW081327221121
622236BV00005B/126

9 781933 846132